Th

Antonia Senior is .... is now a
freelance journalist, ...umns, features and book reviews
have appeared in a number of national newspapers. Antonia lives
in London with her family.

Also by Antonia Senior

Treason's Daughter
The Winter Isles

THE TYRANT'S SHADOW

ANTONIA SENIOR

CORVUS

Published in hardback in Great Britain in 2017 by Corvus,
an imprint of Atlantic Books Ltd. This edition published in 2018.

10 9 8 7 6 5 4 3 2 1

A CIP catalogue record for this book is available from the British Library.

Paperback ISBN: 978 1 78239 663 5
E-book ISBN: 978 1 78239 662 8

Printed in Great Britain by CPI Group (UK) Ltd, Croydon CR0 4YY

Corvus
An imprint of Atlantic Books Ltd
Ormond House
26–27 Boswell Street
London
WC1N 3JZ

www.corvus-books.co.uk

For Glencora and Elishna.

PART ONE

LONDON

April 1652

THE MOMENT THE SUN DISAPPEARS, LEAVING BEHIND ITS burning rim, Patience Johnson understands that she is being called.

Around her, people have frozen like statues before an iconoclast's hammer. A shadow has spread. Silence has settled. London streets are not supposed to be so still. No trundle of carts. No chattering. No calling out of cabbages or oysters. No screaming from the milk-sellers. No cooper clanging or butcher thwacking. No hammering from the coppersmiths or pewterers. No laughing. No bells. Even the pigs and the dogs are quiet. The hush is an urban roar of fear and wonder.

They look up, up to where the sun should be. Necks are cricked, mouths hang open. Behind her, someone prays – the familiar words whispered and echoing in the stillness.

Do they know what it means, or is the truth clear to her alone? It is a sign from Him. The knowledge sizzles, but she feels detached from it, as if she is floating up, up towards that spherical halo that shimmers just out of reach. She is being called. The portent unpeels her, laying naked her soul – her unworthy, eternal soul.

Her eyes sting. She remembers her mother telling her she will go blind if she looks full on at the sun. Will she go blind if she looks at a sun-shaped sign, at a message from Him? She is giddy, as if she's spun too fast in the dizzy-spin game she used to play with her sisters in the orchard. She closes her eyes and finds her sisters there, spinning and spinning and falling. Laughing.

Opening her eyes, she sheds the memory as a distraction. Looking up. What should a person do, she wonders, on being given a sign directly from the heavens? Should she curtsy? Pray?

Onions catch and burn as the sausage man lets his charcoal burn too fierce. The bitter, jagged smell fills the street.

A white-capped woman falls to her knees, the mud splashing up her clean skirts. Another falls, and another, until all the street is kneeling. A veteran with one leg tries to kneel, but catches his stick on a cobble and loses his balance. He lands heavily, his jagged stump hitting the ground first, and he gasps with the pain of it.

The first woman to kneel glances sideways at him and flaps her hand in his direction as if shooing a stray cat. Patience moves to help him, but catches sight of his mottled, angry face and decides against it. She kneels instead, taking refuge in the miracle, offering the grizzled old soldier the courtesy of ignoring the awkwardness of how he rearranges his limbs.

Before the sun disappeared, all was normal. They had all been bustling along the street. Patience had slipped out alone. Not far, in this still unfamiliar city. She likes to walk, to watch. But it is so easy to get lost, no matter how you cling to the spire of St Paul's as a waymarker. Once, when she was deeply lost, she could still see it all the time. She kept following streets that veered off in the wrong direction or came to unexpected ends. All the time, she could see the spire pointing decidedly to the sky like a maypole as she meandered round it in frantic, ever-decreasing circles.

This time, she had not wandered far. She loves her nephew, but the constant, whining demands of a four-year-old grate on her twenty-year-old nerves. She needed to escape, to be alone. To hear her own silence, rather than the chattering of her nephew.

She had looked in the shop windows, caught the trailing ends of conversations, pitied the ragged ranks of the beggared. She picked her way with more certainty across the treacherous cobbles – aimless and bored by her aimlessness.

She became aware of a strangeness. A cloud covered the sun; so much was usual. But something was not quite right about the light. It seemed heavy, too pressing. The air was chilled, and as she shivered, the cloud moved on. In its absence, the sun appeared – but a strange, sinister sun. A black shadow was creeping across its face, dragging gasps and sighs from the tiny people below.

An eaten sun. A swallowed sun. Radiance devoured. In the beginning, there was light. There was light. The unremarkable miracle of the sun. And in the end? What?

When did the end begin? Time has no meaning on this darkening street. There is only a terrifying present and the fear that the sun will not reappear. Certainties shift and falter. If the sun can vanish, what else is safe? Who is safe?

Patience, her senses alight in the darkness, can hear the mumbled prayers. She can smell the shifting mud, as the people around her rock on their knees, stirring up the filth and releasing its stench. She puts her hands up to feel the darkness draped over the city. Goosebumps pock her skin; the hairs on her arm, on her neck, bristle. It is cold; a damp, probing coldness.

What does it herald? What glories, what terrors?

How will I become part of the great happenings? she wonders. How will I take my place among the saints? She imagines the alternative – being shunted aside as the world is broken and remade. It is not to be borne.

Her childhood was on the edge of things. She was clothed and shod and fed. She watched the ravages of the war from afar; the blood that spilled in every corner of the land never stained her, or those she loved. Her sister-in-law, Henrietta, was killed on the day the king died. But she didn't count – Patience barely knew her. She is helping to raise Henrietta's motherless son.

The squire's son, they say, was emasculated by a Royalist musket shot. But he was hidden away, and defied the local children's attempts to spy on him through hedges, to shiver in prurient sympathy at his despair.

No – the war ripped apart strangers only. Patience played and danced her way to adulthood, cocooned as the world turned upside down. She paused at sixteen, aghast, when she first visited London and realized that life was happening elsewhere. The heat and burn of living had bypassed little Patience as she picked blackberries in the autumn sun.

It will not happen any more; she will not let it. She will not be left out of the coming battles. Not this time.

'Test me, Lord,' she whispers into the darkness. 'Take me into your service. Let me prove myself.'

A sudden thought. What if this is it? What if this is the Coming itself? Not a sign of glories to come, but glory itself stepping down from heaven in the shadow of a shrouded sun? She looks around frantically, searching for something, anything that might give her a clue. She feels drunk, pickled in wonder and fear. Her heart beats loudly.

At last the shadow begins to recede. Patience risks a glance heavenwards, and sees the curve of the reappearing sun. It is so bright, so reassuringly, blindingly bright, that she wants to shout her praise. She feels light with relief; sun-blessed. It is not the Coming, then. The world is reappearing in the light. It was a sign, and she will have time to make her mark, to take her place in what is to come.

The shadow pulls further back, leaving only the dark spaces that belong at midday – under the oyster-seller's cart, beneath the overhang of the houses that lean across the street to bristle windows at each other, below the unconcerned cat who stretches and curves his back, pushing the livid sores on his exposed skin towards the emerging sun.

She counts herself blessed. To have seen, and to have understood, such a sign! It must mean He has a purpose for her. She cannot be left out as the world is remade. Not this time.

Patience looks around. The street re-emerges from the darkness looking much as it did before the miracle, and yet the change is there. People are looking at one another with penetrating stares. In London, strangers do not look directly at each other's faces, she has learned. The only way to live with so many higgled on top of each other is to pretend that you are alone. The alternative is to be crushed by irritation at other people's slowness, or their speed, or their loudness, or their quietness, or their general, careless impingement on your own existence.

But now these strangers look at each other, mute. They study each other's faces as the shadow recedes, as if looking for clues on how to react. Should they be scared, or hopeful? With the shadow fully gone and the sun shining, the white-capped woman, the one-legged veteran, the pockmarked oyster-seller, the godly matron, the apprentice boy, the soldier and twenty-year-old Patience Johnson look at each other nakedly.

Patience turns away first, dissatisfied. Why look for others to tell you what to think, especially when the sign is so unmistakable? What else can it mean, this demonstration of His power? It is a warning and a promise. He is to come again, she thinks, near skipping down the street back towards her brother Will's house. She knows the way without thinking.

She is unerring in her path. The chosen one. The blessed one. She gabbles silently to her Christ. The Christ who is coming again. 'Let me be your servant in your coming, oh my Lord. Grant me that. Let me do your work. In what is to come, let me *matter*.'

Will Johnson stands in the street, looking up at the re-emerging sun. Blackberry, his son, clutches at his coat and buries a sticky face into his father's neck.

Will hears the prayers around him increasing in volume. He sighs. What nonsense will be talked as the sun reasserts itself? What endless, frothing streams of piss? He wishes he could find a cave and seal himself up inside until the absurd ranting passes.

He kisses the boy's neck absently, and wonders why his response to this great astronomical vision has been so muted. He imagines himself young, before Henrietta died, and how transported he would have been.

He asks his dead wife a question. Why can't I feel it in my heart, Hen? A total eclipse, for all love, and yet I cannot feel it. Is it your fault for leaving, love?

His son stirs, wrapping into his father. 'It's over, little Blackberry. The sun is back, see.'

'Where the sun go, Dada?'

'It did not go anywhere, my cherub. It was there all the time – just hidden by the moon.'

'I like the moon.'

So did your mother, his father doesn't say. He stands for a while, watching the city fall back into its well-worn grooves. As if nothing has happened.

He wishes the boy were older, so he could explain it all. Explain the elliptical orbits that led the moon to cover the sun, and the glorious, wondrous miracle that is natural philosophy.

'Auntie Imp!' the boy cries out, and Will sees his sister walking towards them. She smiles at Blackberry. She will not tolerate her childhood nickname from anyone but him now. Patience, named more in hope than foresight, earned the nickname Imp early and it has lingered.

Will stumbles on her name, the Imp rolling on his tongue before he forces out: 'Patience. You saw it, I suppose.'

'I did!'

There is something unusually animated about Patience. He has the absurd sense that the sun, in re-emerging, has worked its way beneath her skin to make her glow. She seems almost to hum with energy and light.

'Spectacular, was it not?'

'It was,' she says. Her voice drops to a hush. 'It was a sign.'

He arches an eyebrow, knowing with a sibling's cruelty that this will irritate her. 'It was a natural phenomenon.'

'Call it what you will, brother, but I tell you I felt His breath on me when the sun disappeared.'

'Truly? And did all the hundreds of thousands of people watching with you feel His breath too? Or was His sign for you alone?'

She blushes. He feels his cruelty then, and considers retreat. But really, is it not a kindness to shake this nonsense from her?

'The moon's orbit brought it between us and the sun, Patience. That is all. No signs, no miracles, no revelations.'

She crosses her arms and looks at him, pugnacious and defensive of her new-found revelations. 'And who spins the moon, and spins this world, Will? The rule of the saints is coming, I tell you. Everyone knows it. The rule of the Antichrist is done, and the saints will take their place. Then He will come. It is a sign.'

'So the dead king was the Antichrist?'

'Don't be obtuse, Will. The Pope. The king and Archbishop Laud were merely his agents.'

Will thinks back to the king on the scaffold. He remembers the groan of the crowd as his head fell. Fear of the future hung over all their heads like a giant corporeal question mark. And he remembers the hurried kiss he gave Henrietta as she rushed away to where a twitchy youth would shoot her dead.

The last time he saw her alive. It is more than three years ago. Three years. How is that possible?

Something in his face worries Patience. He hears her voice as if from a distance. 'Will, are you well?'

He forces a smile. 'We shall not agree on this,' he says. 'Let us be friends, for all love.'

She grins back at him, and the tension between them deflates like a bladder ball. He loves that about his little sister – her temper is quick to rise but quicker to ebb. He remembers her as a child, wearing all her emotions on her face and cycling through them in quick succession. She could never bear to see those she loved upset – she took their sorrow on her tiny shoulders and wept with them. She hasn't changed much, he thinks. He puts an arm around her and pulls her in tight.

'Hello, little Berry,' she says to her nephew, their noses touching. 'Imp, Imp,' he squeals.

At the end of the lane, where the cobbles meet the filth of Fleet Street, there is a commotion and the three of them turn to watch. A man is walking, surrounded by people.

He is tall and soberly dressed. His dark hair is cropped close into his nape. He pauses and raises his arms, turning to face his followers so that Patience can see the long line of his nose, his square chin. His dark eyes, which seem to reach further than other eyes, flick momentarily over the heads of his followers to seek hers.

She is open-mouthed, she finds, and brings her lips together quickly.

'We must heed Him,' the man calls in a rich voice, warm like dark broth. 'He is calling us. We must fear Him, we must rejoice in our trembling.'

He looks at her again with a half-smile on his lips and she feels Will's hand tighten on her arm. The man leans in to his followers. With a voice pitched just far enough to reach her, he says: 'He sends a sign, we must listen. For closing our ears means opening our souls to the Antichrist. Where He calls, we must follow.'

Patience whispers an echo: 'We must follow,' and in the febrile atmosphere of the lightening street her soul seems to lift, detach and float.

She hears Will sigh beside her; a puff of despair and irritation. She will not hear him. Why be grounded by his pedantic refusal to see the whole sky? Why crouch when you can soar?

CABO VERDE PENINSULA, AFRICA

April 1652

CAPTAIN SAM CHALLONER IS HUDDLING IN A TINY, STINKING hut. His eye is pressed to a crack in the wall, and he can feel the scratch of it against his cheek. Outside, a circle of locals jostle and spit invective towards the cowering British. Their skin is filmed with the dust raked up by their feet. One man raises his bow and sights down the arrow towards the hut. Sam pulls back, although it is impossible the man can see him; he is but an eye blinking though a hole.

'Jesus, Captain,' says a voice behind him; a low quaver. 'How will we get out?'

'Have faith,' says Sam.

He turns to look at them. Five of them shrinking into the corner. Three seamen from the *Supply*, one of the boys – Tom, is it? – and his coxswain, Butcher.

'Faith in the Lord, sir?' asks little Tom, his eyes huge and frightened in a small freckled face.

'And will the Lord rescue us from this fucking hut?' growls Butcher. 'Halfwit.'

The boy bristles, but discipline keeps him mute. Good, thinks Sam. It's harder to keep the men and boys in check ashore – they have notions that the captain's authority needs sea spray to keep it awesome. He is not long in command of the *Supply*, and he is not convinced by it. A lubberly tub that creeps to leeward. He feels guilty thinking so of his ship, his first command. But worse than the crabwise scuttling in a puff of breeze are the men. The *Supply* is a captured Commonwealth ship, and though its crew have sworn their oath to King Charles II and their general-at-sea, Prince Rupert, Sam is not sure of their loyalties.

There are a handful of true British parliamentarians, who cast him sullen looks and mutter behind his back. The rest of the crew are local men, dredged from the ports in *Supply*'s long cruise of these waters.

Still, he'll be lucky to see her again. They may dissemble all they like to a new captain. Sam Challoner will be bleached bones in the African sun.

Faith, the boy said. We must have faith.

'Never mind, Tom,' he says, smiling at him. 'I meant faith in Prince Rupert, but a little succour from the Lord can't hurt.'

'The general-at-sea will be long gone, sir,' says one of the men – the one with the ugly scar down his face.

'What's your name, sailor?'

'James Fowler, sir.'

'Where did you get your scar?'

'Naseby.'

Sam is about to claim brotherhood; about to say, yes, I was there too. He is about to slap a familiar arm about the man's shoulders, and talk of the horror of fleeing Cromwell's Ironsides.

Then he realizes that, as a seaman from the *Supply,* the man was doubtless on the other side. It was a loyal sword that carved open James Fowler's cheek, not a rebel pike.

An awkward hush falls on the hut. He looks at Fowler, and the man stares back. Hard brown eyes that give nothing away. Even here, thinks Sam. Even in a hut in Africa, surrounded by men who want to kill us, ankle deep in filth and bowel-griping scared, even here the old wounds fester.

'The general looks after his own,' says Sam.

'That's why we are here, sir,' agrees Butcher.

One of the crew, a native of these parts, had come ashore to visit his relatives, who had prevented him from rejoining the ship. The general-at-sea had ordered Sam in to take him off again. A trained topman is not a man to lose ahead of an Atlantic crossing. But Sam's boat had capsized in the surf; and the bedraggled English seamen had waded from the shallows to find themselves surrounded by hostile men.

Butcher nods, and says again: 'That's why we are here.'

Fowler snorts.

Butcher turns on him, squaring his shoulders.

'What? What? Be hanged, you whoreson.'

'Peace, Butcher,' raps Sam.

They all know it is Butcher's fault they are here. Their ordered planned approach to the shore, muskets primed and trained, was scuppered by the coxswain's untimely inability to remember a single damn rule of small-boat handling. One minute Sam was standing at the stern, viewing the hostile natives down the barrel of a beautiful, God-kissed musket. The next there was salt water in his nose, in his eyes. His legs were up, head down. Bubbles rising. The useless, sopping musket a dead weight in his hands. A numbing crack to his head from the upturned boat.

The noddle-headed, useless scummer. He eyes Butcher. Should he disrate him, if they get out of this? Break him?

'Sir, sir.' The boy Tom has his face pressed to the crack. 'There's boats. Can see 'em over there.'

'Move.'

Sam looks through the hole. It takes a second for his eyes to adjust to the sunlight. He can see 'Captain' Jacques, the local interpreter who had jabbered to the hostile villagers, calmed their brimming violence, and led the waterlogged would-be rescuers to this hut. Jacques is still talking to them, his hands outstretched and palms facing down.

Sam notices that even thousands of miles from home, on this sun-baked coast, the same hand signals mean 'calm down, breathe'. Father and Henrietta would like that, he thinks. But his father and sister are dead. Will he ever stop noticing things he would like to tell them? He thinks of the small nuggets of life we offer up to coax smiles from those we love.

Beyond Captain Jacques, there are boats braving the breakers. And in one he thinks he sees the chief himself. Prince Rupert of the Rhine. General on land and sea. Now privateer, fighting a deadly small war against the regicides' mighty navy. Dressed as if to a tea party with a countess, flicking the dust from his lace cuffs into the hungry surf.

'Tom,' he says. 'Your eyes are better than mine. Is that Rupert himself in the flag's cutter?'

He switches places with the boy.

Tom pauses. 'It is! It's the general, sir. Oh, sir, them waves are vicious. They're going for it, sir.'

The men in the hut lean in towards the boy, waiting.

'They're through! Perfect landing, sir. Oh my eyes! Perfect!'

Fowler looks at Butcher, smiling. The big man ignores him, twisting his body away from the scorn.

Sam elbows the boy out of the way. His eye blinks into the blinding hole, and as his vision clears, he sees the general-at-sea striding up the beach, his hand resting on the pistol at his hip.

'Rupert looks after his own,' he says softly. Oh my general.

He turns back into the hut. 'Cutlasses out. Let's go. I'll not have him find us skulking in here like a pack of mongrels.'

They stand at his back, and he pushes his way out of the hut, into the glare of the sun.

Captain Jacques listens to the headman's tirade, nodding and tutting where required. He turns to Prince Rupert, who stands a little apart, wiping his forehead with a dust-stained handkerchief. The harmattan, the hot wind that blows from land to sea in this late dry season, picks up the dust and dances with it. The heat is thick.

Behind the general-at-sea is the small African boy they found after a skirmish last year, lost and alone. He trips after Rupert now, sticking tight to the big man's shadow, just as the dog, Boy, used to. The lad clicks his tongue in disgust at the headman's words, and spits violently into the dust. He must share a tongue with these fellows.

Sam wipes his forehead with a grubby sleeve. He has lost his hair tie, and the back of his neck is sweat-slimed under the thick raggle of hair. He thinks pointless thoughts of cool streams and cloths dampened with ice. He remembers the waterfall near Kinsale, back in Ireland. Swimming under the rush of it, to let it tumble in an icy deluge over his head. He nearly choked on the blessed fresh water as he laughed aloud at the joy of it.

The headman has stopped speaking. Prince Rupert half smiles politely. He looks as if this is a meeting of great diplomats, not a half-arsed engagement on a forgotten scrubby beach.

Captain Jacques clears his throat in the silence and looks ruefully at the prince. 'This one says, your greatness, that kindness was given you and was spat on. Peace be upon you, great one, I am sorry for this anger. This one says that the little boat with the fat man steering' – he points out into the bay, where a flotilla of small boats now bobs beyond the breakers – 'stole one of his beloved canoes and killed one of his men. A nephew, begging your lordship's indulgence. His sister's favourite son, Allah bless her. Sorry, your, um, holiness, but he says that he will keep one of your men. A white slave would make him a big man, your greatness.'

Sam smiles. Christ knows where Captain Jacques learned his English – presumably at one of the trading posts along the coast where a bloat of European merchants risk sweat and syphilis to vie for trade. Somewhere with a shaky grasp of honorifics. I would be dead without him, he thinks, and looks upon the African with a vast goodwill, an almost lovesick smile on his face.

He catches Rupert's eye and forces the smile down.

The negotiations go back and forth. At last the terms are agreed. Butcher and the boy Tom are sent to tell the pinnace of the *Defiance* to let go the native canoe. The group on shore watch as Butcher runs the cutter alongside the pinnace. The figures aboard are stick men at this distance, moving in jerky silhouettes

18

against the darkening sky. The native canoe is lowered into the swell beyond the breakers.

'This one, may Allah spit on his wife's womb, says you may go,' says Captain Jacques.

Rupert nods. 'Thank him for his generosity,' he says, in the thick German accent that has never been tempered by all his service in the English cause. 'Add whatever words you think fit.'

'This one says he will hold one back until his canoe reaches land, your nobleness.'

Sam looks at the ranks of villagers ranging up against them. What are the odds? he wonders. Ten to one? More?

'I will stay, sir,' he says, his lips moving before his fear catches up.

Rupert nods. 'Good man. Captain Jacques, we want assurances. Tell him that this officer is dear to me, and I will kill those who hurt him.'

A stream of vowels and clicks, and it is agreed upon. Rupert and the small band with him walk to the shore, to the beached longboat.

'We will get beyond the breakers and back oars,' says Rupert. 'When the canoe returns, can you swim to us?'

'Yes, sir,' says Sam. He learned to swim in the Thames upriver from London, with mud sucking at his ankles and his brother Ned holding the other end of a rope tied round his waist. He is not a strong swimmer, and he looks nervously at the big waves.

'Good man,' says Rupert again, and suddenly he is gone. Sam fights to stop himself running after his chief, throwing himself at the long legs as they stride away. Rupert climbs into the boat, which scrapes its way across the shingle and sand, into the froth of the sea. Through the breakers now: shivering precariously on the rise, crashing murderously on the fall.

Sam turns to see an argument between Jacques and the headman. Suddenly a clutch of natives rush to the water's edge. They begin firing arrows at the longboat. Jesus wept, thinks Sam. Oath-breaking bastards. They mean to take me for a slave. A slave. He begins to run forward, but hands grab him and pull him sideways. He cannot believe this is happening. It cannot be so. Thank Christ for this dry mouth, he thinks, as his bladder relaxes with fear. Not a dribble.

What a time to care about such trivialities, with the slaver's whip poised above his head. But if there is one thing Sam has learned in a decade of fighting, it is that the outward show bolsters the inner man. If you piss yourself, you are as good as surrendered. His breeches are dry, and a pox on their double-crossing heads.

Rupert's men fire their muskets. The report of the guns echoes in the heat. One local man falls forwards, his head half gone, grey stuff oozing from his open skull as he crumples into the surf. Some of his fellows dive into the sea then. Confident, muscular dives. As the guns fire again, they duck under the water. Arrows sail over the swimmers' heads to thunk on the boat's straked planks and pock the unsettled sea. They will swamp the boat if they reach it. A handful of muskets are useless against this weight of hostile enemies.

The beach is a riot of shouting and fighting. Sam realizes that there are different groups at work, and fighting between the locals themselves. The hands pulling him sideways are rough and insistent, and he finds himself in a thicket, the fronds scraping at his skin, pulling at his shirt.

A hand is clamped over his mouth; a huge arm encircles him. He struggles to breathe and tears leak from his eyes. Oh Jesus. Oh Jesus.

He hears a high English shout. Captain Jacques.

'The watering place, your nobleness. To the watering place.'

Sam doesn't understand. He gags on the hand that clenches his mouth. It smells of fish and dirt. He wrestles his head to one side, trying to scream.

Captain Jacques is beside him suddenly, shouting into his confused brain. 'Calm. Calm. I rescue. Stop this fucking struggle.'

Sam lets his limbs go limp, and his captor slowly releases his grip.

'Come away. Come away,' says Captain Jacques, and they limp away into the snagging bush.

The watering place at which they stopped a few days past is four days' walk through the bush. Sam walks with leaden legs. He finds a despairing rhythm. Will they be there? No they will not. Will they be there? No they will not. Right leg, left leg; right, left. Will they? No.

The harmattan sucks the moisture from the air. His mouth is dry and his lips are cracked. There is a desolation in his spirit to match the featureless coast. His stinging eyes follow the steady trudging of his feet. Iridescent birds caw unheeded; pink suns settle, unremarked on, into purple seas.

One sight rouses him from his torpor. A little inland, with the sea at their backs, they stumble across a lake. But such a lake. At first Sam thinks he is dreaming, a strange and hallucinatory dream rooted in his empty stomach, his aching legs and his despair.

How can water be pink?

But there it is, stretching ahead of him. A great and vast expanse of water, pink as . . . pink as . . . He cannot imagine how he will describe it to his fellow sailors, if he ever sees them again. The storing of an anecdote is a sliver of hope, and he works at it. A lake, then, like a crushed strawberry; but such an English analogy seems absurd here, under this great ache of bluish sky. White heaps of sand are piled by the shoreline – or at least so he imagines until Captain Jacques encourages him to dab a wetted finger into the nearest pile and take a taste. Salt. Pure salt.

They make camp, eating a salted fish they buy from a local with a salt-crust glitter to his skin. But as the sun begins to sink, the pinkness of the lake deepens and curdles into a darker colour until it is blood, blood red.

Sam closes his eyes and begs for sleep. For a man who has seen what he has seen, a blood-red lake is a cruel practical joke played by the Almighty, who is doubtless pissing himself up there at Sam's excessive discomfort. An illusion is all. He will lie here in a salty pyre, and the blood-red lake will not creep up in the night to lick at him. It will not come to claim him for a brother.

Oh Jesus, let me sleep.

Let me sleep.

They arrive the next afternoon at the watering place. The tumble of a fresh-water stream, and beyond it, an empty ocean. They are at the western edge of the world here. An elastic imagination could think a ship would sail off the edge of that horizon; drop down in a plunge of briny fear. Sam settles in silence on the rocky foreshore, eyes straining towards the flat line at the sky's edge.

The wind is not dead set against them – Rupert's pathetic fleet should be here, if it is coming.

Captain Jacques collects driftwood, looking at him with an unreadable face as he passes. Sam sits and watches the waves, willing the pattern of their suck and crash to calm him. It does not work. What if they do not come?

'They may come,' says Captain Jacques as he builds the driftwood into a pyramid. As if he has read Sam's mind.

Captain Jacques strikes the flint and catches the spark in a nest of straw-like twigs. He places the smoking bundle into the heart of the pyramid. He blows, gently. For a big man, he can move with surprising grace. It is still warm, but the dying light promises a cool night. They will be glad of the fire soon. Besides, it keeps away beasts. This bloody place, Sam thinks. God's blood. In every bush lurks something malevolent. Plants, animals, men: all created with one aim – to bring about the premature meeting of one Captain Sam Challoner with his Maker.

Sam stretches his aching legs out towards the flames. He feels the growing heat through his boots, and thinks of all the fires he has camped by. In England, God bless it and keep it, he knew night after night of a hot face and a freezing arse as he fought the rebels. But there were no venomous snakes or ravenous insects there to add to his woes.

Perhaps, he thinks, we just underestimated the wildlife. Imagine being menaced by a badger. He grins, but then a swell of homesickness catches him. He longs – *longs* – for the sharp sip of the year's new cider. For the smell of a fire-black sausage. For the hoppy, sweaty press of life inside a tavern. For English girls with sarcastic mouths and laughing eyes.

Will he ever see England again? Even if he leaves this God-cursed coast, will he be forever an outlaw, fighting a forlorn, hopeless war against the might of the Commonwealth? Rupert's pirates' war against the Commonwealth navy and merchant ships is a comedy. A wren's piss in the ocean.

What choice has he? Besides, the pissing matters to the wren, if not to the ocean.

He watches Captain Jacques lift a lit stick from the fire, brandishing it at the dusk-drawn shadows like an oversized link-boy sparring with ghosts.

The man straightens suddenly, looking out towards the sea. 'A ship,' he says, pointing. Sam jumps to his feet and looks along Captain Jacques' outstretched finger. There, like a tiny handkerchief dancing on the sea, is a sail. Too far to name it for certain – it is a smudge in the gloom. Please God, let it be the general-at-sea.

Sam settles down for the wait. He has been long enough at sea to recognize that an extended stretch looms before any action. A man who stays wound tight in the slow sail towards an enemy broadside will find himself running mad. He wills his tight nerves to loosen. He rolls his head in circles to release his shoulders.

Captain Jacques squats down next to him, throwing the smoking stick into the fire.

'You prince too? Like big man Rupert?' he asks.

'No, my friend.'

'Rich?'

Not a pot to piss in, thinks Sam. 'Aye. Beyond measure. Rivers of gold on our land,' he says. 'Lakes.'

Captain Jacques chuckles. 'You remember old Captain Jacques, hey? Hey?'

'You will have my gratitude for life, Captain,' says Sam fervently.

Jacques settles himself companionably, crunching into the stony ground. 'You have the wife?'

'No,' says Sam.

'You should marry, my friend. Family?'

Sam thinks on this for a minute. Does he have a family? His mother died in birthing him. His father was condemned as a Royalist traitor not long after the fighting began. Almost ten years ago now. Christ. Ten years. Sam had not waited to see him hang, but fled London to join the king's cause. Not politics nor God made him fight. No, it was love and anger, mingled in the flesh of his dangling father.

'I had a sister,' he says. 'Henrietta.'

He can't remember when he last said her name. He watches the fire; even the wood here smells different as it burns. The sounds of the bush creak and rattle around him, but he is too tired to be afraid. Would Captain Jacques be frightened if I tipped him up in Fleet Street? he wonders.

'A sister?' prompts the man, in that strange sing-song accent.

'She was killed in the war. I was in London, sent to try to spring the king. I was hurt. She sheltered me. My brother, Ned, who fought for the Parliament, brought troops to capture me. I escaped, she did not.'

Sam is watching the ships coming closer now; he is nearly sure that the big three-master is Rupert's flagship. They are coming for him.

Captain Jacques whistles between his teeth. 'Your brother, hey?

You will kill him now.'

Sam thinks of the letter he received from Henrietta's husband Will. The crumpled edges of it after he had scrunched it and smoothed it again. The terse, bemused prose. Ned killed in the fighting in Ireland. An English casualty sinking into the blood-soaked ground of Drogheda, where Cromwell slaughtered the rebellious papists in their hundreds. Behind the brevity of Will's note, he imagined a similar maelstrom of reactions. Grief. Confusion and anger, certainly. Relief, too, that the reckoning was no longer coming. A simultaneous sense of being cheated out of that same reckoning.

'He is dead now.'

'So many dead,' says Captain Jacques. Sam can see him shaking his head in the amber glow from the fire. He looks up at the huge, star-stippled sky and the sharp moon. The sail is not visible now that night has fallen. But it is out there somewhere. And at dawn they will launch a boat, and welcome him back into the brotherhood. Backs will be slapped and tales exchanged, and the chief might ask him to share a bottle of captured port.

Sam sighs, closing his eyes. It is grand to be alive.

But I am alone, he thinks. He wonders idly if somewhere there is a girl waiting for him. A girl not paid for in a passing port. A girl he can laugh with. To whom he can say, one night I was lost under an African sky and I dreamed of you.

Fool. You are alone, he tells himself. You have no one to call your own. It's an easy truth to forget in the dank of the ship, where men and officers crowd and stoop in tiny spaces. Where the way a man laughs can grate on your nerves so sharp you think you might have to kill him. Where the laughter with your mates in the still air of a night watch is bolder and brighter than any possible on shore.

Here, surrounded by foreign tongues and a foreign land and noises and smells that make no sense to him, his emptiness is clearer.

I am alone, thinks Sam. Alone.

LONDON

May 1652

THE PREACHER'S NAME IS SIDRACH SIMMONDS. SIDRACH Simmonds. She twists it on her tongue in the hour before dawn, when Blackberry and Will are asleep. Trying it out like a new gown. He is a teacher at a gathered church that meets in Swan Alley. He was an officer in the New Model Army from its inception, but left after the recent campaigns in Ireland.

This much she has found out from Hattie, the butcher's wife. She is an old friend of Will and his dead wife Henrietta; and she knows people across the city.

'He's a Fifth Monarchist,' says Hattie, looking up at Patience over the sausage casings. Everyone calls her the butcher's wife, but it has become a hollow title. The butcher never came back from the wars, so Hattie runs the business. Her seven-year-old daughter Anne helps. She holds the long loop of cleaned intestine straight as Hattie squeezes in the mixture of meat, crumbed bread and herbs. Anne's face is thin and serious. She straightens a kink, looking quickly at her mother, who says: 'Good girl.'

Patience watches Anne's face melt into a gap-toothed smile. It is one of the girl's most endearing qualities – her still face is drawn to the point of melancholy, but her happy face is infectiously joyful. Patience grins back at the child and feels as if it is the first unforced smile she has known since she saw Sidrach Simmonds stride down the sunlit street and call to her soul.

She should be doing something already in answer to that call. She should be living her bigger life. Not skulking. Not trapped in a perpetual dress rehearsal for life's colourful masque.

Hattie is recounting the degrees by which she has gained the information. Someone's sister's husband. Patience is not really listening. The trail does not matter, only the treasure.

She hoards each nugget she learns of his life. She takes them out when she is alone. Buffs them and ponders them. Is this the clue to him? How can I get close to him? Her plan is vague, unformed. She dare not think of exactly how Sidrach Simmonds is going to unlock her future; she just knows that it will be so. God's whisper in her heart on that fateful day has not left her. The elation she experienced with the returning sun may have faded, but the resolution remains; the absolute determination to count.

'A Fifth Monarchist,' says Hattie again, squeezing the meat into its casing with each emphasized syllable. 'You know. Them that believe in the rule of saints. The coming of Christ.'

'We know He is coming, Hattie. The Bible says so. Many believe He will come soon,' says Patience.

'Many prate nonsense, true. But these folk believe that they alone are the saints. And they must prepare the land for Christ's coming. By force if needs must. As if blood enough has not been spilled. Noddle-heads the lot of 'em.'

Patience makes a non-committal noise. She has learned from her brother to be guarded about her beliefs. Anyway, she is not yet convinced that she knows what those beliefs are. She thought she knew everything. Then she came to London. What a child she was, what a fool. Now she is twenty, she knows better.

'Listen, Patience,' says Hattie, straightening. She puts her hands in the small of her back to stretch it out as she says: 'Be careful. They say he is a man of great and forceful character. Great charm. Handsome, too, in his way.'

Patience thinks about the eyes that met hers; the fierce burn of them. The even planes of his face. His broad shoulders. She shakes her head, exasperated. It is not his form she finds compelling. Not frivolous concerns of face or muscles. It is his soul she admires. His great and Christian soul.

'Do not worry about me, Hattie. He does not know I am alive.'

'Best keep it that way. These radicals, dangerous, they are. All that certainty, all that conviction. It chews up a man's kindness. Heartless, some of 'em. The charmers, they're the worst.'

'He is godly, Hattie. How can you think he would not be good?'

Hattie smiles at her. 'There's goodness and there's kindness, and they ain't always the same thing.'

Hattie looks down the long stuffed line of intestine, prodding it in places, looking for weaknesses. Satisfied, she nods to Anne. The little girl, with great seriousness, ties the knot in the end.

'You're so green, Patience. He's a man grown. About thirty, I'm told. You are a girl. You don't know the world.'

Hattie is measuring out the links by eye, twisting them deftly to create the sausage and pack the filling still tighter. Concentrating, she doesn't see the flush in Patience's cheek. She doesn't see the girl's clenched fists, her frown.

'Talk to your brother,' she says, folding the links into a neat loop. 'He will tell you.'

Patience thinks she might scream. 'I must be off, Hattie,' she says tightly. She turns and pushes her way outside, into the sunlight.

Too young, too simple to understand? Does God talk only to old people? Is wisdom earned by years alone? It is preposterous. Outside, she unclenches her fists, suddenly aware that her fury could seem like a spate of adolescent temper. It is more than that. It is a justified rage. She clasps her hands lightly behind her back. Determined on her course.

She will go to Swan Alley. She will attend the meetings of this gathered church. And she will make up her own mind about the beliefs and the character of Sidrach Simmonds.

John Bradshaw stops to contemplate a pigeon. A grey, miserable thing. 'Well, Johnson,' he says to Will. 'Even the pigeons are woebegone.'

'And can we blame them?' Will starts walking onwards. They are not the only strollers in the park this morning; the first warm day of summer has drawn Londoners out to wander the grass like escaped moles, twitching their pallid faces towards the sun.

Bradshaw lengthens his stride to catch up.

'How fares the Rump Parliament?' asks Will. 'I have not been following events as I should.'

'Safer for a man's sanity to look the other way.' Bradshaw emits a strangled noise that Will interprets as derision. 'More than three years since we removed the monarchy, and still they have done nothing. Nothing.'

Will remembers Bradshaw, who was the presiding judge at the king's trial, pronouncing the sentence. The look of bullish awe on his face as he laid the sentence of death on his own sovereign. He has since been president of the Council of State, the body charged with implementing the will of the Rump Parliament. An important man – a rich and powerful one now. Why has he summoned me here? wonders Will. To take the air with him? There must be something deeper.

Bradshaw sighs. 'We had the chance, Johnson, to remake the world. And what do we do? We squabble. We plot. We intrigue. The reform of the Church has stalled. The legal reforms have stalled. The blasted MPs cannot even agree on how to dissolve themselves and call new elections.'

Will raises his face to the sun, trying to draw from it the energy to care. 'Little wonder,' he says. 'How many MPs stayed away while we tried the king, only to creep back when the cruel work was done and resume their seats? How many? So now we have the same old brew of independents, radicals, demi-royalists and Presbyterians growling at each other. Few true republicans.'

'Aye,' says Bradshaw. 'But there ought to be some ground for agreement. You know my views, Johnson. Complete freedom of worship. Let men choose their path to salvation. I accept that is too heady for most to stomach. But can we not at least agree on the iniquity of tithes? It's common ground. Yet even that recedes the instant the Rump turns to it.'

'But ministers of God cannot live on prayer alone, sir,' says Will.

Bradshaw waves an arm, as if this is accepted but irrelevant. He has the politician's disdain for detail, Will thinks.

Will does not point out the Rump's fatal weakness to Bradshaw. The Rump must fail. Its primary purpose now is to dissolve itself in favour of a new settlement. The army, stuffed as it is with republicans and religious radicals, is implacable on this point. But if the Rump goes to the people to elect a successor, the people will not choose the republicans and radicals who will satisfy the army or most of the Rumpers. Stalemate.

The players in this great political game perpetually act in the name of the people, Will thinks. Who are the people?

In London, this great fury of a city, some questions burn violently. Who shall rule? Who shall check that rule? How shall we worship? He imagines the questions bellowed straight down the old Roman roads that escape the city – and how they must lose their heat the further they travel. Smaller questions must burn with a lesser intensity away from London's flame. What shall we eat? Whom shall we love? How shall we face death?

Burning questions to the questioner; irrelevant to the body politic.

So, thinks Will, the Rump Parliament is penniless, divided and unpopular. But what else do we have?

They turn inwards to retrace their steps. Beyond those trees is the place the king died. Will shivers. He remembers again the sound of the falling axe, the grind as it sliced through flesh, the thwack as it landed on the block. He remembers the groan that rose from the crowd – a great spontaneous sigh of grief and fear and awe. It seems to him sometimes as if that groan has never really ended; as if the sad tail of it stretched and stretches still, echoing softly under all their furious scrabbling for a settlement.

He shakes his head to clear it of fancies. He realizes they have been silent for too long, each mulling their own perspective on the deadlock.

He asks: 'What of the army? General Cromwell?'

'Furious,' says Bradshaw. 'Wondering why we fought and toiled and died so that the Rumpers can sit idle.'

'Some stir themselves quick enough when there are sequestered Royalist lands to be bought cheap,' says Will.

Bradshaw looks pained, and nods his head sadly.

'True enough,' he says. 'Well, Johnson. You are wondering why I asked to meet. A friend has need of a secretary. He wants a young man. A lawyer not wedded to the law as it stands. A friend to reform. One with friends in the Temple and at Westminster.'

'I am not in need of a salary,' says Will. 'My practice is in reasonable health. Although I thank you for thinking of me.'

Bradshaw stops and looks at him. The sun is on his face, drawing out the lines and the strain around his eyes, the silver threaded through his thinning hair.

'Stay, Johnson. Do not be so quick. You have not yet heard on whose behalf I am acting.'

Will wants to shrug. It cannot matter which of the city's grandees needs a dogsbody. He quells the gesture – it would be impertinent. He respects Bradshaw. He smiles instead and inclines his head, inviting the completion of the offer.

'I am acting for the general himself, Johnson. He would have you in his service. It is Cromwell who needs a man.'

~ ~ ~

The room is close-packed. The plain whitewashed walls leap with mingled shadows, arms raised, palms outstretched. A range of people. Artisans and goodwives, soldiers and poets. The first preacher is the pastor, Jeremiah Capp. A dry, bookish man with watery blue eyes. Patience watches him gather himself as he begins to talk – the nervous clearing of his throat, the anxious swivelling eyes.

His voice is stronger than expected. He talks with great sense of the coming of Christ, of the responsibility of the elect to prepare a path for Him. He talks of the king's death and the vanquishing of the Pope in England, this blessed land. The slaying of the Antichrist paving the way for the Lord's return.

Patience finds herself nodding her agreement. But she is aware of the length of his talk; aware of the shifting of her weight from foot to foot, aware of the creeping pain in her lower back. Her thoughts drift, to her lovely, sad brother. To Blackberry, whom she loves, and his serious face as he sounds out his letters. She thinks of her chores; her instructions to Mary, the one maid they keep in the household. The new linen they need; the airing of the cupboards for moths. It is an effort to pull herself back to the words.

There is a pause when the pastor finishes. A swell of expectation in the room. A whispering and shuffling. It makes her think of the May Days of her childhood: that moment as the band prepares itself to play and feet ready for dancing begin to judder and tap. Here, there is something powerful in the containment of the excitement. Like a poacher's trap wound to breaking point.

On to the box steps Sidrach Simmonds.

He begins quietly. There are no nerves here, no awkward throat-clearing. A quiet certainty; a graceful confidence. The room sucks in its breath to hear his words.

Yours is the power, he says.

Yours is the duty.

You carry the Lord's hopes with you, His breath in your ear, His hand in yours.

You are the chosen. Only you.

His voice rises up and up, drawing them in, holding them. The first preacher spoke to their intellect; Sidrach Simmonds calls to their souls.

In the candlelight he looks young, innocent. The light glides across the dark sheen of his coat. In the pauses, his eyes drink in the room. Once, they alight on her and she feels lifted – as if by looking at her he is pulling her on to tiptoes, stretching her.

His voice is sinuous. She finds herself trying to work out if it is the words themselves that enfold the listener, or the voice, or some alchemical combination of the two.

The Lord will guide you, he says.

He will find His place in your heart.

You will know His joy as your own.

She looks around her and sees the rapture in other faces. For a heartbeat she is disappointed. His power is not for her alone. But she upbraids herself quickly. These are my brothers and sisters in Christ. She closes her eyes to concentrate.

You are the light amid a crooked generation, he says.

The words dance in her head as if they have always belonged there. As if he is not talking, but merely shining light on the words already alive inside her. The joy Patience feels is unexpected. She looks around at the weeping, shaking crowd and feels a great surge of love. She is unmade and she is made again.

Yes. I am the light. I am the light.

Afterwards, still reeling, she hovers by the door. She knows no one, but she wants to talk, to share what she has felt. Besides, she cannot bear to go home yet. Blackberry is in bed, asleep, and the adults will not be able to borrow his gaiety. She will sit with Will, his unhappiness lolling by the hearth with them like an uninvited guest. She will talk too brightly, too loudly. If she talks of this evening, of Sidrach Simmonds, which is all that she can bear to speak of, he will lean back and lift his brows and roll his eyes. She cannot go back, not yet.

Shyly, she looks about her, trying to invite conversation

A middle-aged woman catches her eyes and smiles. Her dress is plain but of good quality, with a deepness to the black. There are tiny stitches at the shoulder in a colour that does not quite match. Her hair is drawn back from her face, pulling her thick eyebrows upwards into a curve. She has kind eyes, Patience decides, as the woman peels away from her conversation and comes over to her. 'You are new here,' she says. As Patience nods, she smiles. 'I am Marigold Capp,' she says. 'My husband is the pastor.'

'I am happy to meet you,' says Patience. 'My name is Patience Johnson.'

She feels bolder now she has spoken.

'I saw you, caught in Mr Simmonds' words, Mistress Johnson.

He is a persuasive teacher.'

'He is inspired by the divine,' says Patience, with a rush of enthusiasm. Marigold Capp looks awkward.

'Sidrach is a man of much . . .' She waves her hands, and runs out of words.

'I wasn't sure,' Patience says. 'Is it allowed, that I just came in? I didn't know anyone to invite me.'

Marigold lays a hand on her arm. 'Allowed, yes. Encouraged even. But to join our congregation takes a little more. You must prove your state of grace, my dear. Only the elect are permitted.'

'How do I know? If I am elect?'

Marigold looks baffled momentarily. Patience bites her lip. That was the wrong question, obviously. Only the elect reach heaven; their presence called by the divine. The elect know they are elect, among the godly – she knows this much.

She thinks of her father in his quiet country vicarage, studiously avoiding theology. Following the prayer book, praying on Sundays. Performing baptisms, marriages and deaths with a benign, wilful mediocrity.

She speaks quickly into the pause. 'I mean, of course, I behave as if I have God's grace. But how do I know for sure?'

'I think, my dear, that you need to meet my husband.'

She draws Patience into the hubbub of the room. Arms are waving, voices are rising. In one corner, a man is almost shouting. He has a thin white face. He looks like a voluble parsnip, Patience thinks. She laughs at herself, just as they come to a stand in front of the pastor, and Sidrach Simmonds. They turn to look at her, frowning at her fading smile, and she wilts. She has made herself appear silly; frivolous. These are serious men.

Be strong, she tells herself. The woman she will become does not quail at strangers, does not falter.

'This is Patience Johnson,' says Marigold. 'She is newly arrived among us.'

She bobs to them, casting her eyes down at their shoes. The pastor's are scuffed and old; Sidrach Simmonds' shoes gleam as if licked clean.

'You are welcome,' says the pastor. 'Did you enjoy our service?'

'Very much,' says Patience. 'I believe I understood it. I believe so,' she repeats, sounding uncertain to her own ears. Sidrach Simmonds looks directly at her, holding her eyes with his. 'Well, Patience Johnson, there is a beginning in all understanding. And the beginning is the word.'

His eyes flicker around the room. He shifts his weight as if to leave.

'Do you live close by?' asks the pastor, in a voice that signifies he does not care overmuch.

'Yes,' she says. 'With my brother. I keep house for him. His wife died.'

There is a pause. Sidrach Simmonds looks down at his cuffs, pulling a speck of white lint off the black.

'Yes,' she says again, too brightly. 'He is a lawyer. But he has a new line of work soon starting.'

'Mmm,' says the pastor, turning towards his wife.

'He is to be one of the private secretaries to General Cromwell.'

'Cromwell?' says the pastor. All three of them turn back towards her.

'Yes. He starts on Wednesday next.'

A tut from Marigold.

Sidrach Simmonds says: 'We do not use the old names here. They are pagan-inspired. You must say the fourth day of the second week of the seventh month.'

'I am sorry. I did not know.' Another nugget not to offer up to Will's disdain, she thinks.

'It is of no consequence,' he says. He seems to look at her as if for the first time. Weighing her. He holds her gaze for an eternity. She is giddy with it.

'You will learn, Patience Johnson,' he says. 'You will learn.'

Here he is. Will swallows. He clenches his fists and finds them moist with sweat. Standing outside a door waiting to meet the man himself. The man who holds England's future in his palm. For as much as the MPs debate and the radicals rant and people persuade themselves otherwise, the army is the final arbiter of power in England now. Its lord general sits behind this door. Will feels like a schoolboy waiting for a beating.

There is shouting from inside the room, but the thick oak blurs the words. Abruptly, the shouting ends and the door opens. Will starts at the sudden movement. A man comes out. Tousle-haired and smiling-eyed, he looks at Will and grins. 'Johnson?'

Will nods.

'Marchamont Nedham.'

They bow. Will knows him by reputation – he is the broadsheet man. The writer of news and views, currently producing the *Mercurius Politicus*, the Parliament's newsbook.

'The lord general begs your attendance,' says Nedham. He moves closer. 'Careful,' he whispers. He blows out his cheeks and shakes his head, to illustrate his point. Will smiles, taken by the man's droll charm. Nedham sweeps an arm towards the open door, then saunters away. He is practically whistling.

Will steps forward into the room. A man stands by the large window, his back to the door. He is a broad silhouette – his plain dark coat blurred against the light from the window. He turns, and Will catches the lingering fury on his features. Drawn brows, reddened skin – the strength of his face is a punch.

Will begins to stammer something, anything. But the man's expression clears. A sudden smile, wide and artless. The reddish hue remains, and the impression of energy contained by will. He walks forward.

'William Johnson? I am Cromwell.'

Will bows, murmurs something.

'Forgive me,' says Cromwell. He reaches out and clasps Will's shoulder. No flinch? How strange, he thinks as Cromwell pulls him further into the room. 'I was out of countenance,' says the general.

He looks at Will with clear eyes, set in a gnarled face. Will feels an absurd urge to please.

He has been silent for an age. Bewildered.

'It is no matter,' he says.

Cromwell stares at him. Will knows that he presents a confusing figure. After Henrietta's death, his hair turned white. He does not know how long it took to turn. Those days are too much of a blur. All he knows is that one day, he looked in a mirror and he was white-haired. Shockingly old.

He has a young man's face, and an old man's hair, and eyes that make women want to coddle him. He does not want to be coddled.

Cromwell smiles again, and it transforms him. A man would go a long way to win a smile like that from his general, thinks Will.

'I must beg your forgiveness once more,' says Cromwell. 'This letter will not wait.'

He waves a hands towards the large oak desk. It is thick with paper; letters and pamphlets and bills all higgled together. An inkwell sits in a roughly cleared island, droplets from it freckling the dark wood.

'You will understand now, Mr Johnson, why I require your services. I have army business, Council of State business, Parliament business. I drown in business, sir, and I am need of a raft.'

'I hope to be useful, sir,' says Will. He has lost his eloquence. He is a fool.

As Cromwell returns to the desk, Will wanders to the great painting on the wall to the side of them. A Roman general sits on a chariot. Behind him, a long-haired boy holds a laurel wreath in a hover above the man's short curls. Below him, a horse capers and infants wave leafy fronds.

Will can hear the rough scrape of Cromwell's pen as he studies the painting. He is drawn always back to the Roman general's oddly strained face. He tries to look elsewhere, but cannot. The scraping has stopped, and suddenly Cromwell is just behind him.

'Julius Caesar,' he says. 'A fine work, is it not? One of a series of nine by Andrea Mantegna. The remaining eight are at Hampton Court. They work together as a long frieze showing Caesar's great triumphal procession through Rome. I had him moved here to keep me company.'

'It is a fine painting, Lord General.'

'Almost the last of the late king's paintings. I will try to keep it from being sold. It would fetch some thousand pounds, I am told. But Caesar there. Look. He helps me think on power and hubris. On the dangerous seductions of vanity. Look at him, Johnson. "Ha," thinks he. "Look what I have done!"'

Cromwell lends Caesar a pompous boom, which suits his own deep, scratchy voice. Will smiles. But that is not what he sees. Caesar's face looks frightened, almost. Contained panic. 'Look what I have done' is a whispered lament. This Caesar already understands the price that power will exact.

Will pulls himself away from the picture, turning to face his new benefactor. He says: 'The sale of the king's goods has raised bounteous funds, I have heard.'

'Not enough. Ah, Mr Johnson, to see the beauties, the glories, we have sold. Some lewd pieces, to be sure, that will better hang in a popish court. This, the jewel, and its eight sisters. These we will keep. But the rest? Gone. Lord, to think of all the blood and treasure spent in our cause. We must make sure it is not in vain.'

Will nods, accepting his complicity in the cause. As ever, it is easier to let other men assume they know his politics and his God. He has no strong convictions. He is a hollowed-out player on this stage.

He still does not quite understand why he accepted the post at the heart of the godly ranks. Perhaps because it would be unthinkable for a young man of his status to refuse such an offer.

Will is accustomed to behaving how a theoretical young man of his position would be expected to behave. He acts from within the daze that shrouded him on Henrietta's death. The lawyer who cheerfully nods his head to colleagues as he strolls through the

Temple is not real. The brother who watches his sister's growing infatuation with the millenarian preacher is not real. The father who stoops to kiss grazed knees is the most shameful masquerader of all.

Cromwell clears his throat, breaking into Will's reverie. 'Bradshaw recommends you highly, as does your old master John Cooke. Bradshaw says you are discreet, hard-working, serious.'

Am I? Will considers this description of him. If so, I'm not sure I always was. I used to laugh, did I not?

Cromwell is looking at him, as if in judgement. Suddenly he smiles and nods. Will feels an unexpected flicker of relief.

'You will have two hundred pounds a year,' says the general, turning back towards the desk. 'You will share an office with the Council's Latin secretary, from Monday. And you will be utterly discreet. Does that meet your approval, Mr Johnson?'

Will mumbles his acceptance. He understands that the interview is over, and as he backs out, he realizes that now he will pull on another mask: ambitious secretary to an ambitious man.

As he closes the door, Cromwell sinks back behind the desk with an audible sigh. Behind him, Caesar looks down on his triumph with his inscrutable, deadened face.

WEST INDIES

June 1652

*S*WALLOW. HOW SHE DESERVES HER NAME. SHE FLIES ACROSS the water, spreading her great sails, swooping to meet the pitch and fall of the sea.

And what a sea! A cycle of blue and green and turquoise and a blind of white, white sand at the water's edge.

Sam loves the night watches. The rock of the ship like a lullaby; the whispering rush of the white-frothed water under the stern. Above, the masts roll and only the white of the sails is visible in the gloom as the cat's cradle of rigging fades to black. The stars are still, impervious as the rocking of the sails frames one patch of sky and then another, picking out their indifferent beauty.

The men are wraiths in the darkness; a patter of bare feet on the planking. Burned already by the Caribbean sun, their faces are indistinct. Only the gleam of teeth and the yellow of an eye to mark them out.

Below, the men in their hammocks sweat and swelter. On deck there is always this delicious breeze, kissing their damp brows, filling the sails. Lifting a quiet, unthreatening swell from the warm sea.

The ship is a quiet cocoon. It is impossible to believe in elsewhere, inside the dark embrace of deck and sea and star-flecked sky. Impossible to believe in a man's brains spilling on to an African foreshore. Impossible to believe in the storm, last year, that sent the general-at-sea's last flagship down to the deep with three hundred souls weeping aboard as the sea closed over them. Impossible to believe in the pestilence that lurks on these beautiful shores, waiting to send a man mad with fever and delirium. Impossible to believe that this sweet, God-blessed sailing can ever end. Impossible to believe in home.

One night, he stands next to the helmsman and growls at his inattention as the head comes up a trifle and sails lose their taut beauty.

'Sorry, sir,' says the man at the whipstaff. Sam looks at him more closely, peering through the half-light cast by the lantern. James Fowler from the *Supply*. That tub is long gone – she crept off towards the horizon when her captain was floundering on an African shore, Fowler left behind in the confusion. The mutinous bastards sailed back to proffer their arses to Cromwell, most like, leaving the erstwhile Captain Challoner kicking his heels on the flagship, volunteering for night watches to stave off the boredom.

'Settling in, Fowler?' asks Sam.

'Aye, sir.'

Sam looks up at the rigging. The topgallants are set, to take advantage of the light wind and open water. Lord, the beauty of it. He yawns widely. He is tired and still pissed, he thinks, from a convivial dinner in the gun room. Two hours' sleep he had.

Enough to take the edge off the port before he was called from his sweat-drenched cot.

He holds his face towards the breeze and closes his eyes. He wrenches them open again. Stay awake, Challoner.

'You were at Naseby?' he says to Fowler, remembering their conversation in the hut on Cabo Verde.

'I was.'

'As was I. Cavalry. Prince Rupert's regiment, of course. A sad day.'

Fowler smirks. 'Depends on your point of view, sir.'

'True enough. My brother was there too. Served under Holles.'

Fowler turns to look at him. He keeps his grip on the wooden pole that steers the ship. One man can do it, in these light seas and winds, but he needs strength and concentration. 'Your brother, sir. He was not Ned Challoner? I had not thought . . . I mean . . . You are not . . .'

Sam rescues him from his floundering. 'Yes. Ned Challoner. God rest his soul. You knew him?'

'Served alongside him, sir. Owe him my life two times over. More, probably. A good man.'

Sam nods, although he is still not sure that his brother was a good man. A man of strong convictions, who put his cause before his family. Did that make him good, or bad? Or does that distinction depend on your belief in the cause that drove him? Lord, he is too pissed to work this one out. He wipes his forehead with his sleeve, and tries to will himself sober.

'I was with him when he died, sir.'

'Good Lord,' says Sam, looking afresh at Fowler. He is a small, wiry man. His face is lined and burned, and the hair above has receded a fair way. He could be any age from thirty to fifty – impossible to tell. There is a nasal twang to his vowels, and a way of speaking that suggests scorn, despite the disciplined politeness of the actual words.

'In Ireland. I'd fought for him all over, sir. I was his troop sergeant at Naseby. Knew where you stood with him, you did. Hard, but fair. Knew his onions. But at Drogheda, something happened to him. Afterwards, after he died like, I left. Fed up of waiting to be paid, I was. The new officer, he was a green prick, begging your pardon, sir. I signed on to the *Supply*. Know my way around boats.'

'What do you mean, something happened to him?' Sam draws closer. There's a strange intimacy about talking on deck in the night watch. Men speak softly, as if afraid to send their voices booming out into the dark shadows.

'Ireland was hard. Drogheda. Fucking horrible place, sir, begging your pardon. It was a normal siege. You know the thing. Mostly boring, sometimes bloody terrifying. We offered terms. They refused. Talked sharp. So anyhows, we took the town. Cromwell in charge, course we would. The man's a genius.'

He pauses suddenly, and looks around, wide-eyed. It will not do to talk of Cromwell on this ship with anything other than scorn and vitriol.

'No matter, no matter,' says Sam. 'Please, continue.'

'Well, sir. You know how it is. If a besieged town refuses terms, they suffer for it. Stands to reason. When we was through the walls, the general he ordered that one man in every ten be put to the sword. And the priests. Fair's fair. He ordered Ned to take charge of it. Like a bleeding slaughterhouse it was, sir. Lining 'em all up. Stopping the waiting ones from squealing. And the women outside keening. Singing in that funny language. And the begging, sir. Only some of the bastards knew how to die like men.'

Sam feels entirely sober now. He leans against the mainmast, feeling its solidity. He tries to picture Ned's features, but cannot conjure the adult brother. Only the small, freckled face of his childhood play-fellow.

'After, like I say, he were different. Quiet. Uncertain. I had to shoulder some of his work, to stop the whole bleeding troop collapsing. "Was it truly God's work?" he asked me once, sir. "'Twas orders," said I. Leaving it there.'

He falls silent, and Sam, despite the urge to run away, is forced to press him.

'What happened?'

'Well, afterwards, we was scouting out beyond the Pale, and we was ambushed. Stupid, small scrap. And he . . . Well, sir. It was like he had no fight left in him. Stood there, he did. I saw. Let himself be cut down by a heathen lad. A boy really.'

'You buried him properly?'

'Of course, sir. He was properly missed, sir.'

Someone mourned him, then. Oh Ned. Oh my poor brother.

The bell rings then. The watch is over, and the spell is broken. Sam nods his thanks and farewells to Fowler, as the men relieving them clatter on to the deck.

He stays above awhile. He is not ready to sleep, nor for the stifle of his tiny cabin. He stands at the taffrail, watching the water rush under the stern. The sky is lightening. The daily routines of the ship are beginning behind him. The rapping of feet on deck, and the waisters gathering to holystone the decks. The animals are waking up, adding their squeals and clucks to the gathering cacophony. And soon there will be a sun, rising hard and bright on the horizon, smearing the sea and sky with its insistent pink and reds.

MIDDLESEX

July 1652

𝓑LACKBERRY STANDS ON A FALLEN TREE, PULLING HIS long skirts up out of the way of his boots. He looks towards Patience with a wide triumphant smile, before taking a tremulous step forward. His boots slide on the damp bark; the sun, though bright, cannot fight its way through the canopy.

He loses his balance and falls. He lands heavily, silently. Looking up, he sees Patience start towards him with a look of concern and opens his mouth in a wail of anguish. She rushes over and pulls him in. 'Shh, now, little soldier.'

'The boy is not hurt,' says Sidrach Simmonds.

She turns to look at him from her awkward crouch. He is tall, rigid as one of the trunks. Capp, the pastor, stands beside him and seems slight – insubstantial. Behind them, Marigold Capp and her two solemn daughters walk slowly onwards.

'He is not,' Patience agrees. 'I was perhaps . . .' She trails off. Blackberry stops crying, burying his face in her shoulder, wiping his nose on her dress. She tries to brush off the slimy stain without

Sidrach Simmonds noticing, but when she sneaks a glance up at him, he is looking away.

His face is in profile, and she stares longer than is necessary. There is a nobility to his features, she decides. A modern Seneca.

She kisses Blackberry, and he grins at her, bouncing back already. 'I like woods, Auntie Imp.'

'What is that the boy calls you?' asks Capp.

'Imp,' she says, standing. 'A stupid nickname from home. From impatience, you see.'

'You must teach him otherwise, my dear,' says Marigold Capp. 'Anyone listening might mistake the name, and its bearer, for a witch's helpmeet.'

Patience begins to laugh but sees their faces and checks herself.

They walk on, Blackberry running ahead. She finds his exuberance trying. The wood echoes with his cries. 'Look, Auntie! Help, Auntie! What's this! Watch me! Are you watching?'

On it goes. She can sense Sidrach Simmonds' irritation. She can almost see the tremor in his skin when the inevitable happens and Blackberry calls out in a high treble a phrase he must have picked up in Hattie's shop: 'God's blood, Auntie Imp!'

She hopes they have not heard, but their faces betray them. Capp looks serious; Marigold as if she has buried her nose in lemons. The smallest Capp girl, four-year-old Martha, giggles. Sidrach Simmons turns to look at her and she falls silent, so that the only sound in the wood is the absence of chat and the sly call of a cuckoo.

'A lovely notion,' says Patience brightly. 'To leave the walls behind and stroll here.'

'Does it remind you of home, my dear?' asks Marigold Capp, God bless her.

'A little. We have fields by us, mainly. But beyond the village there is a wood where we walk sometimes.'

'Your father has a living there, I believe,' says Sidrach Simmonds. Not a question, but a statement.

'Yes. Not a large parish, but he is happy.'

There is a pause; an unasked question.

'He is not political,' she says. 'We were lucky. We avoided most of the worst of the wars.'

'In these days,' says Capp, 'a man of God must also be a man of politics. If we are to remake the world for the Lord's coming, we cannot hide away in country backwaters, grateful for a good crop.'

'I agree,' says Patience, and perhaps she is too loud, too strident, for Capp looks surprised and Sidrach Simmonds turns to study her with an unreadable expression on his face.

'My dear,' says Marigold, linking arms with her husband. 'There are some matters I would talk to you about. Boring, domestic affairs,' she says, in an apologetic aside to Patience.

They draw behind. Blackberry is sauntering ahead. A stick for a sword. Playing at being Lord Cromwell, no doubt, laying waste to the rebellious Scots. She is alone with Sidrach Simmonds. What if she says something stupid? Something theologically absurd?

She wants him to speak first, to prick the tension. But he smiles a half-smile and lets the silence stretch. 'Blackberry wants to be a soldier, I think,' she says.

'Yes. A strange nickname the boy has.'

'His mother gave it to him before she died. It stuck fast. He is called Richard, for his maternal grandfather. He died in the wars. So too did Blackberry's uncle Edward. In Ireland.'

'Are there none of them left on his mother's side?'

'Blackberry has an uncle. Samuel. He is on the Continent somewhere, I think. With Prince Rupert. I have not met him, of course.'

'A grandfather and an uncle for the king. The boy is of Royalist blood.'

'He is four!'

They fall silent again. Patience chastises herself. She does not quite understand why Sidrach is displeased with her; she only knows that it is so.

She speaks first, again. She asks about his family. He has none, it seems. An only child, his mother and father died of fever when he was a boy. He was raised by an ancient aunt. Her modest possessions and his parents' have all passed to him.

He seems to like talking about himself, and it is safe ground. She cannot be stupid in front of him if she asks short questions about his life. The king raised his standard when the young Sidrach was but eighteen. He was aimless and without profession. Joining the fight seemed the obvious path.

'I was a foolish youth. The army made me. It taught me of brotherhood. Of duty. Most of all, it brought me to the Lord's grace. I was a worm. A weak and foolish sinner. In the New Model Army I found the Lord, and He found me.'

'And you were lately in Ireland?'

'Yes.' A bald, solitary reply. A drawing-in of brows. She has touched on something uncomfortable again. But this time he speaks: 'And now I find myself a youth no longer. My thoughts turn to Whitehall, my heart to Christ. And my home? Well. There is a vacancy, I think, for a woman at its hearth.'

A violent, ragtag collision of caught breath and beating heart. She does not know how to reply. She feels sucked into something momentous. This is what she wanted, was it not? But now the Capps have stopped and they are upon them, and the talk softens to mundane things. The weather and the harvest. The possibility of rain.

The tavern is full. Clerks and secretaries and scriveners; the quiet men who stand behind the booming power players. Will sits with his room-mate, Milton. He takes a short sip from his tankard and waits for the other man to speak. Milton is older than him – early forties, perhaps. He has a long, shrewd face. His eyes seem sore – he rubs at their red rims in a habitual gesture. They water almost continuously. Is it a physical affliction that makes his whole demeanour seem melancholic? The word in the corridors is that his wife has recently died, but their friendship is too new to probe.

Two men drinking in a tavern after work. Two dead wives. Two cold beds. Will grips his tankard all the tighter.

'Well,' says Milton. 'And how do you find it? Shoulder-man to our lord general.'

'Interesting,' says Will.

'How so?'

Will pauses to summon his thoughts. He has learned in the past week that Milton is frank and disarmingly honest. He expects his conversations to be sharp-pointed.

Before he can speak, a man breaks in, throwing careless greetings at them and sitting without being asked. Marchamont Nedham. 'Well met, gentlemen,' he says. 'And how is our lord treating you?'

Will is momentarily confused.

'Cromwell,' says Milton.

'The mighty warted one.'

'Nedham.' Milton raps the name as a rebuke, but he is amused, too.

'Ignore him, Johnson,' he says. 'He's a scoundrel.'

'Ah, but you love me, my serious friend.'

The two men grimace at each other briefly, before Nedham turns to Will.

'Well, Johnson. Have you learned yet that the mighty one is our one topic of conversation? His moods. His fancies. We pore over him as if he is a lover.'

'Closer than a lover, in your case,' says Milton.

'Aye, well. I'm yet to meet a woman who can string me up for treason as he can. So therefore none worth the same scrutiny.'

'Leave the treason alone, then.'

Will watches them spar. Milton says: 'You know, of course, that our friend here turned monarchist some years back. Wrote thundering apologies for the king.'

'God rest his soul,' says Nedham. To be mischievous, more than from conviction, Will thinks.

'But now you are a Commonwealth man?' he asks. Nedham waves an ambiguous arm.

'Our friend here,' says Milton, 'found he miraculously converted to the idea of the Commonwealth inside Newgate,

58

where he found himself on the king's demise.'

'A proper Saul you have before you, gentlemen. That place was remarkably persuasive,' says Nedham, unabashed.

'Did you meet the king?' asks Will.

'I did. He gave me a royal pardon. My first job was to write furious prose to accuse him. My second to write furious prose to praise him. And now . . . Well. Milton here would like all men of letters to believe every word they write. My job is to convince all men to believe every word they read. The truth belongs to he who pays for the ink. Damned pricey, ink.'

Will finds himself smiling. There is something twinkling and irrepressible about the newsbook man. His irreverence is disarming in these days where talk is deadly serious.

'Come, Nedham,' says Milton. 'You will have the boy believing in your nonsense. Nedham is a serious thinker, Mr Johnson, when he applies himself.'

'Deadly so,' agrees Nedham, with an exaggerated, wise nod.

'We even,' says Milton, 'are in agreement at times. We are in the same mind on the possibility of liberty existing only within a republic.'

Will stares at Milton. Not so long ago, the word 'republic' was to be whispered. Even the killing of the king came not from principle in most men's eyes but from pragmatism. A cruel necessity to end the stalemate. How fast the world turns.

'Now,' says Nedham, deflecting the talk as if to spare Will from using the word himself. 'Tell us. How many potentates have you served?'

'The one. I saw the king. At his trial. I never talked to him,' says Will.

'Nor like to, now, where he is,' says Milton. A rueful smile, like a tapster admitting her best ale is sour.

Will says: 'You have met the king, Nedham, and you have met Cromwell. Cromwell has a force, a presence to him. Near him, I feel young, foolish. Keen to be approved. Is that a function of his office, or of his person?'

Nedham draws breath, as if considering. Milton says: 'A shrewd question. What do you say, Nedham? The man or the title?'

Nedham becomes more serious than Will has seen him. Beneath the charm is intellect, deftly hidden. 'What presence the king had was a function of his office, not of his person. But Cromwell? Milton, what do *you* say?'

'Physically, they are opposites,' says Milton. 'One slight, one broad. Cromwell is a big man. Powerful.'

'Powerfully ugly, too,' says Nedham. 'The impact of a man's physique is important, sure. And yet there's many a big, ugly man in the shadows.'

'Perhaps part of it is that we know their stories,' says Will. 'The king's only story was his birth. His power was a function of that birth. Cromwell's power is all earned. He came from nothing, from nowhere, and that counts.'

'Yes,' says Nedham slowly. 'But there is something more, is there not? Personality, and how it affects the men in his orbit. Cromwell's temper is fiercer than other men's, and his sweetness sweeter. So we caper and prance to avoid the first and earn the second.'

'And his sincerity,' says Milton. 'He believes, even when others doubt it, that God works through him.'

'I often think sincerity walks hand in hand with foolishness.

But not in the Lord Cromwell's case,' says Nedham.

'Though he is not a great scholar,' Milton says, with a shake of his head.

'Nor even a great thinker. A great soldier, I am told, by people who understand these things,' says Will. They all nod sagely into their tankards. Nedham pours the last of the jug of ale.

'No matter how great Cromwell is,' says Nedham, 'we must guard against him. We must be wary of self-seeking great men in this newborn republic. The greater they are, the more threat they are.'

We will wrangle this question all evening and not be bored, thinks Will as they call for another jug. Another sign of the Lord Cromwell's power. He tries to pin down the analogy flitting in his head.

'Magnetism,' he says. 'Magnetism, gentlemen. Thales of Miletus broached the idea that magnets have souls, and it is this that gives them the power to move iron.'

Nedham looks blank, but Milton smiles. He leans forward, lips parted. His palm slaps open on the table, and the rattled tankards judder. 'Leading us, Mr Johnson, to the question posed by the Lord Cromwell. Magnets may or may not have souls, but does the opposite hold? Do some souls act as magnets? Is Cromwell's such a soul?'

Will smiles, and Nedham leans back in his chair. He whistles. 'Gentlemen,' he says. 'I think this calls for a bigger jug.'

After the next meeting of the church, Sidrach Simmonds draws her into a corner. He turns those eyes on her. They twist her stomach.

She is trembling, still, from the sermon. She feels the hot breath of God. He is coming. There is no doubt.

'Did you understand today, Patience Johnson?' he asks.

'I did.' She hopes he can see the earnestness in her face. She does not know how to express her sincerity. She wants him to understand her, to feel the answering call of her soul.

'Of course you did,' he says. He smiles, and it occurs to her that it is the first time she has seen him smile. He has been serious, almost severe. His face is warm now, lit from some place within that she longs to know.

Over his shoulder, she can see the faces of the saints. A half-smile from Marigold Capp, their eyes meeting across the room. A stare from one of the Mason sisters. She flutters around Sidrach; Patience has seen her.

Patience stops herself winking at the disgruntled Mason, with some difficulty. Be serious, she tells herself. Be worthy.

She concentrates on Sidrach. The moving of his lips.

'. . . we will be chosen, Patience. You understand this. We, who need Him, will be needed by Him.'

How? She wants to ask for particulars, but she is afraid that if she speaks, this sharp intimacy will smudge. She is close enough to smell him. Nutmeg?

'. . . and the Lord's light, Patience! Imagine it. Can you even come close to it – the brilliance, the purity?'

She nods.

'And you understand, Patience, what is coming. We will be tested. We will be called. What point, what purpose, did the late bloodletting serve, if not to pave His way? He will need bearers for his olive branches. He will need our hearts to be open, to be pure.'

He lays a hand on her arm, lightly. She looks down at the neat nails, at the long fingers. It seems almost proprietorial, this gesture. She does not quite know how to respond. She smiles up at him, hoping that her warmth will be evident.

The summer is fading into autumn and the sun is bright but low behind them. Their shadows stalk ahead on the stony track, melded together and lengthened by the angles of the light.

'You are beautiful,' says Sidrach Simmonds.

She blushes, casts her eyes downwards. She is so nervous, she might be sick. She berates herself: you have waited all your life for a man such as he to make love to you, and now you will vomit on his shoes. Breathe, you ninny. Breathe. He cannot see her face, only the bowed top of her head.

'You are modest. That pleases me,' he says.

She swells a little, enjoying his approval.

He takes her hand and tucks it into the crook of his arm, and they walk onwards.

Behind them, the Capps keep their distance. This walk has become a settled thing. Taken once a week on Friday afternoons, out in the fields beyond the walls. Each walk a step closer to something.

He helps her across a stile, handing her up and over. She could do it herself – she was bred amid fields and fences. But she takes his hand and thanks him, and steps lightly into the mud. Only a year or two ago, she would have jumped down, laughing as she sank to her ankles, sucking her boots out to chase a sister down a tree-lined path.

She finds she has not let go of his hand. His palm is cool to the touch. She feels as if her own hand is burning.

'Yes,' he says. 'Beautiful. Young. Healthy. No fortune, as such. However . . .' He pauses, as if weighing her.

She draws a breath, and finds she cannot exhale it.

'You must know, Patience,' he says, 'that I am moving towards a decision regarding you. It is time, I think, for me to take a wife. A helpmeet. Someone to stand by me in what is to come. A mother for my children. I have chosen you, Patience Johnson.'

Oh, the blessing of the Lord! Chosen by such a man.

'I will do you honour,' she says. She looks up at him with blazing eyes.

'Good, good,' he says, quietly. He doesn't look at her, but scans the horizon for the Capps. He tightens his grip on her hand.

SOMEWHERE NORTH OF
THE VIRGIN ISLANDS

September 1652

*T*HIS IS NOT A LARK, NOT ANY MORE, THINKS SAM. THIS IS not the same sea. This is not the same balmy world he has come to expect and love. This is – and he will admit it only to himself in a whisper in his cot, drenched and shivering and starving – fucking terrifying.

The hurricane hit two days ago. A sudden slam of wind and rain, whipping the seas up into staggering peaks and troughs with unbelievable rapidity. They had time, just, to take in all but one sail – the course on the foremast. Strong, new canvas, thank God, whose white face is keeping them scudding along with the screaming wind at their backs.

They can scarce see ten feet beyond the taffrail in the gloom and rain. Only the sounding of the near-sacred bell tells them if it is night or day. *Swallow*'s master is in irons below, awaiting punishment for the enthusiastic buggering of unwilling ships' boys. But even that excellent navigator would be lost in this tumult, with the ship making leeway at incredible speeds, and the stars and moon shrouded in thick cloud.

Lost on this violent black sea, the *Swallow* climbs the peaks and drops into the troughs with a gallant heart that seems to foresee its own death. Each peak feels impossible to climb; each trough is impossible to escape. The fear of being swamped is constant, and yet familiarity does not deaden it – just ratchets it up so that a man's nerves are screaming, screaming red.

Out there, somewhere, the squadron's other ships are alone too. God help the prize crews on the handful of captured ships they have taken in this leisurely cruise, trying to face this storm with a few men and a hold full of furious prisoners.

Sam lies shivering in his cot, clinging on to its edges to avoid falling to the deck or slamming the ceiling. He is drenched. All his clothes are drenched. Where he is dry, he itches from the salt. His stomach feels completely empty, and his mouth is parched. They are on half-rations of what cold food can be rummaged – no lighting the galley fires in this weather. He pulls the thin blanket over his head. Prayer will have to substitute for sleep, and he mutters the Lord's name again and again, until he is not sure if he is blaspheming or praying.

A ship's boy appears at his door.

'Please, sir. Your watch, sir.'

Sam looks up. The boy is ashen, ridiculously small. One of the poor little mites the master preyed on, no doubt. He looks thoroughly and utterly miserable.

Sam sways himself up. He reaches for his boat cloak, which is stiff with salt where it is not still dripping wet. He grunts his acknowledgement at the boy. Lord, but the effort it takes to rise. The bare bones of him are crying to lie down again. To give up. They will not survive this. Better to be below, suffocating under tons of water, than be offered the false hope of that open sea.

But he sees the small face looking at him, and he makes himself smile, and he makes his legs creak straight so that he is standing. He makes himself take the two steps towards the cabin door. He makes himself climb the ladders, to emerge on the deck into the howling, murderous wind.

He reaches for a lifeline and half walks, half pulls himself forward to where Prince Rupert is standing next to the binnacle. Every time he has come on deck, the prince has been here. God alone knows when the man sleeps. Sam nods at him; the general smiles back tightly.

'You must rest, sir,' he shouts. Rupert shakes his head impatiently. The wet curls of his hair stick to his forehead. Sam turns and looks along the run of the ship, at the huge forecourse straining at its reefs, at the towering wave ahead of them. Up they climb, up and up, and at the top, where the force of the wind is unchecked, there is suddenly a new sound. A shrieking, tearing, ripping sound that promises new horror.

The foremast course is splitting. The wild end of it flaps, flicking an unfortunate sailor over the side of the ship. His white face is visible for one heartbeat, before he disappears. The ship falters, the bow quivers.

Rupert is screaming at the men nearest – they need to get some sail on the stump of the mizzenmast; something, anything to help keep some steerage on her. Behind him, the whipstaff groans at its tackles and the bosun sends men running to clap on. They must fight the sea, fight the bare-rigged *Swallow*'s desire to turn beam-on to the wind, letting the sea curl over their heads and take them all down.

'Sam!' screams Rupert. Shit, thinks Sam. Not me. And why is the German bastard using my given name? Rupert points forward.

The great sail must be contained. Its wild contortions are playing with the wind.

Oh Jesus.

Sam gestures in an arc to a bunch of the nearest men, and beckons them on. The bosun, thinking quickly, hands knives and axes to those who reach for them. A few do not move, but shrink back, cowering and refusing to meet his eyes. But the reckoning must wait.

Sam hurries forward, letting the downward slope of the pitching deck help him in his rush, and hoping that at least a few of the bastards are following. His booted feet slip-slide on the planking, and he wishes he were barefoot. He glances behind – a handful of men, thank Christ, including Fowler. The man is naked to the waist, with water clinging to the grey hairs on his chest.

The split in the sail is diagonal, reaching up from the belaying pins near the deck on the port side to the yard itself on the starboard. Sam throws himself upon its trailing edge, trying to get the living, wet mass of it under control. A handful of them now, clawing at the wet canvas, pushing it back towards the bottom of the foremast. There is Fowler at his side, and he is pointing upwards to the starboard, where the tattered sail is still spread towards the wind. Catching it, filling with its howling mass and pushing the *Swallow*'s head away from safety.

There are not enough of them to hand the mass of sail upon the deck and to haul on the clewlines to pull the bottom of it up to the main yard. How is it hanging on at all? Sam wonders. A sliver of sail is left attached at the top and a broader piece at the bottom. But that sliver is enough to kill them all.

It must be cut.

He looks around to see who he can send, but the men are all grappling with the sail, cutting away awkward lines and using their bodies to weight it down.

It must be him. Oh Lord, oh Jesus.

He runs to the windward side and grasps the rigging, swinging himself up and out. He looks down; he cannot help himself. Down to the black, hungry sea below – so far below. Look up, Sam. He grips the hemp with slick hands, thanking the Lord for the scratch of it, which helps a man hang on when the wind is tearing, tearing at him. Trying to pluck him like a dandelion and send him soaring away.

He climbs as fast as he can. The faster he goes, the quicker he will be down. He is at the yard now, and he manages the awkward swing out and round to find his foothold on the line that runs beneath it. The bucking, leaping wet line that he must inch along. The ragged end of the torn sail flaps below him, so loud it's like a drum in his head urging him out, out and along. To the very edge of the yard at last. Clinging on with one hand, his feet swinging wildly to and fro on the line, he reaches for the axe in his waistband. He hacks at the sail's fastenings. He is practically over the sea here. If he falls, he will brain himself on a gun, bounce off and drown quickly, if he is lucky. Hack, Sam.

It is giving! It is working. He whacks one more time with his axe at the tangle of sail and cordage. It gives, and falls, taking a heavy block with it. Sam watches over the top of the yard as the block falls to the deck, pausing on the way to dash out the brains of Fowler, who is below, blood streaming now from his open skull and down his naked chest.

For four days they run before the wind on the scrap of mizzen sail. Four days, with the wind never abating, and the sea never dying, and the men on board parched and starving, and sleeping where they fall in nightmarish huddles.

For four days, the shocked blaze of Fowler's face through the gloom haunts Sam. The way he still stood there, with half his head gone, and the grey matter leaking. Until, at last, he swayed and bent and toppled. Then his corpse rolled about the pitching deck, bouncing between gun carriages and the mast like an awkward skittle.

At last the wind begins to die from a scream to a bawl. The possibility begins to emerge that they may survive this, if they can get to land and find food and water. Rupert, his face a fatigued skull, releases the pederastic master, promising him his life and making him swear to leave the ship's boys alone. Just find us a harbour, Rupert commands, and the man nods his head and wets his parched lips with a swollen tongue.

And he does, by God.

They glide one day into a natural harbour. The water is choppy, nothing more. The high peaks surrounding the bay block out the worst of the wind.

It is over. They will live another day. On this night, they will anchor and set a harbour watch and allow all the men that can to sleep. Glorious, longed-for sleep.

Sam, released from duty goes below. His legs are trembling and his eyes are on fire with exhaustion. He longs for his cot, the gentle bob of the quietened sea to lull him to sleep. But when he pulls open the door to his cabin, there is something in there. A shape. He takes the lantern from the wardroom table, and holds it up towards the darkness.

The ship's boy. He can't even remember the poor lad's name. Hanging by the neck.

Sam closes the door. Holmes is on watch – he'll take his cabin.

LONDON

Autumn 1652

'**T**HIS WILL BE YOUR HOME, PATIENCE,' HE SAYS. SHE
turns to smile at him, but the low sun is behind him – she cannot
see the expression on his face, and she is blinking blind as he
pushes open the door. The gloom is palpable, a thick darkness
that she blames at first on the sun-blindness. As she steps across
the threshold, she realizes that this is the nature of the house. A
place of dark panelling and drawn curtains. Further inside, past
the stairs, a shadow moves and a floorboard creaks.

'Sarah,' he says, without further explanation. He takes hold
of Patience's hand and grips it tightly. 'Oh my dear girl,' he says.
'How blessed we will be.'

He seems a little giddy, and if she did not know his thoughts
on sobriety, she would think him drunk. Gripping her, he leads
her from room to room. She is pulled from hall to kitchen –
an excited blur of possessions and features. A trunk from his
grandfather, a painting of his uncle, a sword – mounted – that
Sidrach wore at the Battle of Worcester to defeat that hound
Charles Stuart, the Old Tyrant's son.

He guides her in front of him on the stairs, and then pulls her round to face him. He is on the step below and they are on the same level. His good mood is infectious. That heat and light that can hold a crowd, that can make grown men weep for their Maker – all of that is focused on her, Patience Johnson. To be so chosen! She watches his dark eyes travel over her, and the slow smile that spreads across his face is the greatest affirmation she has ever known.

'Sidrach,' she breathes, and he kisses her cheek with cool lips. He moves up past her, and pulls her along, throwing open a door. Inside is a bed, with heavy curtains of embroidered greens.

He leans in to whisper in her ear, and she feels his hot breath on her skin. 'We will make babies here, Patience.'

She feels a flutter of fear and excitement. The dark mysteries of the marriage bed await. Wraiths bend and flicker in her dreams, but she is not clear on what will actually happen. Sidrach will show her. He will be her teacher.

She is frightened he will kiss her here, with the bed behind them like a promise and a threat. She hopes he will kiss her. But he grabs her hand and pulls her on and on, though a succession of rooms.

'Please don't change anything without asking, my darling, my own sweetheart,' he says. 'It was my parents' house, and I have long had it to myself since their death.'

She nods, solemnly.

They come into his study. It is book-lined, with a heavy desk against the wall. If it were her room, she would have the desk by the window. She walks over, and looks towards the street. There is a boy sitting across the road. He is slight and grey-faced. He looks up towards the house, and it seems as if he is looking directly into the room. There is something absurdly touching about the mismatch between the skinny raggedness of his body and the intensity of his stare. What is so absorbing? What draws his eye to this house?

Behind her, Sidrach is talking: 'Please, Patience. Do not touch my books. What need will you have for books, my own girl?'

He walks behind her, and puts his arms around her. The boy is still staring towards the gape of the windows as Sidrach presses her back against his body. He whispers: 'I cannot wait to begin our life together. One week, that is all. I will tell you of your duties. How things must be done. Oh my darling Patience. You will be good, will you not, my dear? A good and dutiful wife.'

'Oh yes, Sidrach,' she says. She wants to turn and see his face, but he is holding her firmly, arms wrapped around her waist. She looks instead through the window at the little boy, who gazes towards the house as if he would lap the timbers in search of cream.

WHITEHALL, LONDON

December 1652

CROMWELL'S FIST SLAMS INTO THE WOOD. THE DESK shudders. Papers shift and totter. A glass falls, slowly, splashing red wine across the shuffle of papers.

An oath hovers in Cromwell's mouth, a hard consonant forming. He looks across at Will and smiles, just evading the profanity. He has a ruefulness, apparent, Will knows, when he is caught being less than perfectly godly.

'No matter, Lord General,' says Will, stemming the tide of wine with his handkerchief and glancing towards the manservant hovering behind them. 'No matter. Jem will see to it.'

'My apologies, my apologies,' Cromwell mutters as Jem comes forward. He holds up the sodden paper.

'This is beyond rescue, I fear,' he says.

The bill is wet and pulpy. Black tears of ink slide down the face of it.

'It is no great loss, Lord General,' says Will.

'No.' He presses his thumbs to his closed eyelids, as if trying to gouge out the dark circles beneath. They are a permanent smudge now. Marks of work and lack of sleep and windows kept shut against the cold, fresh air.

Jem moves to dab the wine from the general's plain black jacket. He is waved impatiently away. Retreating to the hearth, he throws a fresh log on the fire. Sparks fly, bright. It is gloomy in here, although it is barely midday. Gloomy outside; the rain is a sad mush of sleet and ice.

Will shivers. His thoughts flit to Blackberry. He hopes the new nursemaid has him wrapped warm against this weather. The boy is feverish and full of cold. Melancholy. He misses his aunt. Mrs Simmonds, as they must think of her now. That man could let her see more of them, he thinks.

Something of his thoughts must show on his face. The general has stopped his pacing and is staring at him.

'All is well, Johnson?'

'Yes, sir,' he says quickly.

'Hmm. So now. This bill. Another sad fudge. The army will not wear it.'

'Not the radical soldiers,' Will agrees. 'They want complete freedom of worship.'

'They will not get that.'

'No. But they will not settle for much less. An end to a state church. No tithes. No parishes.'

'We can grant them liberty of conscience. Why is that not enough?'

Will shrugs. The general knows as well as he does that the Rump MPs will never offer enough to satisfy the religious sects. The Anabaptists and the Fifth Monarchists. The Enthusiasts and the Griddletonians. The Ranters and the Seekers and the

Muggletonians. Even the bloody papists.

'They have no kindness of spirit, these sectaries. I tell you, Johnson, they rant about freedom but will not extend the same courtesy to one another. They would tear out each other's throats, were I not standing between them.'

He is working himself into a fury again. Will puts a placatory hand up towards him, and says: 'It is exhausting, no doubt, to be a bulwark.'

'It is. It is.'

The lord general sinks heavily into a chair. 'Set up a meeting, Johnson. Between the officers and some of the more obdurate MPs.'

'Another one?'

'Yes, blast it. Another one. At the Speaker's house, if he'll host. Neutral ground. Go on, now. Leave me.'

Marchamont Nedham is in his room, hands stretched out towards the fire. His cheeks are crimson. Will notes, for the first time, the suspicion of broken veins in the older man's nose.

'Ah, Johnson. And how is Old Noll today?'

'Frustrated. Irritated by the Rumpers and by the Fifth Monarchists and the rest of them.'

'Bearing it well, is he? Calm? Song in his heart and a whistle on his lips?'

Will grimaces, and Nedham's deep laugh echoes in the narrow, cold room.

'Ah,' says Nedham. 'Who can blame him. Vipers. The Rumpers out for themselves. The sects at war with each other. I just theorize about trying to settle it all. That poor bastard has to *do* it.'

Will nods, moving in towards the fire. He is chilled just from walking the long corridor. He feels his shoulders loosen as the heat finds him.

'Do you know what I heard?' says Nedham, looking over his shoulder theatrically.

'Not being Cassandra, I do not.'

'Bulstrode Whitelock was heard telling someone – I shall not say who – that Cromwell discussed the post-regicide settlement with him.'

'So he would. They are friends.'

'Aye. But Whitelocke says that Cromwell talked of the possibility of a new settlement with "something of the monarchical" in it.'

Will whistles, looking across at Nedham. He sees his glee at being first with the news, and feels a rush of affection for his friend.

'Think about it, Will. The Rump cannot call elections, for it knows that out there in the shires, people will vote for men even more backward-looking than they are. The army will not stand for it – they cannot serve a Parliament made of demi-royalists. But neither will the army support the Rump, as its members prevaricate on religious reform and line their own pockets with confiscated Royalist property. There is no check on the Rump. None at all.'

'Bar the army.'

'And its head.'

'He would not. He could not. Could he?'

'If not him,' says Nedham, 'then who?'

'The younger son of the late king.'

'He swore on his father's severed head that he would not usurp his older brother's crown. No, Will. If something monarchical is to be our future, then there is only one something monarch possible.'

Will shakes his head. He watches the leaping flames.

'I do not think he wants it, Nedham.'

Nedham snorts. 'You are a gentle soul, Will. Just because your worst, most violent nightmare is to be thrust into power . . . well, that means little. Most men are more grasping than you credit them.'

'Some men are less so than you think.'

'Perhaps.'

'You are correct in one sense, Nedham. If there is to be a Julius Caesar in our new republic, it can only be him. And even if he does not want it, all men will assume that he does.'

'Poor old Noll,' says Nedham.

A rushed knock at the door. Jem bounds in, out of breath. 'Has changed his mind, he has. Wants you now, Mr Johnson.'

'Give Caesar my regards, old fellow,' says Nedham as Will scoops up his ledger and bustles back down the long corridor.

Patience stands in the dark hallway by Sidrach's door, pulling a thick winter shawl across her shoulders. Our door, she admonishes herself. Not Sidrach's door – our door.

She feels the sudden weight of the knowledge that this will be her front door until they carry her empty husk out of here. She looks at the heavy panelling and the dark sheen of the wood. The thick and forbidding heft of it. And beyond that wood, a street that smells of grime and smoke and offal, of accumulated filth and splattered piss. Of the sores on the veterans' festering stumps and the yeasty, hoppy run-off from one thousand breweries. How nonchalantly she made the decision to abandon the countryside and the dreams she once had of her future, which smelled of fresh-cut wheat and the pressing of apples.

If she has children, where will they play? Where will they climb and swim?

She is being absurd. She has Sidrach. The fiery preacher. Man of God and political ambition. Through him, she has a place in the great re-imagining of England.

This house is grand in its gloomy way. She must put aside her qualms; find her courage. This is the melancholy made inevitable by the excitement of the wedding. Just a few days into her new life – of course it will feel unusual.

She pulls the shawl tight, and into a knot across her chest. It is cold out today, but sparkling. She loves a cold, bright day, and she saw the glare of it through the bedroom window and thought to flee into it.

Where will she go? Beyond the walls? Or closer, to watch the boatmen shoot the bridge?

'Patience.'

She turns to see him standing at the top of the stairs, looking down at her. His face is in shadow, and she smiles towards it.

'Husband!'

'Where do you think you are going?'

'I am not sure. What a beautiful day it is, Sidrach. Do you not think?'

She reaches for her hat. He walks down the stairs towards her, and the boards creak beneath his tread.

'It may be so, Patience. But I told you, I am busy today. I cannot go out.'

She laughs, placing the hat on her head. 'But I will be just fine by myself. I might see Blackberry. Take him for a picnic. You said you were busy, Sidrach. I thought I would leave you in peace.'

He is close to her, and she looks at him. The scowl on his face makes her stomach lurch. She has offended him. What has she done?

He reaches out and yanks the hat away from her. It catches a couple of strands of hair, and they come away from her head too. She gasps at the pain of it.

'My wife does not gallivant about town. My wife does not sit in the mud to eat her food. My wife goes out when I go out. Do I make myself understood?'

'Yes. But Sidrach . . .' She stutters to silence as she watches his face lose its handsome sheen and turn bleaker, uglier.

'Sorry,' she said. 'I am sorry. I did not think.'

'No,' he says, loosening the violence in his face. Unleashing a smile that makes her sigh with gratitude. 'No, you did not. You have a husband now, darling girl. Who loves you. Who has vowed to look after you. And you have vowed to obey him. Run along inside and keep busy. Perhaps we will venture out later, after I have written my sermon.'

'Can I help?'

He laughs, walking away and back up the stairs. She watches him go, and the minutes and hours ahead close in upon her, suffocating her.

'Blackberry!'

She kneels, her arms outstretched.

He cannons into her and she wraps her arms around his thin body. She thinks, not for the first time, how apt is the name his mother gave him. He smells sweet, but with a background sharpness, like pickling juices.

'I miss you,' he shouts into her shoulder. 'You're gone.'

'I am sorry, little Blackberry.'

She pulls back to look into his face. There are tears, and she knows he hates crying. He looks at her with fierce, brimming eyes. She pushes back his hair from his wet cheeks and cups his face in her hands.

'Beautiful boy. I am here.'

She feels a hand fall on her shoulder and she stands, quickly.

'And here is your Uncle Sidrach,' she says. Blackberry looks bemused by the sudden change of tone. He is caught between two expectations of him, and he hovers between them. How transparent children are, thinks Patience, helplessly. She remembers the pale skin of his bare back, and how the visible veins meander around his spine.

Sidrach's hand is heavy on her shoulder.

'Make your bow, Blackberry,' says Will, walking forward. He stands behind the boy, grinning at her.

The boy folds himself in two.

'Hello, Richard,' says Sidrach to Blackberry. 'Johnson.' He bows his head to Will.

'Simmonds,' says Will.

Patience hears herself babble: 'I have cooked a goose. The geese have walked in from the fens only this week! Hattie got one for me. Imagine that, Blackberry! All those geese walking all that way. Sage and onions, Will, like Mother makes.'

'Apple sauce?'

'Of course. And bread pudding, my Blackberry. Just for you.'

They keep the conversation light, general. A determined, relentless stream on geese they have known and eaten. The proper time to kill a fattened bird. The correct stuffing. The recipes of mothers and grandmothers. Apples. The orchards they scrumped from as children. The new ale Patience has bought in – Morning Dew, they call it. The impossibility of brewing the household's ale oneself with London water as it is.

The goose is picked over until only its bones are left. Sarah, the maid, scoops them up for the stock pot. The bread pudding is reduced to crumbs. Blackberry, full and querulous, has been persuaded to sleep a while.

Outside, the light is fading. Patience lights the candles. Will looks younger in their glow. She can't see the dark circles under his eyes or the still shocking whiteness of his hair.

'It seems strange, to see so little of you,' he says suddenly.

'I am sorry,' she says, not looking at Sidrach.

'While we were becoming properly acquainted as man and wife,' Sidrach says, 'I thought it best that Patience should concentrate on her own household.'

'But she could visit sometimes. Perhaps when you are working?'

'But what if I need something? My dear Johnson, you should see how I labour over my sermons, how tired I become as I struggle daily with man's blindness. With his obstinate, crass refusal to see the will of his Maker. Daily I wrestle.'

He sighs, and moves his hands as if grasping an obdurate sinner crouching in front of him.

'And what would become of my task if I were to look up and call for a drop of something, or a bite of something, only to find my wife has gallivanted away?'

'But surely—'

'Will,' she says sharply. 'My task is to help Sidrach. He has a great need of me.'

'Indeed I do,' he says. He closes his hand over hers.

'Already, Johnson, I find that I cannot do without your sister. Now, I must ask you a great favour.'

Will gives a non-committal grunt. His fingers tap on the table.

Sidrach leans forward, his hand still wrapped around Patience's. His face wears its most winning smile. 'Well now, Johnson. I would like an audience with the lord general. I have much to tell him, much to suggest.'

Will puts his hands in the air, fending off the request. 'The lord general is a busy man, Simmonds. I can't arrange audiences for him on a whim. I could, perhaps, arrange for you to preach to the Rump, and if Cromwell likes what he hears, an audience is possible.'

'My dear Johnson. You are like a brother to me. You work for the general. I say that an audience is easily arranged.'

'And I say that it is not.'

Patience feels Sidrach's hand tighten on hers. She looks mutely at Will, asking him with her eyes to oblige her husband. Will looks away – he does not see her silent entreaty. A bitter silence falls.

Will stirs himself, looking at Patience. 'I had a letter, Patience, from Henrietta's brother Sam,' he says. 'From Montserrat! He is with Prince Rupert still. You know he served with the prince at

Naseby, and before, I believe. He tells me he has sailed to the West Indies. And to Africa.'

'Africa! How I would like to hear him speak of it.'

'You are not likely to meet him, Patience,' says Sidrach, sharply. 'My wife and a pirate. For piracy was his intent, I suppose. Like his master, the devil Rupert.'

Will smiles. 'Ah. I think he would call himself a privateer, Simmonds.'

'A pirate.'

Will smiles at Sidrach. His smile is a gauntlet. He watches the other man bristle.

'And how,' says Patience, eyes flitting between them, 'is your work, Will?'

Sidrach breaks in: 'Cromwell should sweep those godless swine aside. What is he thinking, letting them swive and enrich themselves while the Lord's work is waiting?'

'He is thinking, I believe, that he is subject to the will of Parliament.'

'Nonsense. What is Parliament's will, man's will, set against the will of our Lord?'

'And who decides the will of our Lord, Simmonds? Him? You?'

Patience stands abruptly, moving towards the fire. She throws another log on to the flames, and the crackle and spit of the catching wood fills the room.

'And Mrs Cromwell, Will,' she says, brightly. 'Have you seen her?'

'I have. She is elusive. She has had separate staircases built at Whitehall, so she can get about unseen. But I have taken a meal with her and her husband.'

'And what is she like?'

'As you would expect.'

Patience tries to imagine it. A settled country goodwife, picked up by fate, tumbled round, and set upon a demi-throne at the heart of things.

'She must be pleased,' she says. 'To be given the chance to help a great man at a great task.'

Sidrach laughs. 'I do not think a man such as Cromwell needs help from a woman.'

She stares at him. Her face stings, as if from a slap.

Not long afterwards, Will takes his leave. She walks him to the door. He carries Blackberry, his thin limbs flopping heavily.

Will kisses Blackberry's flushed brow. He says: 'Mother says that now he is older, I should put him out to foster. Says it is peculiar, a father living alone with his boy.'

'Will you?'

He shakes his head, in a manner so ambiguous it could mean anything. She lets it go. She watches him thinking about saying something. She feels dizzyingly weary, and when he shrugs, turns and walks away silently, she is utterly relieved.

Behind her, she can hear Sidrach's steps echoing in the empty house. She stands by the door watching Will leave, Blackberry's head lolling on his shoulder and their breath smoking in the freezing air.

She lies still. As still as it is possible to be. If she moves, he will call her a whore and slap her. Although if that happens, he does finish quicker. She stifles a bitter laugh. Laughter might make her body move.

Lie still. Don't look as if you are enjoying it. As if you could enjoy it. Oh Lord Jesus. No wonder your mother was a virgin. As if something pure and beautiful could come from this ridiculous act.

Think about something else. Anything.

She thinks about the other Sidrach. She thinks about the low coo of his voice as he tells her she is beautiful. She is his own, and only his. His precious one.

Now, in the darkness, he shifts, pushing at her from a different angle. Patience stays still, thighs spread, but muscles clenched so that her whole body is taut and painfully rigid. She thinks of relaxing her limbs, but he might confuse that with wantonness. Stay still, Patience. Stay still. Think of tomorrow's meal, and the next day's leavings, and the ale to be bought and the washing day that looms ahead of her.

She remembers playing house with her sisters. They lined up their rag dolls and fed them elaborate meals of twigs and grasses on curling leaf plates. She thinks of how quickly they used to get bored and move on to other games, leaving the rag dolls tumbling down and the leaf plates rolling in the wind.

He is mumbling to himself as he grunts and shudders. Like this, he bears no resemblance to the other Sidrachs. Not the loving one who kisses her and vows to keep her safe. Not the public one who charms men's souls. She loves standing next to that man at events, the acknowledged helpmeet. She relishes her share of his pomp. She enjoys the envious glances of women whose husbands cannot move crowds nor articulate God's will.

Nor does this huffing, grinding, *ridiculous* man resemble the other Sidrach. The one she has glimpsed once or twice. She calls that Sidrach out of his hiding place. He is conjured up by her ineptitude. Her inexperience. Her fault.

She will not think of him, that Sidrach.

She retreats to thoughts of her household book. She loves it; the soft leather of the outside of it. The scraps of wit and wisdom she has scratched into its thick, creamy pages. The place where she keeps the recipes her mother has passed on. The stews and brews and mulls, the salves and potions and poultices.

Perhaps she will have a daughter to whom the book can pass. She imagines this theoretical daughter; her fierce, mischievous face.

Take 12 spoonfuls of right red rose water, the weight of sixpence in fine sugar and boil it on hot embers and coals softly, and the house will smell as if were full of roses.

He is getting faster. Rubbing, rubbing at her. His head is pressed into her shoulder, his teeth biting at her nightgown. The curtains of the bed are parted slightly, and she looks out beyond him to the window and the black sky. A cloud shifts and she can see the moon. A thin sliver of white. She dislikes full moons, now; prefers the darkness.

Outside, she can hear a city fox barking, and then the yowling scream of a she-fox mating. It sounds like a child in distress. She thinks of the boy who begs outside their house, and how his eyes fix on the walls. Poor boy. Is he safe from the foxes? she wonders. They are hungry too. Another scream pierces the night. What would Sidrach make of it if she started to yelp like a vixen?

The thought makes her laugh, despite herself. She feels her body quiver. His face lifts from her shoulder, looms above her in the darkness. His hair falls in ragged strands about his shadowed face. 'Slut,' he spits. She turns her face away from the dribbling mouth. 'Whore,' he says again, in a vicious whisper. He doesn't have time to hit her. He gasps and shudders.

Thank God. He is done. He pulls himself out of her. There is a silence as he turns away and arranges the blankets, and then: 'I do not expect my wife to whore herself, even to me, Patience.' He is using his measured, reasonable voice. The voice she would use to chastise a recalcitrant child. She thinks of how it would be to scream like a vixen; to scream and scream at the moon and never to stop.

'Charity!' Sidrach shouts the word. His fist slams into the lectern. He leans forward, bringing them into his grace. His voice drops lower. 'It is your duty. It must be your soul's desire. Does not it say in the book: "Let your light shine before others, that they may see your good deeds and praise your Father in heaven"?'

He leans back. His eyes roam from person to person. They pull towards him as one. He whispers into the clamorous silence of the church: 'Do you want to find Him?'

Oh yes, she calls back with her soul. She looks at him – at his fierce eyes and his skin aglow with the passion of his words – and she feels that surge again. Of awe and the unquenchable thirst to be approved by him.

She looks around the room and sees the crowd leaning towards him, the parting of their lips and the yearning of their souls, and the great godlike stature of the man she can call husband. Pride is a sin, she tells herself. A sin. And yet look at him, oh my Lord. Am I not blessed? Is he not the pinnacle of your creation?

WHITEHALL, LONDON

February 1653

'A NAVAL OFFICER HAS ARRIVED FROM PORTSMOUTH, Lord General.'

Cromwell's head snaps up from his papers. 'Well?'

Will shuffles forward. 'Blake has engaged with de Tromp in the Channel. It is still ongoing. The Dutch are trying to convoy their Mediterranean merchantmen home. Three Dutchmen are sunk, one burned. We have lost one, and three have reached port in Portsmouth, too damaged to continue.'

'Which three?'

Will hesitates.

'Lord help me, Johnson, which three? Where is General-at-Sea Blake now? Where is the wind?'

Will steps backwards as the rage breaks over him. Cromwell advances, his face aglow. 'The wind, man. Who has the weather gauge?'

The weather gauge, thinks Will helplessly. He knows better than to interrupt.

'Damn me, Johnson, who is winning?'

Will has reached the door now. He feels behind his back for the handle. It is solid and cold to the touch.

'I have the messenger outside, Lord General,' he says, pulling at the door.

'What are you waiting for then, man? Bring the fellow in. Let us hope he knows his larboards from his starboards. Those Dutch creatures do, Lord help us.'

Will escapes, and ushers in the young lieutenant. The boy pulls himself upright and squares his shoulders. He looks as if he would rather face a Dutch broadside than cross the threshold of Cromwell's room, which reeks of the general's impatience.

It is small wonder the general is beside himself. Since the defeat to the Dutch navy in November, England's Channel has been governed from the Hague. If this attempt to wrest control back from the Dutch fails, the consequences for the fledgling Commonwealth will be catastrophic.

Behind him, the door is wrenched open again. 'Get Thurloe here,' barks Cromwell.

And then, more quietly: 'If you please, Johnson.'

Will, searching out Milton, hears that he has stayed at home. He walks out himself to tell him the news. Thurloe, the secretary to the Council of Foreign Affairs, is closeted with Cromwell. Will had found him thick in conversation with Sir Henry Vane, the treasurer to the navy. Thurloe's sharp face clouded at Cromwell's summons; he glanced sideways at Vane.

Vane nodded, as if to give permission. He looked drawn, anxious. Well he might – this new fleet under Blake had been conceived and built by him. Carpenters and shipwrights on double-time across the south coast for months. Ships still jury-rigged slipping from their moorings with the pitch scarce set in the plankings. Ships cost money; wars demand hoards. The screw turns ever tighter on Royalists' estates. But it is still not enough.

Walking through St James's towards Petty France, Will smiles at Thurloe's discomfort at being summoned like a boy by Cromwell in Vane's presence. An ambitious fellow like Thurloe must be at war with himself – to which star should he hitch himself?

The relationship between Vane and Cromwell is turning increasingly vexatious. Vane has emerged as one of the most influential Parliamentarians. But his ideas are dangerous; revolutionary. He believes in complete freedom of worship. He is said to have sympathy with the more extreme sects, to have failed to condemn the Ranters and those who believe that England's soul can be remade with all men equal in the sight of law and the Lord.

Will breathes in the icy air. How he enjoys escaping, just for a little while. The intrigues and politicking depress him. He thinks of Nedham, and the man's glee at machinations that leave Will saddened. He has a sudden insight, one of those thoughts that come on a man when he is walking on a cold, clear day: Cromwell is still a soldier at heart – he believes in the power of plain speech, in honour and in providence. Vane is a politician: he believes in layered speech and in expediency. Does that make one of them a fool and the other a knave?

No, it is not so simple. Will thinks of his late father-in-law, who believed that good things could come from yoking man's baser instincts to a common cause; and that terrible things could come from too much honour, too much simplifying.

Turning in to Petty France, he thinks, not for the first time, how glad he is to be a great man's servant, and not a great man.

At Milton's house, he is ushered in by a harassed maid and taken through to the bedroom. A stoked fire rages, and Will feels the heat strike him as he walks in. His fingertips tingle as his skin lurches from cold to hot, and he smacks his hands together. Milton is sitting up in the bed, a makeshift writing desk balanced precariously on his knee. His head whips round at the sound of Will's hollow hands clapping and he regards him with an expression on his face that looks, perhaps, fearful. But what does Milton have to fear from him? Then it strikes him, in the long, silent minute before the maid announces his name. Milton can no longer see at all; the man is completely blind.

Will walks forward in a fog of pity and embarrassment. Should he mention it? Should he talk of it at all? He announces himself, hesitantly.

'Johnson,' says Milton, tersely.

'I have news,' says Will, quickly. 'A great sea battle is being fought in the Channel. Blake has caught de Tromp trying to sneak the Dutch merchant fleet through the Channel.'

Milton pats the bed beside him. Will sits, trying to avoid the worst of the ink stains. He answers the older man's eager questions. He tries not to stare at his eyes, which have lost some of their redness and gained a sort of milky sheen. Why should I not stare? he thinks, irreverently. Milton cannot see me staring.

At last they reach the end of the scant news about the Dutch. They agree that nothing more can be said before more news comes, and then fall to picking apart the small bones again.

Silence hovers. 'Your eyes. Is it,' says Will, sifting his way through the possible phrases, 'permanent?'

'They think so.'

'I am sorry, Milton.'

'Yes.' He rubs his eyes in the habitual gesture Will knows. 'They are trying to press an assistant on me. Some halfwit with a child's Latin, no doubt. I have asked for Andrew Marvell. Do you know him? No. Well, a young man. A fine poet, if a little naive in his expression. A good Latinist, more to the point. He will not irritate me.'

He reaches out a hand and Will takes it. 'You will come and tell me, Johnson. What happens in the Channel. I feel trapped here. Headaches. I need to know. To be connected. I am an island here.'

There is something amiss. Looking through the glass, Patience sees grown men running. She sees clusters of people huddling in fierce conversation. At the centre of the strangeness is the beggar boy. He sits on the street, his arms wrapped around his legs and his head resting upon his knees. Poor little thing.

From below her, a figure emerges from the house. Sarah. She bustles away down the street, not sparing a glance for the little boy who sits so forlornly opposite.

Patience listens for the silence. For the strange empty echo of a house with no one else there. Sidrach is out, too, somewhere. She gathers herself – her great and unbearable boredom weighed against her trepidation.

Before she can talk herself frightened, she runs down the stairs. She grabs her shawl and heads for the kitchen door, slipping through it into the alleyway behind the house. Pausing by the corner wall, she checks the street for Sidrach or Sarah, feeling absurd and gleeful all at once.

Crossing, she slips next to the boy, crouching down next to him. He moves his head sideways, looking at her.

'Who are you?' she says. 'Why are you always here?'

In answer, he closes his eyes, and she sees for the first time the greyness of his skin and the birdlike thinness of his limbs. His lips are a chilling blue.

Without thinking, she picks him up. He is as light as Blackberry, for all that he is at least five years older. He is uncomplaining as she pushes the door of the kitchen open with her foot and places him by the fire. He does not speak as she takes a bowl and ladles into it the hot broth straight from the stock pot that bubbles there on its tripod. He just looks at her with large, trusting eyes, like a runt left out to die.

She hands him the bowl and he takes it, still looking at him. He begins to shiver violently, and the broth splashes out and dribbles down his arm.

'Shh,' she says. 'Shh, boy. Let me help.'

She sits on the floor next to him, her legs crossed under her, and holds the bowl to his lips. He drinks a little. She is worried he will be sick. She remembers nursing a starving lamb, and how tentative she was about feeding it too much milk while its hunger was larger than its stomach.

'Lie down, boy,' she says, placing a thick wool blanket next to him. He lays down his head, and looks at her one more time with the big eyes before closing them. She pulls the blanket across him, and sits in the darkening kitchen listening to him breathe.

~ ~ ~

'What is that?'

'A boy, Sidrach,' she says, jumping out of her seat and standing to look at him.

He tuts impatiently.

'I beg your pardon, Sidrach. He was outside. Near death, poor thing. Starving and freezing.'

'You have brought a ragged beggar boy into my house. Are you entirely stupid?'

She hangs her head. 'Charity. You said it. In your sermon.' She risks a look at his face. It is turning thunderous. 'You will be able to tell the congregation. That you saved a beggar boy. They will admire you for it.'

He pauses, looking at her and then down at the boy again. She can almost hear him thinking.

He sighs. 'He sleeps in here. Only until he is well. And if he steals anything, I will flay him, so help me.'

'Oh Sidrach. You are so good, so kind. Thank you!'

He grunts, and turns to leave. 'Just a week or two,' he says.

Patience crouches down next to the boy and pushes the hair back from his forehead. He murmurs a little in his sleep, and half-smiles.

Victory. The lord general's beatific air returns. God is at his side once more. Who can doubt it?

Will watches – amused, awed? – as Cromwell seems physically to grow. He broadens and straightens, as if pulled heavenwards by God's favour.

He looks down at Will with a broad smile that seems to imply that the destroyed Dutch fleet is somehow their achievement, somehow down to their moral rectitude. De Tromp scuttles back to Holland because Cromwell and Will are locked in an angelic circle of grace, which can allow only for victory. From a chair in the corner Elizabeth Cromwell watches her husband. We all watch him, thinks Will. Anticipating his wants, heading off his anger, hoping for his praise. It is exhausting.

'Honour my wife with your company, Johnson,' says the general. 'I will be with you shortly. The Lord will wait no longer for my praises.'

He leaves the room, and the close air seems to sag, like a kicked bladder.

'And how is your boy, Mr Johnson?'

'Growing ever taller, madam.'

He stands by the window and glances out to the old tennis court, now unkempt and straggling, towards the Banqueting House.

'I am told,' she says, standing and drawing nearer, 'that from this very window, you could see the king being led out to his death.'

'These are comfortable lodgings,' says Will. The keeper of the palace used to live here, in this grand house attached to the back of the Cockpit – Whitehall Palace's now disused theatre. This room, the Cromwells' private chamber, is large enough to be imposing and small enough to be warm.

She looks at him with shrewd eyes. 'You do not like to talk of the late king's death?'

'I do not. I beg your pardon. It was the day my wife was killed.'

'But the two deaths were not related.'

'Were they not?'

Why are we talking of this? I do not want to talk of this. He looks down at her. No man would call her a beauty. She has yellowing skin and too many chins. He tries to imagine her young, but fails, entirely. Perhaps she emerged from her mother with grey hair springing from its ties, with a mouth that droops at the edges, caught in a criss-cross of lines. She has lived in the shadows of her husband. What must he have been like, straining at his life of quiet provincialism? Impossible. Exhausting: that word again. Cromwell simply cannot fathom that other men do not have his capacity, his drive. Does he demand the same from his wife as from his acolytes?

She is watching him closely, and lays a hand on his arm. 'Your small drama is lost beside the bigger one.'

'Ah but that is the point, madam. Tragedy is a matter of perspective. The sun looks small because it is far away.'

'There is no sun today,' she says, looking past him to the window.

'Rain is likely, I think.'

She grins at him, almost mischievous.

'Rain!'

'Perhaps.'

They turn back into the room, listening to the silence. Listening, he realizes, for the heavy pound of Cromwell's footsteps.

'And does your son like the rain, Mr Johnson?'

'He does. His mother . . .' Will trails off, catching himself. Better not to speak of uncomfortable things.

'This place,' she says, with a shudder. She walks to the fireplace and throws a log on to the flames. She stokes it expertly. Will thinks to call a servant, but it is done now.

'Through that wall,' she says, pointing, 'is the old theatre. Just think, Mr Johnson, of the sins and the carnality and the looseness. The vileness. And before that, the cockfights. With drunkenness and gambling and blood. The blood!' She throws her hands up in a quick and violent motion. As if in despair at the sinners of the past.

'There is some irony, madam, in your husband and yourself being lodged here. In the Cockpit.'

'There is no irony, Mr Johnson. Only providence.'

He bows.

With another quick turn away from dangerous ground, she says: 'How is Mr Milton?'

'Completely blind now, I am afraid.' Is that providence, too?

'And no wife to help him. He wrote a disgusting pamphlet once. In favour of divorce. It was, I am afraid, beyond absurd. Matrimony is holy.'

Will thinks of Patience. She is slowly closing herself, folding inwards like a tulip in the night air. He says nothing, just bows and smiles ambiguously. They pause. Then to Will's relief, from outside the room comes the sound of heavy footsteps and the light whistle of a man who believes implacably that God is on his side.

Patience pushes the bloody rag down under the bubbling surface of the water. The handle of the long wooden spoon is hot to the touch. She grips it, thinking strange thoughts of plunging her hand into the pot. Imagining the pain, the blisters popping their way on to her skin.

'More coke, missus?'

She surfaces.

'Oh. Yes. Thank you, Tom.'

The fire beneath the pot is faltering. She smiles at the boy.

'It is here, the coke,' he says. He has a strange, sing-song accent. His words are ordered in a peculiar way. He has had a hard life, so much is clear. Brutal. There are bruises lingering among the freckles that cover his body. Fingerprints pressed into the pale skin of his upper arms.

There is a quiet intimacy to the kitchen. The fire is warm, and the steam rises from the boiling pot, carrying the metallic tang of the blood as it washes away into the pinking water.

Sidrach is out of town and will not be home until tomorrow.

She sits in the chair by the fire, watching the boy as he pours the coal and pokes the fire. He has quick, neat movements. There is a contained grace in him that would suit a girl. It has been more than a week or two, but he has made himself useful and there has been no talk of his leaving. He veers clear of Sidrach, and takes on the messier, smellier tasks from Sarah, who tolerates his presence. The skin is stretching on his skinny limbs as he fills out and loses his greying tinge.

'Do you have a mother, Tom?'

'No, missus.' The boy laughs, without mirth.

'I do. Shall I tell you about her while you clean the shoes?'

He nods, and sits on the floor next to the fire, folding his skinny legs. He reaches for the black and the brush, and looks up at her. There are copper glints in his hair, caught by the fire. When he came, his hair seemed a dull, dark grey. But he has been washed, since then.

'My mother smells of caramel,' says Patience. 'I think perhaps from making jam. Or perhaps there's just a sweetness that belongs on her skin. She's sharp in her manner, though. We don't cross her.

'Father's a little scared of her. We all are. I used to think, Tom, that if dragons came for us, or trolls, my mother would beat them all back with her rolling pin. Stab monsters through the heart with her gardening shears.'

He smiles, showing the gap in his teeth where he's lost a couple to illness or a fist.

'You will make a fine mother,' he says.

She is taken aback by his unexpected forwardness. She glances at the pot and the boiling telltale rag. Not yet. Not yet.

A knock, suddenly, on the door. In bustles Marigold Capp, her pale face forced to a blush by the freezing air. She is settled by the fire; the rag pot is deftly moved out of view and a posset set on to warm. There are fresh-baked biscuits, the way Sidrach likes them – with a touch of cardamom.

Tom has folded himself into a shadow. It takes a minute for Marigold to notice him. She looks at him sidelong, and turns suggestive eyes on Patience. 'Tom,' says Patience, taking the hint. 'Will you run to Hattie, the butcher, and ask for some marrow bones?'

He jumps to his feet, nodding his eagerness. She gives him the coins, and smiles her encouragement as he spins and runs for the door.

'So,' says Marigold, as soon as it slams shut. 'That boy. How do you find him?'

'Biddable,' says Patience. An ally. A smile-in-waiting.

'Strange child . . . I'm not sure how far you should trust him. It seems to me, my dear, that the boy sidles his way into

Sidrach's gaze. He sits there looking worshipfully at him during the sermons.'

'That would certainly work with Sidrach,' says Patience. She laughs, but gets nothing back from the other woman. Marigold disapproves of levity. Patience wonders whether Jesus was so serious.

'Do you think Jesus laughed, Marigold, when he conjured the loaves? Do you think, when He returns to govern us, that He will smile?'

'Patience, do not presume to imagine what Christ's rule will look like.'

'And why should I not? Is that not what Jeremiah and Sidrach do? Do they not believe themselves to be sweeping the ground for His approach?'

'But they are men, dear. They sweep. We follow.'

'Does Jeremiah sweep? I cannot imagine it.'

'A metaphor, Patience. Do not be obtuse.'

I am not being obtuse, she thinks. She pokes at the fire to hide her sullen, rebellious face. I am making a joke.

After Marigold leaves, Patience allows the indolence to envelop her again. She pulls her legs up to her chin, and watches the small leaps of the coals' flames. Behind her, Tom is busy about his task, polishing the great silver candlesticks that Sidrach inherited from some ancient aunt.

Sarah, the maid, is cleaning in the other rooms. She is older than Patience – in her thirties. She has kept house for Sidrach for years. She bobs at Patience when required. Does her duty. But in all these months of living in the same house, Patience and

Sarah have not progressed beyond formalities. In her dreams of playing house, there was an apple-cheeked maid who became a friend; smiling confidences over the pounding of kneaded bread.

She spies on me, Patience thinks. The thought catches her by surprise.

'You are from the north, Tom?'

'Yes, missus. But then on the colliers. Sailing into the Pool mostly.'

'And was your family caught in the late troubles?'

She turns, and catches an expression on his face that she cannot read. He does not reply and she decides not to press the question.

She will go to bed early, she thinks. Push her limbs into the unfamiliar wide spaces of an empty bed. No sisters, no visiting cousins.

No husband.

She hugs the anticipation to herself as the household winds down towards bedtime. Lamps are lit and fires are stoked and a hush falls on the street outside as darkness falls.

There are many jobs she has not done, relishing her rare idleness. She has not made tomorrow's bread, nor checked the brewing ale. She has not made up a batch of the tonic that Sidrach likes to take for his liver; even though it takes a fair amount of boiling and straining and boiling again. I will get up early, she thinks, and do it all tomorrow. Tomorrow.

She sends Tom off to his truckle bed in the corner of the kitchen. She ruffles his hair as she does it, and he pulls away startled, like a cat stroked unawares.

In the bedroom, she leaves her skirt and bodice heaped on the floor. A small act of rebellion that pleases her hugely. In her shift and bare feet, she skips across to the bed and climbs in, pulling the musty blanket up to her nose. What joy there is in this big empty bed, she thinks. She feels the leaden weight of her tired limbs, luxuriating in not being pawed at.

She pulls the bed curtains closed and thinks to daydream a while, to float herself away to home, where the otters play in the river.

She might have been asleep – she is not sure – when she hears his tread. Beyond the curtain, the heavy footsteps seem maddeningly precise. He does everything with care, her husband. Places his feet just so. Closes doors just so. Walks up the stairs just so.

The door creaks open. In the gap in the curtain she can see the gleam of a single candle. She screws her eyes tight shut. Perhaps she is dreaming. Perhaps he is not here.

'Patience. Patience.' The curtain is pulled violently back. 'I come home to a house in darkness. No food. No welcome.'

'We were not expecting you. I will get up and—'

'No. Stay where you are.'

She can't see his face, in the darkness, and it is hard to read him without visual clues. His voice is as usual measured, calm. He reaches out and pulls down the blanket.

The cold air raises goosebumps on her skin. She presses her back limply against the mattress, trying to shrink away from him when there is nowhere to go. He reaches out an arm and his hand finds her face. He draws his palm across her cheek. In the darkness, she has no face to study, no eyes to read. Which Sidrach is it? She doesn't know, she can't tell. She is off balance. Falling.

'Well now, my pretty wife.'

She wants to exhale, deeply, but she lets her breath out in tiny incremental heaves instead. Be motionless. Do not move. Try not to upset him.

He moves his hand slowly down her face, her neck; pushing a finger into the hollow at the base of her neck. Trailing his fingertips down the skin of her chest, pushing aside the collar of her shift, finding a breast. His breathing is becoming deeper, more defined. She can hear it clearly above her heart's hammer.

'Dearest,' she says. Her voice sounds as loud as a cannon in the quiet room. 'Dearest,' she says again. 'It is my monthly time.'

The hand is pulled away abruptly.

'Again?'

'Yes.'

'Have I not done my duty by your body?'

'Yes, Sidrach.'

'Have I not covered you, and cherished you? Am I not blessed by Him? Am I not His voice before His coming?'

'Yes.'

He stands. She cannot bear the contained tone of his voice; its even cadence. Fury would be easier somehow, breaking over her. Cleansing, perhaps?

'Patience. Barrenness is the Lord's curse. Does it not say in Exodus that God has the power to open and close the wombs of women? Your closed, sour womb must therefore be a mark of your shame.'

She does not know whether a yes or a no is more dangerous, so she stays silent.

'Stand.'

She stands. Her eyes are closed; her feet cold on the floor. She knows that he is there, breathing heavily. She can feel his breath hot against her cheek as he whispers in her ear.

'Shame on you. Shame. Shame.'

When the punch comes, it is worse than the anticipation. He drives his fist hard into her stomach, and she crumples. Pain; pain like a cloudburst.

'Up.'

She pushes herself upright. She will not cry out. She will not. She stands, biting her lip, waiting for the next blow.

PARIS

April 1653

SAM CROUCHES BENEATH A CUCKOLD'S WINDOW, HOLDING his chief's long cloak and his sword. Above him, drifting out with the candlelight, are the pants and squeals of an enthusiastic woman.

His legs are stiff, but a strange lassitude is on him and he cannot find the will to stand. The brandy lurches in his stomach, threatening to somersault its way back up his throat. If he closes his eyes, the earth heaves. He fixes his eyes on the stars, trying to hold himself straight.

He can hear Rupert now, groaning away like a diseased goat. At least it's a woman, not a duel. He has been impossible since the inglorious end to their privateering, limping back to the Continent with a handful of pathetic prizes and half the fleet lost. Rupert has recovered some of his strength, prostrated as he was by fever. Or so Sam judges, based on the noises coming from the window.

But here they are, back to this half-life of exiles in a court without a kingdom.

Poor, irrelevant, fractious. They have only their swagger to maintain their status. Rupert swives and duels, Sam standing by his side. Priming pistols, placating husbands, plying the brandy. Staving off the great and wearying boredom. Dabbling with the prince's discards.

Rupert is thick in intrigues against his old enemy Hyde, the adviser to Charles II. Charles, meanwhile, whores and gambles and plays them off against each other. Agrees with everyone to their face, sowing confusion and discord.

They need a war. Or a miracle.

Or something else.

The flowers that twist up the wall beneath the window smell strong, almost lemony. His father would have known their name, perhaps. He used to love his garden. There's some Commonwealth man there now, no doubt, pissing on the roses.

Sam pulls off his glove and reaches out. He rubs a petal beneath his thumb and his forefinger, feeling the softness of it. He puts his hand to his face and breathes in its scent. The room above will smell of sex and candle wax, of the countess's heavy, musky perfume, of Rupert's mix of horse and sweat. Sam shudders.

Loyalty. He has been loyal to the prince for nearly ten years. He loves him like an older brother. More, perhaps, than the brother he lost. Disloyal thoughts, but how can a man weigh loyalty in the wake of the wars?

Somewhere a dog begins to bark. It might be the count coming back from the gaming rooms. He follows the king's lead, surrounding himself with yapping dogs. Sam should stir himself, rouse the prince. Coitus interruptus.

He does not move. Could he return home? Ask his sister's

widower to help him petition for a pardon? Lord. Could he settle into a life back in London? He tries to conjure it up in his head. The sound of carts trundling on cobbles, of merchants shouting, of children shrieking. The smell of the sour Thames.

How can he go home? On what money? He has no trade but soldiering now. He would have been a merchant but for the wars. He feels his age. He is rising thirty, and what has he to show for it? A lost war. A string of women he has had to pay for. Loyalty to a prince as lost as he is, who is himself loyal to a king without a kingdom. So much for the past; what of the future? Indecision weighs on him. In battle, he can make quick decisions. He is prized for it by subordinates. Better a quick decision made in the heat and fury than a slow one, however good. But in this, the great question of his life's purpose, he can make no decision.

He rocks back on his heels, and blocks his ears to his prince's shuddering cry. A crow, frightened by the noise, breaks from the leaves above his head and caw-caws, flying into the night.

WHITEHALL, LONDON

April 1653

CROMWELL STANDS AT THE CENTRE OF THE COCKPIT. ON one side of him are the officers; on the other a band of influential MPs. Outside, darkness. In here, a riot of candlelight that catches and bounces between the gilt mirrors hung round the octagonal walls.

The lord general's face catches the light. He looks tired, as if the dark-ridged circles under his eyes are sliding down his face. Someone is speaking in a loud nasal voice from the Parliamentary side of the room. The arguments are circular, and Will can no longer make the effort to listen. Cromwell, too, looks pained as the voice drones on, closing his eyes and moving his lips. Calling on the Lord, Will suspects. And does He answer?

They will talk themselves hoarse, round and round in a circle. At the centre of the circle is the parliamentary bill necessary to dissolve the Rump Parliament and elect new MPs. All agree that such an outcome is necessary – few agree on how it can be achieved. What qualifications should be set on new members?

What guards should be in place to ensure that only the godly are able to sit in the house?

Or as Nedham pithily says, who shall guard the guardians?

There is Major General Harrison, among the officers, leaning back in his seat. His eyes are large and intent under a blunt fringe of hair. He looks as if he is listening, but he is one of those men who listen only for the pause into which they can begin to lecture. A Fifth Monarchist – in thick with Patience's husband and his fellow fanatics. He is popular in the army; the rank and file suckle at his promise of Christ's return.

Will spies Major General Lambert, Cromwell's second-in-command in the late Scottish wars. Lambert is young, Will's age or thereabouts. His eyes are restless, appraising. A man, says Nedham, who has never knowingly underestimated his own abilities. Clever, though. And dangerous.

There are factions within factions here. The broad split may be between the army and Parliament, but within each contingent is a rainbow of views.

Nedham is next to him, his nib scratching furiously, until at last he stops and leans in, whispering: 'All this hot air, Will. I believe I may faint from lack of breath.'

Will grins. He whispers back: '"As long as earth supports the sea and air the earth, so long will loyalty be impossible between sharers in tyranny; and power will resent a partner."'

Lucan. Will has read and reread his *Civil War*. To think of all the hundreds of years that have passed since the poet wrote those words, he reflects, and still we wrestle with the same problems. How should one man exercise power over another? What price should be placed on freedom, and what price on peace?

Everyone here believes – or hopes – that these are questions that can be resolved for ever, rather than renegotiated endlessly with each successive crisis. They are wrong, thinks Will. Lucan, poor Lucan, knew that failure was inevitable as he opened his wrists and watched the shock of his own blood clouding into the warm water.

Here in the Cockpit, the officers face the MPs, with Cromwell straddling the divide – for once in a literal as well as a metaphorical sense. But his presence is diluted in this room full of men who count themselves rooks, at the very least, in this affair. There are ghosts here, too. Of the cockfights and the plays; simulacra of the present real drama in which lives and souls are wrestled for.

The MPs sit side by side, none daring to wear his hair too short or too long. All in coats that vary from dark brown to black. Will has lost track of the currents of hatred, ambition and rivalry that flow beneath this uniform surface. Vane is there, watching Cromwell. Both believe the other is playing Caesar; each believes himself a noble Antony. At stake is the republic.

The door to the Cockpit flies open, interrupting the speaker mid-flow, much to everyone's relief. There in the doorway is Arthur Heselrige. He is dramatically breathless and travel-smeared. He waves as if to say *carry on*. He takes out a handkerchief and wipes his forehead. *Don't mind me*, he shouts without words. He looks expensive. His fingers sparkle with jewels and a servant follows him in dressed in ostentatious velvet. The silver buckles on his shoes catch and glisten in the candlelight.

'And here is Cato,' whispers Nedham.

Heselrige is the self-appointed guardian of England's fresh-minted republic, the leader of the Rump and the very large thorn in Cromwell's very large backside. Dealer in Royalist estates, whose confiscated treasures stick a little to his hands as they run through them. Each age gets the Cato it deserves, thinks Will. And ours is a venal embarrassment.

'We were discussing,' says Cromwell, looking pointedly towards Heselrige, 'the bill.'

No need to ask which bill. The bill that will dissolve the Rump and allow for elections. But what elections, administered by whom and when? And how, God help them, will these elections return men committed to reform when the electorate want no such thing?

Heselrige is the guardian of the bill as it stands, steering it through the committee stage.

'The bill,' says Heselrige, affably. He adjusts his cuffs and, with deliberate slowness, takes his place. Members shift and move for him, and the muttering ripples around the room.

'We have proposed an interim body; an appointed godly council to oversee these elections,' says Cromwell.

'And that is necessary? Why?' says Heselrige.

'We all fear,' says Vane, 'that unfettered elections will return Presbyterians and neutrals and even, the Lord save us, those who support the man over the sea who calls himself our king.'

There are nods.

'We need time,' says Cromwell. 'Time to bring God to the hearts of the unconvinced. Time to heal the scars. The people of this land will choose the godly path, of this I am sure.'

'But while we wait,' bellows an officer, 'these men of Parliament do nothing, nothing. No reform, no godliness, no attempt to win souls.'

There are roars of assent at this from the officers; clucks and tuts from the MPs.

'A temporary assembly,' shouts Cromwell into the hubbub. 'To draw up the terms of the elections. Otherwise—'

'Otherwise they will find a way to prolong their own power,' says another officer, sitting next to Harrison. His face is purple, the veins popping red in his spreading nose. He points at the MPs, and his rage seems to transmit to the finger, which shakes and quivers.

'Shame. Shame,' come the cries, and Will, whose eyes are closed and stinging with tiredness, cannot tell which side calls shame on the other.

A hush falls, and he opens his eyes. Heselrige is standing, a half-smile on his face. Oh, but he is a wily one. He was one of the five members the dead king tried to arrest in the crisis that sparked the late wars. He was not cowed by the man Stuart and he is not cowed by Cromwell, who can reduce lesser men to a sloppy pottage. His refusal to be intimidated is in itself powerfully intimidating.

'I was seventy miles away, gentlemen. Strange, is it not, that no word of this assembly reached me? And yet, at last, a little bird told me of it, and I have ridden my poor horse into the ground to be here. To tell you this. The work you are set upon is accursed. Accursed,' he shouts over the jeers. 'What did we fight for, gentlemen? Your plan has no legitimacy. No legality. We do not represent the will of the people as it is. We are a purged Parliament. You talk of purging still further. To what end? We did not fight for this.'

'We did not fight,' shouts Harrison, 'so that we could sink back into ungodly ways. The Lord is coming, gentlemen. With your quibbles, Heselrige, you are blocking His path. Spitting on His designs.'

'Do you lecture me, sir, on His designs? And are the rights and liberties of the English people "quibbles" now?'

'Can you ask that of me, sir?' says Lambert. 'To whom is your Parliament accountable? Where are the checks on your power, which you choose to wield in the pursuit of fripperies?'

Cromwell, still standing in the middle, raises his hands as if he can push the dissent to one side. 'Gentlemen,' he says. His voice is pitched low and sad. Both sides crane in to hear him talk. 'Are we to throw away the mercies we have been shown? Are we, by our jarring and fighting with one another, to cast all aside?'

He leaves the questions hanging. His great leonine head sinks towards his chest, and he sighs.

'A break, gentlemen, and can I suggest we use it to ask for His light.'

The room breaks into cliques and groups, with men manoeuvring their way between factions or sticking doggedly with their neighbours. Like a country barn dance, with a malevolent caller and the only music the clicking of heels on the theatre's dusty floor.

Nedham leans back in his seat. 'Well, Will. What do you make of it all?'

'All passion, no sense. I do not see how they will agree with each other, or sell that agreement to the people.'

'The sell to the people will be my job. As for the rest – what else is politics but the grinding of men's convictions into something universally palatable?'

Will nods and then nudges Nedham. 'Look,' he says, nodding towards the centre of the Cockpit, where Cromwell, Vane, Heselrige and Lambert have formed a tight knot. Harrison has spied it now, from among his cronies at the far side. He is bustling forward to break into the charmed circle when it dissolves of its own accord. He is tight-lipped, furious.

'Gentlemen, we have reached an accord,' shouts Cromwell, and the chatter ceases. 'Progress on the bill will be halted.' He looks towards Vane, who nods. 'We will discuss further this question of an interim government.'

'More talk,' whispers Nedham to Will, as the assembly lets out a strange collective sigh of relief and disquiet. No decision is better than the wrong one, perhaps. But the frustration and irritation is visible on every face, and as they file out into the cold spring air, each man looks as if he has been forcibly fed an unripe plum. A squinting, sour line of men disperse to their homes or to their lodgings.

Cromwell is alone in the empty theatre. He droops a little; his eyes are unfocused. He has turned inwards, communing with himself.

'Do you need me, Lord General?' Will's voice is absurdly loud. This place is designed to amplify, to make sound more intense. Cromwell looks at him as if across a great divide.

'What? No. Yes. I . . .'

He pauses. Will moves towards him, talking softly as if to a somnolent Blackberry. 'I will come with you to your chambers, Lord General. If you need me, I will be there. I will have Jem douse the lights in here. We do not need them, for the night is done.'

Cromwell nods, and allows himself to be chivvied towards the back door of the Cockpit, one of the many that lead into his private rooms. They pass the rusting machinery used to propel fairies and sprites through the air. A weight tied to the end of a scenery rope swings, creaking, as Will brushes past it.

They make for the chamber where Elizabeth Cromwell waits, drowsing by the fire. She starts as they enter, looks at her husband's face and immediately stands, ushering him into a chair.

'I will fetch you something, my dear,' she says.

'Shall I call one of the servants?' Will asks.

'I will do it myself,' she says sharply, and he understands that she is annoyed by his question. He is too tired to work out why that should be.

As she leaves the room, Cromwell looks at Will with red-rimmed eyes.

'The whole weight of the cause, the cause for which better spirits than I fought and died, rests on this business in hand. On this parcel of biting, snapping fellows finding a means to reflect His will.'

He retreats into himself then, and Will knows enough of his chief to be silent. He turns to look out of the window. It is a clear night, with a bright moon. Henrietta loved the moon. The familiar sadness catches him by the throat, shakes him.

He notices two figures standing near the ruins of the old tennis court. They are shadowed, and it is dark, but he thinks he knows the shape of them. They stand conspiratorially close as if to whisper sweet nothings in each other's ears. Vane and Heselrige.

~ ~ ~

The messenger comes early to the Cockpit. Cromwell, in a workaday suit of plain black wool and grey stockings, is in a knot of officers and a handful of MPs. They are threshing out the details of the hiatus; almost agreeing and pleased with themselves. Cromwell looks younger than he did last night. He watches the good-natured debate with an avuncular eye.

The Cockpit is gloomy; the small windows allow in only a faint wash of daylight. They are meeting here, rather than in Cromwell's more comfortable study, because they anticipate a crowd. But the small thicket of men is huddled in the octagon's centre, leaving an echoing space around them.

Will is uneasy, even before the messenger whispers in his ear. Where is Vane? Where is Heselrige? Why are there so few MPs here? He spots one or two of them; known army sympathizers. The officers laugh, suddenly and loudly, the sound filling the dusty corners of the old theatre.

The door creaks open; from the outside, not from Cromwell's quarters. A clerk comes in as the laughter ebbs. Will recognizes him; he's something to do with the foreign affairs committee. He looks young and ashen, and Will watches him look at Cromwell standing among his officers and stay where he is. One foot out of the door, one in.

Will walks over to him, and the young man is visibly relieved.

'Thurloe sent me. Can you tell the lord general,' says the young clerk, in a low and confiding tone, 'that they are sitting in the House. Now. Scores of MPs. Debating the bill.'

Will swallows, looking across at Cromwell. He doesn't need to ask which bill. The clerk looks ready to flee. They both know the rage will break on them. Will nods, and walks forward.

He delivers the message clearly, and watches the slower MPs and officers trying to absorb it.

'But we have agreed to delay,' says one. Baffled.

'To pause. For the cause,' says another, befuddled into an absurd rhyme. No one smiles.

Will is watching Cromwell, waiting for the outburst. Harrison is turning a beetroot purple. Others of the officers clench white knuckles on sword hilts. All of them are aware of Cromwell, so aware that most cannot look directly at him. They look at their shoes, at the door, at Will.

Will forces himself to meet his chief's gaze.

'Send the messenger back. I do not believe this,' Cromwell says, with a devastating calmness.

The remaining MPs look at each other, and Cromwell leans back, watching them silently.

'We must . . . I mean. It is our duty to . . . to . . .' says one MP with jowls that shudder over his lace collar as he speaks. They judder to a halt as he runs out of words and courage.

Abruptly he bows and heads out of the room, followed with some alacrity by the remaining MPs. Cromwell is left in a tight circle of officers. They stand in silence, waiting for orders. They seem, to Will's non-martial eye, to have shifted and shaped themselves into rows and ranks. All of them are reflecting Cromwell's contained violence, and the cumulative effect of such control seems to vibrate in the very air of the Cockpit.

~ ~ ~

The second messenger comes. The bill is being debated, with a view to being passed in haste. For months this bill has bounced back and forth between House and committee. And now?

Cromwell remains silent and the officers confer rather than listen to the awful pause. The speculation is wild.

'What is in the bill now that they must rush it through without us?'

'What does it matter? Self-serving, indulgent bastards. They mean to prolong themselves.'

'The biggest attendance in the House for years.'

'And is it a coincidence? No. Planned. To wrong-foot us.'

The officers throw words about, groping for sense. Cromwell seems to listen with one ear, his face impassive.

A third messenger.

Sir Henry Vane is among those driving the bill on. Sir Henry Vane, who last night, in this room, agreed to pause.

Cromwell's neck turns a blotchy red. A warning sign. But the rage Will expects does not quite materialize. Instead there is a heightening of this cold ferocity. An imprisoned rage that seems to thrum visibly beneath his skin.

This is the Cromwell of Naseby and Worcester. This is the Cromwell Will has heard about but not seen; who could charge bare-headed and armourless into a sea of murderous mutineers and bring the ringleader to his knees.

'Harrison,' he raps. 'A troop. Loaded muskets.'

Harrison nods, running for the door.

Cromwell slowly dons his hat. He pulls on his gloves deliberately, finger by finger. He walks to the door, seeming never to doubt that they will all fall in behind him. This is, after all, a military operation. They will follow, so he must lead.

Outside the door, the morning air hits Will with its brightness and freshness. The stale Cockpit behind them, they stand for a heartbeat in the sunshine, waiting for Harrison's assembled troop to arrive.

They come, grim-faced. Martial.

'Lord General, is this wise?' Will forces himself to ask the question.

Cromwell grunts – an acknowledgement and a dismissal. He is a fixed point of rage; there is no way through. Will falls back, letting the soldiers overtake him. They march onwards towards the House, their implacable leader at the front. Will wants them to run; to expend some of this cold fury. But they advance with slow deliberation, falling into step towards the enemy in his lace and silver buckles.

Will thinks of Blackberry. The army is seizing power, and he finds, as he watches the soldiers go, that he does not think of England's fate. Of high politics and the tortured question of how to fill the king-shaped hole in the country's soul. He thinks instead of his son, and the milk-white skin at the nape of his neck, and the chances of keeping him safe if the political tumult rains blood again.

Sidrach comes into the kitchen with a rare bounding energy. The door is flung aside, his hands are clapped and there is a smile on his face so wide she is reminded of a yawning ferret.

She glances down at Tom, who is crouched by the coals, frozen still in the act of blowing on the embers. He would be a comical figure in any other kitchen; his cheeks puffed out and his eyes wild. It's a face that would make Blackberry laugh, in that exaggerated full-body guffaw that young children throw themselves into.

'Well!' Sidrach's voice is a cheerful boom.

'Husband,' she says. 'You are happy?'

'The news, my dear. Such news. Cromwell has listened to Harrison, that godly man, that saint. Together they have thrown those godless fornicators out of Parliament. Cast them off like the flapping old women they are.'

Patience sinks slowly into a chair. Parliament dismissed? The questions whirl. On what authority? In whose name? What will come next? She knows better than to articulate the questions; she can't bear the ridicule.

But Sidrach is too puffed, too bouncing with the possibilities to need prompting. He talks on.

'And Cromwell, they say, is to appoint a council of godly men. Imagine it. A Sanhedrin. As it was ordained in the book. Oh, the sinners and the drunkards and the fornicators will see something now, Patience. Oh, they shall see. A sword of burning fire. We will clear the way for Christ's return. We shall do His work. Just as we laid waste to the papists in Ireland.'

There is a clatter as Tom drops the scuttle. He flinches, an arm rising ready to protect his face, but Sidrach is too glowing to notice.

'The bawds and the adulterers and the thieves. Oh Patience! We will scourge them all. We will lay down the palms for His return, and the sins of the world will be undone by us. They are fools, Patience, who think that His coming does not need us. But we must clear the way.'

He is pacing the kitchen now. His measured step has become a bounce, his arms windmill, and she is afraid. She has learned to anticipate his every mood, and this one is new. She does not know what it means, and the not knowing is the worst. The great uncertainty that keeps her teetering on the lip of a precipice not of her own making.

He stops, suddenly, as if struck. 'Perhaps I might be chosen. Perhaps . . .'

He resumes pacing, shaking his head as if to clear it.

'We must be fierce and bold, Patience. For when He comes, he will smite the nations that are unprepared.' He pauses, looking at her with a sharp smile. 'That's the Irish done for, the bog-hogging papists. Ha!'

Patience tries a tentative smile back, and nothing happens.

'He will rule with a rod of iron, and so must we. It says as much in the book, do you see? "He treadeth the winepress of the fierceness and wrath of Almighty God." Blood will flow, Patience!'

Oh, the pain of keeping silent. Oh, the swallowing of all the rebukes and retorts she can feel trembling on her tongue. The obvious, stupid flaws in his plan. The God of her father is a kind

God who weeps for man and does not bleed him. We have spilled enough blood, Sidrach.

She bows her head so he cannot see her face. Cannot see the fury mounting. A rage that centres on herself, on her own stupidity. She thought that by marrying Sidrach she would help shape these events, be close to the whirligig of power. But in reality she has denied herself even an opinion, a voice of her own. Stupid, thoughtless child that she was.

He kneels next to her and takes her hands, pulling them towards him. The sleeves of her dress ride up, and they both see the bruises on her arm, the purple blush of finger marks.

Leaning forward, he kisses the bruises with an unbearable tenderness.

'Dearest Patience. Dearest wife. It is all for you. For your soul. For does the Bible not say that wives must submit to their husbands as unto the Lord? I am teaching you to submit from love. Love of you and of the Lord.'

She watches him kiss her marked skin. Looking up at her, he says: 'You are learning, my loveling. "But I suffer not a woman to teach, nor to usurp authority over the man, but to be in silence."'

I can trump you, she thinks. I can read. *Let every one of you in particular so love his wife even as himself.* Beat yourself, Sidrach. Let the bruises flower on your own skin. Love yourself as you love me.

But all the defiance is inside. She is silent as he grins and chirps to himself, and on the surface she displays all the compliance he wishes for; she is a mirror through which he cannot see.

FETTER LANE, LONDON

June 1653

I AM HOME, SAYS SAM TO HIMSELF, AS THE GREAT BELLS TOLL above his head.

It seems a meaningless sort of a statement, and he laughs at himself. Where is home? He stands on Fetter Lane, looking across at the door of his father's house. It has been repainted a dull grey, and the sunlight sinks into the grime on the windows.

He stands motionless in front of the house, while ghosts flit in and out of the door. His father, a genial lunchtime wine haze settled about him, saunters down the steps and out into the lane. Ned, his brother, pulls the door closed with a careful click, and looks around to see if he is being watched and judged. Poor old buttoned-up, God-fearing Ned. Last comes Hen, smiling. Pausing to tilt her face to the sun. Looking left and right with quick, restless eyes. Stepping out with a sure step, certain of adventure. Only the truly curious can find excitement wherever they are, he thinks. Lord, how he misses her.

The pack on his back is heavy. Stuffed with all his worldly

goods. Around him, people scurry with purpose. Debating and talking, selling and buying. Moving from point A to point B, thinks Sam. I have no points. I am pointless.

What is the purpose of a pun if you cannot share it?

What now?

Where will he go?

He thought that all would become clear when he reached London. He thought that he would know what to do, how to live. He was half right. There was a joy in leaving Paris, in walking away from that stale pit of intrigue and boredom, where courtiers flock around a sensualist crown-less king. Where wives are attempted for something to do; the more violent the husband, the more delicious the risk. Where feuds are amplified as a distraction from the great and enervating ennui of being young and rootless and purposeless.

Until, at last, came the day when Sam tried to rise at noon and found he could not. The sun was high and angry, wilting the exiled English. Sam lay naked, sweating. The windows were open wide, the curtains were limply still. Not in the least tired, he made himself go back to sleep, for want of anything else to do. He succeeded in forcing a fitful, damp dreaminess.

On waking, he found it was still the afternoon. He thought about rising. But why? He thought about lying there alone until he wasted into a skeleton. He thought of all the corpses he had seen, all the broken, empty carcasses of men. Looking down at his pink, sweating skin, he thought of all that lay beneath, and how often he had seen it pulled inside out.

Home, he thought. I will go home.

And here he is, standing on Fetter Lane. Being sworn at for getting in a haulier's path; stepping backwards into an urchin, who swears at him too with thick London vowels and a thoroughgoing knowledge of God's anatomy. He walks on, turning his back on his father's house, where some fat Puritan whoremonger probably sits eating cheese and letting out sanctimonious farts, which waft up to the room that was once Sam's.

He heads down towards Fleet Street, reflecting that an aimless body in London is like a carthorse in a cavalry charge. He is hungry; is that the place to start? He will find a pot house and ask for an ordinary. He thinks of the small stash of coins hidden about his person, and how quickly they will run through his fingers if he is not careful.

Here he is, on an aimless Saturday in London. He walks up and along past St Paul's. They still stable some cavalry horses here, he has heard, though not in such numbers now the wars are done. He tries to imagine the great nave he knew as a child rigged as stables, with dozens of horses clattering on the stone floor. As he passes the old church, he catches a familiar scent – of hay and dung and sweat. It triggers a hotchpotch of memories: horses and battles; the feel of his hands on a sweat-slick neck, threading fingers through a coarse mane. The peculiar pulse of life and love under a favourite horse's skin.

He turns in to Moorfields, thinking to walk a while in the shade of a tree or two. There a man can find quiet enough to contemplate his next move. But everyone in London has had a similar plan, it seems, and the place is jammed. Small children everywhere; harassed adults sweating and claiming to enjoy the weather. The laundresses and bleachers have staked the sunniest side, and great sails of white linen lie limply to dry in the sun. There is a wrestling match in one corner, drawing jeers and boos at present for some misdemeanour. Along the central path, the book-sellers call and holler, fighting with the ballad-sellers to be heard.

He finds a low wall and sits. He watches a boy with a stick pretending it is a sword, fighting a tree and calling it 'papist'. He watches two pretty girls walking by, and he tips them an easy smile, which they pretend not to notice. They walk on, heads close and giggling.

It is, he thinks, remarkably the same. He expected something different. Some mark that the world has been turned upside down – that these are a people who killed their king. Apparently, Old Noll is to announce his new assembly soon. At present there is no government. No one is in charge, bar Old Noll himself, the scheming bastard. Itching to be crowned. King Warty-face, the peasant monarch.

A small boy stops in front of him, bending over to smell a flower. There is a woman with him, and he finds himself watching them. The boy is still in his dresses, but looks close to breeching. She is dressed severely; godly from the lace at her high neck to the ends of her blunt-cut fingernails. But her face! Freckled and somehow cleaner than other faces, with a shine on it that comes from within. A face full of mischief and light. Sam thinks of the ladies of the French court; of the king's latest mistress, who is beautiful but blowsy, all proffered tits and painted lips.

The girl smiles at something the boy says, and her teeth are white and even. Absurdly, Sam is reminded of his first and loveliest warhorse, who died beneath him at Naseby. A horse who was beautiful and loyal, and so full of heart that she ran until all her blood was spilled and still she ran some more. For him.

He laughs at himself for being such a ridiculous cavalryman; comparing this pretty girl with a horse for all love. His attention wanders. There are other people to watch; other girls to admire. But then the boy raises his head and looks at Sam with green eyes set beneath a chestnut fringe, and the rest of London falls away into so much chatter.

Patience watches Blackberry bending to smell a flower, and smiles. How strange his childhood is, hemmed in by London's walls. She is to take him to the countryside soon, to stay with his grandparents.

Sidrach assented to the trip with a preoccupied wave. Cromwell is drawing up plans for his new council of the godly. Her husband is keen to keep Will happy, and to keep distractions such as Patience at bay. He has not laid a fist into her for weeks. She is off balance, waiting for him to notice her again. Fear lies cold on her soul; sometimes a light smear and at others a great suffocating drift.

But today. Today there is sunshine, there is Blackberry and there is the promise of home, tomorrow. She tilts her face to the sun and thinks of home. How the berries will be fruiting, and the grass will be new-cut, and the brook will be low and barely bubbling.

'Excuse me, miss.'

She comes awake from her reverie. A man. An unshaven man, with salt-thick bedraggled hair and a tanned face that marks him out as no Englishman. Wrinkles he is too young for web the corners of his eyes. Once a soldier, clearly.

'I have nothing for you,' she says, grabbing for Blackberry. London is full of men like this: penniless, sometimes limbless.

He looks wide-eyed at her, then laughs. A great infectious belly-slap of a guffaw. 'Bless your kind heart, miss, I don't want charity.'

His voice is cultured, refined. She looks closer and sees that his clothes were fine once, dandyish even. His boots are polished and worn. 'Damn my eyes, miss, but I must look a sight worse than I thought. Here was I thinking I was quite the thing, strolling about.'

'I am sorry, I . . .' She trails off, confused. But his good humour is catching and she finds herself smiling back at him.

'Never mind, miss. I shouldn't be accosting ladies in the street. But I have a question. May I?'

She nods. Blackberry has slipped his hand into hers and looks up at the man with intent eyes.

'Were you a soldier, sir?' he asks

The man squats on to his haunches, looking the boy in the eyes. 'I was. And a sailor. I am not long back from the West Indies. I saw gales and shipwrecks and natives. I ate coconuts and flying fish.'

Blackberry's eyes are huge and round. His hand grips tighter in Patience's palm and she squats down too, so that the three of them are a strange tableau of little people around which the throng must divert on their Moorfields perambulations.

'He is teasing you, Blackberry,' she says.

'Blackberry?'

'It is my nickname, sir. Given to me by my mother. Did you see a mermaid?'

'I did not. But I heard one singing one night. Beautiful sound. Like a sighing. Dying of love for me, I shouldn't wonder. Sighted me through the porthole.'

'Now he really is teasing,' says Patience. 'Come, darling. We must be at home.'

She straightens herself up. He remains crouched down, looking up at her with a face that catches the sunshine.

'My question?'

'Well then, if you are quick about it.'

He smiles and says: 'Is the boy's real name Richard?'

She nods. Blackberry, too, nods emphatically. 'Is he magic, Auntie Imp?'

'Blackberry,' she says, admonishing him. But the man only laughs.

'Aye, little man. And was your mother's name Henrietta?'

'Yes. But I do not remember her.'

'Oh little man. She's watching you, don't doubt it. And so proud of you, all tall and handsome. I saw her once lift you in the air and blow on your tummy and tell you her heart would break for the love of you.'

Blackberry looks frightened now. He reaches to tug at Patience's skirt. Breaking eye contact with the man and pushing his hair back behind his ears with quick fingers.

The man stands, rueful. He strokes his chestnut beard and says: 'Sorry, miss. I didn't mean to frighten the boy. It's just . . . Seeing him unexpectedly. It's thrown me right off course.'

'Who are you?'

'Samuel Challoner, miss. Brother to the boy's mother. And if I may ask, who are you?'

~ ~ ~

They walk back through the city towards Will's house. Blackberry has taken the arrival of a lost uncle with all the equanimity of a five-year-old.

He keeps up a running commentary on the scenes they pass, leaving Sam and Patience to grin at each other over his chattering head. '. . . There's the book-seller. My mama worked in a bookshop during the wars. A woman working, sir. My father says she loved books. Do you love books, sir? Do you read lots of books? My uncle Ned was killed in the war in Ireland. Did you know him, sir, my uncle Ned? Uncle Sidrach said that he was smiting the papists for God, but my father says that's all stuff and nonsense—'

'Blackberry.'

'Sorry, Auntie Imp. There's the wine shop, sir. Do you like wine? My father . . .'

Sam watches the boy as he talks. He looks at the serious, earnest face; the freckles and the green eyes. The ghost of his mother, walking and strolling in the sun, collecting its light in the gleaming chestnut strands of hair. It is astonishing, yet not. A prosaic miracle. There must be some Will in the boy, but try as he might, Sam can't remember much of his brother-in-law. Will came into their lives when Sam's was full to the brim; with his apprenticeship, with his drill for the trained bands, with his enthusiastic discovery of women. Some ten years ago; more perhaps.

Sam was running with the Roundheads then, in the early skirmishes. Before the bastards hanged his father.

'. . . but Uncle Sidrach says General Cromwell will tread the ungodly into the earth, sir.'

'I hope not,' says Sam. He mimes being crushed by a giant foot, and is rewarded with a laugh from Blackberry, and a reluctant smile from Patience.

He is confused by Patience. Should a Puritan girl look so ready to laugh? Should a Puritan girl look so unbound, somehow, as if she is close to skipping with each step? Should a Puritan girl have such kissable lips?

'Uncle Sidrach?' he asks.

'My husband, Mr Challoner. Sidrach Simmonds. A preacher.'

'Oh,' he says, neutral. Her lips can be as sweet as a cherry, but they are not for him. The last thing he needs is some godly preacher calling brimstone on his head.

'What are your plans?' Will looks across at the man opposite, seeing his resemblance to Henrietta and feeling the catch in his throat.

'As I told your sister, I have none. My general has neither men nor ships. And I am done with fighting.'

'You serve the Antichrist,' says Patience.

'Do I? Lord save me.'

'The Lord does not like sarcastic calls upon him.'

'Does he not? And do you have His ear? I think, Mrs Simmonds, that the God who made this world was a sarcastic cove Himself. Do you not agree?'

Patience begins her retort, but catches Will's eye and falls silent. Sam seems huge, impossibly vibrant. He is all broad shoulders. The walls seem too small to contain him; she can better imagine him at sea, facing down a storm, than she can comprehend his actual presence in this dusty room. His face is mahogany, set with white teeth.

'Do you have any money? Anywhere to stay?'

'A little. And no. I was thinking to throw my lot in with any servants of the true king I can find.'

'God's blood, Challoner,' says Will, visibly flinching. 'Don't talk of Stuart in that fashion here. You'll have us all hanged.'

'I beg your pardon, Will,' says Sam, and he means it. He thinks of little Blackberry – asleep now, with flushed cheeks and an innocence radiating from him like a reproach.

Patience looks pleased, as if Sam's apology is a mark in God's favour. Which is provoking.

'The Act of Oblivion pardons me, even if you do not, Mrs Simmonds.'

'You are still liable for fines for treasonable acts,' says Will.

'Perhaps.' Sam laughs. 'They may try to fine me as much as they like. I have nothing to give. My father's property has been sequestered and spent.'

'You must stay here,' says Will. Sam begins to protest and Will leans forward, pitching his voice loud. 'Listen. You are Henrietta's brother. I love her. Loved her. I insist.'

'How will it play out with your employer?' asks Patience. 'He's a traitor.'

Sam stands quickly, and the chair clatters to the ground. He says nothing, just looks at her with something approaching contempt. She finds it strangely disconcerting. He walks to the window and leans out, as if finding an unlikely succour from the still air of a London in heat.

'Your employer?' he says, turning back into the room. 'I thought you were a lawyer, Will?'

'I am working as a secretary. For the Lord Cromwell.'

'Old Noll,' splutters Sam. 'Old Noll. I'll be buggered. Beg your pardon, Mrs Simmonds. But Old Noll.'

'Who will not take kindly to Will harbouring a Royalist.'

'I'll square it somehow,' says Will. In truth, he is a little nervous. About squaring it with Cromwell, but more about having this man share his space. He knows his house is quiet; knows it is dry. He knows that when Blackberry is not there, the silence is an echo that pulses. But Sam is huge and loud and vigorously present. What else can he do? Sam is laughing now, at the thought of cosying up to Old Noll, and his eyes crinkle so like his sister's that Will wants to sink to his knees and curl into a despairing ball.

He stands. 'Wait here,' he says, as if Sam has somewhere else to go.

As the door closes behind him, Sam looks towards Patience.

'I beg your pardon if I offend you, Mrs Simmonds.'

'You do not. Your politics, however. Your godlessness. These offend me.'

'How do you know I am not more beloved of the Lord than you?'

'Please.'

'That is what I love about the godly,' says Sam. 'You preach a good sermon about humility and being the Lord's arsewipe and all that. But you're so damn certain you know His mind. Me? I know that I know nothing.'

'At least you know that.'

'Ah, Mrs Simmonds. I know lots of things. I know how to make stroked dogs whimper with pleasure. I know how to suck the marrow from a bone. I know how to lick the last of the wine from the rim of the cup. I know about living, Mrs Simmonds, and I let the next life take care of itself.'

'You will burn.'

'Will I? I daresay. But so might you. And at least I will have had some joy before I become toast. At least, Mrs Simmonds, my soul will sing in this life, if not the next.'

'Your soul is singing the devil's tune, but you cannot hear it.'

They fall silent, waiting for Will to return.

I am not so severe as this, thinks Patience.

I am not such a cavalry buffoon as this, thinks Sam.

Will comes back into a silent room, and looks from one to the other. The air is charged with something. Patience looks as if she might cry. She raises an arm to push her hair back, and he sees a fading bruise on the skin underneath her wrist.

'I have something for you. To start you off,' he says to Sam.

He holds out a pouch, and Sam opens it. Inside, a pair of earrings set with rubies, and a necklace to match. He pulls them out, and even in this gloomy room, they seem to gleam.

'Your mother's,' says Will.

'But these should be Blackberry's.'

'Blackberry will be provided for, Will. Henrietta was keeping them as a surety against misfortune, or until our fortunes revived. Our fortunes are settled, and I do not have a daughter. You must have them. Sell them. Use the money to make money, somehow. Perhaps you will find you are your father's son. In business, I mean.'

Sam looks up at Will, struggling to adjust. He is too used to being alone. Too accustomed to the soldier's knack of smearing everything real with a protective sludge of irony and bluff.

'Thank you, Will,' he says. 'Thank you.'

LONDON

July 1653

WILL DRESSES WITH CARE. HE INSPECTS HIS BEST COAT for fluff and lint. He rubs his shoes to draw out an extra gleam. He actually looks in a mirror, an activity he generally leaves for women and Cavaliers. The face that stares out at him is older than he remembers. A sad, grey face. Is this really me? he wonders. Is this how people see me?

He snorts derision at the philosopher in the mirror. He puts his hat firmly on his head, at right angles. The tall crown of it breaches the edge of the mirror.

'You are lovely, Father,' says Blackberry behind him.

Will turns to see the boy in the doorway, still in his nightgown. He clutches a scrap of blanket; a mouldy, threadbare thing that he will not do without at bedtime. Will's mother says it should be burned. Will's mother says the boy must learn to put aside such things, now that the breeching is near. But Will watches the boy pull the blanket to his face and lean a cheek against it.

'It is an important day, Blackberry. A man should look his best as history is made.'

The boy comes into the room, and climbs on to the trunk at the foot of the bed. He perches there and looks at his father with serious eyes.

'Uncle Sam says Oliver Cromwell wants to be king.' He stumbles over the name.

'Well, Blackberry. It is not that simple. It never is. Today he is calling an assembly of good men, and they will decide how we will be governed.'

'Did Oliver Cromwell decide who was good and who was bad?'

Will checks in his task, his coat only half on and the sleeve trailing on the floor. He still thinks of the boy as a collection of bodily functions wrapped inside a kissable skin. That there is a thinking mind inside that small skull comes as a shock.

'Yes,' he says simply, still on the back foot, struggling for balance.

Blackberry nods. A serious, grown-up face that makes Will's heart shatter into fragments. He cannot bear it. Cannot bear the weight of love. Cannot bear the possibility of more pain.

'Run along now, Blackberry. Find Nurse.'

The boy nods, and rolls off the trunk in the most complicated way he can devise. Will reaches out a hand to steady him, but he is up and off, the light patter of his footsteps hardly stirring the air of the house.

It is only after Will has left the house, pulling the door behind him and feeling the still air of a summer morning on his skin, that he remembers Blackberry is off to the country today to stay with his grandparents. London in this heat is no place for a boy, with disease bubbling through the cracked paving stones, pestilence a smirr on the foul-smelling Thames.

He tries to think of the day ahead as he walks towards Whitehall. Tries to think of the tasks he will need to perform for Cromwell, who even now will be pacing whatever room contains him, excitement hovering about him and infecting all who approach.

But all he can think about are the different ways a small boy can find to die: falls from trunks or trees that can crack a skull; plague sores flowering on pale skin, coughs that can rack a thin body until blood runs like spittle.

'I am leaving now, Sidrach,' says Patience.

He looks up from his bible. His eyes are dark, with pooled black shadows beneath them.

'To my parents'. You remember? The Capps are to accompany me partway.' She is babbling at him. Terrified he will change his mind about letting her go. He has been in a vicious temper since the names for the Nominated Assembly were announced, and his was markedly absent. Other Fifth Monarchists have been called.

Will tells them that the wags of London have already nicknamed this new assembly the Barebones Parliament, after one of the members, Praise-God Barebone.

It is today, the first meeting.

He stands and walks past her, out of his study. Down the stairs. He is still silent. The thump and creak of his steps echo through the house. She follows. Why did she not just slip out? Stupid. She is too stupid, too provoking. Why must she always make him angry?

He strides into the kitchen. Tom is blacking boots by the fire. When Sidrach enters, he stands, abruptly. Scared.

Finally Sidrach speaks, in a heavy, ponderous voice. 'Are you still here, Patience? Be off, woman.'

She gathers herself. 'God keep you while I am gone, husband,' she says.

'And why would he not? Am I not His? They will know it, Patience. Those knaves and blackguards. Those beasts pretending to be men.'

He is winding himself up. She sees Tom's face behind his shoulder – the sullen white scowl.

'And you,' says Sidrach. 'My wife. My wife. Going to pick daisies in the country while England's soul is at stake. The beasts and the devils and the harlots sucking at her blessed soul.'

He catches her arm with one hand; the other is balled into a fist. He pulls it back, low to catch her stomach, and she can see on his face the beginning of the smile, the relief he seems to feel when he first makes contact with her. She flinches and closes her eyes. The blow does not land.

Opening her eyes, she see Tom. He is holding on to Sidrach's wrist. There is a look of horror on his face, as if he cannot believe what he has done. He lets go. On Sidrach's fine lace cuff – his best – Tom's blacked thumbprint is horribly visible.

They all stare at it, mesmerized.

Patience breaks the moment first. 'Sidrach. No. No, please.' But he is grabbing hold of Tom's arm, pulling him towards the fire. He is pushing his small, grubby hand towards the red-hot charcoal. Tom is stumbling, his feet scrabbling for purchase on the floor, sobs mingling with a garbled stream of apologies.

The room smells ripe, suddenly. Of burning flesh, and piss, which dribbles down the boy's leg and puddles at his feet. Sidrach lets go, dropping Tom to the floor, where he huddles and weeps. With a look to Patience that she cannot read, Sidrach strides out of the room.

Cromwell has them. All 138 of them, crowded into this room, lean into his words like snakes being charmed. He stands with legs planted wide, turns this way and that. Throws his gaze upon a man here, a man there, until each saint in the room feels as if Old Noll's eyes rest upon him alone.

Will stands at the back, pressed into the wood panelling. The council chamber was full before Cromwell arrived with a coterie of followers and officers. The table sits solidly in the middle, taking space. Behind each seat, men stand and mill. Cromwell stands at the head of the table, leaning against the chair. I will be quick, he tells them again and again. But he is not quick. He talks on into the hush. The chamber is headily hot; it smells of horse and sweat. And hope, Will thinks, fancifully. He lets himself become carried away. Lets himself feel a part of something great, something glorious. Beside him, Nedham, who came early and commandeered space enough, scratches furiously with his pen.

We have not earned sufficient reward for the blood and treasure spilled, says Cromwell. We won the war but we have not won the peace. The godly are yet to rejoice in their triumph.

There are nods and harrumphs of agreement.

I will not advise you, says Cromwell. I will pray for you to find wisdom.

Now Will wrenches himself free from the tide. He plants two feet in the swirl of rhetoric and refuses to budge. Not even love for his chief will let him move. Let him have my heart, he thinks, his inner voice sounding surly and rebellious even to his own ears; he will not have my intellect.

For this is nonsense. Cromwell is talking nonsense. Can he believe it himself? Every man here, nodding and smirking, already believes himself wise; believes that it is the fellow next to him who needs help from the Lord to find his brain.

You. You have been chosen and called, says Cromwell. For all the rest are not yet ready to do His work. 'Who can tell how soon God may fit the people for such a thing? None can desire it more than I. Would that all were the Lord's people.'

Will leans back further, feeling the hard ridges and bumps of the wall digging into his back. He thinks of his youthful passion for natural philosophy; how clean and clear it was compared to this. Observe, hypothesize, experiment. He thinks of Francis Bacon's belief: that a man who starts with certainties will end with doubts, but a man who is content to own his doubts will end with certainties.

This room is all bullish certainty. The power of this puffed-up, puffed-out self-aggrandizing could carry a carriage to the moon.

Cromwell leans into his speech, carrying all but Will inexorably onwards. 'I confess I never thought to see a day such as this,' he calls low into the ears of his acolytes, 'when Jesus Christ should be so owned as He is this day, in this work. Jesus Christ is owned this day by the call of you, and you own Him by your willingness to appear for Him.'

But, thinks Will. But. But. Jesus Christ did not call them here, my lord general. *You* called them here.

~ ~ ~

At home, Patience is wrapped in her parents' affection. She finds herself treasuring the tics that grated on her pre-London self. The way her father clears his throat before a speech. The way her mother cocks her head over her sewing. The precise kiss Father plants on his wife's cheek as he bids her goodnight. The soft voices as they talk of mundane things. Of brewing ale and buttermilk. Of Sunday's joint and Monday's tasks. Of prayer and sleep.

She watches the gentle currents that link them as they go about their individual days. She watches her mother's sharpness balanced by her father's sweetness; his placidity tempered by her passion. And for the first time she wonders about what lies beneath and what came before. Did they fit so well together before they knew each other? Or did it come from knowing each other and growing in time?

She feels stupid and heavy. She despises herself for despising this when she was last here. Before the crack of Sidrach's palm across her cheek wakened her to the possible joys of quiet love. Of gentleness.

She thinks of Tom, left behind with Hattie while his hand heals. She thinks of Hattie's eyes as she smeared the lard on the boy's livid skin, and the lie that dangled in the room like a hanged corpse. An accident. A stupid accident.

Her mother's eyes follow her here. 'I am well,' Patience tells her, twenty, thirty times a day. 'I am happy.'

She knows that her pinched face betrays her. But she will not lay her white-hot misery on them. She has wounded them enough in the past, with her great and ridiculous disdain. She will not compound her sins.

On the last day, she comes close to breaking.

They are picking raspberries in the garden, the last of the summer's fruiting. Later comes the harder work of the preserving, but for now, there is the sun on her back and the light wind at the nape of her neck. There are bees nosing in the flowers, and the scent of summer is spread, thick and luscious, across the garden. Blackberry is ferreting in the bushes. He is intoxicated by the greenery, the space, the possibility of adventures. His face is stained red with raspberry juice, and now some fresh excitement calls him elsewhere.

They can hear her father's voice through the open window of his study. He likes to practise his sermons aloud. It used to irritate her, but she listens now to his deep voice with pleasure. She does not follow the words, just the cadences of his voice.

Her mother picks a raspberry and eats it, smiling across at her.

'Delicious.'

'Mmm.'

'You leave us tomorrow, Patience dear. Will you take our dear love to William? He will be missing Richard.'

Mother never will call Blackberry by his nickname.

'I will. I do not see him often. I am . . .'

Forbidden. Banned. Lost.

'. . . busy.'

'Well, my dear, you must make time. What is there but family that matters?'

A pause. Patience thinks about going home, and shivers in the bright sunlight.

Her mother says with studied casualness: 'You have been married some time now. Any sign of . . .'

She lets the question trail away, popping a fat raspberry in her mouth to cover the awkwardness.

'No.' Patience is short. She wants to head off this conversation. If her mother asks more, she will crack. If her mother shows sympathy, she will crack. The merest touch of a maternal hand to her cheek and she will weep and weep until the garden is watered by her tears.

But her mother just smiles a forced, bright smile. 'In the Lord's own time, my dear,' she says, moving on to new canes, humming a tuneless song as she goes. Over her shoulder she says: 'And if you are blessed, Patience, you will learn that it is not sufficient to love your children. You must be fierce for them.'

Patience smoothes down her rising panic, and breathes deeply, inhaling the heady summer smells as if for the last time. She must hide the shame of her bruises; the marks of her failure and her stupidity.

LONDON

August 1653

WILL RETURNS HOME TO FIND PATIENCE AND SIDRACH sitting with Sam. The air in the room is close and hot. He had planned to throw off his heavy coat, his collar and cuffs. To lie on his bed with the window open and the curtains pulled back, and a book about the stars to distract him from the grubbing of man on earth. He is half-cut already; he shared a flask with Nedham after watching Cromwell address the Barebones. They are beginning to look mutinous, and Cromwell is increasingly irascible and hard to please.

He wanted sanctuary. Instead he must watch Sam and Sidrach circle each other like wary fighting dogs. Why don't they just sniff each other's arses and be done with it? he thinks as he pours the wine. He knows he is sullen and peevish, but Blackberry is not here to be set an example on stoicism, and Will had planned to indulge his misery today. To cosset it with a decanter of wine and honey cakes, eaten in that cool bed so that crumbs dropped on the linen sheets.

Instead there is Sam's voice, which is loud and pugnacious, picking up a thread dropped when Will entered the room: 'Yes, Mr Simmonds, I have met His Majesty on several occasions.'

'His Majesty? Do you call him that? My dear sir.'

Will lifts his head from his glass. 'Sam,' he says fiercely. 'I have asked you repeatedly to call him Charles Stuart under my roof. Even when the boy is not here.'

Sam inclines his head graciously. He smiles at Will, a smile that seems to say, I know you are miserable, dear fellow, so I shall indulge you. Will finds it deeply provoking.

He turns away from the smile, and drinks deep.

Patience stands from her chair and walks to the open window, looking out into the street. The hubbub of a day's trading goes on uninterrupted. Oysters are called and sold, sausages are sizzled, leather is worked, cheese is rolled, geese are herded, pigs are slaughtered, coins are begged and traded. The clang of the blacksmith's hammer sounds through the street in a regular beat.

'How much do the people care,' says Patience, 'that their fate is in Cromwell's hands?'

'Not much, I would say,' says Sam. 'What difference does it make? The beer still needs brewing.'

'Why should we care what the people think?' says Sidrach. 'Most are godless. Fornicators and liars and bawds. This new assembly will pave the way for Christ's return, despite them. They will thank us when they sit at the Lord's side.'

Sam rises and walks to stand beside Patience, looking out of the window. She feels the air between them shiver with his nearness. It is because of his size, she thinks. Because he is like a caged bear in this little house.

'In his speech, the lord general said that the people must be given time to find their way to godliness,' says Will.

Sam laughs. 'Good luck with that, say I.'

Patience turns to him. He is disarmingly close. 'How can you laugh? These are souls.'

'How can you not laugh? What else is there? Is anyone naive enough to think that if Cromwell and Harrison and the rest preach at us long enough and hard enough we will all fall to our knees?'

'You are godless. I pity you.'

'I am not godless, Mrs Simmonds. I believe in your God. I just do not believe he wants us to crawl like worms when there is music, and wine and love and song. Did he not make those too?'

Sidrach Simmonds stands abruptly, so that Patience and Sam both turn to face him. Will watches Sidrach's gaze shift from one to the other.

He waves an impatient hand at them, as if they are children. 'Tsk. You are both deluded. We do not need to wait for the people to be ready. We must force it. Prepare the ground, by the sword if necessary. Christ is coming. Babylon must fall.'

Sam swallows his retort and turns back to the window, leaning out and letting Sidrach's sermon wash over him.

'. . . Does it not say in Jeremiah, "I have seen thine adulteries, and thy neighings, the lewdness of thy whoredom, and thine abominations on the hills in the fields. Woe unto thee, O Jerusalem! Wilt thou not be made clean? When shall it once be?"'

Will sinks his cup of wine and reaches for another. He is losing patience with arguing, debating. Men believe what they want to believe. Turning their minds is so rare, and so unlikely, that arguing for different versions of heaven seems pointless. Futile. He drinks too deep, and the wine has not been decanted long enough, so that the dregs catch in his teeth and fur his tongue. He spits into a handkerchief and thinks of a time when this room was silent and still.

As he sets down the cup, he catches Sidrach's monologue.

'. . . Did not the prophet say, "Awake ye drunkards and weep"?'

Sleep, ye drunkard, and evade the weeping, thinks Will.

In the absence of contradiction, Sidrach clearly believes himself persuasive and ratchets himself up. Arms are wildly deployed, his forehead is furrowed.

'. . . "Repent ye, the Kingdom of Heaven is at hand." Not my words, Mr Challoner. Not my words. The Bible. Matthew.'

Patience watches Sidrach and the flexuous spill of his rhetoric. She listens to him pile quotation upon quotation. Beside her, she knows that Sam is deliberately impassive. She watches her husband with his eyes, rather than the eyes of a persuaded congregation.

Can it be possible, can it really be possible, that Sidrach is a little absurd?

Will cannot help himself. It's the wine. 'Sidrach, dear fellow. What does this Kingdom of Heaven actually look like? How is it governed? No one can tell me.'

Simmonds rounds on him and begins to quote. Will recognizes his mistake. He has an empty cup, and an empty decanter, and once you have set Sidrach off, really it's too difficult to stop him.

The Kingdom of Heaven will be a kind of paradise. It will be virtuous. It will be, to use one metaphor beloved of the saints, like a treasure found in a field.

Sam puffs his cheeks out in an exaggerated sigh. Patience has an urge to elbow him. Sidrach is still directing his diatribe largely at Will, who is sinking further and further into his chair, as if he hopes to hide in it.

'. . . And Mathew tells us that "the Kingdom of Heaven be likened unto ten virgins, which took their lamps, and went forth to meet the bridegroom".'

'Ten virgins, hey?' whispers Sam to Patience. 'Perhaps I'll drop in after all.'

To her amazement, her utter surprise, she finds herself beginning to laugh. She tries to stifle it, to swallow it whole, but it grips at her stomach and forces its way out until she is laughing helplessly. Sidrach stops mid-parable and glances at her quickly. Lord help me, she thinks, looking at his face. She walks towards him, away from Sam. Her hand is raised in a placatory manner, but he scowls at her. Her arm drops limply to her side.

Sam catches Sidrach's expression and has an unfathomable urge to throw himself in front of Patience to shield her.

Will sinks, with immense gratitude, into a boozy snore, dropping his cup to the floor with a violent clang.

WHITEHALL, LONDON

October 1653

'THE MOON DID NOT STAY HONEYED FOR LONG,' SAYS Nedham, as they wait outside Cromwell's door. Inside, they can hear shouting.

'The first time I stood outside this door, he was shouting in your ear,' says Will.

'Lord help me, Will. But I love it when he shouts at someone who is not me. Who is it this time?'

Will shrugs. 'Some of the members. He is trying to clash heads together. Make them agree.'

'It is like making wine from dew. You tried to tell me, Will. That the Barebones was doomed.'

Will smiles, leaning against the wood panels. He rests his head back and closes his eyes.

'I know, old fellow,' says Nedham. 'You do not want to be smug. But you're failing. Do you think the chief believed in it?'

'The Barebones? Aye. He has a kind of innocence, our lord and master. Believes in people's goodness. Believes that if you give them enough rope, they'll rig themselves a hammock.'

Nedham jerks a thumb at the door, through which they can hear the lord general's rising fury.

'Innocent as a lamb, our Oliver.'

'You know my meaning, Nedham.'

'Do I? Does anyone know what his game really is, Will? Do you? Do I?'

The door is pulled roughly open. Will and Nedham push back against the wall, as a column of men exit in a sort of buzzing silence. Growl-faced and looking straight ahead. They are waiting to round a corner, perhaps two, before unleashing their grievances to each other.

When they have gone, Will and Nedham enter the room, each angling ostentatiously to be behind the other. Cromwell is at his desk, his head in his hands. Will feels immediately guilty for his play-acting, and glances sideways at Nedham before approaching the general, slowly and a little warily. He kneels by his side.

'Sir, are you quite well?'

Cromwell lifts his head and looks at him with bloodshot eyes.

'Where will it end, Will?'

'I do not know, sir. Nedham is here.'

Cromwell looks over Will's head at the newsbook man and smiles. A strange, forced smile. 'Nedham. Can we postpone, man? I am . . .' He pauses, lost in the middle of a sentence. 'Tired,' he says eventually, with an emphatic nod.

'Shall I get your chaplain, sir?' says Will.

'My chaplain. Yes. Thank you.' He sits up straighter, palms face down on the desk as if to push himself upright. 'Sometimes,' he says, 'prayer is both an answer and an admission of defeat. Go on then, Will, fetch my chaplain. I am in great need of him.'

~ ~ ~

Later, Will sits alone at the top of his house. There is an attic here, with a round window set into the eaves. Through the window he can see the rooftops stretching and smoking, the gathering coal smear hanging over the city. He can see the pinkness of cloud as the sun sets somewhere lost to view. There is a black and white cat on the roof opposite, arching its back and settling down for a dusk nap.

It is quiet up here. He looked in on Blackberry on the way up. He was asleep already in the room next to his nurse. Will never sees the boy now. He fobs him off in the morning as he rushes out towards Whitehall. He comes home late and tiptoes through the quiet house, avoiding the nurse. He hopes she is kind. How can he know what secret lives she and Blackberry lead when he is not looking on? There must be a tutor soon. Get the boy reading, and starting off on his Latin and Greek. He will ask Milton.

He thinks of Blackberry. His white skin and serious eyes. His furious energy.

He whispers to Blackberry when he is asleep. Wine-soaked words of love and sorrow.

Ah, he sighs, spiralling into the pointlessness of it all. The great unfathomable nothingness. Where is God? The sky over London is a hash of colours. Blues and pinks, blotches of white and tunnels of gold. Where is He? Will sips at his sack, letting the sweetness fur his tongue. He closes his eyes and tries to imagine having a depth of faith like his chief. He tries to search for it, inside his blindness. What would it look like, feel like?

If he cannot imagine a faith so strong, so muscular, perhaps it does not exist. Perhaps it is just what people say they believe. If the spirit is working in Sidrach and in Cromwell, why does it say such different things? If it is not, and yet they both claim its authority, then are they fools or cynics?

Who dupes whom in this great game of God?

He drinks deeply again, his eyes still closed. He tries to imagine Christ on His cross, surveying them all. What does He make of it all?

Downstairs, a door clatters loudly shut. Sam. Will opens his eyes. The sky has lost its riotous colours and is a dusky smudge.

Last night they got drunk together. Maudlin, weep-into-your-pot pickled. They talked of Henrietta.

Will feels too raw, too flayed from the conversation to go downstairs yet. Perhaps he will hide up here a pace longer. I love my sister, Sam had said. But the boy needs a mother. You need a wife. Let her go, Will. Let her go.

He drains his glass; reaches for the bottle. The answer, he knows, is not at its bottom. But what else is there to fill the long evening? Perhaps Sam will leave again.

Will sits listening for footsteps and banging doors. All he hears is the silence, and the voice in his head wheedling: 'Let her go.'

The knock at the door is loud and violent.

Patience, curled in the corner of her room, ignores it. She hears, as if through a sheet of dimpled glass, Sarah's footsteps and the opening of the door and the gruff sound of a man's voice.

She rests her head on her knees and pulls them tight with her arms. She closes her eyes. The wooden floor beneath her is hard and cold, but she cannot the abide the thought of any softness. Her body hurts. She breathes with the pain.

But the footsteps come closer and there is a knock at the door. For you, says a voice, distantly. For you.

'It is Mr Challoner.' This she hears, and she raises her head.

'Tell him I will be down shortly,' she says. 'Rouse out something to offer him from the kitchen.'

She unfolds her body warily. It cricks and cracks back into place. She is astonished it still works. It seemed broken.

She crosses the room to the glass, and checks herself over. There are no marks on her face; he tends to aim for the body. She smoothes down her hair and straightens her dress and dredges a smile from somewhere deep inside.

Downstairs, Sam fills the room as completely as she expected. He stands by the empty fireplace, broad and at ease. His shipboard tan is fading to a more English pallor, but still he looks healthy. He is vibrant, incongruous – like a diamond, he catches the room's dim light and shines it back at her.

'I come to bid you and your husband farewell,' he says, without preamble.

'You are leaving?'

'I hope so. I have an interview with someone Will knows, who will secure a passport for me. I do not want to leave and find I cannot come back.'

Sarah comes into the room, graceless and unsmiling. She sets down a decanter and some stale-looking biscuits. They are silent as she backs out of the door. There are no sounds of retreating footsteps. Patience imagines her ear pressed against the door, squirrelling away information for her master.

'I am sorry you are leaving,' she says. She is being polite, she tells herself.

He nods. 'I will be back. I have a notion to increase my small capital.'

'How, may I ask?'

'I know the court in exile, and the clusters of men who keep the old cause. They are pining, Mrs Simmonds. Pining for home. Many have young children who have never been on these blessed shores, who grow with French accents, or Dutch ones. I have a notion I can trade to them; carry to and fro.'

'They could come home. You have.'

'It is not so simple. Many feel it would be a betrayal of . . .' He stutters over the name. 'The man they call king.'

'And you do not?'

He sighs heavily. 'Have you read Thomas Hobbes, Mrs Simmonds?'

'I have not.'

'Ah, you are surprised. I do read the odd thing that is not a muster manual.'

She inclines her head, smiling at him.

'Which is not to say that I understood all of it. Most of the book went sailing over my head like a misfired shot. But the essence that matters is this. Hobbes is a monarchist, Mrs Simmonds. But not because he believes as many of the exiles do that Charles Stuart is anointed by God.'

'You have met him? Charles Stuart, I mean.'

'I have lived near him, and hunted with him, and watched him at play. And he is a fine man. But touched by the divine?' Sam laughs broadly, and it is so infectious that Patience joins in without quite knowing why.

Laughing hurts, and she has a moment of rage so fierce she almost cries out. Sidrach has made laughing painful. As if the humiliation were not quite enough on its own.

Sam's voice breaks in, as if from a distance. 'Are you quite well, Mrs Simmonds? I beg your pardon, I am boring you with all this talk of philosophers.'

'No,' she says, fiercely. 'You are not boring me.'

'No? Well. Hobbes says that man is a wolf to man, Mrs Simmonds. Without a common power to hold all men in awe, there will be no propriety, nor right to property. We will be in a constant state of war.'

'So a king is necessary to hold our baser nature in check?'

'Exactly so, Mrs Simmonds.'

'And where is God? He made us in His image. This Mr Hobbes assumes that we are all venal, all bestial.'

'And are we not? Forgive me, madam, but I have seen much. And little of it makes me think that man is a congenial beast. You live a sheltered life, Mrs Simmonds, and thank the Lord for that. You do not know of violence, of pain.'

She feels the blush hit her cheeks. She has a sudden urge to confide. To lay her head on Sam's shoulder. The blush spreads across her skin. She is burning.

Sam is pacing the room, threshing out his thoughts while he walks. He seems not to have noticed her flaming cheeks, the pulse beating in her forehead like a drum.

'Hobbes has come home to England. Because, you see, Mrs Simmonds, the consequences of his argument are that it matters not who exercises the power; only that power be exercised. It is,

I confess, attractive. To be allowed to be loyal to a system, not a divine monarch. I can keep my loyalty intact, a private thing, and live peaceably in this new Commonwealth.'

He stops and grins. He reminds her of Blackberry suddenly.

'I know your objection, Mrs Simmonds. 'Tis all gammon I swallow, because I want to be convinced, because I am glad to be home. Glad to be no longer in the wars. I do not know, I confess. I do not know even my own mind.'

She is beguiled by his rueful admission. She is used to men who wear their certainty like an armour.

'But what of God and His love?' she asks. 'What of His son's coming? What place do they have in your philosophy?'

'My philosophy? Well. I think we have fought enough over God's design, Mrs Simmonds. Seas of blood have been spilled in His name. And if He comes again? It seems to me that no one can agree on what He will want from us. To be sin-free? But did He not forgive the sinners? We seek to do His will, but we can't agree on what His will is. It all ends in misery.'

'So we should ignore His will?' She is shocked, breathless.

He looks at her, holding her gaze. 'That is about the sum of it. Until He comes and tells me what He wants, I'll doff the cap on a Sunday and leave it at that.'

They look at each other. She is awed into silence. She feels as if they are teetering on a cliff edge together, but she cannot quite say why or how. He turns away and the vertigo eases. She sits, heavy and lumpen, the edges of her bruises clashing and jolting her into a fresh spasm of pain.

'It is good to talk to you of these things, Mistress Simmonds,' he says, oddly formal suddenly.

'You do not think philosophy beyond a woman?'

He laughs. 'Not I. You did not know my sister very well, I recall. Twins, madam. One slow and dopey. One clever and deep. One who read philosophy and history for joy. The other who was beaten by his tutor for being dim-witted while he dreamed of horses. No, Mistress Simmonds. I concede all ground on this to women. I love a clever woman,' he says, looking down on her with a broad smile that suddenly falters at its edges.

'Well,' he says, all cavalry bluster suddenly. 'I must be off. I am due at Whitehall to see this friend of Will's.'

She stands on weak legs. Holds out a hand. It feels ominous, this gesture. She is aware that something will happen. Some unnamed, momentous thing. When he takes her hand, bending over to kiss it like a Frenchman, she notices as if from a great height the shock that jolts her. She is relieved it is not worse. She thought she might seize up, or faint, or fall.

She is all normal politeness. All stately Puritan ice.

'Goodbye, Mr Challoner,' she says, exactly as if it does not matter to her at all.

Sam is still thinking about Mrs Simmonds as he is ushered into Thurloe's office. Still thinking about her face, and the planes of it. Her smile, and the quick flashes of temper that set her eyes to gleam at him.

He is still thinking about her as he makes his bow, and it is with a wrench that he pulls himself to the present. He sees Thurloe's eyes upon him. The man is disconcerting, and Sam finds himself stumbling over his words.

Thurloe nods as he speaks, nods as Sam gives a potted history of his war and his peace. His relationship to Will Johnson, secretary to the lord general. Then he sits back in his chair, pressing the tips of his fingers together into a steeple shape. His eyebrows rise at the centre, giving him a quizzical air. His hair falls to his shoulders in a disarray that could be artful. He lets the silence settle. Sam will not be intimidated into filling it.

'Well, Mr Challoner,' says Thurloe.

Captain Challoner, thinks Sam, but merely inclines his head graciously.

'I am minded to give you a passport. The Commonwealth, I think, has no reason to fear your wanderings. From the plan outlined by you, I think you will want to come back and forth between London and the Continent.'

'Yes, Master Secretary. For trade purposes. I was never political.'

'Yet you joined the late king.'

'After the Parliament hanged my father.'

'He was a traitor.'

Calm, Sam. Calm. Don't punch the fellow in the mouth. Don't make him swallow those big yellow teeth. Calm.

'He was not. But perhaps, Mr Thurloe, we differ in our definitions. And now is the time for Englishmen to look to their similarities, rather than play up their differences. There has been enough of that.'

Thurloe nods. He pulls a paper from a pile, scribbles on it, then signs it with a dramatic flourish. He sets a candle to melt wax for a seal.

'When you return from the Continent, Mr Challoner, I would very much appreciate a visit.'

'Delighted, of course,' says Sam. 'But to what end?'

'Just a chat. Gossip from Charles II's court. Tittle-tattle.'

Sam bridles. The wax bubbles; Thurloe holds his signet ring just above, letting it hover.

'You wish me to spy.'

'Come now, Mr Challoner. I wish you to chat to me about the news that every halfwit Frenchman selling onions to the exiles has already told his third cousin once removed. I ask you to break no confidences. I ask you for no betrayals. Tittle-tattle. That is all.'

Lord, thinks Sam. Does it matter if I say yes? I have proved my loyalty to the king's cause with blood and pain. Tittle-tattle; that is all.

Mrs Simmonds forces her way back into his mind. He wonders what she would say. She is a woman of convictions. Of moral certainties. But she is also one of the victors, and Sam is tired of being part of a lost cause. He is tired of fighting. He wants capital. He wants a home. A wife. Children. A little girl he will call Henrietta, for whom he will buy Greek primers and Latin poetry. And a pony.

He needs this passport.

He pictures a home that looks remarkably like his father's house. He pictures a wife who looks remarkably like Patience Simmonds. This last, unexpected image prompts him to say: 'Tittle-tattle? Why not?'

No bad thing, he thinks, to put a fair stretch of water between him and Patience Simmonds and her impossible husband.

No bad thing, he thinks again, as he rides a shifting, choppy Channel. Behind him, a grey mist over England, like God's smeary thumbprint. Ahead, France. They will laugh at him, the crowd around the king. At the merchant's son arraying his wares like a tinker.

He must be pointed in his sales. In his cabin is a squalling, puking pile of spaniel puppies. English dogs. Cider. Books. Hunting rifles. The cot is stacked high with boxes, but he is happy sleeping in a hammock.

It is a joy to be at sea, if only for a short while. He lifts his face to the cleansing rush of salted air, here on the windward side. The deck slopes away from him, down to a rushing sea. It is cold out here. The other passengers huddle inside, wrapped in furs against the wind easing through the clinkered sides.

Too fast, they push on towards France.

He is not sad, exactly, to leave England behind. It is clear that the Barebones is failing. He does not know what will happen next. His money is on King Oliver. Will insists not. He insists that Cromwell is a good fellow. But how much is that filtered through Will's goodness? Sam smiles to think of his brother-in-law and his nephew. They are the closest thing he has to a family.

The Barebones. He has used the name as everyone does. Unthinking. The Barebones.

He thinks through the layers of flesh and muscle and blood to where his own bones hold him upright. He saw a skeleton once, in Paris. He had seen bones before, of course. Sticking out from splintered flesh; roughly exposed by the cut of a pike. In Paris, however, was the first time he had seen a full assembled skeleton. The bones were boiled clean, and strung together with wire.

At the time, he was pissed and surrounded by fellow members of Prince Rupert's horse. Someone had stolen the skeleton from somewhere. Who knows where. They had given it a hat, and a name: Digby, after Rupert's nemesis amid the king's staff. They had dragged it from brothel to tavern to brothel. Jermyn claimed to have enjoyed a threesome with Digby and a mulatto whore named Renee. Lord, how they had laughed. One of those blurred nights where brio and shame serenade your hammered soul.

Sam sat beside Digby at a table somewhere, feeding him oysters that slimed down on to the floor. Pouring the lees of cheap wine into his mouth, red flecks catching on the boiled white of his skull.

Sober now, Sam thinks, Digby was once a man. He raged and loved and whimpered.

Tittle-tattle, he thinks.

Does it matter, any question of loyalty? Those to whom you proffer loyalty expect it without cherishing it. At the end of it all, whatever you do or choose, you end up like Digby. Except, perhaps, without even the comfort of cheap wine and mulatto whores named Renee.

Tittle-tattle.

There is always the possibility of heaven to focus a man's mind on his duty. But Sidrach Simmonds' heaven is not for me, thinks Sam. He lets the roll of wave and sky fill him with a vivid delight. Why waste this life dreaming of the next? He should not have thought of Sidrach Simmonds. For thoughts of the man lead to thoughts of his wife. Sam thinks she would stand here with him on the deck, clutching the windward rail with wet hands, laughing at the sea.

You do not know her, he tells himself. Like as not, she would huddle below with the rest of the lubbers. No, she would not. He

173

lets himself think of Mrs Simmonds, made safe by her absence and the growing stretch of sea between him and her bright eyes. He imagines her turning a sparkling face on him, parting her lips into a smile that is also a challenge.

He grips the rail tighter, and forces himself to look towards France.

WHITEHALL, LONDON

November 1653

'**K**INDNESS, GENTLEMEN. LOVE.'

Cromwell's voice is low, reasonable. Across the table from him is Sidrach Simmonds, part of a coterie of fellow Fifth Monarchist preachers. Christopher Feake, the firecap preacher from Blackfriars, is at the centre of the group. Alongside him is Major General Harrison, the Fifth Monarchist nearest the heart of power.

Feake lifts his lip in a curl of derision. Sidrach Simmonds flicks his eyes at Will. Love. The word lies on the table between them all, like an embarrassing and maggoty fish.

Will watches Cromwell refuse to be intimidated by them. What is their scorn compared to a cavalry charge, compared to Prince Rupert riding down on you with a drawn sword and a scream and a devil's imp prancing at his side, dog-shaped? He has earned the right, one hundred times over, to talk of love and kindness.

'We all believe,' says Cromwell, 'in the Gospel. In the power and glory of the Lord. So why are we at odds, gentleman? Why can we not work together?'

'Together,' spits Feake.

Harrison lays a restraining hand on his arm. Feake spasms at the touch, and Harrison withdraws.

'Lord General,' says Harrison, his voice pitched to soothe. 'We can all agree on generalities. We believe in the power of God's truth, and we believe that His son is coming again.'

Harrison's influence, such as it is, relies on his position straddling the divide between Whitehall and the religious firebrands in the city and the army. But the stretch is becoming too much even for him; he is a man with a foot in diverging boats, and soon he will have to jump.

'Generalities,' says Feake, his palm pressing down on the table, fingers spread wide. 'Generalities are irrelevant. What matters is action. Detail. What are we doing to prepare for His arrival? What are we doing to clear His path?'

If He is coming, what need does He have of the scurrying of ants? Will sighs, audibly. Eyes swivel in his direction, looking for a scapegoat. He gazes firmly at the floor.

'Leaving aside the Church itself and the question of tithes and parishes,' says Feake, 'why spend the assembly's time on law reform? To what end?'

Cromwell leans back in his chair. 'To make justice quicker and more easily accessible to the common man.'

'What justice? Whose justice? What need do we have of laws made by man, when God laid down the law to Moses?'

Will rolls his eyes extravagantly. Looking up, he sees Simmonds watching him. The man looks thunderous. Poor little Patience. What was she thinking?

He feels a sudden jolt of guilt. Why did he not protest more earnestly against the match? Why did he not lie at her feet, clutching her ankles, stopping her walk towards this man as he stood there waiting to own her? He wonders what she believes now, about the coming of Christ and the rest of it. Most likely she believes whatever she is allowed to believe.

Will sees Feake, Harrison and Simmonds to the door. As he closes it behind them, Simmonds pauses and turns to glare at him. There is anger and contempt in his eyes.

Will, feeling buoyant now that Christ's triumvirate are leaving, winks at him. A cocky, Nedham-esque provocation that feels delightful. He watches Simmonds' fury surge and clicks the heavy wooden door shut. Turning into the room still smiling, he sees his chief's face, and his stomach clenches with fear.

'Smirking, Johnson? Smirking.'

'No, my lord general. I was—'

'You were smiling, Johnson. Smiling as if it amuses you. This great and sorrowful discord between men of God. This misery at the heart of England. This blood spilled and His legacy still at stake, and William Johnson, this great potentate, this great seer, rises above it all to smirk and prance and find it all so damned amusing.'

'No, my lord general. No.'

The word seems to wind the man tighter. His great head ringing with righteousness, with a flattening pulse of rage. Will steps backwards, his hands raised and palms open.

Cromwell lurches towards him. 'I know you are not godly. I do not see you pray. I do not see the Lord's fire in your soul. When will you see, Johnson? When will you feel his breath at your neck?

Is it the devil in you, sir? I thought you sad. I thought you quiet. A bookish, clerkish, mousy sort of a man. But perhaps you are bad. Perhaps the Lord's song cannot find your heart, because the devil already squats there.'

'I. No. Lord General, I beg your—'

'Get out, Johnson. Get out.' Cromwell presses the heel of his palm to his forehead and screeches. His fervour is terrifying, and yet somehow almost absurd. Will reaches behind him for the door handle. He feels the cold metal of it, and wrenches the door open. Pulling it to behind him, he shuts out that fury, that passion.

What just happened?

Jesus Christ. He feels the Lord's name hover on his lips, and stores the irony for the telling of the story to Nedham. He will make a joke of this unfunny thing, for what else can a mortal do when lashed by the wrath of a man with his God on his back?

Patience waits by the fire for her husband's return. She prays, *prays*, that the meeting has gone well. Sidrach has been in a bouncing, trembling mood for days, ever since the summons arrived, abuzz with extravagant plans to tell Cromwell where he is going wrong. Grandiose pledges of actions he will take, of schemes he will implement once he is at the right hand of the lord general, who is only wanting a little good advice before being the herald of Christ he could become.

Tom clatters into the room, his new nailed boots skittering on the stone flags. He carries a bucket of coal in each hand. Seeing her, he bobs his head and grins a wide toothless smile. 'Missus,' he says. 'Perishing cold, missus.'

She sees that his lips are blue.

'Come here, boy,' she says. She sees him look around the kitchen. 'Sarah is out, Tom. As is the master. Do not worry.'

He comes closer, and at a sign stokes the fire higher.

'Sit,' she says. 'Warm yourself.'

He sits, and she throws a blanket around his thin shoulders. He looks sideways at her, a small, shy smile at his lips.

'Do you know any songs Tom?'

'Only what my mother taught me, begging pardon, missus.'

'Sing one to me.'

'It's in the old tongue, missus. My mother. She was Irish.' He says it in a whisper.

'Are you a papist, Tom?' She shrinks a little from him, in spite of herself.

He shakes his head with vigour. 'Not I, missus.'

He puts his hands to the fire, spreading his fingers and clenching them into fists. Pulling them back under the blanket, he clamps them under his armpits.

'What's a papist, missus?'

'Tom! Well then. Papists believe that the Pope is the head of the Church. And that salvation can be bought and sold. And that excess and gluttony are legitimate in the service of the Lord.'

The boy pulls the blanket closer. His lips are losing their blue tinge.

'And what do you believe, missus?'

'I believe that man's relationship with God is a private one. That salvation is the Lord's gift, not man's. That saints and bishops are creatures of man, not God.'

'And how do you know you are right, missus?'

'Well,' she says, and pauses. 'Well.'

She finds that the words fail to come to her tongue as bidden. How *does* she know?

'Never mind that,' she says, utterly weary of it all. 'Sing the song your mother sang, Tom.'

In a low, guttural voice, Tom begins to sing. A sibilant, rhythmic lament, that suits the leaping of the flames, the low red gleam of the quiet kitchen. She watches him sing it, watches him fight to remember the strange words and the melody. Midway through, he falters suddenly.

He turns to her with a stricken face, his eyes wide with a kind of terror.

'I remember the words, but I have forgotten what they mean. I have forgotten.'

'Shh, Tom,' she says. She reaches out to touch him, to smooth the hair back from his forehead. He pulls back, fierce and scared.

'Shh,' she says again, but as the sound ends, she hears something else. Footsteps on the stairs.

Patience and Tom share a panicked glance. Both spring to their feet. Tom shakes the coal from bucket to scuttle, sniffing back whatever misery threatens to engulf him.

Patience crosses to the table, pulling her knife from the sheath at her belt and starting to shred a cabbage with nervous strokes.

Sidrach walks in. She puts on a smile, and greets him cheerfully, even though it is obvious from the first glance at him that things have not gone well. His face is a glower of rage and frustration. He will be looking for a scapegoat, she thinks. Oh Lord.

Somehow it is a relief that the waiting is over. That she knows, now, the worst. That whatever she says, however honeyed her tone, smooth her voice, placatory her gestures, none of it matters.

He rages for a while about Cromwell. About his obstinacy; his refusal to see his role in the coming.

Mutinously, she thinks: and what is his role? To appoint you to some position of great authority? What else would make you happy, oh lord and master?

In her silence, which he takes for granted, he blusters on. Cromwell is a beast. A monster. A dissembling, perjuring villain. He wants to be King Oliver. King Noll.

Tom, trying to escape the kitchen quietly, manages to drop a bucket and it clatters to the floor. Coal dust flies out, settling like black snow on the shined floor.

Sidrach whips round, curses forming on his tongue. Tom's face is misted with fear.

'Husband,' says Patience, loudly. 'Leave the boy. I will clean it.'

He nods, barely mollified. He is winding himself up to strike, and it will probably be Tom. The boy's eyes are wide, his eyebrows almost reaching his scalp. Patience pauses, and then says: 'Will thinks that Cromwell is not as you suppose him. He does not want power for its own sake, or so Will thinks. He says—'

'Will,' says Sidrach, and in his tone he conveys all he thinks of her brother. At least he is looking at her now, not Tom.

'Husband,' she says, mustering her courage, drawing Sidrach off Tom, who has picked up his bucket and is sidling backwards towards the door. 'He is my brother and I love him. And I think you are wrong about Cromwell.'

'You think. You think. You do no such thing, woman. Your place, if you have forgotten, is not to lecture me about Cromwell. Your job . . .'

She blanks him out. Blanks out the words behind the wide and angry mouth, the spittle flying and the lips stretched thinly over his too-large teeth. Behind him, the door closes. Tom has escaped outside.

Patience looks down at her hands, which clutch the edge of the table. The raw, chapped red hands that seems to belong to someone else, to someone older, wiser. He has knocked the cabbage off the table. It rolls on the floor, rocking on its cut stem.

She moves to pick it up, and something about the move provokes him. He pushes her, palms thudding into her chest. Could she say sorry? Ask him to stop? She will not. He will do as he will do. Such is the nature of tyranny. All she can do is find her pride, hiding in peculiar corners.

Nurture your pride, Patience. Own your name. Do not beg. Do not plead. She talks herself into silence then, as the slaps come down like hail.

'You must dissolve the Parliament.'

'I will not.' Cromwell's fist grinds into his palm. 'I will not,' he repeats.

Major General Lambert sighs heavily. His hands sit on his hips.

'Come, sir. My dear, dear sir. You must.'

'You cannot wheedle me into it, John.'

Will feels like an intruder. He is in the corner of the room, holding a sheaf of unsigned letters. They have forgotten him, he thinks. He sidled in this morning, his usual time, with his usual greeting. Cromwell looked up from his desk and merely smiled. The smile lifted the weight from Will, who was nervous about the encounter after the lord general's fury scraped him raw last time.

Relief, yes; but he feels a little diminished too, by how easily he can be crushed or puffed by the chief's favour.

Now he is invisible. He should cough, but he is caught in the room's web of tension. The two soldiers, comrades, facing each other in the fading light. The light of the candles and the fire catching the grooved lines on Cromwell's face, throwing a criss-cross of shadows across his skin, skitting over the dark bags under his eyes. The same light sheens the smooth young skin of Lambert, picks out the shine of his ungreyed, full hair.

Lambert will kneel in a moment, thinks Will. Then I will cough.

'I will not play the tyrant,' says Cromwell.

'I am not asking that. We are not asking that.'

'Who is this "we"?'

Lambert waves a dismissive arm. 'This, this is the answer.' He thrusts a paper at Cromwell. 'Look at it. I beg you. A new constitution. We have not settled matters since the death of the king. This answers that question. I have been working on it.'

'That is where you have been? You were called to the Nominated Assembly?'

'The Barebones?' Lambert laughs. 'That parcel of fools and knaves. Are you not disappointed by them? Are they not incapable of solving the matters that have dogged us since the execution of that man of blood?'

Cromwell nods, conceding the point. The Barebones seems as paralysed as its predecessor.

'Listen, my lord general. Please.' Lambert's voice is a high wheedle. 'We must separate out those who make the laws from those who implement the laws. This we have always agreed. We must have checks and balances on power. A set of scales. A three-legged stool. No one part of government can ignore the other. In this, my plan, there is a Council of State with real power, a Parliament, the judiciary and . . . and . . .'

He shuffles a little, aware of Cromwell's gaze on him.

'And what?'

'A man at the centre of it.'

'A king.'

'No,' says Lambert, hands raised. 'Well then. Perhaps a man with some of the authority the king once had. But less power. Checks and balances.'

'A king in all but name.'

'You are becoming distracted by the naming of things, Lord General.'

'Will,' says Cromwell, suddenly. 'Will, come here.'

Will steps forward, anxious now that he realizes he was never forgotten. He feels tender; nervous that his employer will unleash the fury on his already bruised person. 'Bear witness,' says Cromwell, his voice studied and neutral.

Lambert turns away, drooping.

'Bear witness, I say, Johnson. I have no desire to be king, in name or in deed.'

Will inclines his head.

'I myself invested the Barebones with its authority to sit for one year. Barely six months ago. I will not break that word. I will not be the tyrant that some already believe me to be,' says Cromwell.

Lambert rounds on him, anger catching at the edges of his words. 'For whose sake do you refuse to think about this? Your

184

own? We slide towards anarchy, sir. In Scotland, the Royalists are rising. In London, the firebrand preachers seek to own the republic. What will their world look like, Lord General? What will the rule of King Charles II look like?'

Cromwell seems to grow in size, the great swell of his barrel chest making slight Lambert seem even smaller. 'Do you lecture me on my duty, sir? Do you so presume?'

Lambert, quailing, seeks to deflect him.

'Mr Johnson. What do you say, sir?'

They both turn to look at him. Will recognizes the blotched skin of Cromwell's face, the tremble that comes before an explosion of honest rage. His every sense strains to tell the chief whatever he wishes to hear. To dampen the rage. But is that not the curse of great men? How many suffer by surrounding themselves only with those who twist the truth into a single, arse-licking 'yes'.

'I cannot see Barebones finding a settlement,' says Will, cautiously. 'I do not want to see a monarchy, nor an anarchy.'

The three of them are silent. Cromwell's great head sinks towards his chest. There it is; the present muddle laid out before them. Scylla on one side: the old days of tyranny and popery and kings. The devil's piper playing the tunes in Whitehall. Charybdis on the other: anarchy, blood and more blood. Orphans. Widows. Harvests rotting for lack of men. Beggars and vagrants, and the red-ragged stumps of veterans' lost limbs. The cacophonous squabbling of God's prophets, tearing the land apart. And in the middle of the channel, a parcel of panicking men trying to steer in the dark with no fucking compass.

Will raises his eyes to meet Cromwell's. 'Sometimes, my lord general, perhaps the least bad answer is good enough.'

Lambert waves his piece of paper. Cromwell turns away from both of them. He closes his eyes and looks heavenwards.

'I would be alone, gentlemen,' he says. 'I must think. Pray for guidance.'

Lambert and Will glance at each other and move towards the door. Will pulls it open, to let in a rush of cold, dark air.

'John,' says Cromwell, and both of them stop.

'I will not dissolve the Parliament. I will not, and I cannot.'

He lays a curious emphasis on the pronouns, a heavy and insistent 'I'.

Will notices the look that passes between them, these two men who once stood side by side on the battlefield. These men who are used to each other's ways, each other's orders. As he leaves the room, he hears the thud of Cromwell falling to his knees. The start of his passionate entreaty to his God.

The door to his office clatters open, and Will jumps, splattering ink across the page he has been labouring on. He begins to curse, looking up as he does so, and sees Nedham standing in the doorway.

'Will. You're to come. Come on now, man. Hurry.' He is near hopping with excitement.

Will casts down his quill and stands.

'What is happening?'

'The end, Johnson. The death throes. The start of a new reign.'

'Stop talking in riddles, Nedham, for the Lord's sake,' says Will, as they emerge into the corridor. He looks at his friend; he does not know which way he is supposed to be going.

'To the Parliament, Will, to watch the show. Lambert's done it. Half done it. Some vote or other gone awry, and now he's to clear the chamber with the sword of righteousness.'

'And then what?'

Nedham stops and looks at him. They are still in the midst of a clatter of excited men. Everywhere there are clerks and secretaries: clustering in bands, heading towards the heart of the action. Drawn to the drama, and the carnage, and the promise of England being remade in their sight.

'Then, Will? Then, King Noll.'

Will reels. It is one thing to guess that it is coming. Another for it to come. Here is history, and here, like a pinprick in the firmament, is Will Johnson: private secretary to a king. Jesus Christ.

'Here,' says Nedham, ducking through a door Will does not know. Through a narrow passage shorn of adornments. They are near running, and Will can feel the hammer of his heart; although whether it is excitement or exertion, or a marriage of both, he cannot tell.

Emerging through another door, he blinks and stares. They are in the great hall where the MPs sit. Cavernous and echoing. There is shouting outside, but in here it is oddly quiet – except for the tramp and scrape of the soldiers' heavy boots as they cluster in the centre.

A man walks past, black-coated and ashen-faced. Nedham plucks his sleeve. For some reason, he speaks in a loud whisper – the odd hush of the place demands it. 'Pray, sir. What is afoot?'

The man is clearly irritated to be stopped, but he looks at Nedham and Will, and says, 'There was a motion to dissolve ourselves, gentlemen. Most have gone. Some,' he waves an expansive arm to the benches, where small knots of men sit, 'some insist on staying.'

Will sees Lambert then. Gorgeous in his military finery, he is striding towards a few of the recalcitrant members. His hand is on the hilt of his sword – ostentatiously, he pulls it a notch or two from its scabbard.

'Gentlemen,' he says. His voice is loud and echoes in the chamber. All heads swivel to look. Will feels Nedham grab his arm, feels his friend's fingers gripping through the fabric. Lambert would not draw blood in this place. He would not. Surely?

Lambert's face is malevolent, at odds with the foppish ringlets curling down.

'Gentlemen,' he says again. 'It is over.'

Will cannot see the faces of the men he is accosting – there are gawpers and soldiers in the way. All hold their breath. All wait.

In the pause that spirals on, Will pictures blood running down the central stone of the chamber. Red rivers that stain and besmirch. Perhaps it does not matter – the threat of blood in this place is the same in the eyes of God and man as the actual liquid itself.

He hears a kerfuffle. The last members are standing. Awkward, they push aside the soldiers and make for the door. Their protest is enough to save their individual consciences

'Cromwell as king, then,' he whispers to Nedham.

'What else is left? Perhaps not in name.'

'A reign demanded by the military, not by the people,' says Will. His voice is a little loud, and he draws Lambert's eye.

'You,' says the general. 'Johnson?'

'Yes, General,' says Will, pacing forward.

'Go. Find Cromwell. He does not know of this action.' Will notes the projection of his voice – the direction of the words towards the retreating politicians. 'He does not know,' says Lambert again, loudly.

'Yes, sir,' says Will.

'Run, will you. Tell the lord general that the speaker is coming to resign the powers of the assembly into his care. Tell him that we are coming. Tell him . . .' Lambert hesitates. Will thinks it might be an apology hovering on his tongue – a strange enough thing for a king-maker to say to the anointed king. Lambert colours, and the unfinished sentence trails. 'Quickly now, Mr Johnson, if you please,' he says, turning into the crowd for his back to be slapped and his name to be called.

Will ducks out, into the silence of one of Westminster's long corridors. Through the window, he sees smoke rising from beyond the walls. The citizens are lighting bonfires in the street, to rejoice the passing of the Barebones. Most Londoners do not want to be godly. They want to eat, sleep, love, drink unmolested by politics and politicians. Sufficient blood has been spilled. Those with any left in their veins want to keep it there.

He should tell Sidrach Simmonds this. If Christ Himself does appear, ready to take His kingdom, there are Londoners aplenty who will sniff, sneer and turn back to their tankards.

Now is not the time to share these thoughts with his chief, he thinks, as he comes to Cromwell's office and knocks loudly on the panel.

Inside, Mrs Cromwell is standing near to her husband. She looks as if she has been crying. But she holds her back straight and her head high. Her hands twist a handkerchief over and around itself. Over and around.

'Will,' says Cromwell, coming forward. 'Well?'

'They are coming here, my lord.'

'So.'

It is hard to read him. This man, who was once a small, insignificant, poor outsider in the flatlands of the east, is about to become the lord of three kingdoms. A king in all but name. It is inevitable now. He could not stop it even if he wanted to. It would be unthinkable. What choice does he have now but to bend his head for the invisible crown?

At least he is broad enough to bear its weight.

Mrs Cromwell swallows violently, her eyes starting from her head. She is not stupid. She knows that they sneer at her. She has no cavalry charges in her past, no glorious military successes to help her claim her position. She has red hands from doing her own washing. She has chipped nails. Greying hair. A belly slack from childbearing. There are less prepossessing women with the title of queen, but they were born to it. Well-born women carry a miasma with them that blurs their faults.

She is brave, though, Mrs Cromwell. God love her. She moves over to her husband, lays a small hand on his arm and says: 'God be with you, husband.'

Finding time to smile at Will, she leaves the room. The door shuts behind her with a decisive thud.

Cromwell is lost in thought, and Will can study him. His face is calm, but there is a flicker there of something else. Something triumphant.

He turns to Will, opens his eyes wide at finding him there.

'Such a power of work to do, Will,' he says. If there is a weariness in his words, his manner is all glittering energy. Good man though he is, how can he resist it? The triumph of being the best, of being the first, of being the chosen. If he is the first man in the three kingdoms, it is because God wills it. And if God wills it, how can His servant not feel touched by His glory? He will call himself humble – and be sincere.

His sincerity, Will believes, is real to Cromwell. A companion to the Holy Spirit that whispers in his ear. But others doubt it. Others mock it. How will the part of the lord general's character that believes in his own honesty, his own sincerity, survive the exigencies of power?

He looks past Cromwell, to the painting of the triumph of Caesar, and remembers how he saw it when he first came here. He had thought it a warning; it was a prophecy. He looks at Caesar's miserable face, his sagging shoulders. And again at his chief, who – to no one's surprise – is on his knees and whispering fervent, desperate words to his Maker.

Later, when Cromwell is done, they settle to business. Occupying themselves with the details that serve to camouflage the whole terrifying affair. There is to be a demi-coronation, to proclaim to the whole world that Cromwell is definitely-not-quite-a-king. He issues instructions on the ceremony that have been long pondered. Suspiciously so? wonders Will. He no longer knows quite what he believes.

In Cromwell's list of steps to be taken – from briefing his tailor to moving his household to Hampton Court and setting Nedham loose on justifying the protectorate to the plebeians – there are pauses. He looks at Will almost shyly, as if to test the new power his words have to command.

'I will see Thurloe now,' he says, drawing the interview to a close. 'Will you have the Treasury clerks work up an estimate of costs for the ceremony?'

Will bows his head. 'It will be worth the price. Render unto Caesar . . .' He begins the quote and waves an arm to finish it. He is still smiling when he sees Cromwell's face, and the grimace frozen there.

'I did not set out to play Caesar, Will. I have had much favour from the Lord, but without seeking it. I am not a Caesar. Must I tell you that? Must I be explicit? I did not seek this.'

'I am sorry, my lord general. I did not mean to imply—'

'No. But Will, if you do not believe me, then who will?'

Will thinks of Sidrach Simmonds, who will see Cromwell as a traitor to Jesus's cause. Of Sam, who will smile provokingly and tell Will that the old bastard has always wanted to be king. Of Patience, who will say little but will think of his Mrs Cromwell and her new burden . . .

'My lord,' he says tentatively. 'I think nothing. But it is true that many believe you to have schemed for this.'

Cromwell sighs. He crosses to the window and looks out across the courtyard towards the river. There are only glimpses of it here; its cold grey mass slinking through the frozen city towards the marshlands beyond.

'The Lord knows my soul, Will. He knows the truth of it. As for the rest of them . . . Well. I must bear the burden of their distrust. For that is a part and parcel of ruling. Did he know that, I wonder?'

Will thinks for a moment that he means Jesus. Most unspecified pronouns in Cromwell's speech refer to the holy. But this 'he' is someone else, Will realizes. The king who climbed a scaffold not far from here, and left dragged out by his heels with his head in a basket.

They are still for a moment, as Will searches for the right words. Before he finds them, Cromwell turns into the room from the window, shakes himself free of fancies and claps his hands. 'Well then, Will. Jump to it, jump to it,' he says. He is all hearty efficiency now; the moment is lost.

If this is victory, thinks Will as he hurries out of the room, why does it feel so very much like a defeat?

PARIS

November 1653

$\mathcal{I}$N GLOOMY FRENCH DRAWING ROOMS, ENGLISHMEN GATHER in tight knots to swear and curse the name Cromwell.

He is a dissembling villain, a perjurer. A devil's imp. A false prophet. A salt-brained infinite liar. He will burn. He will hang. He will find his foul usurper's head stuck on a spike.

Sam hangs around the edges of the vituperative crowds.

He observes with interest how detached he is from the anger. He thinks of Will and his quiet admiration for his boss. He thinks of Henrietta, his sister, who believed that there was good to be found in most souls, regardless of politics.

These men, these broke and tatty remnants of the old king's cause, can allow for no sincerity in their opponents, no goodness. When you have lost everything in a fight, all you have left is your hatred of the victor.

'What say you, Challoner?' says a voice from the heart of the crowd. Richard Holmes, his friend and fellow follower of Prince Rupert.

'I? I have nothing to say. We all expected it.'

'Did I not hear, Captain Challoner, that you were close to Cromwell's circle when last you were in London?' Margaret Cavendish, Duchess of Devonshire, looks at him down her long aristocratic nose. It is said that she writes poems and long essays on philosophy. Sam smiles at her. God love a clever woman.

'Your Grace,' he says. 'I lodged with the widower of my late sister. He works for Cromwell. His secretary.'

A dozen eyes turn on him.

He pushes his chin out, feels his thighs tensing on the chair as if to calm a horse before the charge.

'I did not meet Cromwell. My brother thought it wise to keep me hidden away.'

A sigh hovers about the room. They were hoping for tales of the blackguard up close. A commentary on his warts, perhaps, or an impression of his endless prayers.

He stays silent, and the eyes swivel away again.

'And yet,' says the duchess, 'you came back to us. How interesting.'

'I missed eating snails, Your Grace. Garlic.'

She looks at him intently as the conversation moves sideways and he feel his cheeks burning. He hears Thurloe's words in his head, drumming an insistent refrain. Tittle-tattle. Tittle-tattle.

He has sold most of the goods he came with. He has turned a small profit. Margaret Cavendish herself has fallen upon the books; her husband on the hunting rifles.

'What do you say, Johnson?' presses Holmes. 'You were there most recently. Will they rise against him, the hypocritical old tyrant?'

No, he thinks. They will be grateful to him. He promises relief. A respite. A shield from the radicals. A rampart against the vengeful Royalists.

'Perhaps,' he says, instead. 'He is a wart. He is no king. She – Mrs Cromwell – is more fishwife than queen.'

They like this. He knows his crowd.

'He has the army, however, and the rest is gammon.' This from the duchess. He inclines his head to accept the truth of her words. Imagines her dark hair tumbling over his face.

Tittle-tattle.

He writhes, a little, inside his skin. He hopes they will not notice. He feels as if the words are branded on to his face. Tittle-tattle.

LONDON

December 1653

'*H*E WILL BURN. LIAR. HYPOCRITE. VILE DISSEMBLER.'

With each spittle-flecked word comes a hum of approval. Arms are raised, feet are stamped.

Sidrach Simmonds hushes the crowd with outstretched arms. Patience can sense them leaning towards him; their looming vindication hums closer.

'Who would the Lord choose to have rule over us, Jesus Christ or Oliver Cromwell?'

A harrumph of agreement. Patience watches them nod, sigh, shake their approval. She imagines Sam Challoner standing next to her, leaning against a pillar, amusement lighting his face.

Taking His time, this Jesus, hey? she can hear him saying. No hurry, old fellow. We'll just tear into each other a bit more, shed a bit more blood while we're waiting for Him to show his face.

What if He's not coming? thinks Patience.

She sees the room as if from a great height. The nodding, gurning, back-slapping press of people. Quiet now, they bend their heads in prayer. They mumble, gazing down at the floor. Patience's chin lifts, her eyes look heavenwards. Are you coming, Lord? And if not, why not? Why not?

LONDON

December 1653

SIDRACH SIMMONDS IS DISTANT.

With any other husband, she would think that perhaps there was another woman. But his nightly assaults on her continue. They come laden with scorn for her empty womb. Sometimes he puts his hands around her neck and squeezes. Sometimes she wishes that he would squeeze hard enough to put an end to things. At others, the will to live is so strong that she imagines fighting back. Biting, scratching, flailing, pinching, punching, stabbing.

But she stays still and hates herself for it.

Oh, the misery of her self-hatred. The wounds and the bruises she can bear. The scorn and the contempt. But she cannot bear the slow dampening of her fire. All the energy and passion she once knew, which trembled in her limbs and bounced in her toes and soared in her smile; all is leeched. She can see it, but she cannot help it.

In its place is a terrible torpor. A great and enervating lassitude that pins her to the chair, imprisons her in bed, keeps her pulling blankets up to her chin like a shield.

Only fear keeps her upright. Fear dusts and cleans. Fear kneads the dough and brews the herbs. Fear counts the coins and places them, one, two, three, in Tom's outstretched palm. Fear inspects his purchases. It smells the hops and pours the oil. It counts the candles. Checks for slugs and snails in their small town garden with a compulsive eye, because, the Lord help her, a devouring of his sallet seedlings is her fault somehow.

Sarah watches her. The maid, with her long, sour face, feeds the fear even when Sidrach is not there. No respite, then. No relief from the constant drip, drip, drip pissing on her fire.

But most of all, fear makes her a listener. As a child, she was a talker, a chatterer. A teller of jokes and tales. Now she is mute for hours, days, weeks. She is too busy listening for footsteps. Changes in mood. Sharp edges of things that should be innocuous.

Now her intent listening tells her to be wary. He is preoccupied, and not with a woman. He is plotting. Christopher Feake, the firebrand, is here constantly. They whisper in corners. It is to do with Cromwell.

Feake comes for a meal one Sunday, after church. In front of him Sidrach is all uxorious charm. My dear, he says as a constant prefix. My dear, is there salt? My dear, the wine.

His hand closes over hers and she struggles not to flinch.

Feake is charming. He has a pleasant face, good manners. Patience smiles when he talks to her, and answers meekly, eyes cast downwards. Your lovely young wife, Feake calls her. Your delightful wife. Your sweet wife. His eyes flicker over her. Sidrach shifts in his seat. She does not know if Feake's attention will please her husband or enrage him. She wishes Feake would shut up. Stop talking to her. Let her be invisible.

The mutton is melting soft, thank God. The onions swim in the sauce. Feake's chin is shining with grease, which catches in the candlelight and shimmers.

'And what do you think, my dear?' Feake says suddenly, in the middle of a conversation she has not followed. She has been watching Sidrach eat, hoping there will be nothing to find fault with.

'I beg your pardon, sir, I . . .'

Shut up. Shut up. Shut up. Stop talking to me, you greasy piss-pot.

'Why do some people persist in supporting the usurper Cromwell when now is the time to prepare the way for Christ?'

'I do not know, sir.'

'Come, my dear Mrs Simmonds. What do you think?'

She raises her eyes from the table and sees Sidrach watching her. His dark eyes are unreadable. His hand lies open and still on the table.

Feake smiles. She thinks it is supposed to be encouraging, but it looks wolf-like. His teeth are too large for his mouth, and yellow.

'I think, sir, begging your pardon, that people are weary. Frightened.'

'Why are they frightened? They should be humble before the coming of the Lord.'

She nods. It is pointless to argue. Men like Feake and Simmonds never hear.

Simmonds nods too. 'Only those who have something to hide from Him need fear Him.'

'But,' she says before she realizes she is speaking aloud. That one word has earned her a fist; his eyes swivel round to her and promise it. A pox on you, Sidrach Simmonds, she thinks. She says, loudly and with violence: 'People want to feel safe. Safe in their own homes. In their own land. Cromwell gives them that. He promises safety. Men like you, Mr Feake, think that is nothing. A contemptible, low aspiration. But do not underestimate it. Those without safety yearn for it beyond measure.'

It is the most she has spoken in days. The words feel thick and unformed. She watches Sidrach's hand lift from the table; the fingers begin to strike a rolling tattoo on the scored wooden surface.

'Safety,' she says again, limply, slumping into her chair. His fingers roll and tap, roll and tap.

Later, she asks softly: 'Why did you marry me?'

'What kind of a question is that, wife?'

He is soft and limp. Sated. It is the only safe time to talk to him.

He puts a grazed knuckle to his lips and sucks it.

She folds herself into the corner of the bed, new bruises sitting on old.

'Please?'

'I wanted a wife. Children,' he says. He uses the word as a weapon. The room is dark and cold. The fire is a miserly, dying thing.

'But why me?'

He pauses, and then reaches out for her in the darkness. He pulls her into an embrace. Her head rests on his chest and the hairs scratch at her skin. Her arm is trapped under her body. Goosebumps prickle her skin

He kisses her forehead, smoothes down her hair. Pulls the blanket up over her bare shoulder. Throws her off balance with this ridiculous tenderness. She pushes her head into his stroking hand. For where else can she find comfort but here?

'I liked the look of you. Did you see how Feake drooled at you today? Jealous, the dog.' He laughs. Pulls her in closer so that her mouth is squashed against his cold skin.

'There, now,' he says, as she cries into his shoulder. 'There, now. My own wife. Shh. You must work harder to keep the devil out, my dear, that is all. To obey. It is all in love, my dear wife. All in love.'

She wakes in the dark. Beside her, the press of Sidrach's breathing. She shrinks into the blanket, making herself small and quiet. It is morning, she thinks, and she must get up before him, to avoid the clamping of his spider limbs on hers. But it is icy beyond the bed. She will wait to hear him stir, and then she will leap into the violent cold and away from any entanglement with him.

She concentrates on him. On the stillness of his limbs and the sleep-heavy sighs and snuffles. She wonders if it is possible to will yourself dead. To teach your sleeping mind to eschew the misery of waking.

It takes her a second to wrench her mind from its despairing meander. For there is another urgent demand on her attention. A clattering and shouting. Someone is banging on the door.

'In the name of the Commonwealth,' shouts a voice.

She jumps from the bed. The cold beyond the blanket is a shock, and she pulls her thick shawl around her shoulders.

Sidrach is awake. She knows this, despite the darkness. She is attuned to him, to the vibrations of him.

She lights a taper from the embers of the fire. Her hands are shaking.

'In the name of the Commonwealth.' The voice barrels through the house.

She lights the lamp. Sidrach is out of bed, and he is near her. As she turns towards him, she sees his face. He is not shocked, she notes. He is expecting this, whatever it is. And yet good news does not travel violently, in darkness.

'Stay here,' he says, and grabs the lamp from her. He takes it out of the room, and the blackness closes in. She cannot help herself – she follows the light. She curls herself around the door frame, watching as he walks down the stairs and into the hallway. The door is a sludge of shadow.

He opens it, fumbling with the locks. A bluster of snowy wind comes in as the door swings out. Outside there are torches; she can see the leap of the flames and the light catching on the armour of the soldiers standing there.

She cannot hear the conversation. The soldiers march into the hall, and Sidrach backs away on to the bottom stairs. But he pulls himself tall, and she hears the calculated pitch of his preacher voice.

'You call this God's work? This? You are imps, I tell you. Imps of the man who would be king. He has foxed you, led you in the darkness away from the shepherd's fold.'

She cannot see him speaking – only the wave of his hand. But she can see their faces. The young, scraggle-bearded, round-cheeked faces of these soldiers, which blanch and falter as they stare at Sidrach in all his full righteousness. It takes their captain, stepping in behind them, to bring them back to themselves.

'Sidrach Simmonds?' he says, shouldering one of his young men out of the way and tutting with irritation.

Sidrach nods. 'And what of it?'

'You are under arrest. Accused of dissent and dissimulation.'

Patience gasps; she can't help herself. Shock. And – God help her – relief. They are taking him away. Away! She need not feel the scratch of his body on top of her, the dry rasp of him inside her, the slam of his fist. Oh Lord! Oh Cromwell!

At the sound of her gasping, Sidrach turns and stares at her from the foot of the stairs. She shrinks, despite the soldiers gathered around him. She clings on to the door frame, absurdly, as if she might be whirled into his orbit if she lets go. His face is lit from below by his lamp. There is something exultant in him, some great and smug joy that she struggles to understand. It is only as his arms are bound behind him that she understands. How much greater to be Sidrach Simmonds the martyr than Sidrach Simmonds the irrelevance.

A violent knocking on his door brings Will into a sweating, unsatisfactory wakefulness. His mouth is rasping dry. His head thrums, and through squinting eyes he can see that the light is vengefully bright on this winter morning.

He pulls himself upright and fumbles his way to the door.

Patience stands there, a little bedraggled, a little mousy. Her cloak is drawn tight against the chill. A small boy stands in the folds of it.

'They've arrested him. Arrested him.' The rise of her voice

is panic-edged. The boy clutches the material of her cloak in chilblained hands.

He ushers them inside, calling for the maid, Mary, who arrives, flour-smeared and cross. 'A posset,' he barks, raising a hand to calm the coming protest.

Drawing Patience and the boy to the hearth, he sits them down and wraps them in blankets. The fire is laid, but not lit, and he busies himself with that while Patience weeps softly behind him.

'It is the shock,' she says. 'They are searching the house. They bade me leave.'

'And this is?' He nods towards the boy.

'Tom. Our boy of work.'

'Does he not belong at home?'

Patience looks sharply at him. 'He belongs with me.' The boy sitting at her feet shuffles a little closer to her, the blanket slipping from his shoulders. She reaches down and pulls it back around him. The fire is yet to catch in any significant way. They can see their breath streaming in puffed clouds.

Blackberry clatters into the room. 'Auntie Imp!' he shouts and jumps on to her lap, curling himself into her.

She wraps her arms around his thin little body. She moves his hair aside and kisses the irresistible nape of his neck.

'Well then,' says Will at last, when the room is a little warmer and Blackberry has bounced away to the kitchen with Tom in his wake. 'Tell me.'

'They came for him this morning. He was taken to the Tower.'

'Why?

'Agitating against Cromwell. Feake was taken too. They called Cromwell a liar. A perjurer. Worse.'

Will raises his hands, warding the words away.

'Do not worry, Patience,' he says. 'I will talk to Cromwell himself. If I can get close enough to him. He has a power of men about him now. Even if I fail, I think it is just a warning. The sound and fury of the preachers cannot go unchecked.'

'You think he will be out soon?' Her skin is flushed and damp. Hair slicks to her forehead in sticky whorls. She shivers, visibly and violently.

'Are you quite well, Patience? Patience?'

She leans back into the chair, feeling the coolness of the leather against her burning cheek. Will's voice sounds at a distance. Far away. His hair is caught from behind by the fire, burning in a gold halo. Perhaps he is not Will at all, but an angel, leaning over her, calling her name across a great valley. Funny-looking angel, she thinks, and laughs. Laughs and laughs, the peals of it filling her ears and her head and her empty belly, and the sight of his stricken face makes it funnier, even funnier, so funny that she is crying and crying even as he picks her up. Picks her up, her brother, so she can rest her head against the thick scratch of his jacket and smell the day-old wine breath on him. She closes her burning eyes.

Hattie comes down the stairs into the kitchen. There is a dark fury in her face.

'She is in my nightgown, all tucked up, the little dear. You have sent for the doctor?'

Will nods. Tom has run off into the cold street, the fear making him tremble.

'They charge double on a Sunday, the scoundrels.'

He nods again, and clenches a trembling hand behind his back, closing it in on itself. He pours a measure of wine. A long sip, and there it is – the burn of it on his throat, the nausea as it hits his tender stomach, and the promise of trembles eased. His shoulders loosen down, his head feels lighter already.

'It is early, Will. For unmixed wine.'

'Thank you for coming so quickly, Hattie. I know your skill.'

She watches him drink. There's something contained and angry about her. For all her kindness, for all her fondness for him and Blackberry, he finds he is a little intimidated by her.

'He beats her.'

'What?' Will struggles to understand. Who beats whom?

'Your sister,' she says, with an impatient shake of her head. 'And she such a little thing. Such a sprite.'

'Sidrach?'

Will sits on the edge of the table. He grips his cup tighter and takes another sip.

'Did she tell you?'

'Not she. She is raging with fever. Burning.'

Hattie reaches for a cloth and fills a bowl with water from the pitcher. Dipping a finger in, she nods.

'Good and cold.'

She turns to face Will, her eyes blazing. 'She is covered in his anger, Will. Bruises. Welts. Looks to me as if he has taken a belt to her.'

'I did not know.'

'No. He can control his passion far enough to avoid her face. The scoundrel. The miserable, shrivel-cocked devil.'

'Oh,' he says, with a helpless sigh. 'Lord help us.'

Hattie snorts. 'You just keep on asking for help from that quarter, Will, and he'll just keep on ignoring you.'

Will reaches for the decanter. She puts out her hand and grabs hold of its neck. They are close, uncomfortably so. He can see the grey hairs springing from her bun; the speck of blood by her ear that escaped her morning wash. He lets go, and turns towards the fire.

'Listen to me now, Will Johnson. You have two people dear to you in this house. Blackberry and that little whipped girl in the bed upstairs, shivering her misery out. They need you.'

He will not look at her. He searches the flames for something, anything. The pot on the tripod is bubbling with some meaty concoction. Its smell fills the kitchen, making his mouth water. He thinks of his dinner, of Cromwell, of Blackberry. Scattering thoughts in the hope that one will germinate, blocking out Hattie's voice.

'In my experience, Will, too much boozing makes bad men violent and good men weak. Weak, Will. Do you hear me? There's people as need you to be strong. And here's you reaching for the wine a score of times before noon. I will go now. I am done here. I will come later. Think on what I said, Will. Think on it.'

She bustles away, through the back door. A rush of cold air sucks the warmth from the kitchen. Will shivers. He thinks of his work; deliberately and determinedly. He thinks of all the things that must be done to renovate the Lord Protector's new residence at Whitehall Palace. It must be furnished with economical grandeur. There must be velvets and silks and gilt. There must be reds and purples and golds. Servants must be hired and fed. So much to do. So many lists to make.

All is quiet upstairs.

He reaches for the decanter.

Will sits, as usual, next to Nedham. It is the coronation of the not-king, and Will is hung-over to his bones. He is dry-tongued, dry-eyed. He thinks he might croak if asked to speak; he is a withered frog. He listens to the scribble of Nedham's nib in the hush that fills the hall. About them, the scarlet-cloaked aldermen hover. The red coats and buff jackets of soldiers line the walls.

At the front of them all is Cromwell. He is dressed in sober black, with a black coat and black hat. A thin gold band glitters above its rim.

He inclines his head to the Lord Mayor. In an awed, shuffle-free silence they all watch as the Lord Mayor hands Cromwell the Great Seal, which carries the mark of power, the stamp of authority. He holds it tentatively, or so Will fancies.

The mayor presents Cromwell with the Sword of State and the Cap of Maintenance; those archaic symbols of England's kings. The cap is vivid scarlet against Cromwell's black coat. A sword, a cap, a seal. What gentleman does not possess a sword, a cap and a seal? But not this sword. Not this seal. Not this cap.

How strange, Will thinks, that an object can represent so much beyond its physical presence. A tumble of history and myth and promises. Projected hopes. Fears.

Cromwell nods, and graciously returns the sword and cap. He clutches the seal, still. He processes outside behind the Lord Mayor, who walks ahead of him carrying the Sword of State. As they pass Will, he sees the glitter and shine of the exposed blade.

A sword that is too symbolic to draw blood. Is it still a sword? He shakes his head; looks instead at Cromwell. He appears solemn. But who would not? What is behind that serious, tired face? Perhaps, if all the world were not watching, he would dance behind the sword, bouncing with triumph.

As the Lord Protector and the Lord Mayor leave the hall, there is a perplexed silence. Nedham and Will look at each other mutely; then, as the hubbub begins, they smile ruefully. Inarticulate in the face of history.

They turn to leave, and Nedham throws an arm around Will's shoulder.

'How did he feel, do you think?'

Will shrugs. 'Who knows. He did not know, Nedham, that Lambert was planning to overthrow the Barebones for him.'

Nedham stops, and turns to look at Will with large eyes.

'Where was Cromwell in '48, when the army purged the Parliament of men who might balk at killing the king?'

'I do not know.'

'He was travelling to London. He says. Now this is a man who, when there are Scots to kill, can cover more miles in a day than Alexander. Yet it took him days – days, Will – to go a few miles. He arrived too late; the die was cast.'

'What is your point, Nedham?'

'Will, I like the man. I do. I do not doubt that he believes himself sincere. But he is very adept at not knowing things, when knowing them might be awkward for him. He is a master of advantageous ignorance. A useful skill in a politician.'

Outside, the shots ring out, saluting the new Lord Protector. Will flinches at the sudden sound. He leaves Nedham and hurries back to the Banqueting House to meet Cromwell. There are documents to sign before the feast.

As he weaves his way between the crowds, he thinks of that phrase of Nedham's, 'advantageous ignorance'. It will, he suspects, find no place in the official paeans Nedham writes for the new regime. He thinks of Patience, at home with an ebbing fever.

Was he truly ignorant about Simmonds? Did he choose not to see what was before his eyes? If he cannot ferret out the truth of his own soul, what hope has he of weighing anyone else's sincerity?

At Whitehall, he manages to collar the great man himself, sidling in through the crowds of backslappers and well-wishers.

'Documents to sign, sir. My lord. I mean, Your . . .'

Will stumbles over the new titles. Cromwell smiles at him.

'Never mind, Will.' He puts out his hand, and Will thrusts the papers at him. His cheeks are flushed. It is hot and close in here, to add to his embarrassment.

Cromwell leans on the desk, still standing, signing the first document with his usual economy.

Will steps up to him, whispers in his ear. 'The signature,' he says.

Cromwell looks up, and down again. Oliver Cromwell – the name is scrawled on the bottom of the paper. He holds it up to the crowd of men around him. Lambert is there, and Vane. Thurloe, of course, and a score of civil servants and soldiers and MPs.

'Gentlemen. I cannot get it right, it seems. Oliver Cromwell will not suffice now, I think.'

They laugh, amused by him. Satisfied by his humility. Pleased at further proof of their own cleverness in persuading the reluctant gentleman to elevate himself.

It is all, thinks Will, a little theatrical. Or perhaps not. Sincerity is hard to measure in this place; like trying to weigh a cloud.

Cromwell turns to the next document and signs it with a flourish. Will blots it and gathers it up. He holds the new signature up to the light.

In spiralling, confident loops: 'His Highness, the Lord Protector'.

LONDON

January 1654

A JUMBLE OF TALONS. SAM SCREAMS, WARDS THEM OFF. HIS hands are a wreck of blood, which drips in vivid purple on a grassy floor. The beast. The beast returns, flames flicking from its nostrils like a lizard's tongue. Flick, flick. He will burn. Oh he will burn.

She must stop it. Stop it.

'Shh. Stop what, love?'

She can't speak. She turns her face away; feels the burn in her throat where the words scour her. She will choke, suffocate. Someone help her. Help him. Oh Sam. Don't let the beast roast you. Why don't you call for Jesus? Call for Him. He will forgive you. He is the God of light, of love.

So why has He sent the beasts to claw at Sam, to shred at his skin? To paw and paw at that merry face with spiky claws that draw the blood in ragged lines?

'Shh. Patience. Patience.'

Why is Hattie here? Why isn't she helping Sam? Hattie's big,

217

capable hands and her wickedly sharp butcher's cleaver. Cleave the beast's head from its shoulders. Bring it down. Down.

Oh God. Oh God. Where are you? Why have you forsaken me? Why have you left me? Did I not try to be good? Did I not try to do your will? Why do you let him hurt me? He hurts me. Hurts me.

'He is not here. Darling child, can you hear me? He is not here. You are safe. Safe.'

Cool hands on her forehead. A cold rag. Lord, oh Lord, that feels like heaven. The coldness sliding on her skin; the scratch of the fabric. Safe. I am safe. Lord love me. Lord love me. I am safe.

'Sleep now. Sleep.'

A face. Inches from her own. Wide eyes, white skin, brown freckles.

'Don't die, missus. Don't die. Please don't leave me.'

Am I dying? I am burning. Is that the same? Where will I go? At least I will escape him. Is it wicked to not want to cling on to this life, this gift from our Father?

What if this burning is a foretaste? Oh Lord. Am I not to know your face? A woman who was elect would not wish herself dead. Would not wish her husband dead. I am wicked. Hell. Oh Jesus. Save me from the fire.

'Please, missus. Please.'

Tom, shh. I can't bear your pain too. I do not have the strength. See? I cannot even talk to you. Shh, Tom, shh.

The world is a muffled grey. She can see Will's lips moving; watch Blackberry's face melting into a soundless wail. She cannot hear them.

Will?

Can you hear me?

She is a bird trapped inside her own skin. She tap-taps on the inside of her skull, but he cannot hear her.

He reaches out and strokes her cheek. She can feel it. She can feel the warmth of his palm on her. She tries to speak. Something is grunting, groaning. Something is making a strange keening sound. She would look for it, but she cannot move.

'Close your eyes, Patience. Close your eyes.'

Her mother. Why is she here? Why is her mother here? Her mother belongs in the country, lavender swirling about her and bees humming.

She closes her eyes. It feels better. She might sleep, she thinks.

'He beats her,' Will says, reaching for the decanter again.

'Beats? Strong words. Patience has always been . . .' His mother pauses. 'Wilful.'

'Can we be clear, Mother. You are saying that Patience has earned his fists?'

She waves impatiently at him. 'That is not what I said. But do not be a child, Will. Many a wife is corrected by her husband. What of it? She must learn not to anger him. She joined herself to him in the sight of God.'

There are holes in her logic, but Will finds he cannot face pointing them out to her. It is too much trouble. Besides, Patience is deep in her fever. She has barely eaten or drunk for ten days, and Sidrach is still in gaol. A place of violence and illness. It is entirely possible that, one way or another, the issue of Sidrach and Patience will resolve itself.

219

His mother darts around his kitchen with impatient haste. She lays out the ingredients for the broth in neat rows. A boiling fowl, some herbs, a handful of winter greens. She wipes down as she goes, keeping things as ordered as she can. A contradictory broil of precision and impatience. A slim woman held upright by an invisible rod that keeps her back straight and her shoulders square.

'What will we do, Mother, if Sidrach is released?'

'We? Nothing. He is her husband.'

She hears his silent scorn – a mother's magic.

'Will, I love your sister. As I love you. She is a good girl, and yes, I could wish her a different husband. But husband he is. Once done, it cannot be broken. Where would we be if vows were malleable? If marriages could be wished away? Chaos. Anarchy. She must bear it. Women have borne worse.'

He hears variations on this argument often. He has heard it this week, in fact. Necessary evils. It is unarguably true. Yet sometimes the truth is blindingly miserable. How glorious to believe in utopia. To think that heaven on earth is imminent if we just reach, fingertips stretching, a little further.

Will craves a little of that gullibility. A belief in utopia. For Patience's sake, and the sake of this bloodied, chaotic land.

It seems to him that political life in the new England is an incontinent pissing on the ideals that brought it into existence. And yet, without the dampening drizzle, all would burn. This, he thinks, is the condition of man. Caught, hapless, between flames and piss.

So what, he silently asks his balm, his jewel-deep crush of grape and booze, is the point of protesting any of it?

~ ~ ~

Her surfacing is abrupt. She wakes, fully aware and held taut by her confusion. Where is she? At Will's. In his bed. She recognizes the grey coverlet, and the raggedy ends where it trails the floor. She is dressed in a linen shift. The bruise on the inside of her arm is yellowing; she must have been lying here some time.

She hears the handle turn on the door, hears its sharp, ominous creak. She shrinks into her blankets. The door opens a fraction, then pauses. She waits, breath inhaled. A small boy's head pokes around it.

'Blackberry!' Her throat is parched and it emerges as a croak.

He sidles into the room.

'They said I shouldn't come in. Why can't I do whatever I like, Auntie Imp?'

She pats the bedclothes and he crawls on next to her, burrowing into her shoulder.

'We cannot do as we like, little Blackberry.'

'But why?'

'Because we must all live together. And if all men did as they liked, there would be violence and war.'

'But there *was* a war. I know. My mama died.' He says this seriously, as if it is a great truth he has learned.

She thinks about telling him of the Ranters, one of the sects spawned by the wars. If we are chosen or not chosen for heaven at birth, say the Ranters, then our actions have no consequence. We may drink, fornicate, lie, cheat, steal with impunity. How do you explain such a creed to a five- year-old? How to tell of the misery that ensues, of the women left penniless and alone in anarchy's wake, as the men dance to the Dionysian pipes?

'Never mind, little Berry.'

'Your voice is funny.'

'I have been unwell. Is your father here?'

'He is with the Lord Protector.' Blackberry stumbles over the words, then beams as he gets them out.

'You are not alone?'

'Grandmama is here. Will I fetch her?'

She nods, kissing his forehead. He slithers backwards from the bed and disappears with a clatter and a shout. Beside the bed she sees a pitcher and a cup. Blessed water. She drinks long and deep.

Why can I not do as I want? she thinks. Why?

Her mother comes into the room, padding quickly across to the bed. She feels Patience's forehead and lifts her up to plump her cushions. She straightens the blankets and the coverlet, then checks the water pitcher and the pot under the bed.

At last she sits on the edge of Patience's bed. Her hands twitch compulsively at the folds in her skirt, and her eyes are fixed at some point on the wall behind her daughter's head.

'Hello, Mother,' says Patience, glad to hear the strength returning to her voice. To her astonishment, her mother erupts into spasms of crying. Her shoulders shake as she buries her head in the blankets, rumpling them with forehead and fists.

Patience reaches out an uncertain hand to pat her back.

'Has something happened?'

Her mother lifts her head. She stares at Patience with streaming eyes.

'I thought I would lose you. I thought . . .'

She loses herself in crying again, and Patience is stunned. She cannot remember seeing her mother cry. This is new, and she is off balance. She slowly pats her mother's back, waiting for the retching sobs to subside.

When at last she is calm, Mrs Johnson puts her hands to her blotched red cheeks and smiles at her daughter. 'My dear, I apologize. Such a spectacle.'

'It is no matter. Was I so bad?'

Her mother nods. Tells her of the course of the sickness: of sleepless, feverish nights and days where she lay like a grey-lipped corpse, life just fluttering beneath the pallid skin of her throat. Of the doctor's rueful, shaking head. Of the letter from Will and the dash down to London.

'Your father wanted to come,' says her mother. 'But his work . . .' She waves an arm as if that is explanation enough.

'You came.'

Patience reaches out a hand and her mother grips it. The light creaks through a gap in the curtains, throwing a single spear of sunshine on to the bed. There is a low fire in the grate, but she can't feel its heat. She shivers, and her mother quickly pulls the blankets up and round her, pushing them in and under her chin.

'How is Will?'

'Busy. The Lord Protector is demanding many changes to Whitehall Palace, and Will is involved in seeing to his whims.'

Patience nods.

'And has there been word from my husband?' She hears her voice crack, and hopes it will not be noticed. But her mother's hand tightens its hold and her eyes turn on Patience. The room is silent but for the crackle and hiss of the fire.

'Will thinks he will be out soon. Perhaps this week.'

'Oh,' says Patience, and that is all she can muster, all that she can find to say.

'Patience,' her mother says, as if to embark on some great revelation. But she loses the wind, and sighs. Standing, she says: 'You should rest, but eat first. I will fetch you something.'

Patience watches her go. She thinks of Sidrach in Newgate. Thinks of him amid the stench and the filth; hungry and thirsty and cold. She feels nothing. Nothing at all.

Later, with the broth warming her from the inside out and the sky an inky blue chink in the curtains, her mother says: 'We must talk. About Sidrach.'

'What is there to say?'

'The bruises. My poor child.'

Patience nods. She draws her knees up to her chest, and the blanket slips sideways. As it falls, they both see the livid mark on her arm, and another on her thigh. She reaches for the blanket and pulls it up under her chin.

'It is my fault. I make him angry.'

'You must learn to soften him.'

'Must I go back?'

Her mother stands and paces the room. Patience remembers being a child – lying in bed at night, the moon high over the fields, hearing footsteps about the house and knowing the pattern of the feet. Her father's long, heavy stride. Her mother's quicker, lighter steps.

'Where can you go? A woman leaving her husband? Patience, your father is a man of the cloth.'

'Is he?'

'Patience,' her mother raps. Patience sighs as her name becomes a command and a rebuke. 'Listen to me. Your father has his position. Will has his place with the Lord Protector. What do you think the Lord Protector believes about women who leave their husbands?'

Mrs Johnson paces some more, crossing to the window and back to the bed.

'A child,' she says. 'You need a child. No sign?'

Patience shakes her head.

'And there are reasons to expect one? What we talked of, before the wedding.'

Patience feels her cheeks burn. You didn't talk of what it is really like, she thinks. Awkward and painful. She says: 'He tells me that is my fault too.'

'Fault,' says her mother, 'is a childish word. Whose fault is it? My fault, his fault, your fault. Leave that aside now, Patience. He should not beat you, of course. But you must not provoke him. God has joined you.'

Patience has the sense that her mother is talking wildly, reaching for the platitudes she has used to discuss other people's children, other people's problems with her neighbours. Be a good wife. Do not make trouble, and trouble will not find you. Did not St Paul say: 'Wives, submit yourselves unto your own husbands, as unto the Lord.'

Patience can picture her mother sitting in the garden with Mistress Greenacre, agreeing with absolute certainty that wives must submit to their husbands, while Patience's father snoozes and smiles in his sleep in his study and Squire Greenacre cowers in a corner somewhere awaiting the lash of his wife's tongue. If she closes her eyes, she can see her mother's certainty, see the sharp nod of her head, the thrumming of her fingers on the old stone table beside the willow tree.

But her eyes are open and she watches her mother flounder. The nervous flutter of her hands as she clenches them on a handkerchief. She hears her say again: 'But God has joined you.' This time it sounds like a question, rather than a fact. An entreaty. As if He Himself might pop down from His cloud and say: 'Don't worry, Mistress Johnson. This time, just this once, I will un-join the unhappy couple.'

Patience imagines the scene as her mother talks on. Imagines the fiery Godhead and her mother's awed gape, and this dusty box room alight with radiance. Imagines the relief on her mother's face as they are absolved of guilt, of fault. So she can go home and shock Mistress Greenacre and the rest of the coven with the news that Patience has left her husband but it is not a sin in this particular instance, in this one divinely absolved case, and she has that from the lips of God himself. Yes, God himself has declared Patience Johnson an exception to the rule that unhappy wives must bear their misery and their bruises with meekness and – a divine chuckle at the pun here, a sort of rumbling, thunderous giggle – patience.

Beneath her pillow there is the crinkle of paper. Will, who believes that words and books are the solution to everything, has thrust a pamphlet at her. Written by his colleague John Milton, it argues that the Bible should not impede divorce. At least, she thinks it does. Its logic is tortuous – the reaching of a man trying too hard to make facts bend to inclination – and she feels too weak and feverish to rise to it. One phrase leaped out at her, and she thinks about it as her mother talks herself in circles. *What a violent and cruell thing it is to force the continuing of those together, whom God and nature in the gentlest end of mariage never joynd.*

The gentlest end of marriage. What is that?

Her mother stops pacing and comes to sit on the bed. She takes Patience's hand, looks into her eyes. 'Courage, my darling. Courage. He may not even survive the gaol. Not that I wish harm on any man, of course,' she says, suddenly flustered.

Patience lets herself cry then. That it has come to this. To an unarticulated prayer for gaol fever that hovers in the room with them, the silent echo to all her mother's bombast. She imagines him dead, coffined. In her fancy, there, standing above the Sidrach-shaped hole in the ground, with a smile unbefitting to a funeral, is Sam. She grins back at the man in her head, at his careless good humour, which beams even in figment form. Accepting that he is there, lounging brightly in her mind's eye, and not struggling to question it, or fight it.

She is still smiling when she hears the tread on the stair. Hears the heavy, precise footfall. Not Will. She recognizes the stately pace of it. Sidrach. The smile slides from her face. Her mother catches the change in her expression and stiffens. They both turn to watch the door swing slowly open.

PART TWO

COLOGNE, GERMANY

October 1654

SAM IS FEELING – AND THERE CAN BE NO OTHER WORD FOR it – jaunty. A good word. The crowd surrounding the king are using it. There's a fashion for slurring French words into English. It is something to do in the long, slow hours shadowing a king who is no king.

Today, now, this year, the sun is smiling on the jaunty Captain Sam Challoner. Sam, in thinking this, squints up at the leaden grey sky and notes the irony.

He is wearing his new doublet, cut from a deep burgundy satin. His collars and cuffs are lace, and although they are not the finest cambric, they will blind the pedant with their whiteness. He looks dapper; if not actually prosperous, then verging on it. Since he arrived in Cologne, following King Charles's court to their new home-in-exile, he has found his feet. John Shaw, the merchant, is the only rich Englishman in Cologne – the rest are penny-pinched aristocrats with fine feelings about trade and the correct disdain for Continental creditors. And Shaw is a friend and former colleague of Sam's deceased father.

'Samuel Challoner,' he boomed, wine sloshing and chins quivering. 'God bless my soul. Come, sit with me and tell me how Richard Challoner's boy comes to suckle at Prince Rupert's empty teat.'

So Sam sat, and let Shaw play the avuncular buffoon, until the two were firm friends. Sam likes the merchant. He likes the double face of the man – the front all bonhomie and bluster, the back all shrewd calculation. It reminds him of his father, and the two faces of the best cavalry officers – public insouciance and private efficiency.

Sam has slotted in at Shaw's right hand. Making contacts, greasing palms, levering deals from speculative wisps. The small amount of capital he accrued from his venture selling English goods to the court has doubled through investments advised by his new mentor. He has laid out a little to look the part, and now he strokes the fine cloth of his coat and sighs a happy sigh.

Yes, life is holding up its end of the bargain for Sam. The German sky is grey enough to sate any homesick Londoner's soul. The Rhine is brown enough to play proxy for the old Thames. And there on the skyline is the unfinished cathedral tower, and the crane next to it, soaring high but unused and useless. An unfinished, botched job that allows a patriotic Englishman to feel a little superior to his German fellows. Give us four hundred years to build a church and at least we'd finish the bloody thing, they say to each other as they pootle aimlessly around the cobbled streets, avoiding their creditors.

No aimless pootling for me, thinks Sam, rounding the corner and coming towards his lodging. I have linen to buy, to sell. I have a fortune to make.

Shaw has a daughter, Alice. She is not bad looking, she is the right age, and she seems to have most of her wits. She has the great advantage of being the eldest of the merchant's gaggle of daughters, in a family with no sons. She is also seemingly enamoured of the dashing Captain Challoner, with his tales of battles and shipwrecks and warring African tribes.

There are two ways of telling a war story, Sam thinks. There is the way you tell it when there are ladies present. Just sufficient gore and peril to elicit admiring gasps. Only the villains die, and it is a bloodless, clean sort of a death. 'I ran him through with my sword, ma'am, and he died sorry he was not an Englishman.'

Then there is the story you tell yourself unwillingly in the dark, silent hours of the night. The true story. The rasp of steel on bone; the slow, jagged dying of a man in pain. The shit and puke and fear. The terror of knowing that you are enjoying his pain, because it belongs to him and not to you.

Sam shudders. Think jaunty, Sam. Think bouncy. He stops at a street stall to buy a sausage. It is long and under-seasoned, not like the ones from home. But it is hot and he is famished. He smiles at the sausage-seller – a matron with a sauce in her large brown eyes – and tries a few words of German. She grimaces, then winks at him as he hands over the coin. No matter; he can get by in French until his German improves. Although Alice has told him that many of the locals do not speak German, only a variant dialect.

He bites down on the sausage, feeling the grease dapple his chin. He thinks again of the true war stories. He would like to tell them to someone. Will, poor fellow, has too much to worry about. Perhaps Alice? He thinks of her apple cheeks and bright blue eyes, and pushes the thought away. Unbidden, an image of Patience springs into his mind. Her lively face and her quick understanding. I could tell Patience how it was, thinks Sam.

Turning the corner to his lodging behind Shaw's counting house, he spies two people loitering on the corner with their backs to him. A man and a woman, sombrely dressed and looking up at his closed window. They are familiar somehow. When the woman turns to him, she reminds him of Patience – perhaps because he has just been thinking of her. She is thinner, older. There is something diminished about her; like the Patience he remembers but with the flame shrouded.

'Captain Challoner,' she says, walking towards him. With a shock of recognition, Sam realizes it is Patience after all. And the man beside her turns towards him and Sam finds himself being greeted effusively by Sidrach Simmonds.

'And so, Captain Challoner,' says Simmonds, smiling broadly over his glass of wine, 'my friends and I thought it politic to leave London for a while. We obtained a pass. No doubt the foul tyrant and his henchmen were glad to be rid of me. I am a considerable thorn in the side of the Commonwealth, and alas, have suffered for my stand.'

He looks modestly down at his fingers, which are clasped together under his chin.

While he is looking down, Sam steals a glance at Patience, who is watching her husband's little play with a flicker at her lips that could be scorn or could be amusement. She catches Sam looking at her and turns away, her attention entirely fixed on an old tabby in the corner of the tavern. It yawns, rises and stretches out its back.

'Your congregation must miss you.'

'Yes, poor souls. But I am needed elsewhere, Captain Challoner. Elsewhere. Great and glorious deeds. Great and glorious.'

He fixes Sam with a stare that could be intended to be meaningful but that makes him look ridiculous. Sam feels awkward and hot. His new collar is tight and pinching. There is a red wine stain on the satin of his coat, from Sidrach's inept handling of the jug. None was poured for Patience. Sam found himself offering, but she looked at her husband and declined in a small voice.

'Why Cologne?' Sam asks.

Simmonds looks significantly across the table at Patience. 'Perhaps, my dear, you would step along to our lodgings and find out if they are ready for us? They are across the road, near to yours, Captain Challoner. Perfectly safe, I think, for my wife to see to it.'

Patience stands, bobs to Sam and disappears out of the door.

Simmonds leans across the table. He closes his body in, rounding his shoulders and dropping his voice.

'This is not for women's ears. We are here to find you, Captain Challoner. To ask you to use your contacts. I think there may be areas of considerable agreement between myself and my friends and yourself and your friends. With regard to the tyrant Cromwell. May the devil take him.'

Sam leans back, away from Simmonds' conspiratorial leer.

'Careful, Mr Simmonds,' he says. 'Careful. Cromwell has spies everywhere. Everywhere.'

He remembers Thurloe's studied nonchalance. The way the man tried not to look conspiratorial as he said: 'Just a chat. Gossip. From Charles II's court. Tittle-tattle.'

Who else is providing Thurloe with tittle-tattle? How many of the men clamouring for the king's languid gaze are secretly betraying him?

Sam has avoided the issue by coming to Cologne. If he goes back to London, there will be a reckoning with Thurloe. It is said that Thurloe is even more powerful now that Cromwell is demi-king. A false idol needs his prophets.

Sam thinks of Thurloe's air of menace, the studied quiet of his voice. That is a meeting best avoided. Know when to retreat and when to advance, by God.

He says again: 'In these matters, care must be taken.'

Simmonds draws back, waving a dismissive hand at the rest of the customers. In the corner are a couple of fat grocers that Sam knows by sight. Further back, in the shadows, a woman of dubious morality is stroking the thigh of an ancient merchant, whose red face is turning purple as her hands reach higher.

'There will not be a spy here,' he says, contemptuous.

Sam fights to keep his eyebrow from arching.

Tittle-tattle.

The words are like a blasted imp on his shoulder, whispering at him whenever he is foolish enough to think himself happy. They will keep him in exile, in this foreign town, when all he wanted was to go home and begin his real life.

Sidrach Simmonds takes a sip of his wine. He makes a face, and peers into the cup. 'Germans,' he says with a shrug.

Sam smiles tightly. 'It was no trouble, finding lodgings?'

'No. I have a friend among the Rhine merchants. I wrote to him from Paris and he has organized rooms. We could have stayed with him, but we may be here for some time.'

'It is not London.'

'No. From what I have seen, it is not a godly place. There are, I am told, some justified fears of witchcraft here.'

Sam looks about the familiar tavern: the upended casks, the veined wood of the tabletops, the sun creaking through dusty windows.

'No more than elsewhere,' he says. 'The good folk of Cologne are more zealous in their prosecution, perhaps.'

'Captain Challoner, you jest. There can be no limit on the zealotry necessary to weed out the devil's work.'

'Perhaps. I am sure you are right. Rest easy nonetheless, Mr Simmonds. You will not find witches sauntering down the street. Plenty of Royalists, though.'

'That is why I am here.'

'You are not turning Royalist, Mr Simmonds?'

Sam means it in jest, but Simmonds looks furious. 'I am not, Captain Challoner. I recognize no ruler but the Almighty.'

Sam flinches. Simmonds can never tell when he is joking and when he is serious. There can be no friendship between two people whose definition of the humorous does not coincide. It makes conversation wearying. Strange then that Simmonds' wife seems to have a humour calibrated with Sam's own. Perhaps her husband is a different man when he is alone.

Sam tries to imagine Patience and Simmonds entangled in an embrace of the best kind; one in which passion and laughter fight for primacy. He cannot stretch his mind that far. It is an impossibility.

He fights down images of Simmonds naked, with long, pale and hairy limbs, like a spider.

He says: 'Not a Royalist, then. But you hate Cromwell more than the king?'

'Charles Stuart is not a threat to England's place at the forefront of the Coming. Cromwell is. Will you help me, Challoner?'

Sam sighs. He does not want to be involved. He thinks of Patience. How much she has changed. Her thin grey face. Why does he care? He barely knows the girl. And yet Blackberry and Will are the closest thing he has left to family. And Patience is part of the circle.

Patience sits on the bed in the unfamiliar room, waiting for Sidrach to finish speaking to Sam. She looks around. Here is where she will be covered by her husband's body each night. Here is where he will press down upon her so she cannot breathe or think. Here is where she will fail to sleep, listening to him snuffle and wheeze. He sleeps deeply and easily. Why should he not?

Here is the window she will stare at on the long nights, waiting for dawn to bring some relief. Waiting for the slow turn of the sky that will herald a new day. Sometimes, she knows, she will fall asleep only when she can see the first winking of daylight.

On this mattress she will keep her head still; fearful that if she moves, he will wake. For if there is one thing worse than Sidrach noisily and reproachfully asleep in the dark hours of the night, it is Sidrach awake.

In her wakeful head, she knows, there will be Sam.

As she saw him, her heart seemed to leap high as a grasshopper. For a sublime long minute she felt entirely free – free to allow her heart to leap and her breath to catch and her legs to tremble. But human hearts are not grasshoppers, and its landing was heavy, and so painful she had to stop and stand. Quite still.

Because there was Sidrach, beside her. His palm fleshy on her arm. And there was Sam's face as he saw her. No delight, nor even pleasure. A strange half-stare that she could not read.

Not that it matters. What is he to her? What can he be to her?

She should rise from this bed. She should unpack their trunk, and sweep. She should find the maid that comes with the lodgings and make herself understood with signs and pointing fingers. The list of things she should do is long and laden.

She will sit a while. Stay still and quiet a while. Adjust to the shadows and contours of this new room, in this unfamiliar place. She falls backwards on to the coverlet, listening to the thwack of her body hitting the mattress. She watches a spider scurrying up the bed's curtain. It hides itself in the draped folds, and she waits, breath held, to see if it will ever emerge.

HOUNSLOW

December 1654

AHEAD, THE HERONS SIT, UNSUSPECTING, ON THE RUFFLED grey water. It is too far for Will to identify them; his eyes are not good enough. Bram, the falconer, clips his horse closer to Cromwell and whispers something up at him. Will watches Cromwell nod. The familiarity of that gesture catches at something in him, that strange tumult of loyalty and affection.

He breathes out heavily, looking away.

Blackberry, his short legs stretched wide across the fat barrelled back of a small pony, says: 'What's happening, Father?'

Will glances towards Cromwell as he shushes the boy. The Lord Protector's shoulders seem tighter, as the sound of Blackberry's voice travels across the flat scrub of Hounslow Heath.

'Shh,' hisses Will. 'Did I not say you were to be quiet if we were to follow the birds?'

Blackberry turns to him with round eyes.

'I beg your pardon, sir,' he says in a loud stage whisper. His most grown-up voice.

Will is pinioned by tenderness. He reaches out and strokes the boy's hair. Blackberry will be breeched soon. He should be already. Sitting astride a horse, no matter how small and slow, his skirts bunching awkwardly. Begging pardon like a little gentleman. It is time.

There is such a melancholy in it, thinks Will. Henrietta should be here holding his leading rein. It should be her planning Blackberry's rites. Lord, when will the should-bes and the what-ifs subside? When will the sharp edges of his pain blunt? Is it a betrayal to even wish such a thing? What will be left of her if he can no longer lacerate himself on his grief?

His grip on the leather is white-knuckle tight, and the pony whinnies, tossing her head and pulling back on the leading rein. He slackens it, looking again at Blackberry and his serious, eager face. Such a heart-rending innocence.

The boy's focus is forwards, where Cromwell is reaching out a gloved hand. On it, Bram places the hooded hawk. A peregrine. A pernickety, grumpy bird of prodigious beauty, who likes her lure cast just so, and nips at unwary fingers.

The jesses are of silk, and the bells are of silver, cast in Milan. Will knows this, as he has seen the receipt, and his eyes started at the cost. But they are a fine, pretty adornment for such a bird. Will and Blackberry can hear the sweet jangle even from where they lurk at the back of the pack of toadies and lickspittles.

Next to Cromwell, to the disgruntlement of many of his followers, is Sir Kenelm Digby. Not only a sworn Royalist, but an actual, declared Roman Catholic. A giant, booming sort of a man. The two had formed an immediate attachment earlier in the year, when the former courtier to Henrietta Maria bent the knee to the

Protector to ask for his lands back. And now, here they are knee by knee, glove by glove. Digby's peregrine is darker than Cromwell's, and smaller. A fierce, fast bird.

Cromwell has a habit of picking up Royalists who share his love of music or hawking. Some find it ridiculous. Hypocritical. Sly.

But Will watches him with Digby. They talk together about Spanish peregrines. About a rare Icelandic gyrfalcon that Digby saw once, and the light in its unhooded eyes. About training Digby's daughters to handle a French merlin, with its dangerous tendency to soar high beyond the clouds. About underrated sparrowhawks. The alphanet that Cromwell saw in his youth, which, as soon as it felt the weak Anglian sun on its unhooded head, flew back to Africa, beyond the shouts and the lure.

Cromwell has always had his hobbies. He has always loved the soar of the falcons and the wild wind on his face. He has always loved the melancholy draw of a fiddler's bow. Once, needing him for endless signatures and following a trail of sightings and suppositions, Will found him in St James's, standing beneath an open window, a rapture on his face like a mystic. Transported by the music as it floated down and out of the window, settling on him like a balm in the chill of the evening.

Now, he clings to his hobbies. They are his raft. He is bucked and tossed by the making of endless decisions. By the countless small betrayals. By the astounding incompetence that Will sees creeping out of Whitehall and along the roads to the provinces. The Lord Protector is buffeted by the leakage between his intentions – God's intentions – and their execution. The emperor says jump, and they hop, or skip, or quibble about the definition of jumping.

Music is his calm. As long as the violin plays, he cannot hear the shrill whistle of dissent and failure. He cannot hear the querulous demand for more leadership and the petulant demand for less. In the silence, imperfections echo; but in the perfection of a soprano's high note, Cromwell can be still.

This is the first time Will has seen him with the falcons, and he recognizes the man's quiet joy from evenings spent on music. Cromwell can be carefree, lost in the small tasks of the hunt. Wrapping the jesses into his glove, whispering nonsense into the hooded ear. Judging the distance and the wind. Arching an eyebrow at Digby, who smiles back – and all the blood of Newark and Marston Moor and Naseby and Worcester can be forgotten in the utter simplicity of this moment. The cry of the heron and the shift of the wind. The slipping of the hood and the jesses. The air catching the feathers of the bird's outstretched wings as she lifts skywards. Lord, thinks Will. The infinite grace of your creation.

Go on, my beauty, on.

Blackberry's mouth is an open O as he watches the two birds take flight.

The herons are spooked out of their frozen stance. Up they soar, with long, slow beats of their wings. Necks cricked, the men below watch them rising higher.

'The falcons are not trying to get them,' says Blackberry.

'Ha!' says Cromwell, loudly. 'Not so, young Master Challoner. They are working their way upwards. Do you see them gyrate through the sky, young man?'

The peregrines, seemingly ignoring the herons, twist and spiral, gaining height fast. The herons' path stays low now, and they swoop over the watchers' upturned faces. Above, the peregrines hover. A point of stillness in the grey sky.

Will is gripping the rein too tight again. Blackberry is holding his breath, a great inward sigh that must break soon.

'Now,' says Cromwell, striking his fist against the pommel of his saddle. Down flies his falcon, as if on command, cleaving the air. It is fast and sharp and deadly as it strikes the bigger heron with clenched talons, knocking the bird from the sky. The second falcon follows, a heartbeat behind. Plunging straight down like an arrow, piercing the flight of its victim.

The herons drop from the sky; a slow, looping fall like a dropped feather. They seem weightless, until they land in successive thunks on the scrubby brown grass. Their once elegant necks are twisted, their orange beaks still strangely vibrant.

'Well done indeed,' says Cromwell, delight in his face. Bram is pink with happiness as his training and skill are vindicated once more. Cromwell leans down and slaps him on the shoulder.

'Did you like that, my boy?' Cromwell says, turning to Blackberry and fixing him with the full force of his joy.

'I did, sir,' shouts Blackberry back, beaming.

'Your Highness,' whispers Will, exasperated. Did he not drill the child on etiquette before they set out?

'Your High . . .' Blackberry stumbles over the word. His lip is quivering as if he might cry.

Cromwell edges his horse closer, the pair of them towering over the little boy on his shaggy pony. 'Never mind, Master Challoner. 'Tis all Your Highness this and that to impress the French ambassador. But between friends, it does not signify.'

He smiles, and Will watches Blackberry's awe turn to worship.

It is clearer cut with a child – Blackberry wears on his face what grown men keep locked away.

'It is settled, then,' says Cromwell, and he wheels round. Digby stands impatiently, already swinging his lure in a figure of eight.

'I beg your pardon, sir,' says Cromwell. The two of them trot forward, ablaze with the thrill and the joy of it all. He looks younger out here. He looks weightless. As if the new first Parliament of the Protectorate, anticipated by him with such relish, were not full of duly elected Royalists and Presbyterians. As if the peace with the Dutch were not straining itself to snapping point. As if there were not plots to assassinate him fermenting in dark corners across England and beyond. As if some of the army officers were not agitating against him.

Now, here, there is only the looping swing of the lure and the call to his falcon, who teases him with an unmoving, blinking stare. There is the wind rushing through the grasses and a first bird bagged and a man at his side who will not talk politics. An illusory freedom, thinks Will. But perhaps we must all succumb to illusions sometimes, or we will run melancholy mad.

The snow is falling. Sam lifts his face to it, and thinks of the white mantle shrouding the ships in the far south, and the great shifting blocks of ice that float there.

A long day. He creaks his shoulders backwards, straightens his spine. He is still trying to hold on to that first flush of enthusiasm for trade. But he has spent the day bounding from counting house to warehouse, in hot, smoky rooms, making small conversation with men who might be useful or might just have been sent by the angels to try his patience.

Patience. As always, when he thinks of the word he thinks of the girl. He has not seen her much. She keeps to her rooms here in Cologne. She is trotted out on occasion, when it suits Sidrach to have a pretty woman on his arm. He has been cultivating men in the king's circle. He can rein in his messianic streak when it suits him. Too much godliness would fright the men whose help he needs.

Poor Patience, he thinks. He is not entirely sure why he feels so sorry for her, such a deep and aching pity. Perhaps it is her serious eyes – which he thought once were made to crease with laughter, but now seem stretched into a wide, lost stare.

Is it Sidrach who makes her so serious? Or was she always that way, and he just imagined the flickerings of someone else? Perhaps he liked the shape of her face, and so imagined it contained a soul to match his?

He has to pass their rooms to get home, and he looks up at the darkened window. He fancies he sees a shadow.

There is a queue at the sausage stall. He can smell the onions and the blackening skin, and he stops. A sausage for his dinner, why not? There is half a jug of that fine ale he was gifted by Madame Shaw. She wants him to marry her daughter, of that Sam is now sure. They have a way of fluttering at him, mother and daughter. An overfamiliar solicitude. Is your wine to your liking, Captain Challoner? Are you too hot, too cold? Have more fowl, more of this fine cheese.

The girl is pretty and vivacious. He owes the father much. And let us not forget her inheritances, Sam, he tells himself. He needs a wife. And yet.

What is stopping him?

He will not think of it now. Now, he will concentrate on small things. The smell of the sausage as it sizzles and spits. The beauty of the city as the fresh snow masks the sludge. The icicle dropping in infinitely slow motion from the milliner's overhanging sill. That girl there, with her hands buried in a large fur muff. How she smiles! He thinks of how much his father loved the snow.

Well then. Tonight is his own. No later supper with his patron. No smarming up to useful merchants. No hanging around on the fringes of the court, watching dead-eyed girls being passed around bored and aimless soldiers.

Tonight, Captain Challoner dines with Captain Challoner. A sausage, a beer and the new book of poetry he has bought. A few years old it is; a collection by Lovelace.

A line comes to him: *Fools dote on satin motions laced, the gods go naked in their bliss.*

Not in bloody Germany in winter they don't, he thinks, chuckling to himself. He watches the smoke from the fire pit curl to the frozen sky.

Patience peeks out of the window. The room is unlit, and outside, the late afternoon is dark. She sinks into the cloaking darkness as she watches Sam queuing for a sausage. His hair is a little longer than before. His cheeks have filled out and lost their tan. His eye catches a pretty girl walking past carrying an absurdly ostentatious muff. She sees the girl notice him without seeming to. She keeps her eyes forward and pretends to find her older companion amusing.

Poor Sam, he is defenceless against such wiles. He surely thinks he has not been noticed – that this girl always smiles so prettily and glides so elegantly. Patience thinks of all the girls who must be circling him. Drawn by his easy charm and good looks. His air of finding himself and the world ridiculous.

Lord, she is hungry. She pulls her thoughts back to her empty stomach, although her eyes still track Sam. Sidrach is in Paris. Meeting someone useful, apparently. He told her nothing much in a meaningful sort of a way, and she knew she was supposed to ask for details. She would not.

'Damn him.' She says it aloud into the hush of the empty room. Strangely, it makes her feel better, and she says it again. And again, louder. 'Damn him and damn his eyes and damn his soul.'

Her stomach growls at her, calling for her attention.

Out of the window, she sees Sam smile suddenly. The street seems to glow with it and she does not understand why people do not stop and smile back at him.

A sausage, she thinks. That would stop my stomach growling.

Before she can stop herself, she grabs her shawl. She takes the stairs two at a time, clattering fast. As she pulls open the door to the street, the icy air hits her, punching the breath out of her stomach.

Quickly, before she can retreat back inside, she half slithers across the frozen street to where Sam stands waiting.

'Captain Challoner?'

'Mrs Simmonds!'

'You are waiting for a sausage?'

'Guilty, Mrs Simmonds.'

'Patience, please,' she says. 'You are practically a brother-in-law.'

She blushes. Silence settles on them.

'Well, Patience, then.'

'Well.'

It is hopeless.

What else did I expect? I am a fool. I am being laughed at.

The queue shuffles forward. The smell of sausage hangs heavily, ridiculously, in the air between them.

'Well,' she says at last. 'Enjoy your meal, Captain Challoner.'

She starts to move away. He reaches out his hand, grabbing hold of her arm.

'Wait. Wait. Please, call me Sam.'

The tavern is dark, and gloriously warm.

At first, they are staccato strangers. Pleasantries falter back and forth. But the plates are cleared and the wine jug empties. It begins to be easier.

'And there I was, in Africa. Thinking I had been abandoned by my prince. The great African sky above me, and all manner of calls and shrieks from the bush.'

'Oh Sam. The fear.'

'Here is the part of the anecdote where I affect a proper disdain for fear. I make an offhand remark about a lion.'

He leans forward, and drops his voice.

'The truth. The truth, Patience. I was frightened. I thought I would never see home again. I have not much in the way of family left. The war saw to that. But Africa? No. Not for me.'

'Why not?'

'Oh, it is beautiful. And some of the natives were fine, fine men. Captain Jacques, that I told you of? He saved my life, twice, thrice over. But the sun never stopped shining. I wanted an English fog. The fragrance of wet grass in the morning. The smell of a sausage.'

She smiles. 'The sausages here smell different. Have you noticed?'

'Is Cromwell warty?'

'Sam!' She reaches out and taps his shoulder. As you would an errant brother.

'Do you miss England, Sam?'

She pulls her hand back – fixes it into place with the other. Pulls it under the table to make it behave.

'I do miss England. But there is nothing for me there. Here, I am making a life.'

'And you are close to home, at least.'

'I am. Perhaps I will go home when I have made some money. Get my father's house back. Be a proper uncle to Blackberry. Perhaps even marry.'

The word ricochets. In the corner, a group of apprentices heckle each other. Their laughter is loud and distracting.

'Well,' says Patience, brightly. 'At least the wars are over. Fear is at an end.'

'It is,' says Sam, looking down at the table.

'No,' he says suddenly, 'it is not.'

'How so?'

'I have a new fear, Patience. One so stupid, so inconsequential, I am ashamed to admit to it.'

She waits. She has a quietness, a way of listening that he finds immeasurably soothing. It is not a passivity. Always, underneath, there is this flicker of energy, this promise of passions and joys untapped.

'It is hard to describe. When I was in the wars, or privateering, I knew fear. But with it came such joy. Such delight in being alive. Such rushes of blood to the head. Sometimes, the fear and the joy were indistinguishable from each other.'

She nods.

He looks past her, his eyes fixed on some point behind her head. She watches the candlelight catching his eyes below the serious crease of his forehead.

'The vividness of war, Patience. I fear its absence. I fear making a mistake, throwing myself from the horse, from the bowsprit, from the roof. Just to feel something powerful again.'

'You fear boredom.'

'Yes. Yes. But that's not quite it. I fear my reaction to boredom. I fear the cavalry officer who is hiding behind the merchant. Because I like the merchant's life, I do. I want a normal life; a safe life. But. But.'

'But,' she echoes. 'But. Sam, you fear the absence of fear. And that is ridiculous.'

He smiles at her, looking fully into her face.

'Ain't it though?' he says.

She imagines, just for a minute, how Sidrach would react if she called him ridiculous. He *is* ridiculous. But he is her husband. Before God.

'Sam, I must go,' she says.

'So soon? Not yet.'

'Her name is Blossom.'

Patience strokes the grey mare's nose. She whispers her greetings, listening to the horse's whicker.

'She is beautiful, Sam. I can really ride her?'

'She is yours for the afternoon.'

He gestures to the stable boy to saddle her up. A second lad rounds the corner leading Sam's horse, Grace. She recognizes him already. She throws her head up, pulling at the leading rein, trying to get closer.

'Hey there, Grace, my Grace,' he says, running over to take hold of her. He pushes his hand into her mane, and rests his forehead lightly on her graceful neck. She was not cheap. He has nothing substantial left. But the prince is stabling her for him, so he is saving money really. And she is the beauty of the world. A horse to swell a man's heart with pride and love.

He looks over at Patience, embarrassed suddenly at his naked affection for the horse. She smiles back at him, artless and joyous.

'I am impatient to be off, Sam. It is an age since I rode. An age. And never on such a fine horse as this.'

'She belongs to Prince Rupert's mis . . . friend.' How ridiculous to stumble over the word. She is not a child. But how lovely she looks when she blushes, he thinks. How edible.

Patience feels herself blushing and curses inwardly

As adjusts the stirrups, she thinks about Sam's words in the tavern last week. A fear indistinguishable from joy.

She is afraid. Afraid of the liquid melt of her limbs when she touches him or even looks at him. Afraid of the dark hours of the night when she thinks about him with a ferocity that sears. Afraid of the possibility of sin; not just her sin – his. Does it not say in the Bible that he who commits adultery, even in his heart, *destroyeth his own soul*?

Oh, she would not want Sam's dear soul destroyed. That merry, bright beacon of a soul.

They are friends, nothing more. He is her brother's brother. And she is alone in a strange land. He pities her, that is all.

They mount their horses and walk them through the yard, out into the street. He takes the lead, and she follows him, through the press of hawkers and strollers and touters. Through the gate the people thin, and there they are at last, outside the town, riding through the new snow. The world is monochrome, beautiful. The trees are bare black against the white winter sky. The river coils in frozen loops. The snow is so cleanly empty it makes Patience want to weep, absurdly, for all the crisp-snowed childhood days she didn't think to bless, to gather up in her memory and keep.

Sam makes her laugh. He tells her stories of the court, of Rupert's needling of the king's latest mistress. Of the misadventures of the king's dogs and the disapproval of his mother. When she laughs, her breath-clouds bloom; when she pauses, breathing in, the cold air sucks icily into her body.

Always in the background is the fear. Of what they are doing here. Of where they are going. But this is fear that is indistinguishable from joy. She has known sufficient fear in her life with Sidrach, she thinks. By God, she will have some joy. Just a small portion of happiness, to make the rest of it more bearable.

She wakes, heart racing. The room is too dark for shadows. She pulls the blankets up to her chin, forces her eyes shut.

The dream she has been having about Sam lingers on. She will not think of it, but she remembers it in the tremble of her skin, the unfamiliar looseness of her body. She will not think of it.

They brand a singeing B on the forehead of bawds in Cromwell's London. In England, the Rump brought in the death penalty for adultery, to Sidrach's righteous approval. She thinks of the hangman's noose. Or do adulterers burn? She does not know. Burning would be apt, she thinks, lying in the darkness and fighting her desire.

What is the law here in Cologne?

What does the law matter? She has not touched Sam. Oh, but she would. How she would touch him and touch him and kiss him, if. If.

And does God not know that? There is no hiding place from His stare.

She thinks of a play she was told of by Will, in which a nun is ordered by a corrupt judge to sleep with him to save her fornicating brother from the noose. What was the girl's name? Isabella.

Isabella turned to this Angelo, this old and venal man, and told him no. Her brother would not want her to lose her virtue, to lose her place with the angels. She will not do it. Patience remembers hanging on the story as Will told it. She was mesmerized by the horror of Isabella's dilemma; transfixed by her bravery in opting to sacrifice her brother's life to save both their souls.

Would you save me? Will had teased. You would not want saving at such a price, she had retorted.

And now she is the Angelo. Patience Johnson is the base creature wrestling with forbidden desire. The damner of souls and tempter of flesh. For the Bible makes no distinction between acting on desire and feeling it. Thou shalt not covet thy brother's brother.

How can she be elect if she feels this passion? How can she take her place in the kingdom, at His son's side?

Sidrach will be coming home soon. She longs for his return. He will save her. The crunch of his fist is now no less than she deserves. Sidrach's spite is not the fathomless, pointless thing she once believed it to be. It is her penance.

WHITEHALL, LONDON

January 1655

CROMWELL'S PATIENCE WITH HIS FIRST PARLIAMENT AS LORD Protector snaps.

'It is Heselrige, confound the man,' he shouts, pacing the room. He pounds his fist against his palm. His rage is so heavily worn, he is like a third-rate character actor. The one who plays the cuckold. Turning to Will and Thurloe, he cries: 'Does he believe he is doing right? Does he listen for His command? Does he kneel as I do, and beg, beg for the Lord's guidance? I tell you, Thurloe, he does not. He simply asks himself what policy he could pursue that would most injure me. And then he is off, worrying at it like a blasted spaniel with a bird.'

Will thinks – but does not say – that Heselrige is a distraction. The deep issues at stake would have felt wearily familiar to King Charles: religion, and the power over and financing of England's armies. The Presbyterian-heavy Parliament wants to break the independent churches. There is a proposal, too, to make Parliament alone responsible for raising a militia. This is a direct attack on the New Model Army. The army that raised Cromwell and is the only body that could destroy him.

Will catches Thurloe's eye as Cromwell rages. The spymaster's eyebrow rises and he shakes his head fractionally. Do not react. Do not fuel it. Let the great soul thrash it out until it becomes quieter. Cromwell paces the office, gesticulating wildly. This mood is dangerous, in so far as it can lead to the white fury that prompts Cromwell to act fiercely, and hang the consequences.

'Heselrige. Heselrige. And if I am so great a tyrant as they say, Johnson, men like your brother-in-law Simmonds . . . if I am so great a villain, remind me why I do not simply arrest this Heselrige. Have him placed on the Spanish Chair. Have him taught some manners. Some respect.'

Are these rhetorical questions? Will moves to speak, but Thurloe catches him with another eyebrow.

Thurloe clears his throat, and Cromwell spins round on him. His bully-boy soldier's stance now. But unexpectedly, he softens. 'Yes, Thurloe. You are in the right of it as ever. I cannot play the tyrant. But to be always accused of playing the tyrant, while not having a tyrant's tools . . . while being bound to Parliament and the Council. Three legs on a stool, not one. Three. And yet I am hounded by suspicion. It is cruel and unjust, gentlemen.'

He is working himself back down from the tempest. Thurloe nods, and cocks his head with an expression of sympathy. Cromwell claps him on the back. 'Yes. Yes, Thurloe. You are right. I must be patient. But Lord, it is trying.'

'You promised the Parliament five months, Your Highness. There are some weeks to run. You must indeed be patient. It would not do to dismiss your first Parliament lightly.'

'Yes. But how I would like to send them running. Then we can begin the great work that must be done. Legal reform. Religious reform. We have this God-blessed opportunity to make His land, and we must wait until this parcel of old women has talked itself out.'

Will finds himself speaking. 'Lunar months, Your Highness.'

'Eh? What?'

'Lunar months. The Instrument of Government promised the Parliament five months. Nowhere did it specify whether you meant lunar or calendar months. By my reckoning, five lunar months are up in two days.'

Cromwell is looking at him with an unreadable expression. Suddenly, he walks over, holds Will by the shoulders. 'Brilliant,' he says. 'Brilliant. Thurloe, make it so. I will go now and think of what I will say to the parcel of rascals as I dismiss them. Good work, Will Johnson. Good work.'

It is a measured, scornful Cromwell who stands in front of the House. It is a Cromwell dripping with contempt. You call me tyrant, he says, and yet you want to enslave others in your vision of the Lord's church. By whose authority?

He asks a sonorous question: 'Is it ingenuous to ask for liberty and not give it?'

Nedham nods by Will's side. This is clever Cromwell, turning their claims against them. He is the disingenuous one, according to Heselrige's story.

Attack them, my general. Lead the charge.

It is a regretful, sad-faced Cromwell who tells the MPs that they are compelling him to act against them. A kind father forced to wield the belt. 'Instead of peace and settlement, instead of mercy and truth being brought together, righteousness and peace kissing each other, by reconciling the honest people of these nations and settling the woeful distempers that are among us . . .'

As he talks, the room shrinks to fit his rhetoric. The MPs wither. Heselrige's neighbours shuffle a little away from him.

'. . . weeds and nettles, briars and thorns have thriven under your shadow. Dissettlement and division, discontent and dissatisfaction, together with real dangers to the whole.'

Yet there is a sullen mood among the MPs. Cromwell may be right about their failures, but it is becoming increasingly impossible for him to cling to his high ground. They may have forced him into it. Fate may be working among men. Providence may be at play. God may be moving in mysterious ways. But there is no wriggling away from the fact that King Noll lacks checks to his power now.

The gaols are full of dissenters – Fifth Monarchists and Levellers and Baptists and Royalists and ragtag others. Cromwell has told Will that to try them would mean disproportionate sentences, according to the law of this land. He says he is protecting them from the consequences of their dissent. Perhaps so. But his protection can feel like a tyranny. These are Englishmen gaoled without trial.

Cromwell may claim innocence – and Will may even believe in that innocence when he is feeling chipper – but they can also see the crown he pretends not to wear on his thinning pate. Its wearer can protest all he likes, yet they can all see its glitter, and how it catches the light of the great hall's candles and illuminates his face. Those warts, that nose, that cragged brow: glowing gold from his invisible heavy crown.

But what else can he do? wonders Will. And, it occurs to him as they all file out in sombre array, if that questions torments me, what must it do to him?

Patience turns the letter from Sidrach in her hands. She folds it once, twice, three times so that it is small and fat and unremarkable. Perhaps, if she makes it small enough, the words will shrink to become meaningless.

There is a knock on the door, and she runs to open it. Here he is, smiling at her.

'Sam!'

'I do not intrude, I hope? Have you eaten? Will you join me?'

She pauses. Her hand grips the door. She thinks of all the joy of being with Sam. And all the pain of not touching him, of not talking about the sinful thrum in her blood when he is close. The talk will be light and bantering and honeyed, and underneath it? The devil dancing in her skin, compelling her closer.

'The large frau across the way has taken delivery of some geese. Who can resist her attempts to mangle the poor fowl? Come, Patience. I need you to laugh at her with me.'

'Well then, Sam. If you cannot laugh at the large frau by yourself, I must help. I must . . .'

She turns away from him, into the room. She places Sidrach's letter on the top of the chest. On it she rests a book, to keep it from sliding to the floor. The letter from Hattie lies on the bed, unfolded.

Grabbing a shawl, she turns to Sam, letting herself be sucked in.

Something in her face makes him laugh, and he looks as if he will reach for her hand. Checking himself, he pulls his own hand firmly behind his back, and his laugh turns into something more rueful.

Outside, the sharp air gives her courage. She says: 'I have received two letters.'

'Yes?'

'One from Hattie. She is worried about Will. He is drinking heavily.'

Sam looks at her. He grimaces.

'I have seen drink ruin good men, Patience.'

'I do not understand it,' she says. 'Why not stop? Why not make yourself draw back from the bottle?'

Sam pauses to check his hat at a passing man. The stranger looks almost destitute – his clothes seem held together by witchcraft, they are so tattered. Yet he holds himself upright, and answers Sam's greeting with a flourish. A penniless cavalier in exile is a pitiful thing, Patience thinks.

'Sometimes,' says Sam as they move past the man, 'we slide towards the things we know we should avoid. Sometimes we are moving too fast, too furiously towards the thing we should not touch. We cannot check the rush.'

She feels the blood run to her cheeks.

'In the late wars,' he says, 'I knew such a feeling. In a cavalry charge, Patience, if you break the enemy, you want to gallop and gallop. To chase your fleeing enemy and make him pay. Pay for your fear, your dead friends, your dead shadow.'

'You do not talk of it much,' she says.

'Do I not? And yet I think on it all the time. No matter. My point is that when you are lost in the charge, it is a momentous hardship to check. To stop. To return to the field and finish the job. Cromwell could do it. Could make his men do it.'

'Perhaps that is why he is King Cromwell.'

'Perhaps. Even those of us who would see him hang would concede his quality. But you spoke of two letters.'

'The second is from Sidrach.'

He pauses. They are outside the tavern. She can see the fat frau through the dimpled window, dishing up a plate. Her face is a queer red pattern through the glass. They can hear her laughing.

'He has concluded his business in Paris,' says Patience. 'He wants me to take ship to England and beg for his pardon and a safe passage.'

Sam whistles. 'It is not safe, Patience. Do you remember Mistress Lee? Her husband sent her to beg pardon for his part in the king's armies. The customs men stripped her naked at Gravesend looking for letters and secrets.'

Absurdly, Patience thinks of her fading bruises rather than her modesty. The possibility of shame on two fronts.

'I will lose your society,' says Sam. His air of dejection makes her perversely happy. 'Must you go?'

'Of course. He is my husband and he wills it.'

'Bah,' says Sam. 'Sid says jump and you leap.'

Sid? She would laugh, but for once Sam's face forbids it.

'What would you have me do, Sam?'

He pushes open the door, and the warmth and light pull them in.

The business of sitting, of divesting themselves of coats and shawls, of ordering, of taking the first sip of a stringent wine: these familiar rituals mask the silence between them.

At last, when there are no practical matters to divert them, Sam says: 'Have you read any of the works of Margaret Cavendish, the Duchess of Newcastle?'

The question is abrupt. Accusatory, somehow. Patience bridles, shaking her head. Sidrach insists that she reads only the Bible, but she senses that to tell Sam that will goad him further into this unfamiliar sourness.

'I know her. She is a wonderful, learned woman.'

Patience knows jealousy then. A quick stab of fury. She drinks her wine, feeling the sear of it on her throat.

'She says that without learning and independence of thought, women are like worms shuffling in the dirt of ignorance. Some men prefer their women in such a condition.'

'You imply that you are different.'

'Am I not?'

'How can you know? Fine words are easy. I am yet to meet a man happy to be outshone by a clever wife.'

'Your brother. My sister was such a woman.'

'And I am a worm?'

'I did not say that.'

Patience looks away, towards the fat frau and the judder of her chins. She begin to cry, and is furious with herself, with Sam, with the absent Sidrach. The indiscriminate rage is building in her, leaking out of her as tears.

'Patience,' says Sam. 'Do not cry. Next to my sister, you are quite the best woman I know.'

'Do not say such things. It is not appropriate.'

'Bugger what is appropriate,' he says. He grasps hold of her hand. 'Patience, you must know. You must guess . . .'

He pauses as she wrenches her hand away. The rage and the hopelessness and the desire make her entirely giddy. She reaches for the cup full of wine, and before she can check herself, she has tipped it at him. Hurled it at his face. She watches the shock and bemusement sit, wine-soaked, on his beloved features. The curl of hair above his eyes collapses damply over his forehead.

People are turning. Watching. The fat frau giggles nervously. Patience stands abruptly, pushing her chair backwards. Wordless – helpless – she runs away.

If Will could write a letter to his dead wife and place it in the hands of an angel he is not sure he believes in; if he could watch that letter flutter heavenwards, gripped in the snow-white hand; if he could know the letter would arrive in heaven, a place he is almost certain does not exist – then he would write of guilt and solitude.

He would write of the unbearable humdrum misery of being the widower of a woman who was alive and fiercely loving. The loneliness of surviving.

He would write of the guilt in the choice he makes every day. The choice he makes each evening in the echoing house to ignore his solemn vows and pledges of the daylight hours. The choice – for that is what it is, he knows, no matter how intense the compulsion – to pour out the first steadying glass. The second lubricating glass. The third for joshing at shadows. The fourth self-pitying. The fifth maudlin. And on to the one he is waiting for. Oblivion. But this is an oblivion that comes with a price. Soiled clothes, and crumpled skin. Blackberry crying out in his sleep unanswered. Shaking hands. Daylight hours spent wished away, in an impatient, irascible race for his first drink.

He is lucky, he supposes, that he is so far removed from his old chief. Cromwell cannot move for scribes and spies and soldiers, following him around and waiting for orders. Will's crumbling is – largely – unnoticed. Nedham watches him, painfully silent, as his eyes water and his hands tremble.

But the further he is removed from Cromwell, the more he feels an unexpected lassitude. He did not crave proximity to power. He prided himself on his indifference to it. And yet in its withdrawal, he is finding himself lost.

This is what he would not say to Henrietta: that his greatest problem now is not guilt or loss or loneliness. It is boredom. It is apathy that gives him the excuse he seeks to reach for the numbing bottle. A great and unnerving paralysis of soul. He is the tiny cockle left behind by the retreating ocean, looking motionless at the sky and waiting for something – anything – to happen.

CORNHILL, LONDON

April 1655

THE SMELL IS QUITE EXTRAORDINARY. A PUNGENT, DARKLY sweet aroma that hangs over the room.

'Here,' says Nedham, and the two of them sit near the dimpled glass of the window. The warmth of the coffee shop has put a steam about the place, misting up the view to the street outside. It gives the room a cave-like intensity. A fire rages in the corner.

A neat, round-faced man wipes the table, and Will allows Nedham to take charge of the ordering.

'It is an age since I have seen you,' says Nedham.

'I am on the fringes now. Do you see the change, Nedham? Since the paltry Royalist uprisings. Since the Parliament failed. The chief is less open.'

Nedham nods, solemnly. They have both of them been immersed in the fallout from the rising. A Royalist call to arms that sent Thurloe scrabbling to his spies, and put the army on alert. Handfuls of men answered the call, rallying to the Stuart cause.

But the rising followed Leveller and Fifth Monarchist agitation in the army. At the centre, Cromwell is an embattled man.

Thurloe, grim-faced and anxious, reminds Will of a farmer with a club and a mole problem. Clunk! An army mutiny quelled. Gah! Up pops a Royalist. Clunk!

The farmer is winning, for now. All the moles are clubbed; sedated if not dead.

Nedham has been writing furious denunciations of the enemy without and within. He too looks exhausted – grey shadows edge his eyes. He leans back on his chair and opens his mouth to speak. But he stops, and looks about the room. He leans forward, bringing his face close to Will and lowering his voice.

'I have seen the change, Will. He is a man under siege. The failure of his Parliament, and the swell of Royalist feeling. It may have been a pathetic thing, the uprising, but it worried him nonetheless. The stakes are high – it is his great design at risk, his great plan. He wants religious unity. An England of Puritan soul and English heart.'

'He has always wanted that.'

'Yes,' says Nedham. 'But I think he is beginning to understand that souls are harder to win than he thought. He will not quite admit it, though. That is why you are on the outside of his circle now, Will. Do you see? You have been close to him. A confidant. If he cannot bring even your soul to a Puritan cleanliness, then what hope does he have with the farmer in Lincoln, the dairymaid in Yorkshire, the goodwife in Bristol?'

'I do see,' says Will. 'I am the seeds of his failure made flesh. But what of you? He keeps you close.'

'He needs my pen. And he never had any designs on my soul –

he watched it flip and flop between king and Parliament, following a purse. But you are a good man, Will. And he cannot bear to have a good man close who refuses to rack himself for God.'

The boy comes with a pot for the two of them. There is a pause for pouring, which allows Will a space to develop his thought. It is a new one – it comes unbidden. He takes a sip of the hot black liquid. It is bitter and aromatic.

'I feel as if the sun has gone in, Nedham. I am cast into shadow. Can I not love the man without loving his God?'

'Not if the man is Cromwell,' says Nedham. He says the name a little too loudly, and heads turn. This is a coffee house, after all. The rule, as Nedham has explained to Will, is that conversation should be general. Their intimacy, the closeness of their heads and their low voices, has been an affront to the house. Nedham grins and leans back in his chair. Will mirrors his action, and they sit wide-legged and open-shouldered, inviting conversation in.

'Well,' says a man on the table next to them. 'I have not seen you gentlemen here before.'

'It is my first visit,' says Will.

'Indeed?' He is of middling height, with thinning brown hair and startling blue eyes that peer out over half-moon spectacles. 'And yet you look familiar,' he says. 'Oxford men?'

'Not for some years,' says Will. 'I know who you are, sir. If you will excuse my presumption. My name is William Johnson, and I am secretary to the Lord Protector. You dined with him last week, with his sister and her husband.'

'Just so. Just so. John Wilkins, sir. Delighted to make your acquaintance, Mr Johnson. And?'

'My friend is Marchamont Nedham.'

'The newsbook man! Capital. Capital.'

He beams at them with great satisfaction and good humour. Will finds himself grinning back.

'How did you find our Lord Protector, sir?' asks Nedham.

'Tolerably spry, all things considered,' says Wilkins. 'Most put out about the intransigence of his first Parliament.'

'They were determined to vex him, I think,' says Will. 'They did so insist on curtailing freedom to worship.'

'Yes,' says Nedham. 'But I daresay that he was more vexed by their constant nit-picking at his constitutional place and theirs. There is much work to be done, and they spent their time gazing at their own buckles. I wonder, gentlemen, if His Highness thinks with pity now on his predecessor.'

The three of them look at each other awkwardly. This is territory too murky to discuss with strangers, and Will pulls Nedham back.

'Nedham, the Reverend Mr Wilkins is master of Wadham College.'

Nedham says the name again ponderously. Then he looks up. '*Mathematical Magick*!' he barks, and Wilkins simpers into his coffee.

'A most prodigiously learned book, Will,' says Nedham. 'Written by Mr Wilkins. It was all the rage in London about the time of the late king's fall. I am afraid, sir, that I was like a babe in the woods amongst your geometry. Words are more my line.'

'It is, alas, a book that many own and few have read,' says Wilkins, sipping at his coffee with a delicate hand.

'Better that way than the other,' says Will. 'Although I confess, I neither own it nor have read it. I was preoccupied at the time of the late king's death.'

'Many of us were, Mr Johnson. Many of us were.'

'My friend Johnson here,' says Nedham, 'is a keen natural philosopher.'

'Indeed? And your interest?'

'The stars, primarily,' says Will. 'But my interest has been in abeyance these last years. I was robbed of my wife, Mr Wilkins. I have found that grief and philosophy do not sit well together.'

'Is that so?' says Wilkins, drinking the last of his coffee and waving for another cup. 'And yet philosophy is also a consolation.'

'Yes, but natural philosophy – by which I mean the close study of the world – requires a kind of optimism, I think.'

The boy comes with hot water, interrupting Will in his thoughts. It gives him time to order them properly, and when the ritual of pouring and sipping and nodding is done, the words rush out of him.

'I mean, sir, that one must view the world – and, I suppose, its skies – with a benevolent gaze to be a natural philosopher. If one cannot feel that the world is worth studying, then it is hard to raise the impetus. Other more urgent matters take precedence. Putting food on the table. Putting one foot in front of the other. Pessimism is too akin to lethargy to allow for useful study.'

Nedham looks across at him, a strange expression on his face. 'My dear fellow. It occurs to me that I have only known the melancholic Will Johnson. Were you quite the joker before the death of your wife?'

Will pauses, not knowing how to answer the charge. He cannot remember, quite, what the boyish Will Johnson was like. He smiled more, certainly that is true.

Into the silence Wilkins says: 'We go through many permutations of character, do we not, in the face of great provocation from the universe. And yet there is an essential spirit that carries through from childhood. Tell me this, Mr Johnson. As a boy, did you gaze at the stars with a passionate longing to know their provenance?'

'I did, sir.'

'And did you spend your pennies on books about the stars? Kepler and the like. When other youths spent on wine and women?'

'I did, sir.'

'And I did not, sir,' says Nedham, and the three of them laugh.

'Then, Mr Johnson, I declare that you are a natural philosopher at your core. Grief has clouded your spirit, and there is no surprise or shame in that. When did she pass away?'

'Six years ago,' says Will, and he is astonished it is so long.

'I will not bother you with trite words about how she would want you to pursue your interests. In my experience anyway, Mr Johnson, living wives are not always keen on their husbands' heads roaming the heavens.'

'And yet you are not married, sir?' asks Nedham.

'Exactly so, Mr Nedham.' His eyes twinkle with the joke.

'And yet,' says Nedham, 'some believe that marital felicity is the summit of man's ambition.'

'What rot you talk, Nedham,' says Will. 'Nedham here believes that the summit of a man's ambition is always commercial interest. Commercial success, he tells anyone unfortunate enough to ask him, is the surest route to a happy soul.'

'And to a happy state,' says Nedham. 'A wealthy England is a happy England. We clothe our commercial ambitions with words of justice or God. But it is hard to be happy with an empty purse. The state is at risk from an empty treasury, and the empty purses of its citizens, and more so from potentates who rob those purses. The best hope for peace is prosperity.'

'It is bleak, your philosophy,' says Wilkins. 'It gives self-interest a primacy.'

'Men give self-interest a primacy, Mr Wilkins. I simply question whether that is a destructive force or a constructive one. I exempt you men of natural philosophy,' he says with a courtly bow, 'from all accusations of self-interest. I knew a man at Gray's Inn who devoted all his spare time, when we students were after pleasures of the flesh or the bottle, in studying the habits of beetles. He cannot have enjoyed such a pastime, so I defer to his noble pursuit of human knowledge at the expense of his very human pleasures.'

'No, Nedham,' says Will. 'You are wrong. If a man spends his time studying beetles, it is because he loves the beetles. You may not understand it, but he is entirely self-interested in his pursuit and therefore reinforces your argument. His self-interest is necessary to the expansion of human knowledge.'

'Is human knowledge enriched by understanding the mating cycle of beetles? No, Johnson, I will not quibble. For the central tenet of your argument is that I am in the right, and that is an argument to which I will always subscribe.'

Wilkins is smiling at them both like a benevolent uncle. 'All additions to human knowledge are an enrichment, Mr Nedham,' he says. 'Be it the mating of beetles or the oscillations of planets. Gentlemen, let me buy you another pot of this excellent coffee, and we will wrangle some more.'

~ ~ ~

In the darkness, Patience thinks of the distance between her and Sam, and the slow turn of the moon. She thinks of the dark Pool of London, where the ships of the world jostle for moorings. The soft slurping of the Thames as it hits the wood and the stones of the foreshore. The babble of sailors in one hundred tongues, and unintelligible in all of them.

She thinks of the river as it leaves London behind. The hulk of the Tower growing fainter, and the smell lessening with the noise. The flattening out of the land and the astonishing quickness with which London fades away. The strangeness of the estuary; its flat greyness, and the wild cries of the birds that live there. And there, the sea that separates them. A dark and inky blue, with a moon path shining silver. Beckoning her away from England. Towards him. Retreating each time she gets closer.

Is Sam thinking of her? Or is he with a woman?

She thinks of him with someone else. His languorous smile hanging over another woman's skin as she – the harlot – lies back and closes her eyes.

There is a kind of exquisite pain in thinking of it.

The empty bed is wide and cool.

Today, Sidrach is coming home.

Eventually she gives up all pretence of sleep. There is sufficient glimmering light to allow her to rise. She walks down to the kitchen. Tom is kneeling by the fire, coaxing last night's embers into a new flame. She watches him, while he is unaware of her presence. He has been happy in the two months they have been here alone.

Sarah, that malevolent eye, has not been here. Her sister died while her employers were on the Continent, leaving a husband and five small children. Much to Patience's relief, Sarah has been absent, playing mother. Patience hopes she is keeping her brother-in-law's bed warm, too. It will lessen the chance of her returning, with her sour sabotage of a face.

Tom has been known to sing while he polishes the silver. He has smiled at small things – a kitten he found in the alley behind the house, a compliment from Patience, the bright spring sun on his face.

But now, with Sidrach's return imminent, he is quiet and somehow smaller. Well done, Sidrach, she thinks. This is the mark of a true tyrant – your shadow is as deadening as your presence.

The fire is built now, and the boy slings the pot in place above the flames to boil.

'Tom,' she says softly.

He turns quickly and tries to smile.

'Come sit with me a while,' she says.

'But . . . but . . .' He waves helplessly at the kitchen. There is much to be done before the master arrives, looking to find fault.

'He will not be here until this afternoon. We have time. I will help you.'

He nods solemnly and walks to the table, sliding on to the bench.

'We have been happy, Tom, have we not?'

'Yes, missus.'

'And now . . . now . . .' She falters. 'Tom, I am looking for a new place for you. My brother—'

'No, missus.' He raises his voice. 'You do not want me?'

'I do. I do, Tom. But you are not safe here.'

'You neither, missus,' he says. He sticks his chin up defiantly. Looks her in the eye.

'My place is here, Tom. But you are not so bound.'

'I am bound to you, missus.'

'Tom,' she says. 'You will still see me. I must insist on this. I will manage it with Sidrach. You will go to my brother's house today.'

He looks wild, frightened. She had not expected this reaction. She thought he would be relieved to escape this house. The Lord knows she would be. How she hates it. The heavy dark furniture. The shrouded curtains. The imprint of misery in every stitch of fabric, every rush, every shadow.

'Can I stay for a small while, missus? I will leave next week, if I must. I would not leave you on the first day.'

She nods, knowing herself too easily persuaded. Is it so weak to want to have her ally close for a little while longer?

He smiles, clearly relieved.

'How do you bear it, missus?' he asks, in such a rush that the words blend together. 'The master, I mean.'

She pauses. 'I do not know. Perhaps I bear it because I must. But . . .' She does not know how to word her reply. She does not like to speak of Sidrach, of the tactics she uses to keep her soul unspliced by him. But she loves little Tom – that love born from a desire to protect, to nourish. And love makes its own demands.

So she says: 'There are those I love, Tom. My brother. My sisters. My parents. You.' Sam! Oh my beloved. 'To them, I willingly, gladly offer a piece of my soul.'

'Me, missus?' He looks at her, wide-eyed. She reaches a hand across the table and takes his. The simple gesture seems to push him over the edge. Tears brim and begin to fall down his coal-tracked cheek.

'You. So, Tom. The tyrant. He can mark me. He can torment me. He can make me miserable. But he cannot take a single bite, a single chunk from my soul. Because souls belong to Jesus, the light of love. And souls can only be offered in love; not taken in spite.'

He smiles at her. She feels courageous, taller. The words are making her brave. And it is just possible that they may even be true.

The morning after his meeting with Wilkins, which stretched late into the night, Will wanders London in a demi-haze. He finds his heart is beating faster. Perhaps it is the coffee. Or perhaps it is the awakening of his soul, he thinks, before laughing at his own pomposity.

Wilkins told them of a club he has founded in Oxford, for the examination of natural philosophy. It is an experimental club that seeks to use method and reason together to deepen understanding of natural phenomena. It has London members too, who cluster around the Royalist doctor Charles Scarborough. A fine mathematician, according to Mr Wilkins.

Could he join? Is he good enough? Clever enough?

He must try to catch up with where he left off. How many more books have there been since Henrietta died? How many discoveries? He has been standing weeping on the bank while the river rushes past unheeding.

He finds himself, unthinking, in St Paul's churchyard. The book-sellers' quarter. It is where he used to meet Henrietta before they were married. For a long time he has tried to avoid it, finding the memories too grating.

There is the wall on which they would sit and talk. He can almost picture her there, enthusiastic about something she has read, her hands waving in emphasis. It is, he finds, a comforting image. There is not the violent lurch of pain he expected.

As if to test his new resilience – like probing a splinter with a needle – he walks to their favourite book-seller. They came here before they were married and after. She even worked here, for a while, when she was alone in London after her father's death. Hidden in the back stacks where she would not frighten the customers.

Later she would bring Blackberry here, and whisper to him of the treasures he would know when he was older. Tales of deserts and seas. Poems of love and loss.

Stars, Will would say. Blackberry will read books about the stars.

He will read what he will read, she would say.

She would squeeze his arm quickly, in case he was wounded. Bury her nose in Blackberry's neck. Squeal, suddenly, at a new title, sitting uncut and pristine, and waiting for her to pounce on it.

Lord, it smells the same. Of ink and paper. Of the dust that settles on the leaves. He feels a familiar flicker of pleasure – and this is not a memory, but a real sensation. A present and future pleasure.

Mr Rowan, the book-seller, rushes forward.

'Mr Johnson. Mr Johnson. Such an age since we saw you last. What a pleasure this is. And how is your boy? Young Richard?'

'He is well, I thank you, Mr Rowan. It is good to be here.'

'And it is good to see you here again, Mr Johnson. I have some

wonderful works in. One in particular that made me think of . . .'
He trails off.

'Henrietta?' says Will, and the man's face looks relieved that
her name could so easily trip from Will's tongue. He nods.

'Thank you. I will look at them. There is a particular book I
would like, however. John Wilkins. *Mathematical Magick*?'

'Yes, yes! It is in the back. I will just fetch it,' says Mr Rowan,
and bumbles off into the stacks.

Will stands and breathes. He lets the memories swirl like dust,
and when they settle, he is smiling.

LONDON

July 1655

SIDRACH SITS WITH A PROPRIETORIAL AIR. HIS LEGS ARE spread, his feet planted wide. He drums his fingers on the armrest, and lifts his chin as he surveys his domain. The kitchen should be hers, her refuge. But here he is, for no reason she can think of, except his desire to irritate. To spray himself across her tiny fragment of space, like a vicious tomcat.

'Well now,' he says. 'Well.'

A space in his words: it makes her feel as if she is falling forwards with her hands tied behind her back.

'You have not hired a maid to replace Sarah.'

'I did not see the need, husband. Not with Sarah only gone temporarily. Tom and I shifted for ourselves.'

'Tom and I? Tom and I, is it?'

'I meant only—'

'I do not need your instruction in what you meant, Patience. I know very well what you meant.'

'I beg pardon, husband.'

'Write to Sarah. Ascertain her intentions. I will hire a new maid if necessary.'

She nods.

'It took you some time to secure my passport,' he says.

'I . . . I applied directly. These things. I did what I . . .' She mumbles on.

'Well, I am here now. What news is there? What of the villain?'

The villain? It takes her fear-spliced mind a pace to catch up.

'Cromwell?'

'Of course Cromwell. You are foolish, Patience. I had forgotten. Well? What news? Will must keep you supplied with information.'

'You heard of Penruddock's rising? The Royalists did not get very far. He has arrested some merchants for importing arms. He has legislated against Quakers and Ranters – those who contest his notion of free worship.'

She had thought the news would rile him. Instead he smiles, and rubs his hands with exaggerated smugness.

'He digs his own grave, does Cromwell. Dig, dig, sir!'

'I do not understand you, husband.'

'No, of course you do not. Perhaps you think I came back for your company, Patience. The joy of our connubial bliss. Perhaps you think that your empty, pointless womb was enough to tear me away from those people of quality I found on the Continent.'

He seems to find this notion deeply amusing. She can feel a prickle of sadness welling behind her eyes. She turns on herself. Do not cry. Do not let him make you cry.

She will not ask him why he has come. She will not fill his expectant pause.

'Are you hungry, Sidrach?'

He nods assent, and she bustles to find the cheese and the new soft bread. She reaches for the jug of small beer. It is empty.

'Shall I get some more from the back, missus?' Tom is at her elbow, suddenly, like a solemn sprite.

She nods, and hands him the jug. 'Quickly,' she whispers. He understands, the Lord bless him. The trick is to give Sidrach nothing to seize upon. The trick is to be muffled in word and deed. A shadow.

She covers the absence of the small beer with a pantomime search for pickles. She breaks her own rules – she is loud and clumsy in her movements to cover Tom scuttling away with a jug that should be kept full. Sidrach is too absorbed in his myth-making to notice their pathetic mumming.

'The Lady Norton was most gracious to me as I left, Patience. Said that I would be heartily missed. Promised to read the tracts I gave her.'

She glances at his handsome, smug face as she sets down the jar. Imagines him smirking at some bored aristocrat. Imagines the soft temper of his voice as he promises brimstone but implies oh-so-lightly that he alone can deflect the wrath of the Lord. The spirit working through him. The sucking, seductive pull of his dark eyes.

She sits down next to him, hoping he will not notice the empty glass.

'Oh yes, Patience. I found some spirits to match mine, even among those who gather about the false king. Spirits sickened by the man who calls himself our protector. Protector! He should look to himself, Patience. Protect himself!'

He leans back into the chair, delighted with himself. She smiles – it seems called for.

Tom comes back, carrying the heavy jug. She silently pleads with him not to spill a drop; not to merit Sidrach's eye upon him. Smoothly he comes over and pours out a measure. There is something awry about Tom, but she cannot pin it down. A sort of pugnaciousness, as if he has moved beyond fear and into some state beyond. She hopes that her husband will not notice and test this new Tom. Goad him to breaking point.

Sidrach continues to talk. She catches phrases, listening only for the gaps where she must nod, or hmm, or agree with vigour. Tom comes to her setting and pours a small measure for her. She glances a silent question at him. He is not looking at her. His gaze seems fixed away from her, into the middle distance.

She drinks the thimbleful, and holds up her cup for more. But Tom's back is turned, and he does not see her. She puts her cup down quickly, before Sidrach notices and turns the gesture against the boy. Before he can curse the boy for incompetence and stupidity, and perhaps, if he is feeling particularly venomous, force a small, grubby hand into the burning coals of the fire.

Lord, the white fog of fear and pain that rolled from the boy that day, she thinks. She remembers the blisters that rose and popped on his skin. The scream. Sidrach's impatience later on when the wounds left the boy clumsy.

She is tired. It is the waiting, she thinks. The toll of anticipating the master's arrival, and all the dissembling misery in these short hours since he has been here.

The wet pucker of his lips as he kissed her cheek, the pinch of his fingers on her upper arm.

She must stay awake. She must not sleep until he sleeps. Yet there he is, yawning too. She watches him dizzily. He seems to sway and droop. Or is it her swaying and drooping? Her head is heavy. A great lolling, heavy thing. She remembers the fever. Is this another such? Is she falling again?

Sidrach has put his head on his arms on the table. If she is falling, then so is he. Where is Tom? Where is he?

Here. A small arm around her shoulder.

'To bed, missus. You are sleepy. I will look after the master.'

'I cannot. I . . . I . . .'

'Shh. I can look after the master.'

She allows herself to be led away. Up the stairs, one trembling foot at a time. She sinks into the bed. Tom leaves her. His absence makes her frightened. She wants to call out, but her throat is dry and she can't. She can't.

Easier to sleep. She lets go, slip-sliding into a mash of images. Sidrach shouting; Sam smiling. Blackberry running forward. Falling. She can't catch him. Her hands are coated in tallow. Sidrach is laughing. She runs at him, striking and spitting and kicking.

She wakes.

It is dark outside, and dark in here. The fire is ember red, but its light does not travel far. The house is starkly silent.

Where is Sidrach? His side of the bed is made and empty. She crawls from under the cover, into the sharpness of the night air. Sitting upright, her head fills with blood. Stand. Walk in a slow shuffle to the door.

There is light at the bottom of the stairs, coming from the

kitchen. She grips the banister, easing herself down one step at a time. She feels as if any sudden movement will send sparks flying in her head. The red and white lightning hovers behind her eyes, waiting for a false move to send her reeling.

Slow, quiet.

Down, down, until at the bottom she can pause. She can wait for the sparks to subside, just a little.

There is silence in the kitchen. No chatter, no clatter. No spit and hiss of food cooking. There is the flickering light of candles, and the fire, and she edges towards it. The only possible way to go is forward and on into that silent and strange space.

She reaches the door. Her brain cannot process what she sees. Sidrach is sitting upright in the chair – his chair – but his head is lolling forward. Tom is sitting across the table from him, an open bottle of Sidrach's best wine in front of him. There is a telltale crust of red wine about the boy's lips, and the eyes that rise to meet hers are bloodshot and wild.

'Tom?' she says. A tentative question.

He jumps to his feet and rushes around to stand behind Sidrach. She sees then that her husband is tied into the chair, a criss-cross of ropes keeping him upright. His sleeping head falls forward.

'You should be asleep, missus.'

'And yet I am not.'

'No.'

He lifts a skinny arm then, and she sees the knife. It catches the light and beams at her. She reaches for her belt, and the sheath that knife lives in. It was given to her by her mother for their wedding.

'That is my knife, Tom,' she says, stupidly, as if that were the pertinent point of this tableau. The tied-up Sidrach, and the wild-eyed sozzled boy, and the strange chemical pounding of her head – and yet this small act of larceny is the detail that snags her.

'Your knife. Yes, yes. And I will give it back. After.'

'After what, Tom?'

'After I kill him.'

She shuffles forward, hand outstretched. His response is a quick and panicked push of the knife towards Sidrach's neck, pressing the sharp point into the skin until it draws blood and both of them gasp at the thick red bead that appears as if by wizardry on his skin. Sidrach snuffles within his bounds, his head still drooping.

'You will not kill him, Tom.'

'Will I not?'

'Please, Tom. Do not do this. You are to escape this place. I told you before. Untie him now, while he sleeps, and he will never notice.'

He shakes his head. Realization clicks in hers. 'The beer? There was something in it? Something from the apothecary?'

He nods. The fog in her brain has a cause, if not a name.

'Do not do this, Tom. Not for my sake.'

'Lord, missus. It is not for your sake, though I do love thee dearly.'

'For whose sake then, Tom?'

He yelps, like a puppy. Tears fall. 'I need to tell him, missus. Him. For whose sake I do this. 'Tis why I did not just slit his throat while he slept. I'm waiting now for him to wake. For him to know why. For him to see my face when he dies.'

He is talking himself ferocious. His face is a jumble of tears and snarls, and she does not recognize him. She cannot see the sweet boy who starts at shadows. But she must assume that boy is here somewhere too.

'I will just sit here, then, Tom, will I?' She points to the nearest chair. Her voice is low and gentle, aware of the shake in the hand that holds the blade. As you would talk to a frightened animal, pushed into a corner. All bared teeth and quivering fear.

He nods. She pulls the chair towards her, and the scrape of its legs on the floor is loud and echoing. Sidrach does not stir.

Suddenly there are footsteps along the street outside. Footsteps that sound loud and booming in this deliberate silence. Through the dimpled window she can see the swing of a lamp. The bellman. 'Ten o'clock,' he calls. 'Ten o'clock and a warm night to come.'

Tom sits next to Sidrach, staring at her. She wants to reach out and draw him in. She settles for a smile, which makes the child cry all the harder.

'Why, Tom?'

He shakes his head. A furious movement, informed by the red wine. He reaches for the bottle.

'No!' Her shout is loud in the quiet house. He starts, nervous, and looks at her.

'Tom, let us not cloud our senses. No more wine, dear boy. Cool heads.'

He nods, and lets his head sink down on to his arms.

Time slows. She has never been good at sitting still, at doing nothing. As the night creeps on, she finds to her astonishment that she is bored. She cannot concentrate her mind's eye, with the knife shining and Sidrach drooping forward. She cannot think of other things – the scene does not allow for such frivolity.

And yet. Yet. She cannot think about what happens next either. This absurd impasse is too difficult.

So she sits and waits for Sidrach to wake up; dreading and longing for that moment in equal measures. She concentrates on listening to his breathing. Is that lighter breath a sign of stirring? Is that twitch in his foot just a dream?

The sky outside begins to lighten at last. She can hear the tweeting of birds.

Tom rises and stretches. He cuts himself a slice of bread. She watches the slow saw of the knife through the crust, and thinks, queasy, about what will come next. She is fascinated by Tom eating as if this is a normal morning.

There is a sudden strangled gasp from Sidrach.

She jumps, feeling the stabbing thump of her heart. Tom tenses. The bread falls to the floor.

Sidrach pulls his head back, moves it from side to side. He looks pained; his eyes are screwed tight shut still.

Don't open. Don't open.

They open.

He garbles something. She makes out the word 'What?', repeated with mounting incredulity.

Tom looks at her. She shrugs at him. The absurdity of it all strikes her, and she nearly giggles. She manages to swallow it, just.

Sidrach looks at her. 'Patience,' he says. His tone is a warning and a question all at once.

'It is not. That is. I.' She retreats into silence.

'Tom.' A bark. 'Tom.'

'Sorry, mister. I mean, I ain't sorry. I'm going to kill you.'

He says the words with a befuddled air. Sidrach snorts. 'Ridiculous boy. Untie me now.'

'I will not.'

'Untie me now, or I swear to the Almighty and His son that I will kill you.'

'I will not.'

Patience, sitting in the chair between them, has a sudden urge to run away. She could leave this scene to play itself out. She could let the boy do what he feels he must. Let Sidrach rub against his bonds. Let the knife strike and Sidrach's sour blood gush. And yet she cannot. She cannot move. And she cannot abandon Tom.

'Patience. Untie me.' She twitches forward at the command. She is so used to obeying him. She sits on her hands to stop them moving towards the knots.

Tom lifts his knife, looking at her down the point of it.

'Do not move, missus.'

She stays still.

'Tell us why now, Tom,' she says, gently.

'Why. Why. Do you know where I was born? Do you know where I was a boy? Do you know where I lived with a mother who loved me and a father who didn't hit me? We had a servant. Now look. Oh, my mother, missus. You would have liked her. Loved her.'

'Where were you born, Tom?'

'In Drogheda. Drogheda.' He says the name again, spitting it towards Sidrach like an accusation.

It means little to Patience. But something in Sidrach's face changes, and for the first time she sees fear writ there as well as anger.

'Not much, Drogheda. Not like London, nor even Dublin. But home, missus. Until the soldiers came. Don't know much about why. They closed the gates. All the men went to the walls. My father, one morning. He went. Just walked on, whistling. Holding a pike. Never saw him again.'

'How old were you, Tom?'

'About seven, missus. My mother, she was frightened. Talked of the devil Cromwell at the gates. Said we should surrender, but the men were too puffed up with the fight. That's what she said.'

'The general offered terms, Tom,' says Sidrach, slowly and quietly. 'The Royalist commander refused. What happened next was the natural course of the war.'

'Natural?' A bitter, mirthless laugh. 'Jesus wept, missus, but the noise. When they came on. The screaming. Shouting. They set fire to the church, with hundreds of men inside weeping for their God.'

'Their God. Papist scum,' Sidrach sneers.

'Theirs is as good as yours. Better. Kinder!' Tom is shouting, and he struggles to bring himself back under control.

Patience watches Sidrach forcing himself not to retort.

'My mother,' says Tom. 'She knew they were coming. She hid me in the coal tip. Kissed me first. The men came in. Held her down. She told them where the money was. The food. She didn't tell them about me. I thought they would let her go then. I could see, missus. A crack in the wood. I could see them tearing her dress. Laughing. Holding her down. She was crying. Turned to look at where I was hidden. She . . . she tried to smile.'

He wipes a dirty sleeve across his mouth. 'The man on her then. He swore at her for smiling. Called her names. And then he collapsed into her. Stood up. I thought it was over. Thought they would leave.'

He shudders. She wants to hold him, but she is motionless.

'He slit her throat.'

He turns to Sidrach. Looks at him and says with quiet fury: 'You slit her throat.'

'Me? And you know this, Tom? I was at Drogheda, yes. But so were thousands of other soldiers.'

'Your mates, they laughed. Then one of them called your name. Said: "If the people of Blackfriars could see you now, Sidrach Simmonds." I'd learned English, you see. My family were known in that town. Rich enough to be tutoring me, not like my cousins. I understood what they said. Heard your name. Another one repeated it. Sidrach this, Sidrach that. I was there, all black from the coal. Coal in my throat, my nose, my mouth. Concentrating on not crying aloud. Then, Sidrach Simmonds, you stood up. Wiped your knife. Swore when you slipped in her blood.

'After, I worked the coal ships. Found out where Blackfriars was. Came to see it. And then I saw you.'

Sidrach looks towards the boy. 'And now this,' he says, the softness of treacle in his voice. 'I still say it was not me. Perhaps you misheard. Coal in your ears.'

'I saw your face,' says Tom.

'War is confusing, boy. Messy. You were frightened. It was dark.'

'I saw your face.'

Patience can see the pulse of a vein in Sidrach's temple. His hands, gripping the arms of his chair, are white-knuckled and red-veined.

'Let us say,' he says, 'that it was me. Which I do not admit. But if it was. Would your dear mother, God bless her, want you to take this sin on your shoulders? Want you hanged for a murderer? No, dear boy. She would want you to untie me. For me to see about getting you some schooling. A clever boy like you, Tom. School, not a noose.'

'She would want vengeance,' says Tom. He says it with force, as if trying to convince himself.

'No, Tom. Do you know what mothers want more than anything? For their children to be safe. Are you safe now, Tom? Is this little scene making you safe?'

Tom begins to pace. He prowls the small kitchen, stopping by the window and turning to Sidrach. The grey light stealing through the glass leaches the colour from his face. She can see the old man he will become, when life has battered him even more thoroughly.

'I have thought of nothing else for all these years,' he says. 'Thought of pushing the knife into your throat. Thought of hearing you beg.'

Sidrach swallows hard. She watches the bob of his Adam's apple. His voice when it comes is even and calm.

'Come, Tom. Change your mind. We can make this better. Let me go. I will not hurt you.'

Tom looks straight at Patience, as if she has an answer. Do not trust him. Do not trust him. She is a coward; she cannot say the words aloud. She screams them in her head. Do not trust him.

The boy walks behind Sidrach. She thinks he is moving to untie the ropes. Lord, Sidrach will spring up. He will kill them both. She can feel herself shrinking into her seat. But then she realizes that he is not untying the knots. He has wrapped a rag around Sidrach's mouth, forcing it between his lips and pulling it tight. Sidrach can no longer speak. His eyes are wild. Sweat bursts from his forehead.

What is Sidrach with no voice?

He erupts suddenly. Rocking and shuffling in his bonds. He lets loose a series of high, grunting protests. Patience closes her eyes. She counts downwards in threes from a hundred and one. Will taught her to count backwards as a child, to get to sleep. Concentrating on something just hard enough to block out the world outside. Eighty-six. Eighty-three. Eighty.

She opens her eyes. Sidrach is still. He is looking with rabid intensity towards Tom. The boy is slumped forward, with his head cradled on his arms. She sees, to her astonishment, that he is asleep.

The knife lies on the table between the three of them.

It has slipped from Tom's grasp. His clenched fist has opened. His head rests on arms that lie limply on the table. Oh, the pity of those thin little limbs and the sharp angles of his shoulder bones. Asleep, his mouth has slackened. His breath whispers in the silence of the room.

She wonders how he can possibly sleep. But he is young. The febrile intensity of the night up to this point has hollowed him out, it seems.

It feels like a lifetime since she was childish enough to slip quickly from the world into dreams.

She wants to reach out and smooth the hair back from his forehead, to tuck the long strands behind his ear. But there is no possibility of movement. It is out of the question.

Tentatively, she attempts to move an arm. Her finger twitches. She is pinned to the chair by fear and indecision. She is not ready, yet, to move her eyes across the table to where her husband sits. Instead, she watches the sleeping boy. Watches the rise and fall of his back. The hair that is caught by each exhaling breath, rising, shivering, falling.

She looks at the whorl of the table. There is flour caught in the deepest groove. White sludge collecting unnoticed in there. Such details have escaped her attention as she bustles here and there.

The knife, oh the irony! The wedding gift. She wears the embroidered sheath at her waist, with a matching purse. Roses and vines and pansies curl around both, picked out in gold thread entwined with red. A bird calls from the centre of each, small and carefully stitched. The knife itself has a steel blade, wickedly sharp.

On this table, she has used the knife to cut. To slice. To pare. To carefully ease the skin off a rabbit. To inch a fillet from a fish. She has pricked its point along the side of a mutton bone, tearing the sinew and releasing the meat. The boy himself has sharpened it, with concentrated precision. He knows how she loves the knife, and he is careful with it.

Or perhaps he knew that he might need it.

A groan breaks the silence. An urgent, look-at-me moan. And another. The rocking, shuffling creak of a chair. She will not look yet. She needs time to think. To decide what to do.

She could do nothing. Sit as still as possible. The chair is hard and cold beneath her buttocks, the edge of it pressing into her thighs. Her back hurts from sitting immobile and hunched over with tense shoulders. Her head is heavy and stupid, raddled with indecision.

If she does nothing, the responsibility will be the boy's. He will wake and pick up the knife, gripping it tight so that the amber swirls on the shaft press into his palm. It will be up to him what happens next. He might fail at the last minute. Or he might push the knife into her husband's chest until it finds his heart.

He will be lucky to find such a thing, she thinks. The thought makes her laugh – absurdly, inappropriately. Without thinking, she looks over at her husband to see if he heard her. He hates her frivolity, hates her habit of finding things funny that should be deathly serious. And what could be more deathly serious than this?

He has heard her. Above the rag stretched between his lips to gag him, his eyes are turned on her. Staring, furious.

Fear flutters in her blood. His eyes flick down to the knife, then back to her.

She should pick up the knife, take it behind his back and use it to saw the rope that binds him. She should use that wicked blade on the gag, careful not to score her husband's skin as she cuts.

The longer she does not do what she should, the more his fury will be directed at her rather than the boy. Would you release a rabid dog from its chains?

There is a third option. She could pick up the knife. She could take the sin from Tom and on to herself. She could push the knife into her husband's chest, to find whatever tiny sliver of heart he has. The boy has a sort of grace, a sort of innocence, despite – or perhaps because of – all he has suffered in his short life. He will be lost to the devil if he does this thing. So will she.

But she would be free. The devil's dancer, yes, but free.

She shivers to think of it, watching her husband's red-rimmed eyes watching her. There is something new in the room; a smell she fails to place at first.

He has pissed himself.

So now there is a further humiliation to spur his rage. She closes her eyes, imagining what will happen if she lets him go, how he will bound from his chair, piss dripping down his leg, fury clenching his hands into fists.

Free. She thinks of Sam, and how it would be if he burst into the room to rescue her. To take away the decision, and pick her up and carry her away. Perhaps this night is her penance for loving him when she is bound to someone else.

He is not coming. It is just her, the boy and her husband. She cannot even pray for guidance. The Lord is not with her in this room. How can He be? At this moment, this great test, she is failing. Her indecision is in itself a turning of her face away from Him. In His light, there is only one decision, and that breaks no commandments, no oaths to her husband. Thou shalt not kill.

No. The Lord is not here with her.

Whatever she decides, she will relive and she will regret. Her husband's eyes bore into her. Snake eyes; venomous. The boy shifts a little in his sleep; his eyelids begin to tremble.

What should I do? Oh my soul, what should I do?

And the knife still lies on the table between them.

Will pushes the decanter to one side. He watches the slosh of the red wine inside the glass, and feels an answering tremor in his skin.

The house is quiet. Blackberry is at his early-morning lessons with his new tutor, a thin, penniless youth called Stephen

Cavendish. Cavendish wants to be a poet, but is stuck teaching Latin to small boys. Will keeps his ears open for sounds of beating. He is not entirely sure that he trusts Cavendish to keep his bitterness hidden.

But for now there is quiet. The only conversation is the unspoken one between Will and the decanter.

I will stop your hand shaking.

You are making my hand shake.

I will soothe your spirits.

You are a false friend.

I will make you forget. I will make you brave.

Will stands, abruptly. He walks across the room and takes up his book. He sits with his back to the wine, aware of it.

Slowly the book creeps into the space left by the booze. Fills his blood with ideas, with notions. The first part of *Mathematical Magick* is interesting enough: a route map for novices through the beauty and symmetry of maths. But this is familiar territory for Will, even if it is years since last he visited. He reads with a fondness, with the shadow of his excited youth at his shoulder.

In the second half, however, Wilkins moves on to more speculative stuff. More specifically, Will becomes entranced by his insistence that man might fly. Wilkins envisages a flying chariot, with beating wings powered by springs.

Will pauses, his mind alive with the notion. He is abuzz with questions and possibilities. Experiment, says Wilkins, is the key. Constant and bold experiment.

Yes, thinks Will. Yes.

So caught is he in Wilkins' vision that he barely registers the knocking on the door. It grows in force and intensity; a violent and insistent knock.

The sudden intrusion of the outside world sends Will's eyes beetling across to the decanter. He grips the arms of his chair and pulls himself upright. He crosses the room not knowing quite which urge he is giving in to.

The knocking is louder. He follows it.

On the stairs, he sees Blackberry's head peeking around the corner of the door to the study. Above him, the tutor's owlish glare. Will smiles reassuringly towards them. 'A messenger, no doubt,' he says.

Word from Cromwell, perhaps. He is needed. He thanks his God that he resisted the call of the wine. He will need to be in good fettle.

'Go back to your studies,' he says to Blackberry. The boy winks. It is a new trick, and he uses it on any and every occasion. A careful, exaggerated wink. Will feels a sober lurch of tenderness towards the boy. He winks back, and Blackberry grins before he pulls his head back behind the door. As it closes shut, Will hears the muffled sing-song of a verb being conjugated.

Amo, amas, amat, he thinks, as he walks down the stairs. *Amabam.* I was loving.

The door is rapped upon again. Whoever it is will wake the whole bloody street.

'I am coming!' he shouts. 'I am coming!'

At the door is Tom, Patience's boy. He looks wild. Red-eyed and unkempt. There is a murky smell of beer and mould rising off him. Will looks at him stupidly.

Tom shouts at him, waving his arms.

'He'll kill her!' he cries, pulling at Will's sleeve. 'Kill her!'

Will tries to make sense of it. The words are so unexpected, so extremely unlikely, that they do not translate into meaning. But he is leaving the house, letting the boy pull him down the steps. He feels a shake in his legs, in his hands, as he is towed away from his door. He tells himself to focus, noting the boy's frantic face.

'What has happened, Tom? Calm down, for Christ's own sake. What has happened?'

'No time,' the boy sobs, shaking his head. 'Run, please, mister. She said she'd let him go. Gave me money to run. I don't want her money, mister. I want her safe. Not dead.'

Dead? A strong word. An improbable word. Will fights for lucidity.

They are moving quickly through the streets. London is lazily stirring itself. Will gives up trying to understand. But the quicker he strides, the calmer the boy seems. And he can understand the essence of the crisis, anyway. All his fears for Patience, all his dislike for Sidrach, are coalescing into an urgency. He runs now.

Their door is closed, locked shut.

He knocks. Bangs on the door. An echo of Tom's earlier urgency.

There is no answer.

'Sidrach,' he shouts. 'Patience!'

'Please, mister. Please, mister.' The boy's incoherent plea buzzes at him, melting into his panic. He takes a few paces backwards and runs at the door, slamming into it with his shoulder.

The pain jolts through his side, but – miraculous! – the wood splits and gives. He is through.

Once inside, he pauses. The house is entirely still. Outside, they can hear the insistent cries of the street hawkers. Pies. Sausages. Oysters. The thunderous trundle of a cart. A drum beats somewhere. A snatch of a woman's laughter, intense and loud, pushes its way into the quiet corners of the hallway.

Tom stands close behind him, peering around his shoulder.

'The kitchen, mister. They were in the kitchen. Oh, she's dead. And it's my fault.'

He lapses into a babble, a stream of seemingly unconnected sounds. Nonsense, perhaps. Or a different language.

'Quiet, Tom.' The boy stops his gibbering, although his breathing is still ragged. Together they step further into the house. The floor creaks as they walk, signalling their presence. No bad thing, perhaps, thinks Will. He shivers. There is something so deadening, so dark in the fabric of this house. Perhaps it is a fancy, but the walls have known misery. Thank God she has not brought a child into it.

Patience.

He forces himself to stop thinking of fancies. To stop thinking how much easier this would be if he was a glass or two into a full decanter.

The kitchen is ahead. The door is ajar. Light spills from its edges into the darkness of the hallway. He grabs a candlestick from the table in the hallway, feeling self-conscious and melodramatic as he does so. It is reassuringly thick and heavy in his hands.

'Patience,' he says softly. 'Patience.'

No answer. He reaches out and pushes the kitchen door. It

swings inward. The first thing he sees is Sidrach, sitting hunched on a chair by the fire. He turns to face Will as he comes in. There is a strange, blank look on his face. It is as if he has expected to see Will. He catches sight of Tom, sheltering behind Will's back. He flinches, makes to stand. Fury flits on to his face. But then his eye catches on something beyond the table, and he hunches back down again.

'She's there,' he says. He points.

Will sees her then. She is lying on the floor. Curled into a ball. Her hair streams across the grey tiles. There is blood, pooling on the floor. Blood on her face. On her limp hands. On her thin cotton shift. There is blood clumping in her head.

'Oh Jesus, Sidrach. What have you done?'

He drops to her side. Her face is white, her skin is cold to the touch.

Tom runs at the man by the fire, beating his hunched back with small, violent fists.

'You devil. Devil. Devil. Devil.'

Sidrach sits through the assault like a placid bull being buzzed by a fly.

Will catches it then. A tremor under her eyelid, a flicker at her temple. A breath. A breath! Not dead. His body almost collapses under the weight of his surging blood. 'Not dead, you son of a whore,' he says to Sidrach. Sidrach raises his head.

'Not? I thought . . .' He trails off.

Will slides his arms under her body.

Sidrach seems to crumple further. 'Thank God. Thank God,' he mutters. He raises a hand to his throat, as if to brush off the shadow of a noose. Will sees the bruises and scrapes on his knuckles. He has a violent urge to smash his own fist into Sidrach's face, to watch the blood spread on him, to hear the snap of his nose breaking.

He must concentrate on Patience.

'Tom. Run for the doctor. Then Hattie. You know Hattie, the butcher's wife? To my house.'

Tom nods. He looks broken, as if the strings holding him upright have suddenly snapped. 'Be strong, boy,' says Will. 'Just for a little longer. Be strong.'

Tom pulls himself upright. As he turns for the door, he pauses, then spits at Sidrach, suddenly and violently. Sidrach starts, and begins to lumber to his feet, the spit sliding down his cheek.

'Stop!' shouts Will. 'Tom. Go. Sidrach – sit down.'

They obey him. Tom runs out of the door. Will struggles to his feet with Patience hanging limply in his arms.

'Shh, little Imp,' he whispers into her ear. 'You're safe now.'

'The bed upstairs,' says Sidrach. 'She belongs here.'

Will looks at him. The strength of contempt he feels must burn hot on his face, for Sidrach turns red and looks down.

'What will people say?' he says sullenly to the floor.

Will cannot dredge a riposte contemptuous enough. Silent, he holds Patience tight and walks away.

Patience is astounded to discover that she is still alive. There is no mistaking the symptoms. Pain. A dry mouth. A thump of blood in her head that slams into her forehead behind her eyes.

Besides, this is clearly Will's bedroom. Books teeter up the wall in piles. She pulls herself upright, dragging the blankets with her.

At the end of the bed, curled like a puppy, is Tom. He is asleep. There is something comforting in the fact that he is so still. She thinks back to his face when she saw him last; his eyes bright with fear and red-rimmed with wakefulness. Sidrach rising behind him.

She closes her eyes. She wills herself to think of something other than Sidrach. But he is there, eyes shut or open. Does this mean that he has won? That she is finally broken?

She cannot lie here. If she does nothing, she will think of him. His face, even more than his fists. How those handsome, fleshy features twist with menace. The coal-burn black of his eyes. The unbearable lurch of failing to placate him.

She swings her feet out of bed. Her toes find the floor and she pulls herself to standing, hauling on the corner post of the bed. Her head spins. She will stay standing. She will.

Over to the boy, whose sleeping breath is quiet and even. She pulls the blanket down the bed and over his thin body. He stirs a little, and she strokes his forehead. He whimpers himself back to sleep. Poor mite. What a story he told. And what happens now?

She leaves him there and walks slowly to the kitchen. The corridor is cool, and she shivers in her shift, wrapping her arms around herself.

There at the table, his head bent over a book, is Will. She pauses for a moment, watching. His hair falls forward over his face, hiding the scoring around his eyes. The forefinger of his right hand is tapping the wood insistently, as it does when he reads something that excites him. Tap tap tap. How they teased him for it when he was a boy.

Will, Will
He makes us ill.
He read a book
Till his finger shook
And he had no ink for his quill.

Who made up that stupid verse? She can't remember.

'Will,' she says. He throws his head up, his finger pausing mid-tap.

'Patience! Sit down, sit down. How are you faring?' He bustles her into a chair.

'What happened, Will? How did I get here? Where is Sidrach?'

'Not yet, Patience. Not yet. Let me bring you something. Some wine? Something to eat. Look. Here is a broth for you. Mary made it. She's gone to the market, but we left it at a simmer. For if you woke up.'

'Was it not certain I *would* wake up?'

'Not wholly. The doctor comes and goes. Looks at you and shakes his head. Hattie, too. Quite a blow to the head you had. Such a deal of blood. Come, eat.'

She takes a few sips of the warm broth to make him happy. Then she reaches her hand up to her head, and feels the lump there, like a misshapen egg.

'Tom has not left your side,' says Will. 'Blackberry is in a rage. Called Sidrach out for a duel. Said you were his aunt and he should guard you.'

She smiles, and he grasps hold of her hand, squeezing it tight enough to make her flinch.

'Do you remember, Will, on Sunday mornings? When Father

used to gather us for bible reading? And we would laugh, and flick pellets of paper at each other behind his back.'

'You were the worst, little Patience. I remember it well. How you yawned at the begats.'

'Jeremiah begat Seremiah begat Feremiah. Lord. You laughed at the rude bits.'

They laugh now, and the pain gripes at her ribs.

'We didn't know we were in Eden,' she says.

'No. But the fall is inevitable.'

'He would catch us messing, sometimes,' she says. 'Do you remember? And he would feign a fury.'

'Make his voice deep. "Suffer the little children. Suffer, indeed."'

She eats some more of the broth. It is cooler, but warm enough to soothe. Will brings her a cup of hot spiced ale. He makes it himself, stirring and muttering. She sips at it. There is something sour at the back. She looks questioningly towards Will. 'Hattie's recipe,' he says. 'She says it will help your blood thicken, after all you have lost.'

She nods and sips some more. She shivers, and he jumps to his feet. He brings a blanket and wraps it around her shoulders.

While he is behind her, and cannot see her face, she says: 'I wanted him dead, Will. Dead.'

He comes and sits next to her. 'And yet, from what Tom tells me, you could have let him die.'

'I could not let the boy take the sin on his soul. I thought of taking it on mine. Oh Will. I was so frightened. Of him. Of dying. Of living with him. I thought to kill him myself. Oh Will. *Thou*

306

shalt not kill. Yet the sin was so deep in my skin – the wanting it, the craving it.'

'And yet, Patience. Yet. You did not kill him. All the saints in heaven would be tempted to kill that man. And you did not.'

'But what now? What now, Will?'

He looks at her dove-white skin. The tremor in her hands, and the great grey circles beneath her eyes.

'Now? Now you sleep again. And when you wake, I will have Mary draw you a bath. And then you will sleep again.'

'You will not let him in, if he comes after me?'

'By God, I will not.'

Sam is struggling to close his trunk. He pushes the lid down again, and manages to snap the catch. Riled, ready to be furious with something, he kicks the wood. He has forgotten he has not yet pulled on his boots, and he yelps.

He is still dancing about the room, swearing, when there is a sudden cough behind him.

He swirls around to face the open door, and there, to his astonishment, is Sir Edward Hyde. A lawyer turned King's right hand. They say that Charles II listens to his voice, even when others shout louder.

'Captain Challoner,' says Hyde, in a manner that is both a question and an accusation.

'Yes, Sir Edward. We have met before, if you will forgive me. After Naseby.'

'Hmm.' Hyde looks about the room. He sees a chair and moves across to it, lowering himself heavily into it. He is running to fat, Hyde. More than one chin jostles for position above his

307

collar. He takes out a handkerchief and wipes the sweat from his forehead.

'Damned hot, Challoner.'

'It is, sir.' Why is he here? Sam begins to feel a prickle of unease. Hyde is one of the king's closest advisers. He is a clever, shrewd man. It does not do to cross him. Sam has successfully avoided him.

'Have you heard of this business with Manning?' asks Hyde, in a tone that suggests he and Sam are old chums, parlaying gossip.

'The spy?'

'That's the one. The whoreson leaked the plans of the last rising to Thurloe. No wonder it was a damned damp squib.'

'What will happen to him?'

'We should hang him. But we're guests in this infernal country and they might not like it. So I fear we will have to content ourselves with banishing him from our shadow court. I would not bet on him lasting long. A bullet in the back, I shouldn't wonder.'

Sam fiddles with the lock on the trunk. He should meet the fellow's eyes, but he can't quite do it. Is he blushing? Christ, he's blushing like a nun. He manages to lift his head, look at Hyde and say: 'I would do it if the chance arose, Sir Edward.'

'Would you now?' Hyde raises an eyebrow. Sam feels the strength of the older man's scrutiny. Thurloe's voice pops into his head. 'Tittle-tattle.'

Can Hyde know? He has not supplied Thurloe with anything. Not yet.

But he is on his way to London, and a reckoning is coming. Inside the chest is the letter from Will.

. . . Forgive me for burdening you with this. But it is so pressing
and so miserable. She was near dead with the beating he gave her.
Yet Sidrach insists she returns to his house. Spouts guff about the
Bible, when it is obvious that it is his reputation he fears for. I
fight him off as best I can, while she is weak. But he has the law
on his side. We cannot afford a deed of separation, even were I to
persuade my parents that putting this marriage aside is the only
course. Oh Sam. I would that your sister were here to advise me.
She had courage enough for these battles . . .

Sam does not know what he will do when he gets there. He
only knows that he must go.

He realizes that he has been silent for some time, and Hyde
is staring at him oddly.

'Tell me about your brother-in-law,' says Hyde.

'Will Johnson? He is a good man.'

'He is a regicide. He helped kill the king.'

'Yes, but—'

'There can be no buts in this. He helped kill the king. You
stayed with him in London.'

'I did. I had little money. He offered.'

'He writes to you here.'

'How do you know that?' Will is becoming irritated by this.
Only the tethering of his conscience to that word *tittle-tattle* is
preventing him from shouting. He keeps his calm, but only just.

'I know what I know. And I also know, Captain Challoner, that
you are returning to London.'

'Just for a visit, Sir Edward. I have business.'

'You are very sure they will let you in. Why is that, I wonder?'

'What do you insinuate, sir?'

'Nothing, nothing.'

Hyde stands, pulling himself out of the chair. He moves towards the window. The small effort makes him breathless.

'Prince Rupert vouches for you,' he says, when his breathing is even.

'And so he should. I fought for him from Yorkshire to the Virgin Islands and back. And I would remind you, Sir Edward, as you seem to know me, that my father was killed by the rebels, and my sister was killed by the rebels' soldiers. My loyalty should not be questioned.'

'You would be astonished, Captain Challoner, at the number of men whose unquestionable loyalty has been bought by Thurloe. The king cannot pass wind without that man knowing of it.'

Hyde looks out of the window, towards the dull blank wall beyond. He is stalling.

'Your brother-in-law's sister.'

'Patience? What do you know of her?'

'We know her husband. Simmonds. He was here, of course. Last year. I had a number of audiences with him. An interesting fellow. Strange, is it not, how these people never question their place in the Lord's design.'

Hyde turns back into the room. 'You love your monarch, Challoner.'

Again, the statement that could be a question. Sam thinks of Charles as he last saw him. At a gaming table. His face slipping with tiredness and the bilious aftermath of too much food and drink. The curse as he was trumped. The consoling whisper of his showy mistress. Around him the sycophants dripping their barbed honey. The circling of men who have known glory, known action, but now clamour for a crumb of favour.

No, thinks Sam. I am monstrously indifferent to Charles Stuart. To the monarchy itself? That, I revere. But is this not the same question we have been fighting about for fifteen years? If not monarchy, then what? If not this monarch, then who?

Hyde is looking at him. 'Of course,' he says. He sounds stupid. Unenthusiastic. He must concentrate. 'I mean to say, my sword is his. My honour is his.'

'Your heart?'

'Sir Edward. I am a patient man. But I have a packet to catch. Is it at all possible to leave my heart aside and come instead to the blasted point?'

Hyde smiles. A chubby wolf. 'I need you to take a message to Simmonds. Tell him, now is the time. Tell him that you will smuggle him out. Afterwards.'

'After what?'

Hyde smiles again, and the sheen on his upper lip makes Sam unaccountably queasy.

'No matter. It is best you do not know.'

'And how will I smuggle him out?'

'You have smuggled in and out before. We will send a boat to Viking Bay. Thanet. You know it?'

Sam nods.

'It will heave-to offshore with the dawn each day of the first week in August. The signal is three long, two short, one long. They will send a boat onshore. Do you understand?'

Sam nods again. 'Why me?'

Hyde shrugs. 'You know the man. You are related to him by

marriage. Your meeting with him will not seem suspicious to Thurloe, who will have you followed. It is serendipitous that you are going to London. Why are you going?'

'You have read my letters. You know why.'

Hyde raises an eyebrow. He takes up his hat and makes for the door.

'Sir Edward, I have not yet agreed.'

'Captain Challoner. Your position in Cologne is entirely dependent on your relationship with the court in exile. You think Mr Shaw will continue his patronage if you are known to be out of the king's favour? He is, as I understand it, already smarting from your failure to court his daughter.'

He takes his leave, and the room is strangely cavernous in his absence. Sam feels a curious absence of rage. He sits heavily on his trunk, and raises a rueful smile as the lock catches itself. Thurloe in London; Hyde in Cologne. Somehow he is playing a double game, when he tried so hard not to play at all. But why bother with rage? Does a pawn fume at his fate? Or does he just limp forward, dumb and miserable, waiting to be sideswiped by a rook?

Sam's presence is astonishing.

He sits at Will's table, wide and vivid. Patience watches him reach for his glass, watches the way he knocks back the ale with a kind of joyous relish. She watches him reach for the cheese – how he cocks his head to catch the smell of it. He smiles to himself as he cuts a bit off.

He catches her looking at him. She would expect a grin. A comedic mime – an exaggerated munching of the cheese. Instead, their eyes lock and he looks away quickly. He frowns down at the cheese as if it needs his sole attention to prevent it flying off the table and out of the window.

Is it pity or contempt that is hammering out this distance between them? Her face is still a mess. Purple and yellow fighting for mastery. One eye still nearly closed. Oh Lord, the shame. The shame of being this woman. This battered, feeble mouse.

She stands. She has forgotten the pain that strikes her ribs, sending sparks flying through her body. She catches her breath and he turns to look at her. His face is unreadable. Oddly serious.

Will is talking, about some book he loves. He is flogging the conversation valiantly forward. But she is not listening, and she thinks Sam is not either. Eventually Will stutters to a halt.

Into the great silence between them, Sam says: 'I have something to tell you both. I wrestled with it all the way here. Should I tell you?' His voice is sombre.

'Will,' he says. 'Even knowing this could put your life in danger. And yours, Patience. But it touches you both.'

'A pox on my life,' she says, in a whisper.

'Sir Edward Hyde came to see me. Before I returned to London. I was told to help Sidrach Simmonds in some unspecified endeavour that will help the king. Charles Stuart, I mean. Then I must help to smuggle him to Cologne, afterwards.'

Will and Patience glance at each other. Will looks as if he has been slapped. 'Endeavour?' he says. 'What, for all love?'

'I do not know,' says Sam.

'I do, I think,' says Patience. 'He means to attack Cromwell. The Antichrist, as he would have it. He means to kill him.'

Will looks even more flabbergasted. But Sam just nods. This was his conclusion.

'But why Sidrach?' Will looks between the two of them.

'It suits Charles Stuart's party. Better Sidrach than a Royalist. If he succeeds, the monarch's hands are not tainted. It is a fallout among allies. A Puritan scrap.'

'And Sidrach can get close to him. Through you,' says Patience.

'Jesus,' says Will in a whisper. 'Jesus wept. What will we do?'

The question is unresolved the next morning when Patience awakes in Will's bed. Below, Will and Sam sleep on trestles by the ashes of the fire. Perhaps they arrived at a neat solution after she went to bed. But she doubts it. Some questions can be worried at endlessly and never settled.

Leave Sidrach to it? If he succeeds, Blackberry will grow up in an England sliding towards chaos and blood again. Even if he fails, the violence of the state's revenge could fall on Patience, and perhaps too on Sam and Will. And Blackberry. Cromwell's men will winkle Sam's involvement from somewhere. They will torture it out of Sidrach.

Tell one of Cromwell's advisors? They have no proof. No means of knowing about the plot that does not cast Sam in a suspicious light.

He must be free to return to Cologne, to the capital he has accrued there, to the life he has begun to carve for himself. But Sam is caught between a noose and a lee shore, as he said last night, grinning despite himself. Dear Sam. She pauses on the thought of him, on the flare of regret that he came to London on Hyde's orders, not for her sake as she had thought yesterday afternoon when the door opened and he bounced into the house. Whirled in, a riot of noise and laughter. And then he saw her bruises and stopped, pale suddenly and awkward.

She pushes back the blanket and sits upright. She pulls back the curtain around the bed to let the light in, and hugs her knees to her chest. Sunlight fills the quiet room. It lights on a corner of the blanket, picking out the gold and making it gleam. It was a wedding present from her parents to Will and Henrietta.

She thinks of their wedding and how happy they were. She thinks of her own wedding.

The revelation comes to her suddenly. There is only one answer to their dilemma. Sam and Will probably knew it last night, but were too kind to say it. They must think she is dense, or a coward.

Sidrach must be trapped in the act, with no hint of contrivance from Sam. He must be caught, and Sam, blameless on all sides, must return to Cologne alone. The only escape from their trap is to spring it back on Sidrach.

But they cannot trap Sidrach without knowing his plans. And there is only one way to weasel those from him. She must go back to him. God help her. God save her. She must go back.

LONDON

August 1655

'IT WILL NOT HAPPEN AGAIN, WILL,' SAYS SIDRACH. HE TALKS past Patience, towards her brother. He is all smiles. All genial warmth. 'It was that boy's fault. The confounded boy.'

'Yes,' says Will. He is smiling back, but his eyes are dark and cold. Tom is upstairs. He was shaken when he understood that Sidrach was coming here. That Patience was returning to him. They could not explain why it was happening, this unthinkable surrender, and he looked at her with a silent plea. His hands were trembling and jumping. He wept, and ran from the room. She did not follow – what could she say to make this better?

Her brother will look after him. Poor Tom.

'We have not seen Tom since that night,' says Will to Sidrach. 'He has disappeared.'

'It is not surprising. The cheek of it. The impudence. The damned nerve of the boy, pulling a knife out. Threatening me in my own house.'

She tenses, hearing the rage swelling in his voice. But Will is here, and Sidrach only retreats from his anger. He smiles.

Asks Will about his work. Makes a genial uncle comment about Blackberry. He enquires about the boy's breeching.

This. This is what makes her most furious. He can control his anger. He can, as most adults do, take a breath, swallow down his fury and act as a civilized human being would. But only when other people are watching. Other men.

If he can contain himself, if he can be polite in the face of provocation, why not with her?

She feels strong, suddenly. As if this revelation, and her secret knowledge of his plans, is enough to make her shoulders broader, her mind sharper. She knows, too, that there will be an ending. That the misery of her marriage has a finite span left. She might die – he might kill her.

At least if I die, it will be over. Death as a full stop. She smiles at the absurdity of her logic. Sam would like the joke.

Sidrach catches her smiling, and his face darkens. Quailing inside a little, she grins wider, forcing herself into a smile of wide joy, which unsettles him. His platitudes to Will fade to a stutter. Her smile is true now, feeding off his disquiet.

'Well,' he says. He looks back towards Will. He clears his throat. He is off balance. 'We will be off. Back home with my lovely wife. A new start.'

He ushers her out. His hand is on the small of her back. She can feel it there through the layers of fabric. She looks back at Will.

'I will see you soon, Patience,' he says. 'Soon.'

Outside, the heat is fierce. She feels prickles of sweat breaking out down her back as they walk. The sun is bright in her eyes and she squints painfully. It casts its muting glare on the street, drawing the stink from the ground. Cats and barefoot children mug the shade. The pie man is sweating and puce under his makeshift awning. London is not good at bearing heat.

The smell of the meat juice meets the street stench, and Patience feels sick suddenly. She feels the gorge rising in her throat, and swallows it down, clasping her hands into fists.

They are silent as they walk. She sees a rat worrying at something bloody in the shadows of Grope Alley. It seems less like dinner, and more like a fight the rat might lose. Her sense of broadening out, of courage, has receded. She is, instead, pleasingly numb. The world is a patina to her; she cannot be moved by its sights or sounds. By its terrors or threats.

Sidrach clears his throat beside her, and she tenses. Her fists ball tighter, and she feels her spine curve, her shoulders hunch inwards.

'Patience, I was obviously displeased,' he says slowly, picking at his words. 'Your antipathy when that boy was threatening me. Your failure to intervene. And letting him go. Letting him go! What were you thinking?'

They walk on, turning into the familiar street. She sees the dark windows of the house, barricaded against the heat. She knows already that it will be damply gloomy inside. She knows the heavy ticking of the clock. The background silence in the corridors that makes floorboards creak and doors whine and his breathing sound loud as a death rattle.

She stays silent. His question is, she is sure, rhetorical.

They pause at the steps to the front door. The wood is so dark a brown it could be black, and it catches the sunlight and keeps it hostage.

'But. I was, perhaps, a little severe in my chastisement. I pride myself, Patience, on being a calm man. A man of intellect. I am God's chosen, and I have a duty to behave with forbearance, even to those who do not always merit it.'

There is a movement at a window above them. Patience looks up, shielding her eyes against the sun.

'I have lured Sarah back,' he says.

The door opens, and there she is. Straight-backed and severe. Her hair is pulled tightly back, with none of the fashionable loose tendrils that smack of frivolity. 'Master,' she says, bobbing to Sidrach. She ignores Patience, and for a moment it seems as if she will bar the way, square-hipped and furious. But she draws back and they walk in.

Panic rises in Patience. It flip-flops inside her chest like a dying fish.

Courage. What is the worst he can do?

The door smacks shut behind her.

Sidrach is quiet over dinner. Contemplative. His chewing is loud and it shreds her nerves. She cannot eat; she mangles the meat and prods the vegetables into disorder, hoping that this will disguise her telltale lack of appetite.

Sarah clears the last of the dishes. She is rough with Patience's plate, and a crest of unwanted parsley sauce spills over. It stains Patience's cuff; the startling green of it will be hard to shift.

Patience is staring at it, distracted by it, when Sidrach begins to speak.

'I begged your pardon earlier,' he says.

No. No you did not quite do that, she thinks. But she inclines her head as if in acceptance of an apology.

'My father,' begins Sidrach. He pauses. 'I do not speak often of my father. He beat my mother when she did wrong. I did not mean . . .' He stutters to a pause, reaching for his glass.

'It is no matter, Sidrach,' she says. 'It was my fault. I provoked you.'

'Yes. You did. And yet I believed that you were dead. That I had killed you. That, at least, you had not deserved. Thou shalt not kill, said the Lord. And I very nearly disobeyed him. Believe me, Patience. I have begged His pardon until my throat is raw.'

When he pauses again, she hears the unnatural silence of the house. The menacing stillness. At home, before she came to London, there was never silence. Someone was always laughing or crying or shrieking.

'I pray for a child,' says Sidrach. 'I have prayed. He has not answered.'

'His ways are deep.'

'Yes. Perhaps it is this place, this England. How can we be blessed when we do not do His work? It is, perhaps, a sign. That we must work harder for Him, for His coming. Push forward. Find courage.'

She makes a non-committal noise. She fills his glass, taking care not to spill any drops.

'It may be, Patience, that I have to go abroad. In haste, perhaps. I will send for you.'

'When, Sidrach?'

'Did I not just say? In haste. I do not know exactly when.'

'I beg pardon, Sidrach.'

'Well, no harm. Soon, I think. I must convert some of our possessions into ready money. To start again elsewhere. Somewhere in the Palatine, or the Netherlands. Among godly folk. Perhaps even in America. Would that please you, my dear? America!'

'I would be happy with whatever pleases you.'

America! She cannot conceive of it.

There is a sudden knocking at the door. They sit in silence, waiting for Sarah's head to peer round into the dining room. 'I beg your pardon, sir. There's a Captain Samuel Challoner here. Begging to see you, urgent. So he says.'

Patience hangs on to the table. She looks down at her plate to hide her face.

'You will excuse me, my dear,' he says.

He leaves the room and she stays sitting there, hanging on as if she might fall. She unclenches her hand from the table's edge and reaches for her glass. A small sip to steady her. She twirls the glass round and round, watching the red wine through the distorting crystal. She picks at the green stain on her cuff. She watches the flicker of the candlelight. One candle is nearly burned down to its nub. He is mean about many things, her husband, but not the light. He likes good-quality wax – light enough to read the Bible by.

The wax pools in the lip of its holder. She watches the little flame fight for life as it slides down into the liquid heat.

'Patience.' She jumps; his voice is loud and sudden behind her. Turning, she expects to see Sam, but he is not there. Only Sidrach, standing in the doorway. He walks forward. His face is white.

'Captain Challoner did not stay?'

'No. He . . . he came with a message for me. Nothing for you to concern yourself with, my dear.'

He sits down. He seems diminished, somehow. As if he is being pressed downwards and inwards by some unseen force. He tries for a smile, but it falters on his lips. She can see the child in him suddenly. An unexpected swell of pity hits her.

What happened to him? What failure to love or be loved created Sidrach Simmonds? She fights the pity. Remember what he did. Remember who he is.

'It is done,' says Sam. He sits heavily into the chair. 'Hyde's message delivered. My help pledged. The shy bastard turned white.'

'You think he will do it?'

'He said little. It is a game for quiet fellows, this. Perhaps that is why I am so poor at it. I must see Thurloe.'

'Thurloe? Why?'

Sam sighs. He looks at Will. Can he trust him? Maybe yes, maybe no. What to do? He decides with a firmness learned on campaign. Maybe he cannot trust Will. But he must believe in a world with trust in it. He must believe that Will can put his loyalty to his brother-in-law above his loyalty to the state.

So he tells Will about Thurloe and his request for tittle-tattle. About his failure, so far, to comply. About the reckoning that must come if he is working in theory for both Thurloe and Hyde – and in practice for neither.

'I would be left alone, Will. Left alone.'

Will is thoughtful. He sips his coffee – strange, bitter stuff he downs in gallons. He has taught the boy Tom to prepare it, in a drawn-out ritual of roasting and grinding, sizzling and boiling.

He says it makes him vibrant. Makes him see clearer. Sam cannot stomach it.

'Sam, you must give Thurloe something. I know the man. He is not easily fooled. It would not do for you to be arrested now.'

'I know. I will think of something. Gossip from the court. I will tell him of Manning's arrest – he may not yet know of that.'

Will is silent for moment. He looks at Sam with an inscrutable face, and then leans in to speak quietly. 'Sam. You will not use this affair for the sake of Charles Stuart? You will not engineer it so that Sidrach succeeds?'

'My first aim is to protect Patience. To rid her of that man.'

'Aye, but your second aim?'

'I have not been thinking of it,' Sam lies. He knows that Will must know it is a lie. It is too feeble to be true.

'Will,' he says. 'There must be candour between us. I love your sister. With all that I have. Do not doubt me. She is what matters in this. Cromwell and Stuart? Both may hang, for all I care.'

Will nods, as if Sam has told him something he already knows. Perhaps he does. 'His death will not bring back the king, Sam. His death will bring bloodshed and misery. None of us would thank you – not I, not Blackberry. And certainly not Patience.'

Slowly, the days pass. Patience settles into a remembered pattern. There is not always comfort in familiarity, she finds.

She patters around the house trying to avoid Sarah and Sidrach. She watches Sidrach's face, trying to anticipate the growling that heralds a storm.

She is a watcher of runes, of omens. A soul-shifter who wraps her own moods around his. She must be nimble, relentlessly vigilant. Any inattention can pull the wrath down upon her aching head. It is exhausting. In the evenings, she pretends to read the Bible next to him. Eyes open, she uses the silence as a cover for still, secret thoughts.

She thinks of Sam. Of Will and Blackberry. Of her parents and her sisters. Each enumeration of people she loves is a small victory, a small recovery of herself from the shadow who pads through this house.

Sometimes she thinks of the slim pity she felt for her husband on the night she returned. He has slowly pressed it out of her, like a mangle working the linen. Every glower, every snap, every tut is a fresh press. A fresh wring of that compassionate sliver.

The nights. Oh, Lord Jesus, the nights. Her absence has pepped his passion. Either that or he is determined to get her with child.

Lord. Lord Jesus, she prays as he grinds on top of her. Lord, let me not bear his child. Lord, let me not bear his child.

They sit at the table one morning. His slow, determined chewing makes her stomach turn. A side of soft and creamy cheese sits between them. He moves to cut another slice of bread, and swivels to look at her as she says: 'Husband?'

'Yes, my dear?'

'I think I will visit Will and Blackberry, after we have eaten.'

'You will not.'

'But—'

The knife slams to the table.

'Your brother knows altogether too much about our family. I will not have him laughing at us.'

'Sidrach, I am sure he does not laugh. I know he does not.'

'You will not contradict me, Patience. Every time I open my mouth, you rush in to contradict. Is that the proper duty you owe to me? Oh, the sin of Eve, Patience. Did she not contradict the Lord's wishes? I say again, he laughs at us. And if I say so, it is so.'

He picks up the knife. Half a slice hangs limply from the loaf. It will be difficult to cut the full slice straight now. He looks at her, furious. The bread is her fault too. She can see that he is fraying. She knows that she should not tug at the unravelling ends of his temper.

And yet. Sometimes the strains of submitting are worse than the consequences of dissent.

'I would see him,' she says softly. 'He is my brother.'

'And I am your husband.'

He grabs at her wrist and turns it upwards. She stares at the scrabble of blue veins underneath her white skin.

Slowly he presses the knife to her wrist, letting the jagged edges of it nick her skin. He licks his lips; leans in a little closer.

'You will learn to obey me, Patience. I will not be forced to correct you again.'

He pushes the knife a little deeper. It breaks the skin, drawing blood that swells into beads, like a bracelet of tiny rubies.

'I could cut now. I could cut and cut. The Lord would thank me for unburdening myself of you. I have great work to do for Him. Great work. I am His servant. And you are a distraction. I thought I needed your brother for this great work. Therefore I thought I needed you. But I do not need you, Patience. Do you hear me?'

She is a statue. A frozen woman with a bleeding wrist. He grips her fingers together, and bends them back, so that her wrist arches towards the knife. Cut me. The pain is not so bad. Not as bad as the voice in her ear, the breath on her neck, the nearness of him.

'The world would think you had done it to yourself. Poor stupid Patience. Had to kill herself. Had to give up. She was damned anyway. How could such a fool be elect?'

His voice is throaty and dark; just as she remembers it from that first time she saw him. When his charisma blocked out the street on the day the sun vanished, and she leaped two-footed into his path.

His voice is a velvet threat. He moves even closer, his lips brushing her earlobe.

'And who would miss you, little wife, if I cut now? No one would know it was not you. No one but the Lord. He sees into your heart. He knows you for a cold, barren bitch.'

There is a waft of chill air, which freezes them still. Sarah has opened the door and is backing into the kitchen holding on to two full pails of water.

Sidrach drops the knife. But he is still close to her; he is still holding on to her hand.

'Excuse me, sir,' says Sarah, as she turns and sets down the pails heavily. Water slops to the floor. She looks at them both, clearly wrong-footed by their peculiar closeness.

'No matter, no matter,' he says, with a wide smile. He stands, and puts his napkin on his plate.

'Well then, my dear,' he says to Patience, with a bullish brightness. 'You are to stay here this day. I am glad of it. The silver needs a polish, if you are in want of a job.'

LONDON

September 1655

*P*ATIENCE IS SO STILL, SHE CAN HEAR THE BEAT OF HER own heart.

She presses herself back against the wall, listening to the quiet of the house. The silence that settles on the stair treads, on the wooden floors, in the dead eyes of the portraits of dead Simmonds men.

She shuffles sideways, her hand reaching for the doorknob. It is cold to the touch, shockingly so on this sweltering day. The sun's light cannot find its way inside, but its heat pushes through the thick walls. The sweat is slick on her skin – although where the punishment of the heat ends and the fear begins, she cannot tell.

The click of the door's opening ricochets through the house. She stands and listens to it, trying to still her thumping heart by will alone.

She finds the energy to laugh at herself as she slides backwards into the room as if she is being watched. She is only entering his study because they are both out and she is alone, for once, in the house. So this scuttling is absurd. Still, she cannot help it.

Inside, it smells of him. It reeks of his presence. The joyless books stacked just so. The bible open on his desk. The knife he uses to sharpen his quills glinting at her. The chair turned towards the door, so he can listen for her misdemeanours even as he pretends to work.

She moves towards the desk, not sure what she is looking for. She pulls out the drawers, appalled by the booming scraping sound. Inside the very bottom drawer there is a case. She lifts it out and unlatches the catch. She knows before she opens the lid what she will find there. A pair of dark, long-barrelled pistols.

The knowing is not enough to stop her panicking. She lets the lid fall with a violent clang. As she moves to put the box back where she found it, she spots a paper lining the bottom of the drawer. She pulls it out. It is some sort of legal document; a lease, she thinks. Relating to a set of rooms above an inn – the sign of the Bird in Westminster. Near the Holbein Gate. She has not been in, but she knows it. It is not the type of place where a woman like her belongs.

Nor a man like Sidrach.

Before she has time to think, she hears a noise. A thumping. She pushes the paper back flat into the drawer, and sits the case of pistols on top. Darting to the door of his study, she sidles out into the corridor.

Her breathing is too loud. She can't hear above its jagged wheeze. She fights for calm. She is entitled to be in the corridor. She is safe.

Safe. A strange word to use in this house, she thinks.

The noises come from the kitchen, and she makes her way there slowly.

Sarah is back, and with her is the girl from the butcher's shop. Anne. Hattie the woman-butcher's girl-apprentice. Patience smiles at her, and Anne grins back.

'Sausages,' she says, holding up the packages she is carrying.

'Thank you, Anne,' says Patience. She turns to leave the kitchen, but a thought catches her suddenly.

'Sarah,' she says. 'I've a yearning for strawberries. Could you go for me?'

'Now?' Sarah says. She puts her hands on her thin hips. 'Can it not wait?'

'No, it cannot. And Sidrach is not keen for me to leave the house today.' Patience borrows her mother's sharp servant-berating voice. It seems to work. Sarah looks sour, but she unwraps her apron. She makes to shoo little Anne out of the door, but Patience stops her.

'Wait. I have a job for Anne. You go, and I will talk to her.'

Sarah opens her mouth to protest, but something in her mistress's face warns her not to. Patience waits for the door to close before she moves closer to Anne.

'Should you like to earn a penny, Anne?'

'Yes, missus.'

'Well then. You must go to the house of my brother Will. You know him?'

'Of course. My mother is friends with him.'

'You must give him this message. Tell him I am safe, but Oliver is not. There are pistols. Tell him I am not allowed to leave the house. Tell him I am watching. Do you have that?'

'You are safe. Oliver is not. Pistols. Not allowed to leave. Watching.' The girl's large blue eyes are solemn.

'Good girl. Tell him I said to give you a penny. And you must find reasons to come here to pass messages back and forth. Can you do that?' Anne nods.

As she runs off, Patience feels an intense relief. There is now a slender, girl-shaped link between her and Will. And Sam.

'How was Thurloe?' Will asks the question gently, noting Sam's lack of verve and the nervous tapping of his foot upon the floor.

'He was . . .' Sam pauses, 'exacting.'

'Dear fellow,' says Will, cutting a slice of Mary's veal pie and offering it up. 'Do not take it to heart. We must all make our compromises with power.'

'Oh, I did not tell him much. I do not know much. I am very much on the fringes. But he probed, and I spilled what I did know, and I wonder if I let slip something, something that could be problematic.'

'Do you care so very much about Charles Stuart?'

'Him, no. But Prince Rupert? Oh yes. And those poor bastards sitting out there in Europe wanting to come home, trying to do right, cleaving to their cause. My erstwhile brothers. And now, I wonder, what am I? Who am I, Will?'

'You are a good man. A loyal man.'

But Sam just waves a despairing arm, and takes a bite of pie as if to buy time.

'Peace makes the world so blasted complicated. Cromwell's death would—' he begins to say as he swallows, and then he sees Will's face and he stops talking again.

They turn with relief to the door, which opens to Hattie and the girl Anne. Anne is pushed forward towards them, and she says in a sudden blurt, 'I seen Patience. Mrs Simmonds, that is. I seen her.'

The next day, Thursday, Anne creeps into the kitchen. Patience is sitting at the table polishing Sidrach's silver. The eyes that stare at her from the shiny metal are hooded and tired.

Anne looks around for Sarah, but seeing only Patience, she advances more confidently.

'He sends love, missus,' she says in a rush, as if to make sure she is getting the words right. 'And he says Sam has had word. He is to be at Whitehall steps. Tomorrow, missus.'

As Anne speaks, the answer clicks in Patience's mind. She curses herself for her slowness. Her stupidity.

'Listen, Anne. Go to Will. Tell him—'

The girl's eyes widen suddenly, and she looks behind Patience towards the door. Sidrach's voice, harsh and loud: 'Be gone, girl. No messages. Go.'

Anne looks at Patience in a mute plea for advice. Patience, her heart sinking to her toes, nods at her. Tries to smile. 'Go then, Anne. My dear love to my brother, that is all.'

Anne spins and flees from the room.

Patience watches the door close behind her. She hears Sidrach approaching, and she closes her stinging eyes.

'Tell me again, Anne,' says Will.

'Then he came in and told me to go. Seemed cross, he did, sir.'

Sam is pacing the room. His furious glances at Anne are scaring the child, and her voice falters.

Will gives Anne a penny, and she bobs her thanks. Before she has left the room, Sam is shouting: 'We must get her out, Will! We must go there!'

'And do what, Sam? We need to finish this thing.'

'What if he kills her?'

'He will not. How can he build God's kingdom on earth if he hangs for her?'

'It is too great a risk.'

'Patience begged us to trust her, remember? And she told Anne she was safe. Tomorrow, Sam. Tomorrow it will be over.'

'But we know nothing. Meet at Whitehall steps with a hired boat, he says. Horses waiting at Ratcliffe, beyond the Tower. No more than that. Barely a time.'

Will, sober now for weeks, thinks with mounting urgency of the balm in the bottom of a bottle. I need a clear head, he thinks. Concentrate, he thinks.

'Listen, Sam. The world knows that Cromwell leaves Westminster in a carriage for Hampton Court on a Friday. And tomorrow, this Friday, you are to meet Simmonds at the steps there with a boat. The coincidence is too bald. He will make his attempt.'

'But where from? The bastard does not trust me.'

'Nor should he.'

'True.' Sam pauses to smile, briefly, at Will.

'Courage, Sam. It is nearly over.'

The darkness is absolute.

It has crept under her skin. She has strange fancies that if she were to cut herself, she would bleed black blood. There is a madness lurking close. She senses it.

Her eyes are closed. In her head there is sunshine. There are sparkles on river spray. Light – beautiful golden, velvet light – flickers between the branches of trees.

It is hot down here in the cellar. She cannot concentrate on her mind's eye, and she loses focus. Panic rises. She feels the tremor in hands she cannot see.

Focus.

Sam's face, smiling. Blackberry pretending to be a rabbit, hop-hopping through autumn leaves. Her father sleeping, slack with beef and port.

She tries to sleep, conjuring the ones she loves best as guardian angels. But the darkness is absolute and the door is locked and Patience's angels cannot protect her now.

Sam sits in the damp bow of the boat. The oarsmen have tried to pass pleasantries with him, but his curtness has deterred them. The rise and bob of the vessel surges suddenly, and stinking Thames water crests over the gunwales and splashes his trousers.

He swears.

The older oarsman glances at the other, who clears his throat and says: 'Much longer, sir?'

'I've told you. I do not know. You are being paid for your time.'

'Tide'll turn soon, sir. If you want to shoot the bridge, we needs be off.'

'Wait, damn you.'

He looks to the top of the steps. Should he trust Will with this? Will has never been a soldier. They need to find Simmonds.

Will, loitering near the Holbein Gate, realizes that he has been a complete fool. He thought he would just see Simmonds. Follow him, then fetch Sam to help accost him and have him arrested. But as he looks upwards at the dense overhang of the houses backing on to the street, it becomes clear to him that the man could be anywhere.

Soon – in fifteen minutes, perhaps – Cromwell will come through that gate. He is in a meeting with the Council of State, and Will prepared the order papers. It will not last much longer, he judges. The sunlight has lost its glare, become more comfortable.

He will be unaware of the danger, Will's beloved, difficult chief. Leaning back into his coach seat with relief. Mrs Cromwell beside him, her small hand resting in his. The great craggy face breaking into a smile at the thought of two days at his adored Hampton Court. There will be music, there will be good wine. Perhaps hawking, if he can find the energy in this enervating heat.

But somewhere in these dense shadows lurks Simmonds, who thinks that he can remake the world with one bullet. That his righteousness is a divine command. And Will does not know how to find him.

Sam appears beside him, making his overheated heart jump.

'Sam. How are we to find him?'

Sam looks at the burling mill of people. The overhanging windows.

'I will look,' he says. 'Stay here.'

'Sam. In fifteen minutes, if we haven't found him, I will have to warn Cromwell. Stop this thing.'

Both of them are thinking of Patience and her shackles. And

of an England without a king again, and the torrent of blood that will rush to fill the king-shaped hole.

Footsteps.

Patience presses her ear to the door. Splinters jag at her face.

It doesn't sound like Sidrach. Even if it is him, she cannot bear it in here any longer. Daylight brought some relief, in the slight lightening of the dark. Thank the Lord for that thin line of light under the bottom of the door. But she is thirsty and hungry. She is bored of the constant, dragging fear. Things scuttle in the darkness at the bottom of the steps.

She sits at the top, right by the door. How long has she been in here? At least one night and most of one day.

She must get out before darkness falls again. She must.

'Help!' she croaks with her parched voice. 'Help me.'

She hears the footsteps come closer, and pause.

'Oh please,' she says. 'Please let me out.'

The sound of a lock being turned. The creaking open of the door, which fills the cellar with light. Beautiful, painful light. She squints against its glare to make out a small, unfamiliar shape.

'Missus? Missus, is that you?'

Anne, the butcher girl. In her blood-smeared apron, with the hovering smell about her of sage and thyme.

Will, slumped against the wall under the sign of the Bird, which creaks and moans above his head, looks through the open doors of the gate to where Cromwell's carriage is waiting. The horses are bridled and impatient. The coachman has donned his hat and is clambering stiffly up on to his tall seat.

The Lord Protector's lifeguards are ranging themselves up, ready for inspection by their captain. Will can't make out their faces from here, but he watches the routine of checking kit and squaring shoulders.

God's bones.

Sam appears next to him.

'Nothing,' he says.

Will turns to look into his face. 'I must go to warn Cromwell.'

'If Sid's here,' says Sam, 'he will have seen us together now. Me with you. And if you warn Cromwell, Sid will know that we are in this thing together.'

'Yes.'

Sam shakes his head. They do not need to articulate the obvious fact that he will be a traitor to both sides. Thurloe will know that he was abetting Simmonds. Hyde will know he colluded in warning Cromwell. Both sides will condemn Sam Challoner.

I cannot go back to Cologne. I cannot stay here. I am in limbo.

He feels a moment of vertigo. A strange sensation that sends him reaching for the solidity of the wall behind him.

'I will go to Patience. Get there first and try to persuade her to run with me,' he says.

'She will not go, Sam. It is too great a sin to ask of her.'

'I must try.'

'And I must warn Cromwell. I am sorry, Sam.'

Sam laughs suddenly. 'God's blood, Will. Am I to sacrifice my future for that warty old whoreson? What fools fate makes of us.'

'Aye.'

Behind them they hear the barking of commands and the neighing of a horse. Will pulls Sam into a close embrace.

'Go well, my brother.'

'And you.'

Will feels a new hand on his shoulder, and a voice that cracks and trembles cries: 'You are here!'

They spin to look at Patience – a dishevelled red face, smeared with coal. A wildness in her eyes.

'He is here! Up there.' She points above the sign and they look upwards, as if he will be there floating above their heads. A spectral demon.

'Come. Follow!' she shouts.

Will looks back briefly, to see the large, ungainly shape of his chief walking towards his coach through a corridor of soldiers. Patience and Sam push through the doors of the inn, looking for the stairs.

'You have rooms upstairs?' she says to the potboy, who gawps at her.

'Where, boy?' says Sam, grabbing his shoulder. The youngster, frightened, points to the side of the room, where a door is closed.

'Will. Stay. Watch Cromwell.' Sam's officer's voice is strong and implacable.

Will nods, and Sam runs to the door, pushing against it. It stays closed.

'This is the only way?'

'There's stairs at the back, sir. Towards the river. But, sir, you cannot. I mean, Mr Powell is up there. He pays for privacy, sir.'

Sam ignores the boy's bleating. He steps back and charges the door, which buckles and snaps against his weight.

'Stay here,' he shouts to Patience. But she is damned if she will be told to stay put, now at the end of it all, and she follows him up the narrow stairs. The two of them are close together as they bundle through the door at the top.

A room, sparsely furnished. A canopied bed, and crude paintings on the walls of mythical creatures glumly copulating. A stale, hot smell.

And at the end, Sidrach. His back is to them. He is crouching by the low window. The pane is cocked open, and light spills inwards on to the dusty floor.

As they crash into the room, he turns, opening his body towards them. She sees the ugly bulk of the pistol resting on the sill of the window.

He is rising then, with a face of fury and the pistol in an outstretched hand, turning, turning it towards them so that Patience can see the mouth in its barrel – wide open and ready to spit.

'You bitch,' says Sidrach, scarcely noticing Sam. All his rage and spite crunch into his voice.

She looks into the open mouth of the pistol. She teeters. She looks beyond the metal to the snarl of his face above it. The world slows enough for her to wonder why he hates her so much.

Sam, shielded by Sidrach's hatred for her, is already lunging across the room, his sword out and leaping for Sidrach's wrist. He slashes, and the pistol falls to the floor. Beside it, lying palm up on the wooden boards, is Sidrach's unfurled fist.

Sidrach stands, stupid, looking at the blood fountaining from his wrist. At the missing space where his hand should be. Then he screams, and his face is a wide, contorted horror, and the sound is something demonic, something not of this world. Sam stoops to grab the pistol, and as he does so, he looks out of the window.

There, framed exactly, is the Holbein Gate. And out of the gate comes the carriage.

Below him, he sees the top of Will's head. Will looks up towards the window and Sam shrinks back. There is no sign of recognition in Will's eyes as he drops his chin and moves out of sight, towards the door of the inn.

Behind him, Sam can hear Sidrach sobbing with pain and Patience crying. The carriage is moving forward, beginning its sweeping turn. As it circles, Sam finds himself bringing the pistol around to bear.

Along the long muzzle, he looks through the open window of the carriage directly at the unmistakable profile of Oliver Cromwell. His hat is off. He is mopping his forehead with a startling white kerchief. Beyond him is the dim outline of Mrs Cromwell. Sam regards Cromwell with astonishment. The raggle of shoulder-length hair. The nose that seems a parody of itself. So large, so insistently Cromwellian.

He gazes down the long line of the pistol in his hand, and feels his finger quiver on the trigger. He imagines, for a heady, trembling second, returning to Cologne as the man who killed Cromwell. He thinks of his dead father, and his sister, and his brother; and the ceaseless roll call of his comrades with their souls ripped hellwards and their corpses rotting from Marston Moor to Worcester.

And yet. What price revenge?

Will runs up the stairs. His own sword is in his hands and he follows the screams. Outside, he saw the soldiers suddenly alert, listening as the noise filled the street. He saw the captain of Cromwell's lifeguard snap orders at the sergeant.

He must get to the others before the soldiers do. Help them. He can hear sounds from the top of the stairs. But he cannot work out whose scream it is. It is high-pitched, insistent. Behind him, the inn's customers cluster at the foot of the steps, looking upwards with nervous prurience. Good. They will slow down the soldiers.

'Keep back,' he roars down at them as he runs up the stairs. 'Back!'

At the top, the door is already open, and he rushes in.

Sam is standing at the window, looking into the room, holding the pistol limply at one side.

Sidrach is on his knees, screaming, holding the bloodied stump of an arm to his chest.

Patience glances towards Will. He sees her white face, and the blood smears on her cheek. He does not know whose blood. But no matter.

He leaps forward with barely a pause, turns his sword point-first and thrusts it into Sidrach's throat, so the screams becomes a gurgle and he crumples to the floor.

He can hear soldiers shouting somewhere, and Patience's voice saying: 'He's dead, he's dead.'

'Run, Sam. The other stairs.'

Sam pauses. He nods. 'I did not shoot,' he says, and Will does not understand the words, nor the bemused look on Sam's face. 'Sid,' says Sam. 'Blame me for Sid, Will.' He runs towards the back of the room.

Patience feels Will pull her into a tight embrace. She hears him whisper. 'If there is a sin, it is my sin. Mine. Do you hear me?'

'Yes. Yes.'

She is crying, she thinks, and retching. The blood is pooling on to the floor. And she is free. Free! But her freedom is drenched in too much blood, too much.

Sam looks at her from the door, as she kneels on the floor and pulls Will closer, and he opens his mouth to say something. But then he is gone, and she hears the thunder of soldiers coming up the stairs. And she looks at Sidrach's empty black eyes and waits for the Lord's judgement to strike her exultant heart.

WHITEHALL, LONDON

September 1655

'WILL!' SAYS CROMWELL, LOOKING UP FROM THE PILES of paper on his desk. A smile to light a room, still. But a dulled light.

Will bows. Rising, he pushes his hair from his eyes.

'A sad business, this,' says Cromwell.

He gestures to the cluster of men around him; men whose faces Will does not even recognize. They file out on the command. One pauses at the door, an unspoken objection on his jowly, smug face. Cromwell raises a bushy eyebrow and he scuttles out.

When the door has clicked shut, he says: 'Your own brother-in-law. Thurloe has told me. A pity he died.'

Will manages to pull a contrite face.

'We could have questioned him. The plot thickens. Thickens, Will.'

He stands and walks to the window. Outside, they can see the grey huddle of London in the rain. The soft patter and smear of the drops on the window. 'You must come out to Hampton Court. Bring your boy, Will. He would love it.'

'He would. We breech him tomorrow.'

'So soon! I will tell Mrs Cromwell. She will rouse out a present for him.'

'No need, Your Highness.'

Cromwell turns back to him. 'Will, given the circumstances . . .' He falters.

'I have already informed Thurloe,' says Will quickly, 'that I would prefer, given the circumstances, to return to private practice of law.'

'Good man,' says Cromwell. 'You always were a good man. I am sure we can put business of state in your path.'

'Thank you.'

Cromwell pauses. Will wonders if he should leave. He begins gathering himself to head out, but the Lord Protector starts to speak again. 'Thurloe thinks we should proclaim your brother-in-law's plotting. Use it. We are formulating a plan to put the major generals in direct charge in the provinces. Some may not like it. But there are enemies everywhere, Will. We need to be vigilant.'

'Yes, Lord Protector.'

'There is your sister's good name, of course. He has no other relatives?'

'No.'

'I met him, did I not? A fine-looking man. Intransigent.'

'He was certainly a man of decided opinions, Lord Protector.'

Cromwell nods. Behind him, the rain still spatters the glass. Will thinks of Blackberry's breeching in the morning. After, if the rain holds off, he will take the boy beyond the walls. He has begun asking questions. Why does the moon follow me? Where do the stars go in the daytime?

They will lie, as Will and Henrietta once did, and look at the stars from beneath a blanket. They will talk of the moon, and where the stars go in the daytime. Tomorrow will be a good day, thinks Will. Tomorrow I will let others toast the boy's health and I will avoid the wine.

'I think then we will keep this business quiet. I do not want to give the Fifth Monarchists more reasons to hate me. They seem to have enough already. We have put it about that he died in an altercation with a Royalist. Also your brother-in-law, I understand. He has gone back to Cologne?'

'Yes, Lord Protector.'

'Useful that he has left. It will be better for him, too, if this business keeps out of the way of Nedham's pen. I don't doubt they would hang and quarter him in Cologne for preventing my assassination.'

'That is very true, Your Highness. He is safer if the story is quiet.'

'How strange are His ways. A Royalist, one of Rupert's own, stopping a bullet meant for my heart.'

He pauses, and raises his eyes heavenwards. 'Strange,' he says again. 'Why did he not let Simmonds shoot, Will? Thurloe was unclear on that.'

Will considers telling the truth. 'He wants an England at peace, Your Highness. He has suffered a surfeit of war. And he believes you to be the best bulwark against disorder.'

Cromwell nods. 'A right-thinking fellow. You are lucky in one of your brothers-in-law, at least.'

He walks towards Will and claps him on the shoulder. Up close, Will can see the broken red veins embedded in his cheeks, and the mottling of the grey bags under his eyes. 'We shall miss you here,' says Cromwell. 'There are challenges ahead. People will not like the major generals being set up over them. But the change is coming. We will win the souls of the people, Will.'

Will makes a non-committal noise. Cromwell looks sharply at him.

'We need stability. Peace, as your brother-in-law knows. There is a free and interrupted passage of the Gospel running through the midst of us, Will. Each man can hear it, if he is given quiet. The major generals can guarantee the peace. Then we will win the souls. We won the war, Will. We will win the peace also. Do you not think this is so?'

Will looks at his chief. He looks at the grey streaks in his hair. The clenching and unclenching of his fist. The ink spatter on his right hand, smudged with the thumb of his left. He looks at the bible open on the desk, its pages rumpled. He looks at the appeal on Cromwell's face. The unlikely, unexpected doubt he sees there.

'Yes, Your Highness,' he says. 'I am sure it will be so.'

If I could write a letter to Henrietta and place it in the hands of an angel I am not sure I believe in; if I could watch that letter soar through the clouds, borne by thunderous beating winds, then I would write of love.

I would write of this boy. This boy. This boy you bore and loved. This boy who is neither you, nor me, but some wondrous creation of his own invention. This boy who asks questions and seeks knowledge. This boy with your eyes and my chin and his own bubbling spring of joy.

I would write of the books I will offer to him. Of the diffidence with which I will offer them. Because I would vow this in my letter: to let him read what he will, to let him follow his own stars, find his own Homer.

Then. Henrietta, I would tell you of this night. Of how we are lying here as I once lay with you, looking at the stars. Imagining you. Talking about you. Conjuring you among all the celestial bodies.

The patterns of life, my Henrietta! Do you remember how we once imagined him? Talked of him. Conjured him among all the celestial bodies.

Looking at the stars with you, with him, reminding each other that in the great sweep of myth and lore, the only prick of light that really matters is the love of the living and the dead. Our souls are made for love, my Henrietta. Not for despair. Not for bitterness. Not really. Not at the reckoning.

And our boy. He will grow up in a world replete with all the usual villains: war, disease, misery, grief, boredom, hunger, thirst.

But it is also a world in which men can conceive of flying, my Henrietta. Not as a wish. Not as the fairy tales would have it, on the wings of spirits and dragons. No. Man can conceive of building something in the image of the angels. Something with wings and an engine, and no soul of its own. A machine.

He may build this machine, our boy. Perhaps, perhaps not. I do not wish greatness upon him. I have lived close to greatness, and I have seen the sourness in its belly. But he could fly, my Henrietta. He could feel the rush of wind in his face, like one of Cromwell's hawks. He could soar.

And this I vow, my Henrietta. While I breathe, if he falls I will catch him. But I will not stop him trying to fly.

This is what I would write, Henrietta. That while man is violent and power-hungry and base, he is something else. Man is glorious. Man can dream. Invent. Name and track the stars. Love.

This boy is glorious. Our boy.

In Cologne, Sam is sitting on a bale of cotton in a warehouse by the river. He crumples his letter from Will. It is full of stars, and a strange febrile joy to be alive. The one fact to hold on to is Blackberry's breeching. He is a boy on his way to manhood.

They are far away, his only family.

He has a world of things to do. He must tally off these bales, for a start. He must talk to the captain. He must report to Mr Shaw. There is a reception tonight for Charles Stuart, who is in town, and Rupert himself has sent a boy requesting Sam comes. He can imagine it. The desperate shine of cheap buckles and fake gems. The pouting red-lipped girls. The triple-bluff languor of the under-employed soldiers: a layer of affected sloth that is supposed to mask brilliant industry, which in fact is a bored apathy.

He can imagine the preening of whichever woman has temporary occupancy of the crownless king's bed. The to-and-fro as the mothers and girls weigh relative prospects. Where does Sam stand now that he is on his way to being prosperous? He was penniless and untitled. How will he rank against the titled paupers who will be pecking around the king's cast-offs tonight?

Shaw's daughter will be there, with her new intended. A younger son with an honourable name and debts that stretch from Paris to Brussels. She will be watching Sam as she parades her catch; her jewellery ostentatiously real amid a sparkle of tinted glass. This could have been yours, her eyes will say.

Let her. He crumples the letter in his hand again. No word about Patience. How could Will not have known that Sam would be on edge to hear the least crumb about her?

He remembers her as he last saw her. Crouching low over her husband's body, her hands daubed in his blood. The sweat on her brow. Terror in her eyes.

'He's dead, he's dead.'

He remembers how she touched a hand to her cheek, and recoiled from the blood. The mark left on her skin so vivid against the white of her blood-leached face.

Why didn't he run to her then? Trample on the bastard's bloody body to reach her and lift her and hold on?

So stupid, Sam.

And now, nothing. Should he write? He cannot go back. He will be arrested the instant he tries to return. Thurloe has made clear that his protection extended only as far as Sam's uninterrupted passage out; not his passport back in. As he understands it, the death of Sidrach Simmonds is at his door: Sam Challoner, the rotten Royalist. The traitorous bastard is not to be exposed for what he was, what he was planning. Sam has the Lord Protector's private thanks. What use is that?

He rises, pushing himself upright. The scratch of the jute on his hands reminds him why he is here, and he sets about the day's business. He is not a boy, to rile about unfairness, to mope lovesick when there is work to be done.

~ ~ ~

It is late when the ship is finally loaded, but they have not missed the tide. He helped with the work himself at the end, throwing off his jacket and getting into the heavy lifting. He took orders from an amused overseer, who tutted at his mistakes and slapped his back with an overfamiliar glee.

He is sore from using muscles that do not get used. His hands are filthy. But it was good to lose himself in physical work, even as the local men mocked him gently in their strange dialect. He will hurry home, wash, pull on a clean shirt. Beautify himself as far as possible. The evening's early skirmishes will be beginning already. The gallant advances of the rakes, the strategic retreat of the prettiest misses.

Lord, what a bore.

It is a dull sort of day. A dismal sky, with the promise of rain and a wind that seeks out the sweat cooling on his skin. He lengthens his stride. He will be late. He grins as he imagines the patronizing horror with which the lords this and the viscounts that would view his day. Labouring! Lifting! Tallying!

Ah well. Let them mock. They'll be begging him to spot them money for the gaming tables before the night is out. He thinks of his father suddenly, and the old man's belief that hard work and pleasure were both necessary conditions for a fulfilled life. Dear old man. Sam has never been sorry he missed his hanging, as he galloped off to offer his sword to the king. He is glad he does not have to remember his father choking on a rope. He can think instead of the old man's great growl of pleasure at the unveiling of a good meal and a fine claret.

There will be neither tonight, Sam thinks ruefully. Thin wine and watered gravy.

He will have a glass of his own finest claret as he changes his shirt. He brightens a little at the thought. He turns the corner into his street, his step a little bouncier.

And there she is.

Patience.

Standing in front of his door. A black travelling cloak about her shoulders. The hood pushed back. A formless shadow, turning to him. Smiling at him. His heart lurches like a drunkard.

Patience!

He has said it out loud, he realizes, and he laughs.

'Patience!'

'Sam!'

'I did not see you, after, Patience. I had to run. I wanted to speak.'

'It does not signify. I was not ready to speak.'

'And now?'

'I am here.'

She smiles at him, and suddenly they are holding hands and the grinning is wide enough to hurt.

'We have never spoken, Sam, about this thing between us.'

'This thing?'

'Well then. Shall we call it by name? Shall we call it love?'

He laughs.

'How forward you are, my Patience.'

'It is just a word. I have travelled across a sea to find you. The time for coyness is past.'

'It was not a criticism. We shall have honesty between us, when we are married.'

'Married?'

'Of course.'

'How forward you are, Mr Challoner.'

'Not without cause. Lord, how I have wanted you. What? Why so sad?'

'Was it not a sin, Sam? To love you while I was married to him?'

'Let us walk a little. Down to the river. Where do you stay?'

'At the inn on the square.'

He tucks her hand in the crease in his elbow. He holds it there, tightly. They turn together, and begin to walk towards the river.

'Now, Patience. Perhaps. Perhaps it is a sin. But I do not know. And I do not presume to know. He gave us hearts, did He not?'

'Yes.'

'And those hearts He made belong together, Patience. That much I know. This is what I suggest. Let us concentrate on our own hearts and let the rest be damned.'

Patience stops. She turns to him.

'You are right, Sam. My heart. Your heart. The world be damned. This matters. This and only this.'

EPILOGUE: COLOGNE

September 1658

*P*ATIENCE PULLS HENRIETTA TO HER FEET. SHE REWARDS her mother with a gummy, radiant smile.

'Clever girl,' says Patience. 'Clever girl.'

Somewhere in her belly there is a kick or a punch. A hammering reminder of new life to come. Patience puts her hands on her stomach and tries to feel for the little foot or hand – she can't reach it through the layers of cloth. Why so many clothes? Why can't we just float naked?

Henrietta babbles to get her attention back. Patience smiles at her, and the grin back is so large, so delighted, that she laughs aloud. Poor little Henrietta. She is the centre of their entire world. And she is about to share, to be displaced. Patience hopes it does not worry her too much.

It is an unseasonably warm day, and they are in the garden of their small town house. The grass tickles Patience's bare feet, and Henrietta is completely naked. Her plump, folding thighs and her big belly are a constant source of joy. The whiteness of her skin against the shocking green of the grass is a miracle.

Everything about Henrietta is miraculous. Patience knows that she is comedic in her maternal verve. No child has ever been more perfect, more beautiful, more adored. She knows that this cannot be true, but she does not care. Reason be damned. Henrietta is her baby, her miracle. And the rest of the world can take its mockery, its cynicism, and be hanged.

The garden seems remarkably beautiful today. Perhaps it is because she is happy. The gardener speaks not one word of English, nor even German. He speaks the strange local dialect to her maid, who translates it into halting German for Patience. She has enough now to get by.

He speaks with his skill, however. Late-season flowers drip from baskets. The beds are bright with reds and pinks and purples. In the vegetable corner, beans and peas and marrows hang swollen and ready to be plucked. The apple tree at the end of the garden, trained against the wall, is drooping with the weight of its crop.

There is a rustle as the opening door of the house catches on the plants that threaten to engulf it. She looks up, expecting to see the maid or Tom. But there is Sam.

Her heart catches.

Oh, the small but glorious victory of loving your own husband, she thinks for the thousandth time. Not just the slippery, thumping love of courtship. This is a deeper thing. This is tracing her child's face in his face. This is gratitude for the life that she owes to his existence. This is watching Henrietta's squirming delight at his unexpected appearance. 'Dada, dada.'

Love. What a stupid, imprecise word for such a welter of things.

'Sam!' She says. 'Why are you home?'

'And what greeting is that, woman? How are my beautiful girls?'

He comes out into the garden and bends to kiss her, tickling Henrietta under the chin. The sun catches grey glints in his hair. He pulls a strand of grass from her cheek and sits heavily down next to them.

'Hey, my Hen Hen. Little Pudding Cat,' he says, pulling the baby in for a kiss that makes her babble delightedly.

'Well, Sam? Has something happened? I thought you were expecting a shipment today.'

'I was. I have some news. I thought I would come and tell you.'

She waits. He looks cheerful enough, so she doesn't press. She lets him enjoy the pause before the punchline.

'Cromwell is dead.'

'Dead?'

He nods. She sits straighter.

'How?'

'Details are sparse. An ague, I believe.'

She is stunned.

'Will,' she says suddenly. 'Blackberry.'

'Well, love. Richard Cromwell is named Protector. The men around the king are abuzz with wild schemes to carry Charles home. But it will not happen. How can it? No. Will is safe, sweetheart.'

A flicker of fear makes her shiver, despite the sunshine. She offers up a silent plea to the sky. Please, please. This time. Let me and mine escape the grind of history.

There ought to be more to say. About Cromwell, about England, about the day three years ago when Sam stopped a bullet

357

hitting Cromwell's heart. Which is still, now, despite Sam's efforts. There ought to be more to say, and yet there is not. She kisses him. 'Stay to eat, while you are home. Out here, in the sun? I have those cold chops, and some cheese. I will open a good bottle.'

'How can I resist an hour with my favourite girls?' he says. 'I will go and fetch it, my beautiful whale. You stay here.'

A chop. A glass of wine. A shared joke with the one you love. An apple for afters, picked from a tree that you own. Quiet pleasures, she thinks, as he heads inside to rouse out the wine. Quiet pleasures to be loved loudly and fiercely and passionately.

'Sam?'

'Yes?' He turns at the door, and she revels in him.

'Don't forget the pickle.'

ACKNOWLEDGEMENTS

This book owes a debt to two of my favourite heroines: Isabella in Shakespeare's *Measure for Measure*, and Dorothea Brooke in George Elliot's *Middlemarch*. Both are women attempting to live meaningful lives in worlds that are antagonistic to their attempts. Both remind the historical-fiction writer of the sin of anachronism: pre-feminist women were not as we are.

The seventeenth century is a fascinating era in the development of women's political consciousness. Women were beginning to write radical ideas, but shrouding their work in a passive language of permission. 'God allows me to write despite the fact I am a woman. I do great things for the honour of my husband.'

Margaret Cavendish, who plays a cameo role in this story, is one of the first to articulate a different story. 'I am a woman, and have a right to be heard on my own terms.'

The burgeoning consciousness of women is just one of the strands which makes this such an extraordinary era. The 1640s were thunder, bloodshed and regicide. The 1650s are a quieter, more intricate story of hope and disillusionment.

At the centre of this story is Oliver Cromwell. As bitter, bloody and vile as the English Civil War undoubtedly was, its aftermath could have been worse. Cromwell was a bulwark against anarchy and extremism – a flawed champion of the moderate line. I was expecting a demi-monster, and found someone more nuanced and far more interesting.

Among the most useful primary sources I used to think my way into the seventeenth century were the political works of Milton, and his unlikely chum, Marchamont Nedham. The works of Margaret Cavendish. Of course, Sam Pepys – although his diaries are set a few years later. Thomas Carlyle's editions of Oliver Cromwell's speeches and letters, which are enlivened by the editor's extraordinary and idiosyncratic notes. The mother's legacies contained in Silvia Brown (ed.): *Women's Writing in Stuart England*, are fascinating insights into the domestic lives of women. The poetry of Marvell and Milton for Cromwell, and Lovelace for the Cavaliers. Thomas Hobbes and John Wilkins – for political and natural science.

I have tried to remain as faithful as possible to the events of the mid-1650s. Simmonds' plan to assassinate Cromwell is based on similar plots. For more on the secondary sources, and how this book found its shape, please visit my website: Antoniasenior.com.

As well as the fictional ones, this book owes large debts to a few real heroines and heroes. Louise Cullen at Corvus has been kind and diplomatic in reminding me that plot matters as much as politics. Thank you also to Sara O'Keeffe and Jane Selley.

A huge debt, as ever, to my agent Andrew Gordon at David Higham Associates. Thank you for your advice and support; both are invaluable. On the rare occasions I don't follow your advice, I always wish I had!

This book is dedicated to my sisters – I do not tell them often enough how much I love and admire them both. Thanks also to my mother, Elizabeth Senior, who is my most constant and partisan reader. For beyond-the-call-of-duty babysitting of my trio of gorgeous girls, and for their moral support, I owe a huge thank you to Bill and Sandra West.

Thank you to Nick Roe for sharing his expertise. Thank you to all those friends who have listened to me whinge about the writing of this book: Megan Skipper, Annabel Roe, Clare Moore, Anna Mazzola, Matt Ashton, Sophie Morgan, Charlotte Barratt, Leigh Victor, Neva Chowdhury.

Finally, all gratitude and love to Colin, my husband, who is worried that everyone will think he is the model for Sidrach Simmonds. Colin, I promise, is the anti-Sid; for which I am profoundly grateful.